MIDNIGHT WHISPERS

a novel

CAROL WARBURTON

Covenant Communications, Inc.

Cover design copyrighted 2007 by Covenant
Models Photographed by: Picture This... by Sara Staker.
Background Photo: © Jupiter Images

Published by Covenant Communications, Inc.
American Fork, Utah

Printed in Canada
First Printing: October 2007
13 12 11 10 09 08 07 10 9 8 7 6 5 4 3 2 1

ISBN 978-1-59811-370-9

To wonderful friends in the Adelaide Australia Mission who made our time there so rewarding and enjoyable. May God continue to bless you.

ACKNOWLEDGMENTS

As always, my appreciation goes to Dorothy Keddington and Ka Hancock for insightful suggestions and encouragement that kept me on the right track. Thanks to LouAnn Anderson and Nancy Hopkins as well. I count myself very fortunate to have such good friends. My thanks to Angela Eschler, my editor at Covenant Communications. All of you have played an important part in the writing of this novel.

ONE

The autumn sea crashed against the jutting headland, its spray turning to silvered mist and obscuring the man and horse coming toward me. When the mist dissipated, my eyes took in the outline of his dark jacket and hat, along with the self-assurance with which he sat his black horse. I didn't know him, and yet I felt no fear, only curiosity and a strange mingling of expectancy and wonder. He had come—the man I'd been waiting for. Excitement pulsed along my spine, and I felt an answering quiver run along the back of the mare on which I sat. I patted her neck to quiet her while my eyes remained on the horse and rider. They left the foaming breakers and came across the sand, and just before reaching me, the rider reined in his black stallion and slowly lifted his hat.

"Miss Jessamyne." The tone of his resonant voice made it a statement rather than a question, as if he knew me, though I was certain we'd never met.

My voice quavered slightly. "Yes."

"I was afraid you wouldn't come." The assurance in his tone was edged with wonder. "Who would have thought . . . ?" His voice trailed away as he rode the stallion closer.

I felt a tiny prick of fear, and my mare moved nervously. "Who are you?" I asked. "And how do you know my name?"

Instead of answering, he smiled and lifted his dark brows. His warmth and his teasing manner melted my nervousness, erasing my fear. This peace came so completely that when he reached to brush a tendril of black hair away from my cheek, I did not flinch, nor did I breathe. The world seemed to stop for a heartbeat. Even the restless waves lapping at our horses' hooves stilled. I leaned toward him, and he to me.

A voice crashed through the stillness. "Wake up Miss Clayborne. There's a ship off starboard, and the captain says likely it's sailing to Australia the same as us." Jamie Hewitt rapped impatiently on my cabin door. "Did ya hear? There's a ship. The first we've seen in a fortnight." I stirred, not wanting to leave the soft magic of my dream. When Jamie's knuckles rapped the second time, I slowly opened my eyes. The sight of my cramped cabin banished the last vestiges of the dream. Instead of a handsome man about to kiss me, I was greeted with the sight of Jamie's sister stretching and pushing back the covers of her narrow bunk.

"We're coming," I called to Jamie.

"Why is it Jamie always hears and sees everything first?" young Beth complained.

I shook my head, having noticed myself his penchant for being in the thick of things. "Probably because he never sits still."

"That's a truth," Beth agreed. Although she clearly wished she'd been the one to come with the news, her regret didn't keep her from slipping out of bed to join him.

I turned my head to the wall so Beth could have a bit of privacy. It was something we now did by rote—taking turns each morning and night. Even at eleven, she was as uncomfortable undressing in front of me as I was with her. While I listened to the rustle of her clothes, I thought of the strange turn of events that had put me and Bethy Hewitt together. Father's death and my resulting desperation had played a major part of it, but so had the kindness of the Hewitts.

I didn't like to recall the week when my life had come crashing down. Father's death had been devastating enough, but when Mr. Radnor, the solicitor, said Father had been living on borrowed funds and our home must be sold to pay his numerous debts, I could scarce take it in. How could this be—Henry Clayborne, a gentleman of taste and no small reputation, a pauper?

When I expressed my disbelief, Mr. Radnor had been sympathetic. "I fear it's true, Miss Clayborne. Your father has known this past year that his ability to borrow had come to an end." He made a small regretful sound with his tongue, and his gray mustached lips turned downward.

The parlor, with its windows draped in black, seemed to close around me. "What am I to do?" I whispered.

Mr. Radnor gave another sigh, but when he spoke, his voice was brisk and businesslike. "I've given the matter considerable thought these past days. As I see it, your only option is to go to your brother Robert."

My heart bumped against my ribs in an erratic leap. "Robbie?" It was difficult to say the name of my brother; he'd been disowned some twelve years before.

Mr. Radnor nodded, his eyes watchful.

"Father forbade me to see or speak of him."

"I know." The calmness in Mr. Radnor's face was mirrored in his voice, but his eyes remained alert. "Although I'm your father's solicitor, Robert and I have remained in touch over the years."

I felt the quickening of excitement. "You know where he is?"

"I do." He smiled, the expression making his face look younger. "I also know of Robert's fondness for you, and yours for him. He—"

"Where—Where is he? When can I see him?" In my eagerness my tongue tripped over the words.

"Since your brother now lives in Australia, it will be months before you see him."

"Australia." I breathed the word aloud. Though I'd often thought of my lovable older brother, never had I imagined him in Australia. While my mind searched for snippets of information I'd learned about that far-off land, Mr. Radnor explained about the yearly letters he'd received from Robert.

"Your brother has done well after making a small fortune prospecting for gold. He's married well too. I believe his wife comes from one of Melbourne's leading families. There are children. A boy and a girl." Mr. Radnor paused to withdraw a packet of letters from his brown leather case. "I've kept his letters, which you may have if you'd like. All of them ask about you, and I've taken the liberty of keeping Robert informed of you as well."

"Please." I reached for the letters while my mind strove to change the bold scrawl on the envelopes into a picture of my beloved brother.

"I wrote to Robert as soon as I was informed of Mr. Clayborne's death, but I waited to post it until I'd spoken to you." He paused and fixed me with a kindly eye. "If it's your wish, I'm sure Robert will welcome your going to live with him in Australia."

"Yes, please." Despite the crushing news about the state of Father's affairs, I'd found myself smiling.

So the letter to Robert Clayborne in Australia had been dispatched, and now I was on my way to join him.

"I'm finished," Bethy said.

I turned my head to look at my cabinmate, the present brought sharply back into focus as I took in her plain calico dress and the locks of brown hair that straggled from her nighttime plaits. "Would you like me to straighten your hair?"

Beth shook her head and opened the door. "Mama can do it later."

Even with her gone, I felt a strange reluctance to leave my bed. Was it the dream that had left me feeling not quite myself? Bits and pieces of it floated through my mind—me, Jessamyne Clayborne, who was terrified of horses, sitting on one as calmly as if I'd been doing it all my life. And the man. I recalled his handsome features and tender, half-teasing smile as he brushed a lock of hair from my face.

My hand went to my cheek in an unconscious effort to bring back the touch of his fingers. Why had Jamie chosen that precise moment to knock on the cabin door? Why couldn't he have waited just long enough for me to experience my first kiss? If he had, I might also have discovered the stranger's name. I smiled at my foolishness, and in my mind I could hear Cook from back home giving me one of her scolds.

"What a silly goose you are, Miss Jessamyne. Wishing you could be with a man who doesn't exist. I've never heard such nonsense. What you need is a healthy dose of fresh air, so get yourself up on deck, and don't ye be letting me hear any more of this foolishness."

As if she'd been in the cabin, I followed the advice and went on deck to find the rest of the Hewitt family. As soon as I arrived, Jamie pulled me over to the rail and pointed to the distant ship, sails filled with the swell of wind. The dazzling glitter of early morning sun on the vast expanse of water forced me to raise a hand to shield my eyes.

"Captain says she's a merchant ship with likely a few passengers, same as us. But *The Mermaid* is faster." This last was said with an inordinate display of pride.

I smiled at the flaxen-haired boy whose deeply tanned face bespoke the hours he spent on deck with the crew. I knew his mother worried about the sailors' influence and colorful language, but Jamie's enthusiasm was so infectious that I suspected he had more impact on the sailors than they on him.

"Captain says if the winds hold we'll be headin' into Port Phillip Bay and Melbourne in less than a week." Jamie's "captain says" was repeated so often I wondered how Captain Edwards had time to manage the running of his ship when he spent so much time tutoring Jamie.

"So soon?" I glanced at Sarah Hewitt for confirmation.

"That's what he was sayin' this morning, and to my way of thinkin', it's not a day too soon."

Like her son, Sarah Hewitt's hair was fair, but her most pleasant aspect was her smile, which came as readily as her laughter. Everything about the woman was agreeable, from her rounded figure to her natural fondness for people. I felt certain that most of the female passengers had shared a confidence with the middle-aged woman, knowing in an unspoken way their secrets would never pass her lips.

William Hewitt turned to greet me, his brown eyes teasing. "It's nice to see ya and Bethy on deck so early. If my memory serves me, it's the first time ya've been above deck afore breakfast."

"You're right," I laughed, "and you have Jamie to thank for our promptness. I don't know when I've heard such a racket."

"I didn't want ya to miss seein' the ship," Jamie protested.

His father laughed. "In Jamie's eyes, a ship is man's greatest invention."

I liked William Hewitt as much as I liked his wife. He was tall and pleasant-faced, with touches of gray already showing in his brown hair and beard. Like the majority of the passengers, he was on his way to start a new life in Australia. Hardly a day went by that I didn't see him standing at the rail, his eyes on the distant horizon, as if willing the shore that held his future to show itself among the waves.

Other than the crew, the Hewitts and I were the only ones on deck at this early hour. As I took in the family, I was reminded again of my good fortune in being put with such kind people for the long voyage. Besides being chaperones and shipmates, they had also become my friends. Their warmth had quickly broken the barriers imposed by social class.

Timmy, the Hewitts' youngest, had tired of watching the other ship. Fair, like Jamie, his large blue eyes and rounded cheeks gave him the look of a cherub. But just a few hours in his company had proved that looks could be deceiving. "Come on, Bethy," he said, pulling on her hand. "Let's do somethin' fun."

Sarah Hewitt pulled her shawl more tightly around her shoulders. "It's too windy here for my likin'. Why don't we sit under the awning?"

Her husband and Jamie declined, but I was happy to follow her suggestion, as I'd failed to bring my shawl.

Sarah smiled at me as she settled into a chair. "Can ya believe we'll be in Australia in just a week? I can't wait to see this strange country with black Aborigines and kangaroos and outlandish birds. And, of course, William's uncle." Her smile faded "I've not heard anything good about his wife, but since we won't be sharing the same house, I think we'll get on well."

"I can't imagine anyone not getting on with you."

"I suppose that's true—I've met few people I don't take a likin' to, though there's some I like more than others . . . you especially." She touched my arm—a habit of hers, and one that made me feel all the more included. "I hope we'll be able to see each other after we get to Melbourne. That is, if your brother approves."

"Of course he'll approve," I protested, but a part of me wondered. William Hewitt had been head gardener at an estate in Hampshire, and Sarah had been the housekeeper. As such, they would not have moved in the same circles as the Claybornes. Although we were not at the top of the social ladder, we had been on its fringes. My clothes had been purchased at the best shops, and my attendance at the best parties gave Father and me satisfaction.

Thinking back on my first days with the Hewitts still had the power to make me blush. I had held myself aloof. Always polite, of course, but doing nothing to invite friendship. But Sarah Hewitt was a master at making friends, and Jamie was not far behind. Without quite knowing how it happened, I had relaxed and given myself to their open overtures.

"I wonder what kind of trees and flowers we'll see growin' there?" Sarah went on. "William's been countin' the days till we arrive. Says his hands are fair itchin' to dig in the Australian dirt." She paused, and her voice turned tentative. "Before we get there, it would be nice to hear yer brother's letters again. Then we'll be knowin' what to expect."

I'd read Robert's letters to the Hewitts and some of the other passengers. All had shaken their heads at his good fortune in finding gold, and his colorful depictions of the animals and country had heightened our impatience to get there.

The creaking rhythm of the ship and the breeze blowing under the awning created a pleasant venue for my contented languor. I closed my eyes and let my mind wander back to my dream. I'd had similarly vivid dreams on two previous occasions, and each time pieces of the dreams had become reality—the quarrel between Father and Robert manifested itself first in a nightmare, as had the specter of Father's death. But this morning's dream had whispered of love and magic. Pray God this awaited me in Australia.

Sarah's voice intruded into my thoughts. "Do ya ever worry ya've done the right thing?" Before I could rouse myself to answer, she went on. "When William and I decided to take his uncle's offer of a new life in Australia, it seemed so right. It felt even better after we prayed about it. We were sure it was God's will, but now . . ."

Her tone and hesitancy made me turn and look at her.

"Now . . . it don't seem so right, and sometimes during the night I feel afraid." Her fingers tightened on my arm. "Please, don't be tellin' William. I don't want him thinkin' I've lost faith, which I haven't, but . . ." Her voice trailed away in a sigh.

"Perhaps it's because we've been so long at sea," I said, for it was unlike Sarah to express either fear or loss of faith. Early in our friendship, she'd told me about her new religion. Mormons, they were called, though she'd been quick to explain that Mormon was a nickname, the actual name of the church being The Church of Jesus Christ of Latter-day Saints. Sarah had also been quick to invite me to join them for the reading of scripture and for prayer. Each time I'd refused, and after a while she'd ceased to ask. It wasn't that I was against religion, but rather that I hadn't made up my mind about the matter.

William and Jamie turned from the rail and joined us. "Jamie says he's starvin', and my stomach's tellin' me the same. I'm thinkin' breakfast should be ready by now."

As if he'd heard William, one of the ship's stewards came up the stairs to announce that breakfast was served. Hungry, the children hurried down the stairs with their parents not many steps behind.

I followed at a more leisurely pace, turning for one last look at the passing ship bobbing like a toy boat on a vast expanse of water. My decision to linger was immediately regretted, for when I reached the passageway leading to the dining room, it was firmly blocked by Jeremy Moulton.

I possessed a strong dislike for the man, but he, on the other hand, had taken an inordinate interest in me. No matter where I sat or walked, he never seemed far away, always ogling and making me feel uncomfortable. He was powerfully built and possessed both coarse features and speech. As his gaze slid over me, I quickened my pace, thinking it better to get the unpleasantness over with so I could enjoy my breakfast.

"Miss Clayborne."

I gave a stiff nod, expecting him to move so I could pass. When he failed to do so, I was forced to stop. "Would you kindly let me by?"

"But of course." His withdrawal was only halfhearted, and my long skirt brushed against his trousers.

I shot him a cold look, one that should have made him feel uncomfortable. Instead it brought a smile to his thick lips.

"Did ya know I'm on speakin' terms with yer brother?" His words stopped me, and his smile broadened into a chuckle. "Like it or not, Miss Clayborne, ya might be seein' more of Jeremy Moulton when you get to Melbourne."

"I doubt that." Although I walked away with head held high, his words struck at my confidence. Dear heaven, what was Robert doing associating with the likes of Jeremy Moulton?

* * *

Captain Edward's announcement that only a week separated us from the shores of Australia cut through the sameness of too many days of sun and sea. Passengers who'd been content to wile away their hours at cards or gossip in the salon suddenly found the deck more to their liking. All wanted to be on hand when the ship's mate called out the first sighting of land. Extra chairs were placed under the awning, and others besides Sarah Hewitt asked me to reread Robert's descriptions of Australia. Everyone seemed to walk with a quicker step and speak in a more animated tone, myself included.

On the day we hoped to see land, I didn't need Jamie's knock to summon me on deck. Beth and I were early, but much to our chagrin Jamie and his father were there before us.

"Do you see anything?" I asked as I looked out over a sea of choppy gray water.

"Nope." Instead of being disappointed, Jamie looked excited. "Captain says there's a storm brewin', one that'll likely test *The Mermaid's* mettle . . . hopefully get us into Port Phillip Bay quicker, too."

As he spoke, a gust of wind ruffled the water and filled the sails with a burst of restless energy. I felt an answering quiver in my pulse. Storm or not, we were almost there.

Sarah and others had joined us at the rail. All were as anxious as I to get their first glimpse of Australia.

"Mercy!" Sarah exclaimed when a rush of wind set the ribbons on her bonnet snapping.

"Captain says there's a storm brewing," Jamie repeated. He pointed to heavy gray clouds out over the water. "Ya can see it comin'. Captain says the glass is fallin' too."

Like Jamie, William was intent on the billowy clouds on the horizon. Sarah touched his shoulder. "Will the storm bring trouble?"

William put a reassuring arm around her. "I doubt it. At least Captain Edwards don't seem worried."

But an hour later the wind had strengthened ominously, lifting the sea in rough swells and putting a worried frown on the captain's face. While the first mate stood at the helm, the rest of the crew hurried to lash down anything not fastened to the deck.

"Ye'd best get below deck," one of the crew warned. "Captain's set on makin' a run for the bay where we'll be more protected, but it'll still be a rough sail."

Sarah and I collected Beth and Timmy and made our way down the stairs. I knew it would be useless to try to get Jamie to come. He was stuck fast to the rail with his father, both of them seeming to gain enthusiasm with each gust of wind.

We'd scarcely gotten below deck when the ship's sharp pitch made Beth declare she felt unwell. Since she and Timmy had both suffered seasickness at the beginning of the voyage, Sarah took them to the larger cabin she and her husband shared with the two boys, where she hoped a "lie-down" would make them feel better.

I was left in the salon with Mr. and Mrs. Abernathy, who were on their way to join their son and his wife in Australia. They were an affable couple, and Mrs. Abernathy seemed always to have a smile. Neither of them smiled now. Each time the ship pitched or shuddered, Mrs. Abernathy gave a frightened cry while Mr. Abernathy shot a worried look at the salon's polished walnut timbers.

Several passengers usually occupied the salon, but today only the Abernathys, Jeremy Moulton, and myself sat in the chairs that were bolted to the floor for just such an occasion as today.

Since my most recent uncomfortable encounter with Mr. Moulton, I'd made it a point to avoid him as much as I could. I was aware of him now, his stocky legs splayed out in an ungentlemanly manner. In the dim light, the scar over his left eyebrow gave his broad features a sinister appearance, while his watchful eyes seemed to follow my every movement. I had hoped that once we reached Melbourne I would never see the man again, but his recent words implied otherwise. How had Jeremy Moulton come to know Robert? And more importantly, what would bring my brother to associate with such a man? The questions filled me with unease, a feeling that made me realize it had been twelve years since I'd last seen my brother.

A brilliant flash of lightning, followed by a crash of thunder, brought a cry of alarm from Mrs. Abernathy.

"It's only the storm," Mr. Abernathy assured her, but the quick manner with which he glanced at the porthole made me suspect he was as uncomfortable as his wife.

A rush of rain followed the thunder. A moment later William and Jamie hurried into the salon; their wet shirts clung to their arms, and Jamie's fair hair was plastered flat to his head.

"It's a flood out there," William declared, "but the captain's still goin' to try for Port Phillip Bay."

"Can you see land?" I asked.

William shook his head. "The clouds are so thick ya can't see a thing."

"Mercy," Mrs. Abernathy breathed. "With so many clouds we could crash ashore and not know it."

"The captain knows what he's doin'," Jamie declared.

"I certainly hope so." Mrs. Abernathy reached for her husband's arm. "I'm feeling a little unwell, dear. Will you help me to our cabin?"

Not liking the way Jeremy Moulton watched me, I excused myself as well and followed the Abernathys from the salon. The act took some effort, for the ship pitched and reared like an agitated stallion, and I had to brace myself on the walls of the passageway to keep my balance.

The clouds and rain made my room too dim for reading. For a moment I thought of joining Sarah and the children in the adjoining cabin, but the sound of someone being sick quickly changed my mind. Fearing the storm might last for several hours, I changed into the comfort of my nightgown and lay down on the bunk. The pitching movement of the ship became more violent, making the cabin tilt at an unnatural angle. My eyes snapped shut, and I set my mind on the more pleasant thought of Robert. Twelve years my senior, Robert would now be in his mid-thirties. What would he think when he saw me, a young woman instead of a girl?

A sudden shuddering yaw of the ship stripped such thoughts from my mind. In their place was an uncomfortable dizziness that told me I would soon be sick.

I sat up and grabbed my cloak. Fresh air and a quick walk around the deck had saved me from seasickness when we first set sail. Hopefully the treatment would work again.

Struggling for balance, I reached the passageway, where the violent motion of the ship threw me against the wall. Somehow I stayed on my feet and mounted the stairs, my nausea momentarily forgotten when my leg cracked against a step. Reeling like a drunken sailor, I finally reached the door and threw the heavy bolt from its hasp.

A sudden plunge of the ship flung me out onto the deck. Rain and howling wind snatched my breath and billowed my cloak as I tried to regain my balance and turn back. The ship lurched and fell into a deep trough that sent me scudding across the rain-slicked deck to crash with jarring force against the wheelhouse. My fingers scrambled for a hold on the sodden wall until I found purchase. I laid my head against the wall and looked in horror through the driving rain at the heaving mountains of water that reared against black, lightning-streaked clouds. Why had I left my room?

"Dear God, help," I prayed as a foaming wall of water rushed over the bow then tore at a lifeboat and flung it against the rail. I watched in horror as the rail gave way and plunged with the lifeboat into the heaving sea.

I dragged ragged gasps of air into my lungs, scarcely aware that my hair had been torn from its pins and streamed like sodden strands of rope in the howling wind. I fought to stay on my feet as the ship fell into another deep cavern and a gray cliff of water rolled toward me. It smacked against my knees and knocked me into its wake, sucking me toward the gaping hole left by the splintered railing. Terrified, I frantically grabbed for a remaining post as I plummeted past it and into the roiling sea.

The crashing water sucked me down into the depths, then spewed me up as effortlessly as if I had been a child's toy. I gasped for breath before I was pulled back down, choking and struggling as I fought for life. Another heaving wave threw me to the surface, where my head crashed into something solid. Frantic, I grasped at the object, my efforts as wild as the waves that threatened to suck me back into the frenzied sea. Somehow I clung to the wood, the buoyancy of it keeping my head above water. I breathed in labored gulps of air as rain and water lashed my face. I choked, and for a paralyzing second I almost lost my hold on the wood. My arms felt like aching slabs of stone, and my numbed fingers were losing their grip. "Please, God . . . help . . . oh, please," I gasped, my voice but a whisper.

Just when I feared that exhaustion and the drag of wet clothes would overwhelm my waning strength, I managed to pull myself more securely onto the planking. Gasping, I clung to its width, my arms and legs instinctively wrapped tightly around it. My heart beat out a staccato *thank you* as I struggled to fill my heaving lungs with air.

On some level, I recognized that the boards were a remnant of the smashed lifeboat and that my cloak had been torn away by the battering waves.

The numbness in my fingers had spread to my body, the cold such that I felt as if I were encased in an icy blanket. How long I clung to the planking in that half-stupor of cold and exhaustion and pelting rain, I couldn't say. Perhaps several minutes, maybe no more than a few seconds. I only know that when I next became aware of conscious thought, the rain had mercifully ceased.

As I raised my head, I discovered that one of my eyes was swollen shut. Even so, I was able to make out a sea that no longer pitched so violently. The storm seemed to be lessening.

The sight brought a fleeting surge of hope that was quickly dashed when I failed to see either ship or land. What if the storm had carried me out to sea? Too tired to hold onto the thought, I laid my throbbing head back down onto the board while shivers wracked my body. I fought an overpowering weariness, wanting only to sleep, but something stronger than exhaustion kept my arms and legs clinging to the boards. The pitch and swell of the waves was hypnotic, and soon there was only myself and the heaving water—and the terrible cold.

After some time a shaft of warmth and light pierced through my stupor. I opened my good eye and was greeted by the sheen of late afternoon sun on the water. It took great effort to lift my head, but I was rewarded with the sight of waves crashing onto a shoreline. Hope came again, and though I knew nothing of swimming, I made a weak attempt at kicking my legs to speed my progress. Panic seized me when I almost lost my grip on the planks. Terrified, I wrapped my legs around them again and lay with pounding heart, praying I would be able to hang on until I safely reached land.

The next moments passed in a haze of rolling waves and a terrible exhaustion that ate at my will to stay atop the boards. I wanted to let go and slip into the water where I needn't fight anymore, but each time the impulse came, something stronger urged me to hang on. "I can't," I whispered.

At that moment a wave flung me upward. There was a sensation of flight, then jarring pain as my head struck something hard. Dazed, I laid on the rocks and sand, aware of shooting pain and the warm trickle of blood from a gash on my head. But I was safe. *Thank you, God.*

I was exhausted, and growing unconsciousness pulled me toward a black abyss, but instinct fought the sucking darkness and urged me to slowly drag myself through rocks and debris until I was free of the waves. Every movement brought fresh pain and cloying weariness. My mind tumbled dizzily, and I wanted only to sleep. And then, mercifully, I did.

Two

I dreamed I was on horseback again, watching in fascination from the shore as a man and his horse emerged from a churning gray sea. Water dripped from his boots and the horse's flanks, and a cold wind blew off the water. I shivered, but my fascination with the rider was so intense that I remained where I was instead of seeking shelter. Mesmerized, my gaze followed his undulating course across the wet sand, and I smiled as my eyes drank in the curve of his answering smile. Even so, I was aware that both he and the black stallion were watchful. I wondered at this until I realized we were not alone, that a shadowy presence had wrapped a warm cloak around my shoulders. Before I could respond, I felt myself being lifted and carried away. The jarring movement made me whimper. I struggled to look back, but swirling mist obscured both the rider and those who carried me. The fog rolled in thick folds around me, stopping my mouth and tumbling through my brain until I, too, was swallowed by the mist.

Time passed and pain cut through the gauzy grayness to bring a prickling of alarm. I became aware of voices and felt hands remove my wet nightgown. The strange singsong cadence of the voices added to my unease.

I strove to open my eyes and panicked when only one eye would open. My fear grew at the sight of a brown face peering down at me. A cry of terror pushed past my cut lips.

"It all right, missy."

My head jerked, and I saw several dark-skinned natives looking down at me, their thin brown legs rising like sticks planted in the earth. I tried to sit up, but a woman's hand firmly kept me in place.

"No move," she commanded. Her head, with its mass of kinky gray hair, wavered and swam before my swollen eyes. Yet something in the tone of her voice quieted my fear. My eyelid closed when her warm fingers made a soothing trail over my eyes and forehead. Her touch and singsong chant brought peace and carried me away into deep, restful sleep.

* * *

When I next knew consciousness, warm sunlight streamed through a canopy of branches over my head. For a moment I thought I was still dreaming, for the leaves were oddly shaped and more gray than green. I blinked swollen eyes, the movement sending shards of pain through my head and throbbing body.

The dark-skinned woman immediately materialized at my side. When she bent close, my sight fastened on a butterfly-like creature that hovered just below her neck. Its vivid red and green wings pulsed and shone iridescent in the sunlight, the movement a fascinating whorl.

"Good," she said when she saw my partially opened eye follow the insect's movement. Her smile brought animation and warmth to her brown features.

"Where . . . where am I?" I whispered.

The woman shrugged.

"Please . . . I need to know." When I tried to move, she put a restraining hand on me.

"No," she commanded. "Move make sick."

I wanted to tell her I was already sick and that just blinking made my head throb miserably, but when I tried to form the words, they melted before they reached my lips.

A younger woman handed my nurse a gourd of steaming liquid. "Drink," she admonished. "Make better."

With her help I took several awkward sips of a hot, bitter liquid. Instead of protesting, I meekly swallowed, vaguely recalling I'd done the same during the night. Fear had dissipated, replaced on some level with the knowledge that neither the liquid nor the Aborigines would harm me.

Thereafter I drifted in and out of consciousness, aware at times of strange, silent men with nothing but loincloths to cover their nakedness, watching but not speaking. Through it all was the singsong chant of the older woman and the soft rhythm of a leafy branch as the younger woman fanned flies away from my face. Like the men, the women wore very little, and the two children nothing at all. My brain was too fuzzy to be scandalized or fearful. My only emotion was a heavy weariness mingled with gratitude.

"Thank you," I managed to say the next time the older woman gently rubbed a smelly salve over my face and into the cut in my scalp.

She nodded and adjusted the blanket in which they'd wrapped me. I wrinkled my nose at its unpleasant odor, but, remembering the terror of the waves and the unrelenting coldness, I was grateful for my covering. In place of cold, now all I felt was soreness. Every muscle ached, and I slowly became aware I had sustained numerous cuts and bruises, the most notable being those on my head. I couldn't lift it without experiencing a sickening dizziness. I raised my hand and gingerly touched my swollen eyes and forehead. As I did, I realized my arm was bare and covered with scrapes.

"My clothes," I whispered, pulling the blanket close to protect my modesty. "Where are my clothes?"

"There, missy." The younger woman pointed to a low-growing bush. Draped over the branches were the tattered remnants of my nightgown. "Soon dry."

* * *

Daylight faded into darkness, lit by the pulsing light of a fire upon which something cooked. I smelled singed hair and later the odor of meat. The more pleasing aroma made me hungry. I watched the Aborigines gathered around the fire, heard their laughter and animated conversation. Like me, the prospect of food cheered them.

I opened my mouth as wide as my cut lip would allow as the older woman put a piece of the hot meat on my tongue.

"Roo," she said. "Kanga . . . roo."

For a moment I thought she spoke in her native language, then the memory of Robert's description of the Australian animals slipped into my mind. *Dear heaven,* I thought, but it didn't prevent me from taking a small second bite.

The woman nodded in approval when she saw my weak pleasure in the meat. As she nodded, I caught sight of the butterfly, its colors subdued in the flickering firelight. Fascinated, I studied it more closely and realized that, rather than being alive, it was an ornament attached to a leather thong around her neck.

Aware of my interest in the ornament, she touched it and smiled. "Courage," she said. "Make strong."

Soon after I slept again and did not waken until the sound of excited voices penetrated my mind.

"They come, missy," the younger woman cried. "Big boss woman come."

I opened my swollen eyes to follow her pointing finger. A wagon pulled by a team of bullocks approached with a man on horseback riding at its side. The man was unmistakably white. Good as the Aborigines had been to me, my heart lifted with the knowledge that more help had arrived.

I watched with a happy heart as the wagon came to a halt at the edge of the camp. A moment later the man assisted two women down from the wagon. The women turned and made their way toward me, nodding to the natives who had formed a half circle around the pallet of animal skins on which I lay.

Both women wore broad-brimmed hats that shadowed their faces and made it difficult to see their features. But one woman's hips were broader than the other's, and something in her confident manner led me to believe she was the elder.

Her confidence seemed to desert her when she drew close. "Mercy," she whispered. She dropped to her knees and reached for my hand. "Oh, my dear . . . ye poor, poor lass."

The touch of her hand and the sight of her gray eyes brimming with tears brought an answering response from mine. Tears that had lain dormant during most of my ordeal now broke forth in rivulets down my face.

"There, there . . . We've come to help ye," she soothed as she magically produced a handkerchief from the sleeve of her green dress.

The younger woman knelt beside me and gently dabbed at the swollen corners of my eyes with the handkerchief. "Does it hurt?" she asked.

"Yes," I said, though I would gladly have borne more pain just to have them with me.

"I'm Anne McKade, and this is my daughter Millicent," the older woman said. "We came as soon as Mooney told us his family had found ye washed up on the beach."

"Thank you." The words brought a fresh spate of tears and made me grip Anne McKade's hand harder. She and her daughter brought comforting memories of afternoons spent in the kitchen with Cook. I sensed that these women were solid and good, like Cook and Mrs. Woolsey, my father's housekeeper, and I wanted nothing more than to keep them close.

"Who are you?" Millicent asked. "How did you get here?"

"Jessamyne Clayborne." It felt good to say my name and know my life was about to resume its proper shape again. "I was washed overboard in a storm at sea."

Anne nodded. "And what a storm it was. We felt it all the way to Tanybrae."

While we talked, the young Aborigine woman continued to fan the flies and insects away from my face. When one darted past the branch and lit on my nose, Millicent shooed it away. "These pesky flies are the curse of Australia."

I looked at the Aborigines surrounding my pallet. "They've been very good to me," I whispered.

Anne nodded and smiled at the natives. "Yagan and his family sometimes work for us at Tanybrae. They are good and can be trusted." As she spoke, she released my hand and got to her feet. "You have taken good care of the white woman," she said, addressing the natives. "She thanks ye, and so do we."

The black men who stood at the foot of my pallet nodded, but none of them spoke. I watched them closely, noting for the first time the breadth of their noses and lips.

"This is Miss Clayborne," Anne said. Glancing at me, then at the oldest man, she went on. "And this is Yagan and his sons Wong, Apsin, and Mooney."

Each man nodded as his name was spoken. There was a quiet dignity in their faces, and although the bearded older man did not smile, his sons did.

Weak as I was, I couldn't help but think it strange that Anne treated the Aborigines with such courtesy. Robert's letters had led me to believe many treated them more like animals.

My Aborigine nurse put a hand on my blanket. "I . . . Sal," she said, not waiting for Anne's introduction. She pointed to the woman who fanned me. "Her . . . Toppy."

"Thank you Sal . . . Toppy." I looked at the men, putting faces to names and wishing I had known their names sooner. "Thank you."

"Are ye able to walk?" Anne asked.

"I don't think—" I began.

"No walk. Not good for missy," Sal interrupted.

Although Anne McKade bowed to Sal's wisdom, she lost no time in organizing my move from the ground to the wagon. When she discovered I wore no clothing, she instructed her daughter to keep the blanket pulled tightly around me. Nothing seemed to daunt the practical woman. "We'll remedy yer clothes when we get ye to Tanybrae."

The men picked up the pallet of skins on which I lay. Their uneven gait reminded me of those moments after my dream, and I knew this was how Yagan and his sons had carried me from the beach to their camp. The jarring trip to the wagon made my headache worse, and I was grateful to be laid on a mattress in the back of the wagon.

The bandy-legged little man who'd accompanied the McKades on horseback scurried around, his grizzled face registering dismay each time he looked at me. I heard him tell the men to take care as they lifted me onto a mattress, and later he asked Mooney to help him tie a piece of canvas across the wagon to shade me from the sun.

When he finished, he poked his head under the canvas. "'Enry Twimby at yer service, miss. If'n ye should be needin' anythink, ye 'ave only to ask 'Enry."

With that, he doffed his battered hat and dropped out of view, only to appear a moment later to help Anne McKade into the back of the wagon.

"Henry said he'd drive the bullocks so I can ride back here with ye," she said after she'd settled herself. "Although Millie is good with horses, she can't yet handle the bullocks." She paused and gave me a searching look. "Ye look tuckered out and in need of a sleep. And that's what ye must do, for it'll take us awhile to get to Tanybrae."

"Is your home near Tanybrae?"

"It is Tanybrae." Pride and love folded around the name. "Tanybrae is the name of our station, and a finer one ye'll not find in the whole of the Gippsland."

The Aborigines had gathered by the wagon to bid me good-bye. When I lifted my hand to wave, I noticed that Sal now wore a faded, loose-fitting dress. When the wagon moved, she followed us.

"Sal come too," she called in response to the question she read in my eyes. "Sal help make better."

I glanced at Anne and saw no surprise. "The natives believe Sal has the gift of healing. They travel great distances to consult with her, and she's healed many." She nodded as she spoke. "Tho' that awful salve she's put on ye smells terrible, I'm thinkin' 'tis workin' a magic that'll draw the swellin' out of yer poor face."

"She should ride," I said.

"'Twon't do a mite of good to invite her. Sal doona care for our ways. Besides, she and her people are used to walkin'. 'Tis their way, same as runnin' around all but naked. They ken they must wear clothes when they're around us, but soon as they go on walkabout, they take on their old ways. Some are stubborn about changin' . . . Same as us Scots," she concluded with a chuckle.

I'd noted Anne's accent, and her revelation that it was Scottish made me want to know more about her, but tiredness was stronger than curiosity. Against my will I fell asleep to the accompaniment of Sal's singing and the rhythmic lurch of the wagon.

* * *

I awoke to the motion of Anne shooing flies away from my face.

"I'm sorry," she apologized. "Och, but I hate the pesky creatures. I think they ken and come to plague me all the more."

How good it was to awaken to a white face looking down at me—one that spoke more than a smattering of English, albeit with a lilting accent. Seeing Sal walking at a steady pace behind us, I immediately felt guilty. She and her family had rescued and nursed me with kindness. I would never forget that.

Although I'd slept, the jarring of the wagon made my head throb even more miserably. My muscles and body still ached too. I closed my eyes against the glaring sun, wishing the ride would end so I could be in a comfortable bed. Thereafter, I dozed and tried to retreat from the pain that jumped through my temples each time the wagon hit a bump.

Seeing that I'd wakened, Sal resumed her song.

"Sal be singin' ye a songline," Anne said. "Tho' I have no notion of what it means, I'm sure 'tis part of her healin' magic."

I looked at Sal with interest, wondering about the song she sang while noting the steady rhythm of her legs and the pack she wore on her back. Then her figure grew indistinct, and I slipped into sleep again.

When next I wakened, the wagon had stopped, and Anne was making preparations for tea. Henry had pulled the wagon into the shade of strange-looking trees with thick trunks, the white bark swirled with patches of gray.

As soon as we stopped, Sal climbed into the wagon to check on me, looking deeply into my swollen eyes and telling me to stick out my tongue. "Sleep," she admonished. "Not talk."

Henry pulled a log close to the wagon and straddled it with his bandy legs to drink his tea. Sal refused the McKades' offer of thick slices of bread and a tepid beverage. Instead, she chose a place well away from Henry, where she drank a few swallows from a skin bag she carried on her back.

When we resumed our journey, it was Millicent who rode with me in the back of the wagon. "Mum's up front," she explained, giving me a searching look. "Are you feeling better?"

"A little." I smiled to lend conviction to my words, but the process of stretching my lips made me wince.

"You poor thing," Millicent crooned. She looked to be about my age, and even with the floppy-brimmed hat, I thought she was pretty.

It was easy to follow Sal's instructions to sleep, for the afternoon heat made it difficult to keep my eyes opened. As Millicent chatted quietly, I finally gave in to the drag of sleep, and Millicent's pleasant voice faded into nothing.

* * *

It was late afternoon when we arrived at Tanybrae. The barking of a dog jerked me back to wakefulness.

"We're here," Millicent said, "and none too soon, either. A bumpy ride in this wagon is enough to give anyone a headache. I can imagine what it's done to you."

"It's better than being in the ocean," I replied.

Millicent reached for my hand. "How did you manage not to drown? When you're feeling stronger, will you tell me about it?"

I nodded, though my mind was on a large brown and white collie that barked and sniffed at Sal. From my bed in the back of the wagon, it was difficult to view much of the house. I caught a glimpse of a high-pitched roof and a low-spreading veranda as the plodding bullocks pulled the wagon close to the door. As soon as we stopped, the grassy yard filled with several people whose main interest seemed to be pinned on me.

Sal scowled at them and waved her arms. "Away . . . Away," she said. Two Aborigine girls quickly complied, but the others paid her little heed.

Fortunately, Anne was of the same mind and sent an apron-clad woman into the house with instructions to see that the most available room was made ready. She turned to a man who loitered by the wagon. "George, I'll need ye to carry Miss Clayborne," she concluded.

The burly man stepped closer, his eyes widening when they took in my swollen face. He was dressed in a worn cambric shirt and work boots, and beneath his battered leather hat, side whiskers and a beard covered his ruddy face.

I clutched the blanket tightly around me as George lifted me into his arms. "I'll be walkin' easy so's not to hurt ya," he said.

His gentleness surprised me as he carried me up the steps to the veranda and across its width to the main portion of the house. I was surprised, too, at the speed with which Henry hurried ahead to open the door.

"Through here and into Brock's room," Anne said, leading the way. "There's no time to make up the guest room."

I had a glimpse of windows spread open to the sun, of pastel colors, and of the richness of polished wood as we passed through a large room and down a hallway. George's boots clumped on the floor, and the rasp of his breathing sounded in my ear.

Anne and Millicent were already in the bedroom. While Anne bustled to plump the pillows, Millicent kept the blanket pulled around me as George laid me on the bed.

"Thank you." My attempted smile felt more like a grimace.

"Ma pleasure, ma'am." George kept his eyes carefully fixed on the wall above my head, belatedly removing his grubby hat with large hands as he backed out of the room.

Anne's face filled with sympathy as she looked down at me. "Ye look worn out. How are ye feelin'?"

I sighed and settled into the softness of the mattress. "Better except for my head."

Sal joined Anne and Millicent. She looked long into my eyes, muttering to herself and nodding. I returned her gaze, noting the intelligence in her brown eyes and the age creases in her leathery skin. She touched the cut and bruises on my head, her fingers a soft caress as she gently rubbed my temples with more of the smelly salve. "Need drink," she said.

I wasn't sure what she meant until she returned with a cup of the bitter concoction she'd given me before. "Drink," she instructed.

I wrinkled my nose at the acrid odor but obediently followed her bidding, swallowing awkwardly as she spooned the hot contents into my mouth.

"Mercy," Millicent whispered after Sal left. "She gives me the shivers."

"She does that," her mother agreed, "but there's no denyin' her healin' power. I doot Miss Clayborne would be doing so well if any other Abo had found her."

"I like her," I whispered.

"Aye, but unfortunately there's some in Australia that are downright hateful to the blacks . . . Treat their animals better, they do."

As she spoke, she removed her unflattering leather hat, revealing a thick plait of chestnut hair fastened in a loose coronet on her head. "We need to give ye a wee bit of a washup and get ye into something besides that smelly blanket." She glanced at Millicent. "If ye'll fetch one of yer nightgowns, I'll see to collectin' soap and water."

Fatigue and pain dragged at my brain, and I was content to drowse until the women returned. When they did, their arms were laden with supplies. Besides her nightgown, Millicent carried a sheet and towel while her mother bore a pan of steaming water.

"There," Anne said after she poured water into a basin. "I'm sure a wash and fresh nightie will help ye feel better." She spread the sheet over me in efficient movements. "Now if ye'll unwrap yerself from that blanket, Millie can pull it off."

In no time, the task of removing the blanket was done, and I gave myself over to Anne's gentle ministrations. "I think 'twill be best if we leave yer poor face and hair for another day when yer feeling better."

I nodded and closed my eyes, savoring the smell of the scented soap as Millicent lifted the sheet so her mother could wash me.

Anne gave a little gasp when she reached my legs. "Och, ye poor dear. I've no' seen so many scrapes and bruises. As bad as yer poor arms they are."

"They're from the boards I clung to," I told her.

"Och, 'tis a miracle ye dinna drown."

"It is," I agreed, my heart thanking God for His goodness.

* * *

Next morning I awoke feeling more like myself. The throbbing in my head had diminished, and a distant ache when I stretched was all that remained of my sore muscles.

"How do ye feel this fair morn?" a voice asked.

I turned my head and saw Anne McKade sitting in a chair next to the window. "Better," I answered, my voice stronger than I expected. "But you needn't have sat with me. It couldn't have been a very comfortable night for you."

"There'll be other nights to enjoy my bed. With ye bein' so hurt, I kenned ye shouldna be left alone."

"Thank you for being so good to me." Tears came and I swallowed to control them.

Mrs. McKade left her chair. "There, there, lass. 'Tis the way of us country folk, lookin' out for each other." She patted my shoulder and smiled. "Besides, Millicent was gettin' bored with life at Tanybrae. Havin' ye to talk to and look after will give her somethin' useful to do."

She paused and looked outside. "I promised Sal I'd let her ken when ye woke up." Mrs. McKade bustled from the room, her step brisk, as if the prospect of having something to do invigorated her.

No sooner had she left than Millicent came in. "Mum said you're awake and feeling a little better. I wanted to bring you breakfast, but she said I should wait till Sal has a look at you." She sat down on the edge of the bed, taking care not to jostle me. "You'll never believe the things they're saying about you."

"Saying?"

"And Sal," she added. "She spent the night with Callie and Min, the Abo girls who work for us. They seldom say much, but this morning they're bursting with the things she told them."

I frowned in puzzlement.

"Did you know Sal dreamed about you during the storm?" Millicent gave an excited nod. "In her dream she saw an enormous fish tossed about in the waves. Just before it reached land, it opened its mouth and spewed a white woman onto the sand. Sal could see you were hurt and needed help, so as soon as the storm ended, she and her family went to find you. The dream was so real they knew exactly where to look for you." The excitement on Millicent's face was replaced with wonder. "Have you ever heard of anything so strange? Just like Jonah and the whale."

Something pricked along my spine and sent warm tears to my eyes. Had God heard my frantic prayers and whispered them in a dream to Sal?

Seeing my tears, Millicent reached for my hand. "It's strange, isn't it? Strange and wonderful."

Mrs. McKade returned with Sal. Many new thoughts filled my head as I noted Sal's quiet dignity and the way her gray-white hair curled like a halo around her brown face. When her eyes sought mine, something passed between us—warmth that whispered of time older than memory, yet new and deep too. It came with such force that I knew we would always be friends. Tears came to my eyes, and I saw answering moisture well up in Sal's dark eyes.

"Missy better," she said after a long moment. "Now Sal go home."

"Miss Clayborne can sit up, then?" Anne asked.

Sal nodded. As she did, she touched the butterfly pendant hanging around her neck. "Courage. Be strong."

"Thank you." I reached for Sal's hand, felt its leathery warmth and strength. "Thank you."

Sal took my hand in both of hers, looked closely at the palm, then slowly turned it over to look at the back. "Soon," she said. "Good come soon, missy."

THREE

After Mrs. McKade had seen Sal on her way and sent Millicent on an errand, she returned to my room.

"I wish she would ride," I said. "How can Sal walk so far without shoes?"

"I wondered the same when I first came to Tanybrae, but I had only to look at the Abos' feet to learn why. Hard as nails, they be. Thick too. My son says 'tis calluses they have, same as he gets from workin' with ax or spade."

Sleep and a bowl of porridge had refreshed me, and I used the opportunity to satisfy my curiosity. "Tell me about your family. You mentioned a son."

"Brock's his name. He's away at Melbourne, and who's to say when he'll be back. And ye've met Millicent." She paused and looked out the window. "There was two others . . . a wee laddie and lass. Diphtheria took the bairn before he was old enough to toddle. And wee Alice . . ." Her voice quavered over the name. "'Twas snakebite took her." Anne swallowed, and for an instant her pleasant features hardened. "'Tisn't just flies I hate aboot Australia. There's fierce heat and snakes and wild fires in the summer . . . endless rain and too much loneliness in the winter. 'Tis a hard land ye've come to Miss Clayborne, one that'll test ye dearly if ye plan to stay."

Before I could form any words of sympathy, Anne's voice came again. "Ye mustn't let my maudlin talk put ye off Australia. There's much that's beautiful and good aboot this land. 'Tis wonderful here in the Gippsland. Sometimes the beauty makes me ache with wonder . . . birds that fair dazzle the eyes, and strange animals. I doona regret leavin' Scotland, for 'twas here I wed me Angus, though he's gone now too, God rest his soul." There was a tiny silence. "Angus left me with Tanybrae tho'."

My mind caught hold of Tanybrae and held it like a cushion against Anne's pain—losing the sweet bairn and wee Alice and husband Angus. I looked at her with new understanding. Small wonder there were lines etched around the corners of her mouth and sadness in her lovely gray eyes.

"What about ye, Miss Clayborne? Where do ye come from, and what brought ye to Australia?"

"England. My parents are dead, and I'm on my way to Melbourne to live with my brother."

Only then did I realize *The Mermaid* should have reached its destination by now . . . that is if it hadn't perished in the storm. My mind refused to give the idea credence and concentrated instead on the realization that everyone on board must believe I'd drowned. "Dear heaven," I whispered. "I must let my brother know I'm alive."

"Och—I was so concerned aboot getting' ye to Tanybrae that I dinna think to ask if ye had family who would be worried. I'll tell Henry he must be off to Melbourne as soon as he can get himself ready. He'll need yer brother's direction tho'. Can ye remember it?"

I tried to recall the address scrawled across Robert's letters. All that came was the name of the street. "He lives on Rathdown Street and his name is Robert Clayborne. I'm sure if Henry asks, someone can direct him."

Anne nodded and left the room momentarily. While she was gone, I thought of Robert and the Hewitts and wondered how they'd taken the news of my death.

"How long since the storm?" I asked when she returned.

"'Twas on Tuesday, and today's Friday, so three days."

"How far is Tanybrae from Melbourne?"

"Less than a day, though if we've had a bad rain it can take longer. 'Tis why we came for ye with bullocks instead of horses. Wet like it is, horses woulda had a hard time."

I looked out the window to a sky unbroken by clouds. Hopefully by tomorrow night Robert would know I was alive.

"I'm needin' to check with Hilda aboot tea, but Millicent's dyin' to have a chat with ye. She'll be along directly."

When she left, I turned my attention to my room—or rather Brock McKade's room. The carvings on the bed were bold and masculine, as were the armoire and wardrobe. Twin windows looked out onto the veranda. They were draped in dark blue damask that matched the padding on the chairs. A bookcase and a large painting of horses galloping across a meadow dominated one of the walls. From this I judged that Brock McKade liked both books and horses.

Before I could think more on the man whose room I occupied, Millie knocked on the door. "Mum made me promise not to tire you with my talking. She says I'm as bad as Henry sometimes—which isn't true, but I do like a good gossip. That's one of the drawbacks to living at Tanybrae, no one to talk to but Mum and Brock. But Brock sees that I get into Melbourne so I can go to some of the dances and parties."

She paused and looked thoughtful. "Strange, but when I'm in town I wish I were at Tanybrae, and when I'm here I wish I were in Melbourne. It's like I can't make up my mind. Mum says it's part of growing up, but Brock says I need to stop being so wishy-washy." Millicent didn't seem to expect a comment and went on without pause. "I wish Brock were home so you could meet him. I know you'll like him . . . all the women do. Mum and I can't understand why he's not married. When we ask, he just smiles and says when he finds the right woman he'll marry her in a flash."

"Is your brother older or younger than you?"

"Older. Six years to be exact." She paused, and a pleased smile played at the corners of her lips. "It's nice having an older brother to escort me to all the parties. Nice too that some of Brock's mates have taken a fancy to me. Well, one or two have, anyway."

I could see why. I'd thought her attractive, even under yesterday's unflattering hat. Today she was even more appealing, with tendrils of rich chestnut hair framing piquant features and large gray eyes lit with animation. While she chatted on, I found myself liking her all the more, and had I been feeling more myself, I would have encouraged her to stay longer. As it was, my eyes began to droop.

Seeing them, Millie stopped in midsentence. "Mercy, now I've tired you just like Mum told me not to do."

"It's not you . . ." I began.

"I'm such a chatterbox." She gave me a quick kiss on the cheek. "I'll be back after you've rested."

* * *

After I'd napped, Anne suggested I try sitting up. I managed it with a little help and felt encouraged when there was no sign of dizziness. Anne and Millicent seemed as pleased with my progress as I was.

"Maybe by tomorrow you can try a few steps around the house," Millicent said. "I can't wait to show you Tanybrae."

"Now don't ye be rushin' things," her mother cautioned. "Remember Miss Clayborne's had a terrible ordeal." She paused and adjusted my pillow. "Do ye feel strong enough to tell us aboot it?"

At my nod, she and Millicent pulled their chairs close. My description was brief, for the memory of being sucked into the heaving ocean brought a return of terror. Even though the day was warm and pleasant, shivers caused my body to tremble and made my voice quaver.

"Poor lass." Anne put her hand on my shoulder, and Millicent tucked the covers more firmly around me. After we had talked a little longer, Anne got to her feet. "I wish I could stay longer, but I told Callie I'd show her how I want the last rows of the garden laid out. Callie's one of the Abo girls and a niece of Sal's, I think." She glanced at her daughter. "Why don't ye tell Miss Clayborne aboot Melbourne while I talk to Callie."

"Please call me Jessamyne."

"And you must call me Millie," Millicent put in.

Anne paused briefly at the door and nodded. "'Tis as it should be, for I've an idea the two of ye are of a similar age."

"I'm twenty-one." I said.

"And I'm almost nineteen." Millie's face took on more animation. "I can't wait to introduce you to my friends in Melbourne. They often invite me to stay with them and attend their parties."

"How do you know Melbourne so well?" I asked, seeing a satisfied smile pass Anne's lips as she left the room.

"It was Brock's doing, though Mum played a part too. Brock said I needed to learn there was more to life than riding horses, and Mum agreed. So I went to boarding school in Melbourne for four years." A tiny frown wrinkled her forehead. "At first I hated it, but after I settled in and made friends, I came to enjoy it. Hopefully it will be the same for you—liking Melbourne, I mean. There are dozens of nice shops and several parks. Boat rides on the Yarra River are like heaven."

I tried to picture the days ahead—my reunion with Robert and the beginning of a new life in Australia. I hoped I'd find Melbourne to my liking and that, like Millie, I'd soon make new friends. At that my thoughts turned to my bruised face and the McKades' reaction when they saw it. "How is my face? Does it look terrible?"

Millie gave me a quick look, then glanced away. "Your eyes and mouth are badly swollen. And the color—" Her voice broke off.

"Do you have a mirror?"

"Yes . . . but . . ." For a second Millie looked disconcerted. "What I mean is, do you think it wise?"

Stubbornness overtook my unease. "Yes."

Millie's pensive expression when she handed me a tortoiseshell mirror increased my unease. Lifting the mirror, I gasped. Surely the swollen, distorted face gazing back from the glass couldn't be me.

Too shocked to speak, I could only stare. Where before I'd possessed smooth white skin, now I saw ugly swellings of red and purple. And my hair! I wanted to cry at the tangle of snarled, witch-like hair. I swallowed and laid the mirror face down on the covers.

"I'm sorry," Millie whispered. "I'm sure in a few days you'll look better."

"I hope so." I strove to make my voice light, but inside I feared my face might be permanently marred. Until that moment I hadn't realized what an important part my looks had played in my life. Although I would not describe myself as a beauty, I knew I was considered comely. Compliments about my glossy black hair and deep blue eyes had been frequent and had added to my confidence and sense of well-being. But now . . . I closed my mind against a montage of unpleasant thoughts and took a deep breath. "Do you think we can get the tangles out of my hair without cutting it?" I asked.

Millie's expression was doubtful. "We can try."

The next minutes were painful as Millie worked her fingers through the worst of the snarls. I closed my eyes and tried not to wince. Instead, I diverted myself by asking the names of her friends and if she had a particular favorite among her brother's mates. My tongue tripped over *mate,* for I didn't know if I'd used it correctly.

"There's Christopher Morgan. He's always first to write his name in my dance card, and last time I was in Melbourne, he came by twice to call on me." She reached for the comb to work at another snarl. As she did, Anne rejoined us.

"Are ye sure yer up to all of this?"

I nodded. The thought of Robert seeing me in such a deplorable condition made the pain of making myself presentable a small price to pay.

Anne went in search of another comb, and the two of them worked with purpose at the snarls. Despite the tugging, time passed pleasantly as we discussed the latest fashions and compared Australian life to that in England. I began to think I would fit in very nicely— that is, if my bruised face ever healed.

* * *

I slept again that afternoon and awoke feeling refreshed. Anne had braided the hair rid of snarls, while the rest was gathered into a loose plait so they could finish combing through it on the morrow.

In place of her comb, Millie now carried a book of fashion plates. "I thought we could look at them . . . That is if you feel up to it."

"I do. I always like looking at pretty things."

Together we looked at pictures of the latest fashions, pointing out those we were most taken with and sharing our favorite colors. I watched expression cross Millie's pretty features, took in the richness of her chestnut hair, and thought it wouldn't be long until she fell in love and married.

From there I fell to wondering about her brother. What did Brock McKade look like? Would I find him as pleasing as his women friends did?

The amusement in Millie's voice as she pointed out an exaggerated costume jerked my mind away from her brother. But it didn't diminish my curiosity about him—this man in whose room I sat.

* * *

By the following morning, I felt much better. Not only could I sit up without becoming dizzy, I could also walk and move around the room. Although my first steps were painful, those that followed were less so.

After breakfast Anne returned to my room. "'Tis a bonny morn outside. If yer feelin' up to it, why doona we go out on the veranda to finish untanglin' yer hair." She paused and looked out at a sky devoid of clouds. "I've a notion a wee bit o' fresh air will make ye feel better."

Millie went ahead to arrange cane-back chairs by the veranda door that opened off the bedroom. After I was comfortably seated, Anne draped a shawl around my shoulders as she and Millie sat down. "I doona want ye catchin' a chill."

I scarcely heard her, my mind being occupied instead with the lovely view. Green rolling hills stretched to the misty horizon, all dotted with livestock—the McKade cattle and horses I assumed. Colorful birds chattered noisily from nearby trees, the flash of bright wings among gray-green leaves reminding me that this was Australia, not England.

"It's lovely," I breathed. "But the trees and birds are so strange."

"Och, they're strange, aright," Anne agreed, "but Brock and Millie will be tellin' ye different, for 'tis all they ken." Millie smiled at this while Anne went on. "The big trees with white trunks we call ghost gums, tho' there are some in Melbourne that call them eucalyptus. As for the birds, the white ones with pink breasts are galahs—pesky things they be with their squawkin' and quarrelin', but right bonny when they fly. 'Tis the same with the green and red lorikeets. Some call them parrots. I canna get enough of watchin' their bright feathers flash through the trees."

I nodded in agreement. How would it be to look out my window each morning and be greeted with so many beautiful birds?

"When you're feeling stronger, I'll take you for a walk around the place," Millie said. "But for now we'd better see about your hair."

I suffered through the ordeal of untangling it as best I could, for I was anxious to have it looking better for Robert. Hopefully by evening he would be here.

"Do ye feel strong enough to tell us a wee bit aboot yerself?" Anne prompted. "Ye said yer poor parents are dead."

"My mother was thrown from a runaway horse when I was five. I was with her . . ." My voice trailed away as I recalled my terror and the frantic gait of my pony as it bolted after Mother. "Our groom was able to snatch me from my pony, but he was too late for Mother."

I stared down at the snowy skirt of my nightgown, aware of Millie and that Anne's hands had stilled. "But I've had a good life," I hurried on. "Father and I were very close and, of course, there was Cook and Mrs. Woolsey, our housekeeper, and later my governess."

"Ye had a governess did ye?" Anne asked gently.

"Father thought it was best." I realized now that his decision might well have been prompted by economics. The best ladies' seminaries did not come cheap, and Miss Lovedale had been so eager for a position that her salary had probably not been much. What an ostrich I'd been, never once suspecting that Father's income was not as great as that of his friends. Yet somehow he'd been able to maintain membership in his favorite club and see that I was presented to society.

"When did yer brother come to Australia?" Anne asked, finishing my hair and moving beside me.

I realized I was still a mystery to the McKades, and that living so far from town they were hungry for something new to think and talk about. I didn't mention Robert's and Father's quarrel or that my brother had been disowned. "About twelve years ago. Robert has always been one to seek adventure," I said, which was true. I remembered his numerous scrapes and his impatience with conformity. "I think Australia met his definition of adventure."

"Aye," Anne agreed. "There's many come here for that very reason, my Angus among them."

"How long have you been at Tanybrae?"

"'Tis twenty-five years . . . Brock was just a wee bairn. 'Twas nip and tuck to make a go of it with a few cattle to run and trees to fell, and naught but Henry to help Angus." She paused and motioned to the pasture. "'Twas not as ye see it now. All was a tangle of trees and bush. We lived rough, with naught but a bark hut to cover our heads. When we finally built a wee house with wood floors, it seemed a castle after the hut."

I pictured Angus and Henry working with ax and saw to fell the trees and Anne bringing them a flask of water with one of the children clinging to her skirt. They had paid the price of sacrifice and hard work to build Tanybrae. It must have been difficult in those early years. Millie seemed as entranced with her mother's memories as I.

"Many would have given up, but not my Angus." Anne went on. "He was a fighter, he was, and not afeared of hard work. Had an uncanny mind for figurin' and plannin' too. Every year he bought more cattle, and when we began to prosper, he added the horses."

Anne's fingers stilled, and when I looked up I saw that she was smiling. "When we wed, Angus vowed he'd build me a home as bonny as any I'd seen in Scotland. He was a man ever true to his word, and what ye see today is that promise."

"It's lovely."

"Oh, aye. Like I said, me Angus was a man ever thinkin' and plannin'." She resumed her careful work with the tangles.

"What did you do while Mr. McKade was felling trees and taking care of the cattle? I'm sure you must have been busy too."

"Aye, there was much to keep me busy. Sometimes I even helped Angus and Henry choppin' the trees, but most times I tended the bairns and the chooks and looked after the garden. 'Tis a lovely land, the Gippsland. Berries and fruit and every kind of vegetable ye could be namin' grow like weeds, they do."

She went on to explain the making of butter and cheese, that chooks were what Australians called live chickens, and a myriad of other tasks and interesting details that filled her life. No mention was made of the wee bairn and little Alice, though her voice trembled slightly when she spoke of the danger of snakes.

"When did Mr. McKade die?" I asked the next time she paused.

Her hands stilled again, but Millie continued to work with the snarls, almost with more resolve it seemed. "'Twill soon make five years."

Silence followed her words—a silence peopled with the shadowy wisps of a small bairn and a wee lassie and the terrible loss of her husband.

Millie was quick to put the conversation back on more comfortable ground. "There, this lock is smoothed to the very end." She held it out so I could see it. "You have lovely hair—black as magpie wings and just as shiny. I'm sure we'll have all the tangles out before your brother gets here."

"I hope my appearance doesn't shock him."

"I told Henry to prepare him," Anne said. "Just the same, 'twill be good for yer hair to be properly washed and combed."

"And you can wear one of my dresses," Millie put in. "I'm sure one will fit you."

Their words cheered me, and I took heart at the prospect of Robert's coming. What would he think of me? And just as important, what would I think of him?

FOUR

After an afternoon nap, I went with Millie to the south veranda. My hair had been washed and dried and carefully coifed so as not to disturb the deep cut, which Anne said was healing nicely. The smelly green salve had also been washed from my face. Although Millie offered me her mirror, I declined, wanting to think of myself as I had been, rather than as I was.

From this side of the veranda I discovered that the house sat on a rise, with the barn and outbuildings situated off to the side. Horses grazed in an enclosed paddock, and a belt of trees growing along a small stream offered shade for them and the cattle.

"Isn't it lovely?" Millie asked. "Spring is my favorite time of year."

It took me a second to remember the seasons were reversed in Australia. "Is it always this green?"

"Only in the spring and early summer. Unless it's unusually rainy, by late summer the grass turns brown." She paused and touched my arm. "I know you're anxious to see your brother, but Mum and I are hoping you'll stay with us for a few more days. There's so much I'd like to show and tell you, that is, when you're feeling stronger. You do ride, don't you?"

I shook my head. "I think horses are lovely from a distance, but since Mother's death, I take care not to get too close."

Millie's features fell. "Oh. Though I understand," she assured me. "I've ridden for as long as I can remember. Horses are my second legs and the best way to get around at Tanybrae."

"Does your mother ride too?" I asked.

"She does, though not as much as I do, and of course not as much as Brock. He's always with the horses."

"Where does he go on his trips?"

"Mainly through the Gippsland and to Melbourne, though sometimes he goes as far as Adelaide." She paused and her voice lifted. "Our horse Night Flyer won the Melbourne Cup last year. That's where Brock is now. Helping to get things arranged for the race next month."

Horse racing had never been of interest to me, but I remembered Robert had thought it all the thing. I also recalled hearing that inordinate amounts of money were won and lost at the events. Millie's next words bore this out.

"Brock used the money from winning last year's race to buy new brood mares. If he can win again, he plans to buy more land."

We sat for a few moments in comfortable silence, my eyes taking in the view that stretched before me. Everything was so big and wide at Tanybrae, rather like the vastness of a rolling green ocean.

"Do you have any close neighbors?" I asked.

"Only the Marshalls. Peter and his wife Carrie have been here longer than Mum and Da. Since it's half a day's ride, we don't see them very often. And then there's Wooraronga." Her voice slid awkwardly over the word.

"What a strange name."

"It's Aboriginal. Many places in Australia have Abo names. Wooraronga used to belong to the Somersets, but when they fell on hard times, a man from Melbourne bought it. Since he doesn't live there, it's the same as not having neighbors. Stockmen live there, of course, and a couple to look after the house. They keep to themselves and aren't friendly, so we haven't much to do with them, except Brock. Their sheep keep coming onto our land and eating our grass. Brock had words with their stockmen, but it hasn't made much difference. They're a rough bunch of blokes, a lot different from the ones the Somersets hired."

"How disappointing for you."

"Yes, though you mustn't think I'm lonely or unhappy. There's plenty at Tanybrae to keep me occupied. Like I said, Brock sees that I get into town several times a year, and Mum's thinking to start a school for the stockmen's children—the Abos too. You can't see them from here, but there are several houses at Tanybrae besides our own. We're almost like a little village. George and his family live in Mum and Da's old house, and the stockmen that aren't married bach together in a big room off the barn. But—" Her voice broke off and she pointed to the avenue of trees leading to the house. "Look! Someone's coming!"

A man on horseback cantered his horse toward us. My first thought was that it was Robert, but when Millie stepped to the veranda railing and waved, I knew otherwise.

"It's Brock!" She flew down the steps and hurried to meet him, her green dress billowing out from her slender waist. Her brother reined in his horse when she met him. They were too far away for me to hear their voices, but the frequency with which he looked at me left little doubt that I was the subject of the conversation.

I immediately felt self-conscious, the sensation as uncomfortable as when I'd been small and overheard people refer to me as that "poor child who'd lost her mother." Being uncomfortable didn't stop me from noting Brock McKade's broad shoulders or the easy manner with which he sat his horse. A wide-brim leather hat prevented me from seeing much of his features, but something other than Millie's reference to her brother's good looks told me I would find them to my liking. Such were my emotions that spring afternoon as I first saw Brock McKade—self-consciousness, curiosity, and wonder at whether his lips would tighten with revulsion when he saw my swollen face.

After what seemed an inordinately long time, he dismounted and walked with Millie to the veranda. I lifted my head, trying to picture myself as I'd been before the storm—comely and confident and smiling—but when I attempted to smile, the pain of my cut lip quickly reminded me the memory was but an illusion.

"This is my brother Brock," Millie said. "Brock, this is Miss Jessamyne Clayborne. I was just telling him about . . ."

What else Millie said was lost in my rush of emotions as Brock McKade removed his hat and smiled. For a second I forgot to breathe, forgot everything except that I knew that smile, knew also the high cheekbones and squared-off chin, his features as familiar to me as my own.

"G'day, Miss Clayborne." Not "Miss Jessamyne" as he'd said in the dream. Even so, I recognized the voice, its deep timbre and nuance washing through me like the words to a song I'd longed to sing all my life. For a moment I thought I heard waves crashing off the headland, yet enough of reason remained to tell me I sat on the veranda at Tanybrae and that Millie stood at her brother's side. The breeze blowing off the meadow ruffled Brock's hair, which was thick and wavy and shone like burnished bronze in the afternoon sun. His blue eyes held only concern and kindness, and he didn't seem to notice that I sat with mouth slightly agape or that my face was bruised and distorted.

Questions tumbled through my mind. Did Brock recognize me? Had he dreamed of our meeting as I had? I listened with half a mind as he welcomed me to Tanybrae. "Millie told me of your misfortune. Who would think such could happen? I hope you'll soon be feeling right as rain."

My mind was fully taken with the man, not his words. Although his voice was warm and friendly, he gave no sign that he sensed anything unusual. Disappointment nibbled at my wonder, its bite no more than an irritation as I strove to put my jumbled thoughts into a semblance of order. "Thank you," was all that came out.

"I'm sorry your arrival to Australia wasn't more friendly. The storm and the battering it gave you wasn't one to make you feel welcome."

My ability to make a sensible reply was still lacking, but a small sound from Millie brought me sharply back to myself. "It's . . . it's not what I expected," I began weakly. I took a deep breath and made a better effort. "But your mother and Millie have more than made up for the oversight with their warmth and hospitality."

I watched in fascination as a smile hovered at the corners of his mouth. "Such are the McKades, Miss Clayborne. Country folk who like to look after their neighbors and anyone else who needs help."

"A trait for which I'm extremely grateful."

We studied each other, me sitting in a cane-back chair in Millie's borrowed pink dress, and Brock in a blue cambric shirt with moleskin breeches tucked into serviceable riding boots. Unlike my admirers in England who spent their days behind a desk, Brock was a man of the outdoors, one who seemed at ease with himself and those around him.

Just what Brock thought of me, I could not know, but I saw interest in his blue eyes, and he seemed to have already forgotten my bruised face.

"I was just telling Jessamyne about Tanybrae," Millie said. "Mum and I are hoping she'll stay with us until next week, but—"

Before she could say more, Anne stepped out onto the veranda. "Brock!" Her voice filled with gladness. "We didn't expect you home so soon. Did everything go well?"

Brock nodded. "All the arrangements for the race have been made, a jockey hired and rooms booked for the three of us at the Grand Hotel."

Millie let out an excited squeal. "The Grand Hotel! How wonderful!"

Brock laughed. "It's better than the cubbyhole we put up at last year, that's for sure. But times are better now, and hopefully after Night Flyer wins this year, they'll improve even more." Brock glanced toward the paddock. "Speaking of which, I'd better check on my favorite horse and give Springer here a rubdown and water." He nodded at me. "Miss Clayborne." Another nod. "Mum."

After going a few steps, he stopped. "It looks like we have visitors."

I watched as a carriage emerged from the trees and rolled across the grassland. A horse and rider loped at the side. Millie shaded her eyes with her hand. "That's Henry, so that means . . ."

I struggled to my feet. "Robert."

We stood without speaking as the carriage barreled up the avenue of fig trees and slowed to a halt in front of the house. A man emerged from the black vehicle, his legs long and thick through the thighs, his shoulders wide and filling his dark-colored coat. The features of his face were partially hidden by his hat. Even so, I knew it was Robert, recognizing him by his quick stride as he came toward us.

I moved to the top of the steps and watched as he removed his hat, his steps slowing as his eyes took in my face.

"Egad!" Distress crossed his features, though he made an effort to conceal it, as I did mine, for the handsome brother of my youth had changed to a man with thinning hair and features that showed extra flesh. All this changed when his lips curved into his characteristic smile. "Jessa . . . Is it really my little Jessa?" In three quick strides he mounted the steps and pulled me into his arms.

Tears came as I was folded into his embrace and felt the strength of his sturdy body. "Robbie." Despite the painful bruises, I buried my face in his shoulder. After a moment he set me away from him.

"I know I look frightful," I began, wiping at the tears.

"Who cares about that? The important thing is that you're alive. When the ship's captain came with your trunks and told me you'd been swept overboard, I wouldn't believe him." He swallowed hard, and I saw the shine of tears in his blue eyes. "Ah, Jessa. Do you know how many times I've wondered about you?"

"And me about you. I begged Father to—" The tightening of Robert's hand on my arm reminded me of the McKades. "—to let me come to Australia," I finished. Turning to Millie and Anne, I added, "Forgive me. In my excitement I've forgotten my manners. Robert, this is Mrs. McKade and her daughter Millicent. They took me in and have been very good to me." I looked over at Brock, who, despite being in conversation with Henry, watched Robert closely. "And Brock McKade," I added.

Robert spoke to both Mrs. McKade and Millie as he bowed and took their hands, but to Brock, he only nodded. Brock's nod to him was just as cool. "McKade and I have already met," Robert said to dismiss my questioning look.

With this we went inside the house, the tension between the two men seeming to follow us into the sitting room. I listened with only half a mind while Anne invited Robert to stay for tea and to spend the night, all the while wondering what had happened to cause my brother to be so cold to Brock McKade. Although Robert graciously accepted her offer, his response was not as positive when she tried to persuade him to let me stay at Tanybrae until the following week.

"Yer sister has been through a terrible ordeal, and I'm thinkin' 'twould be wise for her to rest a wee bit longer before makin' the tirin' journey to Melbourne."

"I appreciate your concern, Mrs. McKade, but I'm anxious to get my sister back to Melbourne where she can be examined by my physician and looked after by my wife." His tone was clipped and cool.

"But Robert . . ."

The look he directed at me made me close my mouth. Still weak and not myself, I knew I was not up to arguing with my brother. More than that, I didn't want to begin our reunion with discord. Even so, I felt embarrassed and hoped the apologetic look I gave Anne and Millicent told them Robert's words and actions were not mine.

"I doona ken what we were thinking, wearin' Miss Clayborne out," Anne's eyes met mine as she spoke. "Poor lass, ye look ready to drop."

"I am a little tired." In truth my strength had suddenly left me.

Robert was quick to help me to my room.

"I'm sorry. Maybe we can talk after I've rested," I apologized.

"And if not, remember we'll have the whole of tomorrow to talk," Robert assured me.

I was grateful for his arm to lean on, and in my gladness to be with him again, I quickly forgave him for his rudeness as he and Anne led me to my room.

"Now off to sleep with ye," Anne ordered after she'd seen me comfortably settled on the bed.

I wanted to comply, but the wonder of seeing the man I'd dreamed about residing at Tanybrae kept sleep at bay. How could it be? In my dream, the man astride his black stallion had burrowed his way into my heart. In my waking life, would Brock McKade do the same?

* * *

Feeling much refreshed after my nap, I joined the McKades and Robert for a meal the McKades referred to as tea. Since the afternoon was long gone, the term surprised me, but whether *tea* or *dinner,* I looked forward to it. The sun had set and a lamp cast warm light onto the snowy tablecloth and flowered china.

Robert, who'd been examining a painting of the Australian landscape, came to greet me. "Jessa. I hoped you'd be able to join us."

"So did I. Do you know how many years it's been since we dined together?"

"Twelve, I believe. I counted them on my way here. You were only nine, but look at you now."

"Please, don't." I put a self-conscious hand to my face. "I know I'm a sight."

Robert dropped a soft kiss onto my forehead. "Don't worry about the bruises. They're sure to heal."

Before he could say more, Anne came into the room with a vase of roses and set them on the table.

"How lovely!" I exclaimed, admiring the perfection of the pink heads that spilled from an aquamarine vase.

"Flowers are Mum's specialty," Millie said, following her mother into the room. "You should see her garden."

Anne stepped back to judge the effect of the flowers. "Roses are my favorite, and they do well in our climate. I canna get enough of them." She paused and looked around the room. "Now where's that son of mine? I told him not to be late."

"I'm right here," Brock said, coming through the door. "George and Dan had things they needed to tell me."

"George," Millie laughed. "He always has things to tell you. What was it this time? That one of the mares has the colic?"

My mind was too preoccupied with Brock to pay much heed to the conversation. He'd changed into a white shirt, the collar unbuttoned and without a cravat. The casualness did not diminish his good looks, but rather emphasized his tanned face and damp, freshly combed hair. Despite my admiration, I was aware of the unfriendly look he shot at Robert. What had happened to set the two at odds? I felt Robert's stiffness as he helped me into my chair, saw the tightness of Brock's lips as he bent to do the same for Millie and his mother.

After we were seated, Anne nodded at her son. "Would ye please lead us in grace?"

Brock grimaced, his mood clearly at odds with his mother's request, but his voice after he bowed his head came out firm and respectful.

When he finished, two young Aborigine women carried steaming bowls of food to the table—roast beef and potatoes surrounded by carrots glistening with melted butter.

"I'd like ye to meet Callie," Anne said to me as the taller woman set the platter of meat on the table. I glanced up at a dark face framed by mahogany curls and saw brown eyes appraise me.

"And this is Min," Anne went on, indicating the second woman. "Both are related to Sal and have been at Tanybrae since they were but wee lassies."

I smiled as I met Min's gaze. Her comely features were less animated than Callie's, her dark hair straight instead of curly. Like Callie, she darted quick glances in my direction, reminding me of what Sal had told them about her dream. I turned to Robert. "It was Sal and her family who found and cared for me after I was washed overboard."

Robert's answer was a curt nod, one that told me he thought it a breach of etiquette for Anne to introduce the women. More than that, I sensed he didn't like being served by Aborigines.

"No doot ye'll be findin' our ways more casual than those in the city, Mr. Clayborne," Anne said. "Since we have few close neighbors, we savor the company of those who live with us at Tanybrae."

Robert's only response was to make a careful cut of the beef with his knife.

Brock's voice filled the silence. "Mr. Clayborne *is* one of our neighbors, Mum."

Anne turned and stared at her son.

"When I was in Melbourne, I discovered that Mr. Clayborne and his partner own Wooraronga."

Millie's pretty mouth was slightly agape as she shot a nervous look at Robert. All she'd told me about Wooraronga's stockmen and their rude ways skittered through my mind. *"A rough bunch,"* she had called them. *"Men who let their sheep graze on Tanybrae land."*

"Is this true?" Mrs. McKade asked.

"It is." Robert's voice held no apology, nor did he seem to be discomfited, but acted as if they were conversing of something of no more import than the weather.

Not so with Brock, who set his fork across the remains of his food and gave Robert a long, measured look. "The reason I was late for tea is because one of my men told me your sheep have come on Tanybrae land again. This must stop, Mr. Clayborne. Do you understand?"

Robert's fingers tightened on his knife, and his voice was clipped and taut with anger. "Don't come on high-and-mighty with me, McKade. I told you I'd have a talk with my foreman."

"Then see that it's done."

An uncomfortable silence settled over the room, broken only by the clink of silver against plate and the rhythmic ticking of a clock on the side table. Searching for something to break past the discomfort, I complimented Anne on the meal.

"Thank ye, but I'm thinkin' it should be Hilda ye thank. She's the one what does all the cookin'."

"Wait till you taste Hilda's sponge cake. She made it special for you," Millie put in.

The women joined me in making polite conversation, but Brock and Robert didn't participate. Each kept his eyes on his plate, their expressions sullen. As the plates were cleared, the tension mounted. I breathed a sigh of relief when Brock excused himself before dessert, saying one of the brood mares truly did have colic.

Since Robert wanted to make an early start for Melbourne, he and I retired as soon as we finished our sponge cake and tea.

"Sleep tight, and I'll see you in the morning," he said as he left me at the bedroom door.

Although the strain at dinner had tired me, I didn't easily fall asleep. Instead my mind again slid to the man whose room I occupied, and I saw his tanned face as he'd sat at the table, heard the anger in his voice when he'd warned Robert. I felt torn between the two men—Robert, my long-lost brother and Brock, literally the man of my dreams.

* * *

A chorus of birds wakened me the next morning, their cheerful songs drawing me to the veranda window. Sunlight and dew-damp grass called their own invitation, one that bade me don Millie's pink dress and step outside. A soft breeze ruffled the leaves of the gum trees, and in the distance I heard the lowing of cattle. Breathing in the sharp aroma of eucalyptus, my attention was caught by the sight of a man leaving the barn. When he saw me, his steps veered toward the veranda, making my heart lift as I recognized Brock McKade.

I ran a hand over my uncombed hair, silently decrying the fact that my appearance couldn't be pleasing. Then my thoughts were wholly taken with the man walking across the grass, his long stride and his smile when he took off his hat.

"I didn't expect to see you up at this early hour, Miss Clayborne. By the looks of you, you slept well."

"I did."

"Good." Brock stopped with a booted foot on the bottom step and looked up at me. "Last night Mum told me more about your ordeal in the water. I've felt the ocean's might and seen the size of storm-tossed waves. To think that anyone, let alone a woman, could survive boggles my mind." He paused and his blue eyes held mine. "It took great strength and courage to cling to a plank for all those hours. Not only do you have my sympathy, but my admiration as well."

I was not unused to receiving compliments about my looks, but to have someone of Brock's stature speak of my courage made me feel awkward. All I could do was nod.

Sensing my discomfort, he changed the subject. "You've chosen an ideal time to come to Australia. Mum calls it a bonny time, and I'm a wee bit partial to it meself." His smile and feigned Scottish lilt immediately put me at ease.

I smiled back. "It's lovely . . . strange too. I've never seen such colorful birds, but I'm disappointed that I haven't seen a kangaroo."

"A herd is more likely what you'll see. At least at Tanybrae. Sometimes they eat Mum's garden. If you were to stay instead of hurrying off to Melbourne, I'm sure you'd see kangaroos a plenty." The look he gave me was measured.

"My brother thinks it best for me to leave for Melbourne."

"And what do you think, Miss Clayborne?" He continued to hold me with his steady gaze, one that said a woman courageous enough to stay afloat in a raging sea should have few qualms about voicing her opinion.

"I think that after I'm recovered, I'd like very much to see more of Tanybrae."

Brock's lips lifted. "I'll be holding you to it . . . Mum and Millie too. We'll even take pains to have some roos waiting, maybe even a koala or two."

I laughed for no reason other than that I was happy. Was it just me who felt an undercurrent of excitement beneath his words? Before I could wonder, Millie stepped out onto the veranda.

"There you are. I came to help you with your hair." She shot an accusing look at Brock. "You said you were too busy to take breakfast with us, but here you are talking with Miss Clayborne."

"I came to bid her good-bye." Brock's voice and expression turned bland. "A safe journey to you, Miss Clayborne. Remember you're always welcome at Tanybrae."

"I'll remember," I said, although it would be more than just the invitation I'd recall.

"You see?" Millie declared. "Even Brock wants you to stay."

"To come," I corrected. "And I will after I'm recovered—that is if you'd like me to visit."

Millie's quick hug blocked my view of her brother on his return to the barn. "Do you need to ask? Mum and I were wondering how we could capture you, but perhaps delay is the better tactic. After Christmas would be an ideal time. By then you should be feeling better and—"

"Millie!" Anne came to the veranda door. "Dinna I tell ye Mr. Clayborne wants to be off?"

"You did, and I was about to tell Jessamyne."

With that I was whisked away to complete my toilette and eat breakfast. Questions about Brock followed me, but Millie's happy chatter gave no opportunity to think them through. For the moment it was enough to know he had thought of me.

* * *

An hour later we set out for Melbourne in Robert's comfortable carriage. The excitement of Brock's invitation was still with me.

More than that, I now had opportunity to become reacquainted with my brother and see more of Australia. Although we did not share the same mother, Robert and I had always been close, and I had missed him.

Dressed in Millie's borrowed pink dress, I waved to her and Anne as the carriage started down the tree-lined lane. Settling into the soft cushions of the carriage, I spoke. "What wonderful women."

"Yes," Robert agreed, "but probably not the best for you to associate with socially."

"Why not?"

"They're not quite our kind, especially the brother. I have better things in mind for you in Melbourne."

"For instance?"

Instead of answering, Robert patted my hand. "We'll talk of that later. First I want to catch up on all that's happened to you. Mr. Radnor wrote that you'd been presented when you turned eighteen. How did that go?"

I recalled my excitement and satisfaction when my dance card had been filled at every occasion. "It went well."

"Yes, I thought as much. Even with the bruises, I can see you bear a strong resemblance to your mother, who was considered a beauty, by the way." He paused and gave me a searching look. "Did you form any attachments?"

I shook my head. "None that lasted."

"Good." A wonderful smile spread over his face. "My little Jessa. Have you noticed that your face isn't as swollen this morning?"

"I haven't looked. In fact, I don't want to look again until I'm recovered. You'll have to be the one to let me know when it's time to look in a mirror."

"I'll do that." He rubbed his chin and looked thoughtful. "Mr. Radnor wrote about Father's death and the need to sell the house. What of Cook and Mrs. Woolsey? Were they still with you?"

"They were . . . and both as gruff and dear as ever." I went on to tell him of our tearful parting and my relief when they were able to find new positions. "Now tell me about you. Mr. Radnor gave me your letters, so I know you were fortunate enough to find gold."

His smile returned. "That was a wild time . . . A good time too, since I made my fortune. You won't believe the size of some of the nuggets. I found a vein up in the hills. Though we lived rough for a while, things are now building up along the Yarra, as you can see from being with the McKades. Melbourne is quite a city, and I think you'll like it."

"Your letters mention your wife and children."

"Yes, Olivia." His smile faltered. "I met Olivia after I made my fortune, which brings me to something I need to mention. You see . . ." There was an uncomfortable pause. It lasted so long I grew uneasy.

"No one in Australia knows I was disowned. They think I'm the younger son of a good family. The good family is true, but the part about being disowned . . ." His eyes became unreadable. "It's imperative that this doesn't come to light, especially now. Can I depend on you to keep quiet?"

"You know you can. Aren't we brother and sister?"

"That's my girl. And just so you know, keeping quiet won't hurt your prospects either."

"Do you think I've spent my life telling others about you? Father was adamant that we never discuss you or the situation that led you to leave our home. The truth is, Robert, I have no notion why you were disowned." It was on the tip of my tongue to add, "nor do I care," but something in his eyes made me swallow the words. He seemed surprised and relieved that I did not know. But why? Although I loved the Robert I had known as a child, I realized I knew little about him as a man.

"I knew I could depend upon you." His smile returned, and with it, his charm. "As for Olivia, she does well enough as a wife—good family, lovely manners—and I'm pleased to say we move in the best circles. I'm hoping the two of you will become friends."

"As am I, since I know no one in Melbourne." I thought fleetingly of the Hewitts and decided now was not the time to let Robert know I intended to continue that friendship.

"Olivia and I have two children," Robert went on. "Burdell will soon be eight, and Sophia is six. I have hopes for the boy. He takes after his Grandfather Griffith and possesses his grasp for business. The old man made a fortune in commerce and banking, you know."

"What of you, Robbie? What do you do?"

A satisfied look crossed his features, and he leaned back into the red plush seats. "Land," he said. "I buy up land and then sell it for a profit. I've done well in it too, and I mean to do better."

Something in his voice caused me to look past his smile and note the puffiness around his eyes and a narrow scar on his left cheekbone. I looked for a resemblance between Robert and Father but failed to find it. Although Robert and I shared the same father, he came from Father's first marriage and I from the second. This hadn't made any difference in our relationship. One of my earliest memories was Robert pulling me in a little cart around our garden. He seemed always to be there to spoil and protect.

"You must love your children very much . . . especially Sophia," I said.

There was a slight hesitation. "I do, but she is not the minx you were."

I smiled, remembering the way he used to tease me. "I love you, Robbie."

"And I you." He leaned over and kissed my cheek. "Welcome to Australia, Jessa."

* * *

The rest of the journey was spent in reminiscing and watching the scenery. Robert was proud of his new homeland and acted as if he owned it all himself.

"It's a grand land. So big a man can get lost without even trying. Some have, you know—disappeared into the bush never to be seen again."

I looked out at the rolling expanse of grassland and trees and hills and wondered what it would be like to set out into such a vast world.

"Here in the Gippsland and along the coast, plentiful rain keeps it lush and green, but farther north the rain slackens, so it's not as hospitable. After that it's the outback—miles of desert and rocks and practically no water. I've never seen the bush, but I've heard there's a stark beauty about it. In fact, some prefer it to the coast."

I thought about this as the carriage bumped along the track. It was riddled with potholes, but Robert assured me that when we neared Melbourne the way would improve.

"Do you think we'll see any kangaroos?"

"I can probably arrange that. I've seen kangaroos several times when I've been out this way."

This surprised me, for I'd thought Robert preferred city life.

"Remember I'm part owner of a spread not far from the McKades'."

I turned to look at him. "Why is it you don't like Brock McKade?"

"Not dislike so much as distrust."

"Why is that?"

Instead of answering right away, Robert glanced out the window as if unsure how to respond. "I've heard rumors about him . . . shenanigans his father pulled to get Tanybrae. I don't know all the details, but some say Brock is no better than his father."

My mind filled with Anne's story of the years of hard work it had taken to carve a home out of the wilderness. She'd described her Angus as a man always figuring and planning, but surely no shenanigans.

"It's true that McKade's made a name for himself with his fast horses, but whether or not he can be trusted is another matter." Some of the grimness left his face "Tell me, Jessa, is it any better with you and horses?"

"No, and I doubt it ever will be. But I've found I get along quite nicely without them. Most women spend more time in the drawing room than they do in the stable, you know."

At this point we left the grassland and entered a thickly wooded area. The chatter of birds filled the air, and I caught the flash of vivid green and bright red feathers among the branches of enormous trees.

"Everything's so different, even the trees."

"Aren't they magnificent? The thinner trees are mountain ash, and the ones with white trunks are called gum trees. If we're lucky you might see a koala up in the branches. They feed on the leaves."

Although I watched carefully, I saw nothing besides birds among the gray-green leaves.

"It's a strange country you've come to, Jessa. Did you know gum trees lose their bark instead of their leaves and that the seasons are backward?"

"I knew about the seasons."

We made our way through the forest that formed a canopy over our heads. Lush ferns and undergrowth hugged the sides of the road and brushed against the carriage. In time I grew drowsy and slept, always aware of the sway of the carriage and Robert's comforting presence beside me.

* * *

"Wake up, Jessa. We're almost there."

I blinked and sat up, noting late afternoon sunlight and the press of increased traffic.

"If you look you can see the botanical gardens. They're beautiful at this time of year. Sometimes Olivia and her friends take a picnic lunch and stroll along the paths. On ahead is the government house."

I looked at the imposing edifice, every bit as impressive as buildings in England.

"I've been to the government house on more than one occasion—sat in on a meeting or two with the premier." Pride threaded through his words.

Next he pointed out the Yarra River. I looked down at swans floating placidly on the rippling water as we crossed Prince Bridge. Robert pointed out Flinders Street, then Collins. Both streets were wide and crowded with conveyances of every kind. Brick and stone businesses with flamboyant architecture crowded the sides of the streets, bringing me an instant liking for Melbourne.

Soon the bustle of the city was behind, and we moved along a broad thoroughfare lined with trees and comfortable, well-kept homes.

"Rathdown Street isn't much farther." Robert's tone told me he was also proud of his address, proud too of the imposing edifice before which the carriage slowed. We passed through pillared brick gateposts and onto a gravel drive that curved before wide double doors.

As Robert helped me down from the carriage, I looked up at the tawny brick edifice with multipaned windows marching across both stories. Graceful gables rose to the crenellated rooftop.

"You have done well."

"I told you Australia has been good to me." He took my arm. "Come."

I knew he was anxious to show me his home, anxious too to introduce me to his wife and children. As we entered the house, I was aware of marble floors, a red urn filled with peacock feathers, and wide stairs leading to the second landing.

"Olivia, we're here!"

A tall, matronly woman appeared at the top of the stairs. The style of her drab, green dress was severe, as was her plain face framed by mousy brown hair. Even her expression was unwelcoming. I had expected someone of Robert's age. This woman looked to be at least several years his senior.

Robert spoke when she reached the bottom stair. "This is Jessamyne. Jessamyne, my wife Olivia."

As her gaze traveled over my bruised face, her lips tightened in distaste. At the same time, I sensed her satisfaction in knowing she needn't worry about competition from my looks. Although neither of us spoke, enough was conveyed by expression and glance to tell me that Olivia Clayborne and I would never be close friends.

Five

Tired from the long journey and still not fully recovered from my injuries, I retired early. Before I fell asleep, Robert ushered a portly gentleman into my room.

"Dr. Fleming," Robert said by way of introduction. "I've told him about your ordeal. Although you seem to be doing well, I'm anxious to hear the doctor's opinion of your injuries."

Dr. Fleming looked deeply into my eyes, and then ordered me to stick out my tongue. "Hm," then "Hm" again was all he said, and his nod was so vague I had no notion if it conveyed good or bad.

"How is she?" Robert asked after the doctor had given the scrapes and cuts on my arms a cursory examination.

"Remarkably good. Your sister has a very strong constitution, Mr. Clayborne. Even so, I would advise you to keep her in bed tomorrow so she can recover from the rigors of her journey. After that . . ." We both looked at him expectantly. "After that, she is free to move around the house as much as she is able, although I would recommend that your sister avoid bright sunlight for the next fortnight."

I thought of telling him that Sal's care had played as much a part in my recovery as my strong constitution, but I realized the doctor probably wouldn't take kindly to the information. Moreover, sleep was more appealing than conversation. As soon as they left, I promptly gave in to the sensation and did not rouse until morning.

Although the night's sleep had refreshed me, I was glad to spend the whole of the day resting in bed. Many thoughts filled my mind while I drowsed—my stay at Tanybrae, Anne and Millie, but mainly

Brock. When I remembered his kindness and the directness of his blue eyes, I couldn't see him in the light Robert had painted him. The same was true with Brock's father, and I determined that until it was proven otherwise, I would consider it no more than ill-willed rumor. Just how Robert's feeling about the McKades would affect my desire to visit them, I couldn't know. Since it wouldn't take place for several weeks, I put the problem aside.

* * *

The following morning a tap on my door wakened me. "Master Clayborne said if'n yer feelin' up to it, he'd count it a pleasure should ya join him for breakfast," the maid said.

It was the same girl who'd come with my meals the day before— Dolly she'd said when I'd asked her name—pleasant of face and quick of movement and not much older than myself.

"The children are up and he'd like ya to be meetin' them," she went on. Unlike Olivia, her only reaction to my face had been a quick look of pity. "Like I was tellin' ya last night, I unpacked yer trunks and yer gowns are pressed and ready if ya'll tell me what ya'd like to wear."

Not wanting to force my bruised body into stays, I chose a loose-fitting pink wrapper. While Dolly went to get warm water for my morning toilette, I inadvertently caught a glimpse of myself in the mirror. I was immediately sorry, for the bruises were still horrible, especially around my eyes, and the cut on my lip was noticeable. Even so, I was encouraged to see that the swelling was dissipating.

After I'd washed, Dolly cleverly arranged my hair to cover the gash on my head. "There," she said. "Now no one will see the cut." With that, she led the way downstairs and into the breakfast room.

My brother and his wife were already there, Robert wearing a gray morning coat that emphasized the color of his blue eyes and Olivia in a beige gown that made her swarthy complexion look even muddier.

"Jessamyne." A fond smile lit Robert's face as he came around the table to help me into my chair. As he did, he dropped a quick kiss on my cheek. "I believe I can see more improvement in your face."

"I hope so. It can't be a very pleasant sight for you at breakfast."

"Better a little unpleasantness than you at the bottom of the sea. When Captain Edwards told us you'd been swept overboard . . ." Robert's voice trailed away, and he gave my arm a quick squeeze. "I thought McKade's man was jesting when he brought me the news you were alive."

"Was it the McKades that found you?" Olivia asked.

"No, Aborigines."

Olivia gave a shudder. "Thank God it wasn't me they found. How could you bear for them to touch you?"

"I was so thankful to be saved, I didn't give it any thought."

Olivia sniffed and looked at her husband. "Speaking of the McKades, Papa came by yesterday to say McKade will be back in town next week. He invited you to go with him to have a look at Night Flyer."

I looked up at the mention of Brock. His name and face were in my thoughts more often than I would ever admit.

Robert took my plate to the sideboard and began to fill it. "A capital idea. Neville might like to go with us as well. Since he plans to enter Bruiser in the Cup, he'll probably want to look at the competition." He paused and handed me a plate of omelet. "It's a pity you still have an aversion to horses. The Melbourne Cup is being run next month, and it's all the thing to be there."

"Don't you ride?" Olivia asked.

"No."

A look of satisfaction crossed her face. "Robert and I are often in the saddle, aren't we, love?"

Before Robert could reply, a tall woman knocked on the door and entered with two children. "You sent word that you wanted the children brought downstairs to meet their aunt."

My gaze slid from the woman to the children. Both were staring at me, the boy with interest, the girl with her nose wrinkled in aversion.

Olivia rose from her chair and brought the children to the table. "These are our children—Burdell, who's eight, and Sophia, who's six. Children, your Aunt Jessamyne."

Burdell took a cautious step toward me, his eyes wide and staring. "Did you truly wash overboard into the ocean?"

"I did."

"Is that why your face looks all purple and funny?"

"Burdell." Olivia's voice was stern.

"It's all right. It's a perfectly natural thing for him to wonder." My smile brought an answering one to Burdell's lips. "You look much like your father did when he was your age," I added.

The boy's shoulders lifted, and I could tell he was pleased. By the looks of him, he was destined to be as handsome as his father. Not so his little sister. Plain like Olivia, Sophia had pushed close to her mother and looked at me from the folds of her skirt. For a moment I felt pity that nature hadn't given Robert's looks to Sophia instead of Burdell. Life seemed to deal more kindly with a plain man than a homely woman.

"How are you, Sophia?"

Instead of answering, she buried her face more firmly into Olivia's skirt. "I don't like her, Mama," she whispered. "She looks like a witch."

"Hush, sweetheart. You mustn't talk like that to your aunt." Though Olivia's voice held censure, her expression said otherwise.

Not so Robert. In three quick steps, he took Sophia firmly in hand and brought her to my chair. "You will apologize to your aunt."

Sophia's mouth turned stubborn, and I caught a glimpse of angry tears in her brown eyes. "Sorry," she whispered, but she did not sound sorry, and she looked at the floor instead of me.

"You're forgiven. Perhaps when my face is better, you'll change your mind and we can become friends."

The child's stiff demeanor did not fill me with optimism. Like Olivia, Sophia seemed to wish I had not come.

* * *

After Robert left for his office, Olivia took me on a tour of the house. Wishing to put our relationship onto a better footing, I looked for ways to compliment her. There was much to be admired, for all the rooms were large and tastefully decorated.

"Our home is still quite new. We moved here when Sophia was still a baby. We would have built it sooner, but Robert wanted Mr.

Reed to design it. Papa says he is the best in Australia and told us we had made an excellent choice." She paused and looked at me. "Did Robert tell you that Papa owns the City Bank and that he's twice been elected to the legislative league?"

"I'm afraid we spent most of our time reminiscing."

As if I hadn't spoken, she went on, "I feel we are well matched as husband and wife. Robert brought a good name from England, and Papa has made a great name for himself here in Melbourne. When we held a party for our new home, all of the best families came, even the premier and his wife."

"It must have been an exciting time for you." To change the subject, I complimented her on one of the sofas.

"Mama helped me choose it. Mr. Woodruff has an agent in London who orders the latest styles and ships them to Melbourne."

"How fortunate," I said, not knowing what else to say.

"Oh my, yes! And I have it on very good authority from Mrs. Childs, who recently returned from England, that we are not a step behind them in either fashion or furnishings." She looked significantly at my pink wrapper. "Robert is a stickler for propriety, so in the future it might be wise if you were more fully attired before you come downstairs for breakfast."

I wanted to tell her I was too sore and tender to be laced into corsets and stays, but instinct told me Olivia would neither commiserate nor approve. "Perhaps until I'm recovered, it would be better if I take my meals in my room."

Olivia blinked and looked for a moment as if she didn't know what to say. "That's something you had better ask Robert."

"I will. Now if you'll excuse me, I'm feeling a little tired and would like to go and lie down."

Entering my room, I found that the excitement and good feeling about making my home with Robert had dissipated. I already knew there would be no long talks or friendship between Olivia and me. In fact, if I were any judge of character, I suspected she would do all she could to undermine my relationship with my brother.

Sighing, I sat down in a flowered chair and let my gaze travel over the lace curtains at the wide windows and the matching tester over the bed. The room was beautifully furnished with a blue counterpane on the bed and flowered carpet on the floor—the "blue room" Olivia had proudly called it the night before. As I looked around the pleasant room, I wondered if in time I would come to consider it a prison.

"None of this, Jessa." The words made me feel better. Hadn't I been noted for my intellect as well as my looks? Surely in time it would be the same in Melbourne. Time was what I needed—time for my face to heal and to make new friends. Olivia was not the only person in Melbourne. There would be others to make me feel welcome.

With this bracing thought, I went to the wardrobe and opened the doors. Dolly had filled it with my gowns and accessories. As I looked at the rainbow array of dresses, I was assaulted with guilt. Why hadn't Father told me we must be careful with money? Two new gowns instead of four would have sufficed. The two black dresses made for Father's funeral and the subsequent mourning had been hung behind the others. I moved them to the front. Evidently Dolly hadn't been told I was in mourning.

I suddenly remembered the gray jacket and blue, knotted tie Robert had worn for breakfast. Neither it nor the suit he'd worn yesterday gave any indication he was in mourning. Had my brother's anger at Father been so intense he felt no loss at his death? This set me to worrying about other things. Why had Robert passed himself off as a younger son instead of one who'd been disowned? And why had he seemed relieved when he discovered I didn't know why he and Father had quarreled?

A soft knock interrupted my thoughts as Dolly stuck her pert face around the edge of the door. "Pardon, miss, but would ya like me to bring ya some hot water so ya can have a bath?"

The idea of easing my sore body into a tub of warm water was an inviting alternative to my uncomfortable thoughts. "Thank you, Dolly. That would be wonderful."

"It won't take but a moment." True to her words, she was back in a short time with the water. "Over here." She indicated a small alcove, its interior hidden by a screen painted with blue and white flowers. Behind the screen was a hipbath. Thick towels were draped over a rack, and an array of perfumed soaps sat on a shelf above the tub. When Robert had said he'd done well for himself, he had spoken the truth.

After Dolly had filled the tub and left the room, I undressed and carefully eased myself into it. The water stung my cuts and scrapes, but as my body adjusted, I relaxed and gave myself over to the luxury of a bath—something I hadn't been able to do since I'd left England.

After I'd dried and put on my wrapper, Dolly knocked again. "I'll just see to emptying the tub. Then if ya'd like, I can lay out one of yer gowns and help ya get dressed."

Despite her kindness, I suspected Dolly was curious and that she might also be a talker. "Not today. For now, I think I'll lie down."

"Very well." She gave a curtsey and went to empty the water. As she reached the door, she stopped, her pretty face a study in curiosity under the starched whiteness of her cap. "Everyone's sayin' yer a seven-day wonder. Did ya know all of Melbourne is talkin' about ya? It's even in the newspapers. A miracle, they're callin' it. I want ya to know I'm glad ya didn't drowned, and I count myself lucky to be servin' ya."

"Thank you, Dolly."

"Yes'm." Giving me a quick smile, she left the room.

Her disclosure surprised me. I hadn't thought the news of my disappearance would be common knowledge. This set me to thinking about the Hewitts and my desire to see them again. Did they know I was alive? This was something I needed to talk to Robert about.

It was evening before I had a chance to see him. He came to my room with a puzzled expression on his face. I was reclining on the bed reading a book I'd brought from England.

"What's this nonsense about not coming down for dinner?" The tone in his voice was very like Father's.

"I'm still feeling a little tired," I began.

"Come now, Jessa. I'm your brother and not so green you can put me off with the excuse of a headache or being too tired."

His scowl made me laugh, for he'd always like to lord it over me. "Well, if you must know, the rest of me is as bruised and sore as my face, and the thought of putting myself into my clothes is not to my liking."

"Good. Oh, not that I'm glad you're sore and hurting, but I was worried Olivia might have said something to put you off. It's a fault she has, and you must learn to ignore it as I do."

"Well, she did say that a wrapper was not quite the thing to wear when I was dining."

"Just as I feared." He crossed the room and sat down on the bed. "Don't let Olivia cow you. For all she knows, wearing a wrapper to dine is all the rage in London, and that's what you must tell her."

My laughter joined his and brought release to the tension I'd been feeling. "Do you know how good it feels to laugh with you again?" I reached for his hand and squeezed it. "I've missed you."

"And I've missed you." He raised my hand to his lips and kissed it. "So, no more retreating to your room to take your meals, understood?"

At my nod, Robert looked at me for a long moment, a finger to my chin, tilting my face to one side, then to the other. "Even with the bruising I see evidence of beauty. When you've recovered, I'm sure you'll have many admirers."

I thought of Olivia's plainness and wanted to ask him why he'd married her. On some level, I already knew. One day in Robert's company had revealed that social status and a prominent name were very important to him.

"So, is it settled? Can I expect you to join us in your wrapper for dinner?"

"You may."

Satisfied, he got to his feet. Although the years were starting to show on his face, Robert was still a handsome man. Noting the fashionable cut of his gray coat, I was reminded of his lack of mourning.

"Robert?"

Something in my tone turned his expression wary.

"Why is it you're not in mourning for Father? I know you quarreled, but even so, I expected to find you in black."

He shot a quick look at the door, and finding it slightly ajar, he closed it. "That's another thing I need to talk to you about, Jessa. You see . . ." His voice trailed away and he seemed to search for the right words. "The fact is, there are several things I haven't been entirely truthful about here in Australia. When I was searching for gold, people weren't inclined to ask many questions, but after I'd struck it rich and set myself up in business in Melbourne, it became important that I had a good name."

He sighed and his handsome features turned pensive. "From the start Olivia let it be known that she was interested in me, but her father is a stickler for propriety. He also has connections back in England, and I knew he'd be checking on me if I continued to court Olivia. So . . ."

Robert spread his hands and attempted a smile. "I doubt you know there were two Henry Claybornes in England and that they both had sons named Robert. I didn't become aware of this until I was away at boarding school where I was mistaken for the other Robert Clayborne who, by the by, was the epitome of propriety and later went to India and did well for himself. Knowing it would be difficult for Olivia's father to check for details in India, I gave it out that I am that Robert and that I later decided to come to Australia."

A sick feeling settled in my stomach. "Robbie, how could you?

"I know what a cad you must think me, but it seemed the thing to do if I intended to marry well. And since the other Henry Clayborne died about the time I left England, I can't very well go into mourning for him at this late date, can I? Or you either."

Stunned at Robert's duplicity, I found it difficult to think of anything to say.

"You do understand, don't you?"

"I'm afraid I don't." Robert's gaze slid away, and for a moment neither of us spoke.

"How do I fit into your deception?" I finally asked.

"You are my sister, of course."

"You mean the other Henry Clayborne had a daughter named Jessamyne?"

"No . . . At least I don't think he did. But it's doubtful Olivia's father inquired about daughters, so I'm confident we don't need to worry about it."

A dozen disjointed thoughts tumbled through my mind. Didn't Robert know playing with lies was like playing with fire? I hated the weakness that gaped like a raveled hole in my brother's character. It was one that frightened me and made me feel ill.

"Am I forgiven?" he asked after a moment.

"The ones you should ask forgiveness from are Olivia and her father. Haven't you thought that such might be the proper thing to do? You and Olivia are married and have two wonderful children. What could be so bad about discovering that you were once disowned? There are worse things."

"Perhaps." Robert looked at the window and grimaced. "The devil of it is, I've been thinking to run for political office. If any of this should get out, it would be the ruin of me, especially since I've lied about it for all these years. Besides, I need my father-in-law's backing if I mean to succeed in politics. He'll never give it if he knows I've deceived him."

For a moment neither of us spoke. I didn't like being a part of Robert's deceit. More than that, I feared the outcome.

"Can I count on you to keep quiet about this . . . and to refrain from wearing mourning?" he finally asked.

I sighed and looked up at him. "You know you can, but it doesn't mean I like it."

"I know." His voice was somber. "I'm sorry, Jessa. I hoped you wouldn't have to know."

"Pray God that no one else comes to know," was all I could think to say.

Robert's handsome features were glum, and for a second I felt sorry for him. As he turned to leave, I remembered the Hewitts. "I have a favor to ask of you as well. I became friends with the Hewitt family while I was aboard ship. Unfortunately, I never thought to obtain the address of their new home. I think it's in a place called Geelong—about a day's journey from here. Is there a way you could discover their address from the ship's records so I can write and let them know I'm alive?"

Some of the worry lifted from his face. "I imagine so, although if they read the newspaper, they're sure to know. Everyone is saying it's a miracle you survived."

"It was. And I've thanked God many times. Just the same, I'd like to write the Hewitts and thank them for looking after me on the voyage."

"How can you say they looked after you when they allowed you to go on deck during a raging storm?"

"That was my mistake, not theirs . . . and one for which I've dearly paid. Hopefully your mistakes won't require as much from you."

Unable to think of a response, Robert nodded and left the room.

* * *

Things went better between Olivia and me over the next few days. Not only was she more cordial, she went out of her way to find things to divert me while I convalesced. I could only assume Robert had spoken to her. "Robert said you may use his study when you feel so inclined," she said after breakfast the following day. After some polite conversation, I thanked her again and went at once to explore it. The room was paneled in rich walnut, and its furnishings were heavy and masculine. The sight of numerous bookshelves reminded me of Robert's love of books and the long hours he'd spent reading to me when I was small. The years didn't seem to have diminished his interest. My gaze slid over the gold lettering on several volumes: *A Tale of Two Cities, Oliver Twist, Gulliver's Travels,* all favorites of mine.

Later that day, Olivia also brought me a wrapper. "I thought you might like a change," she said when I thanked her. I smiled to myself, recognizing that even her gift held a bit of censure. But thanks to Robert she was trying, and for that I was grateful.

With Olivia and me both putting forth effort, the week passed pleasantly enough. One evening, Robert broached a new subject. "Olivia and I would like to host a dinner party for you. Since you don't know anyone in Melbourne, it will give you a chance to meet our friends and be introduced to society."

"I've started compiling the guest list," Olivia put in.

My hand went to my face. Although it showed signs of improvement, it was not normal. "I'd hate for anyone to see me yet."

Olivia shifted impatiently. "This won't be for at least a fortnight. Probably not until the first of November."

"By then you should be healed and looking yourself," Robert added.

Now that my concerns had been addressed, the prospect of a dinner party brightened my outlook. Although I managed to fill my hours with reading and occasional chats with Robert and Olivia, I longed to make new friends. How I wished the Hewitts and the McKades lived closer. Although Robert intended to locate the Hewitts' address from the port authorities, letters would not be as satisfying as visits. Patience, I told myself. With that I had to be content.

SIX

Each day I inspected my face for signs of improvement, and by the end of the following week I was rewarded with the sight of features that were almost normal. Other than yellow-green circles under my eyes and around one cheekbone, I looked quite myself. When I joined Robert and Olivia wearing a dress instead of a wrapper, Robert's face lit with pleasure.

"Lovely," he declared as he helped me into my chair. "Didn't I tell you Jessamyne would be a beauty, Olivia?"

Olivia wasn't pleased by Robert's remarks, but his reaction warmed my heart. I'd had quite enough of being the ugly duckling and was eager to resume the role of an attractive young woman. Much of the conversation that evening centered around the upcoming Melbourne Cup.

"The odds are on McKade's horse, but I'm putting my money on Neville Bromfield's Bruiser. I've had a chance to look at both horses, and Neville has assured me Bruiser is sure to win," Robert declared.

"How can you be so sure?" I asked, remembering Anne and Millie's pride in Brock's Night Flyer.

"I'd put Neville's judge of horseflesh over McKade's any day. Besides, he's my business partner. Experience has taught me that Neville is seldom wrong." Robert paused with fork in hand and looked at Olivia. "Speaking of which, how are your plans progressing for the dinner party?"

"Very good. Besides Neville, I plan to invite the Saunders and the Bowens . . . probably the Claytons, as well." Olivia looked at me, her thin smile not quite stretching to her brown eyes. "Both the Saunders and the Bowens have daughters your age. I'll invite them so you can begin to make friends."

I was pleased by her suggestion. I was even more pleased the next morning when Olivia invited me to go for a ride with her in their open buggy. "I thought you might enjoy seeing some of the sights after being confined to the house for the past fortnight." I thanked her excitedly, and a short time later we set out for a drive around the city. It was a lovely spring morning with blue sky and myriad birds singing from the branches of the trees, their songs strange but pleasant, as was the sight of bright clusters of red blossoms on one of the trees.

"Bottlebrush is what we call them," Olivia told me. I gave the tree a second glance, and indeed, the showy blooms looked much like brushes used to clean bottles.

Olivia enjoyed being my guide, as it gave her an opportunity to reveal her knowledge, which was considerable—I had to give her that—but also tedious as she explained each building's history and description. But I was so happy to be outside that I bore her talk with good humor, craning my head from under my parasol to look at Melbourne University, and commenting on the designs of the churches and library.

"We are a prospering city," Olivia said with pride. "Did you know we have over three hundred thousand people? Only Sydney rivals us in size."

My mind left Olivia and fastened on a boy waiting to cross the street. *Jamie!* It was Jamie Hewitt! "Stop! Ask the driver to stop!" When Olivia was slow to respond, I called to him myself. "Please, stop!"

As soon as the buggy pulled to a halt, I opened the door and stepped down. "Jamie! Jamie Hewitt!"

Jamie turned and looked at me, his face a combination of surprise and disbelief. "Miss Clayborne?" He started toward me, his feet breaking into a run. "Is it really you?"

"It is, Jamie."

"But—" He paused for breath, his expression still one of disbelief. "They said you'd been washed overboard and drowned. Mr. Moulton said he saw ya goin' up to the deck and then ya were gone."

"I *was* washed overboard, but then I was rescued."

A look of wonder crossed Jamie's tanned features. "We was prayin' for ya, Miss Clayborne. Mum, Da, all of us said prayers for ya night and mornin'." Tears welled up in his blue eyes, and his arms went around me. "Mum will be out of her mind with gladness, Da too."

Before I could say more, Olivia's voice cut into our conversation. "Send that boy on his way and get back into the buggy, Jessamyne. You're making a spectacle of yourself."

I shot Olivia a quick glance, noting her frown and tightly compressed lips as she leaned out of the buggy. Not liking either her rude words or behavior, I said I'd be there shortly and made a show of turning my back to her. "It's all right, Jamie." I gave him a reassuring smile and plied him with questions.

I learned that the Hewitts were living with relatives in Geelong and had come to Melbourne to pick up supplies for their new home. Realizing I had no notion of how to get to the area of town where he was to meet his family, I told Jamie to climb up with the driver and show us the way.

"Are you out of your mind?" Olivia asked when she understood my intention.

Jamie shot her a nervous look, his friendly face coloring with humiliation. Seeing him hesitate, I put a reassuring hand on his shoulder. "Don't pay her any mind," I whispered. My voice and hand urged him up with the driver.

Olivia bristled, but before she could say anything, I climbed into the buggy. "It's important that I talk to his parents." Remembering Robert's advice not to let Olivia cow me, I met her gaze head on. "If you don't wish to go with me, the driver can take you home first."

Olivia gave an exasperated sigh. "This will not put you in good stead . . . hobnobbing with ruffians."

"Jamie is not a ruffian. He's a delightful boy, and his parents are my friends." Seeing the distasteful look she shot Jamie, I hurried on, my voice tight with anger. "Yes, *my friends,* Olivia. Had it not been for their willingness to share one of their cabins, I couldn't have found passage so quickly to Melbourne."

"Such doesn't require you to include them in your circle of friends," she sniffed. "I strongly suggest you carefully reconsider the matter."

"And I suggest that you drop the matter. They are my friends." My tone was cold.

"Well, they are not mine," she said just as coldly. With that she demanded to be taken home.

After depositing Olivia at the house, we continued on to the store. The drive didn't take long. Jamie excitedly jumped down from the buggy before it stopped and ran into the establishment "Mum! Da! Ya'll not believe who I found! Miss Clayborne! She didn't drown! She's alive!"

Sarah met me at the door, her blue eyes wide and a look of wonder on her face. "Alive?" As her gaze took me in, she pulled me into her arms. "Miss Clayborne . . . Jessamyne! We thought ya was drowned."

"There were times I thought I would drown too, but I clung to a board until I washed ashore."

Sarah hugged me a second time. "The good Lord be praised."

By now William and the rest of the family had joined us. After hugs were exchanged, I told them of my rescue by Aborigines and the McKades.

William shook his head in wonder. "All of us was prayin', but who would believe such a strange thing could happen?"

"I would." Sarah's voice was quiet. "As soon as I set eyes on ya, I knew ya was someone special." She touched my face with a tentative finger. "God is mindful of ya, Jessamyne. Seek him and he'll show ya what he wants ya to do."

Tears filled her eyes as she spoke, and I felt the prick of tears myself. Not knowing how to respond, I hugged her. "Thank you," I whispered. Wiping my tears, I bombarded them with questions. "Now tell me about you. How do you like Australia?"

"Grand . . . just grand."

"'Tis a grand land indeed," William put in. "God's treasure, as some of the Australians like to say. The soil's so rich, I'll not be havin' any trouble growin' things."

While they told me of their new home, I saw and felt their happiness. They were such good people. None deserved happiness more than they. Not wanting to lose contact with my friends, I asked for their address and gave them mine.

"We plan to come to Melbourne at least once a month," William told me. "We've found where our church meets and want to worship with them as often as we can."

"Aye," Sarah agreed. "It's but a small room above a shop, but the members have welcomed us." A soft smile curved her lips. "We've been richly blessed."

"We went to church yesterday, and I met a girl who's just my age," Bethy added.

"I'm so glad." I smiled down at her, remembering the nights aboard ship when we'd shared the tiny cabin. Like Jamie, Bethy showed signs of being much like her mother.

After a few more minutes of pleasant conversation, I realized that the hour had grown late.

"Remember we'll be keepin' ya in our prayers," Sarah said in parting. "I know God has good things planned for ya."

Her words lingered in my mind as I rode in the buggy back to Robert's house. I hoped she was right, for although I had found my brother, I still felt very much alone.

* * *

Olivia had not wasted any time letting Robert know I'd been "hobnobbing with ruffians," as she put it. A short time after I returned home, he summoned me to his study. Suspecting what would take place, I entered the room with a stubborn set to my mouth.

Robert was standing with his back to the unlit fireplace. He wasted little time in getting to the crux of the matter. "Olivia told me the two of you went for a buggy ride this morning and that you stopped to speak to a ruffian from the ship."

"Jamie Hewitt is not a ruffian. He's a bright young boy with good parents who have come to Australia to better themselves . . . rather like you did, Robert."

My thrust made him glance at the door. "Nonetheless, they are not the kind of people you should be spending your time with, especially when you are so newly arrived yourself."

"Since they live some distance from Melbourne, there's little chance I'll be living in their pocket. They were only in town to pick up supplies for their new home."

Although my explanation seemed to satisfy Robert, I sensed that something still weighed on his mind. After a long moment he spoke. "I told you that I want very much to be elected to office, and I'm assured by many that I shall succeed." His eyes lifted to meet mine. "I can't afford to have anything happen that might ruin my chances. But if my sister is seen associating with those who are not quite the thing, it could result in me losing the backing of some very influential men."

The memory of the Hewitts' goodness to me filled my mind. "They're my friends, Robert, and I don't intend to abandon them just because they don't meet with Olivia's approval."

His mouth tightened, and I feared for a moment he would lose his temper. "Olivia said you were stubborn. Not that the trait should surprise me. I well remember that no amount of coaxing would get you inside the stable, nor the schoolroom either if it didn't suit your fancy." The memory of it seemed to soften his feeling. "Very well," he said after a moment. "You may keep in touch with them. In return I shall expect you to be especially nice to Neville Bromfield."

"All right." Although my answer came without hesitation, part of me wondered why Robert thought he needed to ask me to be especially nice to Mr. Bromfield. Wasn't he Robert's friend and business partner?

At the dinner party a few nights later, I wondered again. I had dressed with care and knew I looked attractive in the jade green gown. The black velvet piping at the neck, sleeves, and across the edge of the bustle was especially fashionable. After Dolly helped me with my hair, I applied a dusting of powder to the last yellowed signs of the bruises and descended the stairs feeling pleased with my appearance.

The appreciative look in Robert's eyes told me I hadn't been wrong, as did Olivia's, although her expression was far from appreciative. Then my attention shifted to the handsome man who stood at Robert's side. I knew at once it must be Neville Bromfield. What surprised me was his age. I had expected him to be Robert's age or older. Instead, he did not look even thirty.

"I'd like you to meet my friend Neville Bromfield," Robert said by way of introduction. "Mr. Bromfield, my sister, Jessamyne Clayborne."

"My pleasure, Miss Clayborne." Like Robert, his brown eyes were warm and appreciative.

I found Mr. Bromfield to my liking as well. Although he was not as tall as Robert, he exuded presence. Slender of build with thick black hair and a luxuriant mustache, my first impression was of a man who liked mystery and adventure, like a dashing pirate setting out to seek a treasure.

"Your brother has told me much about you, Miss Clayborne. Not many can claim to have been rescued from the sea by Abos. It's good to see that you are recovered from your ordeal."

"Thank you. Unfortunately, Robert didn't tell me as much about you, Mr. Bromfield. I know only that you are his friend and business partner."

Neville shot Robert a quick glance and smiled. "Yes, Robert and I have known each other for several years. Since the days of prospecting for gold, in fact."

"Was it in Ballarat?" I asked, for I'd heard of the famous gold strike there several years before.

"No, Robert and I didn't come onto gold until some years after the Ballarat gold rush. What we found was closer to home. The upper reaches of the Yarra River was our lucky lode."

I thought it strange that, whereas Robert had been vague about the whereabouts of his good fortune, Neville was more open. Before I could ask him more, Mr. and Mrs. Saunders and their daughter Chloe arrived.

The parents were thick-figured and ordinary in appearance. Chloe, on the other hand, was attractive and willowy of figure with a vivacity of expression that gave me hope we could become friends. Although Chloe was a bit stiff at first, by the time we exchanged a few words over dinner, we began to get on.

The Claytons, a couple with two sons, arrived next. Horace, the eldest, looked to be in his mid-twenties. His brother Percy was about my age. Horace's pleasant features and outgoing manner put me at ease, but Percy had little to say until Amanda Bowen and her parents arrived. It was obvious he was much taken with Amanda, whose blue gown set off her pretty features and thick golden tresses.

After introductions were finished, Robert and Olivia led us into the dining room. It was bright with the glow of gaslit chandeliers, the sheen falling onto the snowy white tablecloth and dancing off the silver. I knew Olivia had taken great pains in planning the evening. The silver-rimmed china interspersed with vases of hothouse flowers did much to set the mood for the evening.

Both Robert and Olivia were in their element—my brother affable and relaxed, and Olivia taking pleasure in her role as hostess. I sensed her dress had been selected with care, the puce silk bodice festooned with rows of knotting.

Everyone was eager to hear the details of my experience in the storm. Forks stilled and eyes turned to me rather than the food, a fact that did not make my sister-in-law happy. Twice she attempted to steer the conversation to other subjects, but each time attention returned to me. I felt a bit self-conscious when I explained my reason for going above deck in such a fearful storm, but Neville was quick to reassure me.

"I'm not a good sailor either, Miss Clayborne. In fact, that's why I hire others to tend to my business interests in England."

I was grateful for his solicitation and could not fail to notice that his gaze frequently rested on me while I chatted with Chloe and Amanda.

"Weren't you frightened when you saw the blacks?" Chloe asked. "I think I should have fainted from fear."

"It was a bit unsettling," I agreed, "but when I realized they meant no harm, I was grateful they'd found me."

"How fortunate that the McKades were able to help you," Mrs. Saunders put in. "Although I've never met the mother, I have seen the daughter a few times." She turned to Olivia. "She went to school with Victoria Thompson, you know. Chloe and Amanda have met her as well."

"Did you meet Brock McKade while you were with them?" Chloe asked. Her cheeks flushed at the question, and she avoided her mother's gaze.

"Only briefly. He arrived at Tanybrae just as I was leaving. I believe he'd been in Melbourne."

"No doubt making arrangements for the race," Neville said. He looked at Robert. "I have it on good authority that besides Night Flyer, McKade is entering a filly this year—a ploy to stack the deck more heavily on his side."

Robert's grimace made me wonder how much money he planned to place on Bruiser. Everything in the room seemed to speak of money, either in words or dress or lavish display of jewelry. I knew even then that the people who surrounded me at Olivia's beautifully set table would have little permanence in my life. They seemed to float like colorful flotsam on the ocean's surface, bright baubles to admire as they drifted past. They were strangers, all of them. Yes, even Robert, whom I already suspected was other than I wished to believe. While I talked and laughed and listened, I felt as if I'd been handed a script to a part for which I wasn't suited. Yearning hung on the edge of my thoughts and words. Where was the role I was destined to play?

Pleasant conversation and music followed dinner. Not only was Amanda pretty, she also possessed a lovely singing voice. It was obvious that Olivia thought the evening a success, and, for my part, I was flattered by Neville Bromfield's marked interest in me.

"Do you ride, Miss Clayborne?" he asked as he was leaving.

"No, I don't."

"A pity, but one that can be quickly remedied, for I keep a full stable and would consider it a pleasure if you would let me teach you."

This was not the first time such an offer had been made, and I was used to making excuses. "You're very kind—" I began.

"My sister had an unfortunate incident as a child that left her with an aversion for horses," Robert cut in.

Neville's deep brown eyes clouded. "I'm sorry to hear that." He paused and studied me for a moment. "Will this unfortunate incident prevent you from accompanying me to the races? The Melbourne Cup is next week, and I'd deem it an honor if you would be my guest for the occasion."

"Thank you. I've found that if I keep a safe distance from horses, I do very well."

"Then I'll plan to see you next Tuesday, Miss Clayborne. I like to make an early start to avoid the crowds. Will ten o'clock be convenient?"

"Yes."

Pleasure showed on Neville's handsome features as he bade me farewell, and I found myself looking forward to the races.

Robert seemed as pleased with the evening as Olivia. "I had a notion Neville would find you to his liking," Robert remarked.

"Mr. Bromfield is younger than I expected. When you said he was your business partner, I pictured him as being older."

"Actually, there are but two years' difference in our ages. Neville holds his age well."

"Why is it that he isn't married?"

Robert shrugged. "Hasn't found the right woman, I guess, though a time or two I thought he might succumb. There was Miss Fullbright—"

"You know she wasn't suitable, Robert," Olivia cut in. "Oh, a pretty enough face, but a reputation that was entirely too questionable. Neville did well not to pursue it further, and I made it a point to tell him so."

"I'm sure you did." Robert shot me an amused look, and had it just been the two of us, I would have laughed.

* * *

The feeling of well-being was still with me the next morning. I awoke early and was on my way downstairs when the sight of a stocky man leaving Robert's study brought my steps to an abrupt halt. My heart jerked as I stared down at Jeremy Moulton. Stepping back onto the landing, I watched him cross the entryway to the front door. The jauntiness in his step was an extension of the smugness I'd glimpsed on his face as he left the study, one that told me Mr. Moulton was extremely pleased with himself.

Although I'd disbelieved his claim to business dealings with Robert, what I'd just witnessed bore it out. My first instinct was to hurry downstairs and confront Robert, but caution urged me to hold my tongue and observe.

Even so, I sought Robert in his study. When he opened the door, relief played over his features. "Jessa, I'm surprised to see you up so early."

"It's not my habit, is it?" I looked around the room, wondering what had transpired between him and Jeremy Moulton.

"Olivia and I were both pleased at how well last night's dinner went. Neville seemed much impressed with you. What did you think of him?"

"I haven't yet decided, though I own he's a very handsome man."

"Neville is noted for his looks. Accompanying him to the races should give you opportunity to become better acquainted."

"I hope so, but . . ." I paused before going on. "I need your assurance that it won't put me too close to the horses."

"You have my word, although when Bruiser wins, Neville will join the horse and jockey to accept the prize. I'll make certain that you remain with Olivia and me until the horses have left the track."

"Thank you." I smiled in an effort to lighten the mood. "You seem confident that Bruiser will win."

"I am. Because of it, I'm staking a small fortune on the outcome."

"Do you think it wise?"

"I do. Neville has an eye for good horseflesh. More than that, I've never known him to fail in any enterprise to which he sets his mind. His mind has been pinned on winning the Melbourne Cup this past year. Mark my word, Jessa, Bruiser will win."

Olivia was of the same mind and referred often to the race during the ensuing days. Since I was curious about the event, I tolerated her condescending monologue with good grace, but when Olivia swept into my bedroom the day before the race, I was taken aback by her boldness.

"I've come to look over your wardrobe," she announced. "Accompanying Neville to the races will put you in the limelight. As such, I feel it my duty to recommend what you should wear. Let me see . . ." She stepped past me to the wardrobe and took out a dress, then another.

I felt my temper rise. I'd never appreciated being told me what to do, especially by someone I didn't hold in high regard.

"This one," Olivia said, holding up the least favorite of my gowns. "It conveys just the right degree of decorum without making you look conspicuous. Yes, the gray should do very well."

"I thought to wear the deep violet," I countered, though in truth I hadn't yet decided what I would wear.

"The gray will be much better, and I saw the very hat to go with it in a milliner's shop yesterday. I almost bought it for myself, but at the last second I changed my mind." She paused and smiled. "It will be the very thing for you. If you'd like, we can purchase it this afternoon."

I strove for tact, but my efforts weren't successful. "I appreciate your thoughtfulness. However, the choice of what I wear will be mine, not yours." I reached for the gray gown and hung it back in the wardrobe.

Shock flicked over Olivia's sallow face. "Really, Jessamyne. Since you have no notion of what is worn at the races, I thought only to recommend."

"Which I appreciate, but I've been choosing my clothes for some years, and I prefer to keep it that way."

"This is Australia, not England."

"Then perhaps I'll start my own style." Picking up my shawl, I went to the door. "Now if you'll excuse me, I'm going for a walk."

Olivia followed after me. "You are much too headstrong for a young woman of your age."

I ignored her and hurried down the stairs.

"Robert will not approve of your going for a walk unaccompanied. Let me call for Polly."

I hurried to the door. "You have no need to worry about me. I'm quite capable of finding my way around." With that I closed the front door and hurried down the steps.

My pace down the street was brisk, my shoes a staccato on the hard-packed path, my breathing rapid. I hadn't intended to lose my temper, but everything about Olivia rubbed me wrong. I'd been less than a month in her home, and we were already quarreling. What would be the situation in two months or, heaven forbid, a year?

I continued on my way, paying little heed to my surroundings other than to note that the day was overcast and to wish for a secluded spot to sit and collect myself.

I traversed several streets before I spied a path that meandered off into a copse of trees. Inside the grove, the noise of passing traffic faded. My steps slowed to a more comfortable pace as I breathed in the stillness and the sharp aroma of gum trees. I hadn't gone far before I spied a smooth log that offered a place for me. Picking my way through ferns and low-growing bushes, I sat down.

From there I had a lovely view of parkland with a bridge spanning a little stream. Taking a deep breath, I let the beauty and stillness enfold me until anger was replaced with calm. I was a goose for letting Olivia get under my skin. Robert said he'd learned to ignore her, and I must do the same. Holding my tongue had never been easy, but it could be done with practice and time.

I sat for several minutes, watching the play of sunlight on the woodland floor and listening to the pleasant song of birds. The unbidden picture of Brock McKade smiling up at me as I sat on the veranda at Tanybrae wove its way through my mind. I closed my eyes in an effort to trap the image more firmly. As I did, I became aware of male voices. Looking through the foliage, I saw two men come over the bridge. Unease shot through me. In my search for quiet, I'd given no thought to the danger of the isolated woodland. If I hurried, could I reach the path without being seen?

Before I could move, the larger man stopped and looked toward the trees. My breathing halted when I recognized Jeremy Moulton. Instinct pulled me more deeply into the undergrowth. I sat very still, hoping I wouldn't be seen.

The men resumed their conversation. Mr. Moulton seemed to do most of the talking, although the smaller person, who looked more youth than man, nodded and spoke from time to time. I couldn't hear what they said, but I was close enough to see Mr. Moulton reach into his pocket and hand something to his companion. After shaking hands, Mr. Moulton walked back across the bridge while the slightly built man started toward me.

My relief at seeing the backside of Jeremy Moulton was replaced by curiosity about his companion. Boy or man, he was no taller than I. Still, I didn't want to be discovered.

I watched him as he drew closer, noting his tight-fitting breeches and riding boots. It was a man, not a boy, his features sharp in their thinness like those of a fox. He was obviously pleased by the transaction with Mr. Moulton and was so caught up in counting a wad of bills he didn't look in my direction.

My mind tumbled with thoughts. What had Jeremy Moulton been up too? And what connection did he have with Robert? Little snippets of gossip I'd overheard about my brother back in England skipped through my thoughts, words describing him as wild and irresponsible. I saw no signs of those weaknesses now—only ambition and smugness. There'd been gossip about Robert and money problems too, but each time I'd asked for further details, I'd been put off. Now I wished I'd been more persistent. I wished too that I knew more about Robert's involvement with Jeremy Moulton. Unease dogged my steps on my way home. *Dear Robert, what are you doing?*

SEVEN

The day of the Melbourne Cup dawned bright and sunny. Robert breathed an audible sigh of relief, for the previous day had been overcast and rainy. "A great day for the race," he declared. He was dressed to the nines in a dark frock coat and tall black hat, and Olivia was not far behind him. I could tell she had again taken great pains with her dress and thought herself nicely turned out in a gown of sienna silk with matching hat and gloves.

I had settled on wearing the deep violet for no other reason than Olivia had said it wouldn't do. I'd always liked it, thinking the checkered violet and white trim around the bustle and hem brought just the right touch of quality to its tailored style. Even Olivia couldn't fault the hat with its wide brim and cluster of roses and violet ribbon.

"You are looking exceptionally nice today," Robert said to Olivia.

She smiled and looked pleased until Robert turned to me. "I fear all the gentlemen will be looking at you instead of concentrating on the races, Jessa. Neville will be an envied man."

"You were always one to exaggerate, but I thank you just the same."

At that moment, Neville came to pick us up in his carriage. Like Robert, he wore a dark coat and trousers and a high hat that made his black brows and mustache all the more striking.

"Miss Clayborne." I read admiration in his eyes as he took my hand and raised it to his lips. I saw it again as he helped me into his well-sprung carriage.

Robert and Olivia had been invited to ride with us. The men were in high spirits, and even I looked forward to watching the race. Although it was still early in the day, the streets were filled with other conveyances, all bent on the same destination as we. Gentlemen doffed their hats and ladies nodded, while drivers urged their horses and shouted rudely at those who tried to cut in.

When we crossed Prince Bridge, I looked down on a river dotted with bright colored punts also filled with passengers on their way to the races. Music floated up from the boats, some ribald and discordant, other melodic, but all of it happy.

"Some are already drunken," Olivia said in disgust.

I'd seen Robert slip a small flask into his pocket, and I wondered if Neville had done the same. What did Olivia think of that? For me it was enough to be in the company of two striking men and a part of the excitement that permeated the air.

"Happy?" Robert asked.

"I am."

"Would you like me to make a small wager for you on Bruiser? I'll supply the money, of course, but the return will be all yours."

"You're still certain Bruiser will win?"

"I am." Robert exchanged a quick glance with Neville. "What do you say, Neville? Is he going to win?"

Neville smiled. "You will not go wrong if Robert places money for you on Bruiser, Miss Clayborne."

"I have heard good things about the McKade horse too. Miss McKade says they have high hopes he will win again."

"She and several thousand others," Robert said. "But those wise enough to place their money on Bruiser will not be disappointed."

I wondered how he could be so certain, but having never attended a race before, I bowed to their greater knowledge. By now the traffic was so heavy we were forced to travel at a slow plod.

"Thousands more come by railcar, and those who can't afford the price of a ticket walk," Neville said when he saw me turn to look at the long line of conveyances behind us. "Last year the newspaper said more than a hundred thousand people attended. By the looks of things, we will equal or surpass it this year."

I was impressed with the numbers, but thoughts about the race were still uppermost in my thoughts. "Since you own Bruiser, don't you need to be out to the race course early?"

"I leave all the race preparations to the trainer and jockey."

By now the sun was streaming down with enough force to make me grateful for my parasol. Dust rose from the heavily traveled road, and the flies rivaled people for numbers.

Olivia swatted impatiently at a buzzing insect. "The flies are one of the drawbacks to coming to the races," she complained, "and they'll be even worse when it gets warmer."

I was too excited to let even the flies annoy me. Neville's interest and smile added to my excitement. What woman didn't respond to a handsome man's flattering attention? Each time Neville looked at me and smiled, I counted myself fortunate.

"Flemington and the racetrack are just ahead," Robert said.

I looked past the line of carriages to a flat, oval area by the river. Hundreds of people swarmed toward it. In a turnaround area close to the track, our driver pulled the horses to a halt, and Robert and Neville got out to help Olivia and me from the carriage.

The crowd quickly encircled us, and I was glad for the support of Neville's arm in the crush of people. Everyone seemed to be dressed in their best—the lustrous silks and satins of the rich a pleasing contrast to the bright calico dresses of the less affluent. Seeing a man and woman with three children in tow reminded me of the Hewitts. Closer inspection proved me wrong, but it didn't prevent me from wishing they could be there too.

Neville was not the least bashful about pushing a path for us through the crowd, and in no time we were there. Robert and Neville left us as soon as they made certain Olivia and I were comfortably settled, Robert leaving to place his bets with the book-makers and Neville to have a final look at Bruiser. During the interval, Olivia introduced me to some of her friends—a Mrs. Folger and her daughter Geneva, and the Morrisons and their three daughters. I was glad to spy the familiar faces of the Saunders. Chloe seemed pleased to see me as well, especially when several young men approached and asked for introductions. I couldn't fail to enjoy the attention, and even the snippets of conversation I overheard about me being washed overboard did not dim my pleasure.

While in conversation with one of the men, I heard a woman's voice call my name. Turning, I saw Anne and Millie McKade making their way through the throng.

"Jessamyne." Millie reached me first, her piquant face showing pleasure. She looked very fetching in a periwinkle blue dress and a hat with swathes of blue netting and flowers. She took my hand and squeezed it. "You are just as beautiful as I thought you would be, though I own you're vastly changed since I last saw you. But Mum recognized your brother and said it must be you."

"I'm so glad you did. How are you?" I looked from one to the other. "It's so good to see you again."

"Doesn't Mum look pretty?" Millie asked. "I persuaded her to buy a new hat. Mum never buys anything new for herself, but I told her she needed to look nice for when Night Flyer wins the cup."

Anne's gown of deep burgundy brought color to her cheeks. Her hat was flattering as well, and I was quick to tell her.

"You're very kind, though Millie didn't have to talk very hard to get me to spend the money. I'd already decided I owed it to Brock not to make him ashamed of his mother. Last year only Brock was certain he would win the race, but this year we're all optimistic."

"As you should be." Guilt flicked at my conscience when I remembered that Robert was placing money for me on Bruiser. "I've heard wonderful things about the McKade horses."

"And all of it true. Brock says he's never seen Night Flyer running better, and the filly looks promising too," Millie said as she rose on tiptoe to look through the crowd. "Brock was here just a few minutes ago. I know he'd like to see you again."

"I think he's gone to check on Night Flyer," Anne said.

I felt a prick of disappointment. Although I'd come to the race with Neville, that didn't mean I'd lost interest in Brock McKade.

Olivia politely cleared her throat, and I realized she had joined us. As I made introductions, I sensed Olivia's disapproval. Fortunately, neither Millie nor Anne seemed to notice.

"I believe I saw you at the Morrisons' party last winter," Millie said to Olivia. "I doubt you noticed me, for I came with Sophia and her brother, but I remember seeing you and Mr. Clayborne. Didn't you come with the Saunders?"

Hearing that Millie had been to the Morrisons' party made Olivia unbend a bit. Before Olivia could say more, one of her friends caught her attention.

"What a minx you are," I whispered to Millie. "You know the very way to wind my sister-in-law around your finger."

Millie giggled. "That's because she's so much like my friend's mother." As she spoke, I spied Robert and Neville making their way toward us. Knowing of the rivalry that existed between the McKades and Neville, I was relieved when Millie and Anne said it was time to take their place for the race. "We're looking forward to your visit to Tanybrae," Anne concluded as she prepared to leave. "Hopefully after the race we can make plans."

"I'd like that," I replied, though I wasn't quite sure how to bring it about with Robert and Neville in attendance. But I waved good-bye and still had a smile on my face when Robert and Neville neared.

"It's almost time," Neville said when he reached me. He tucked my hand around his arm and walked to the railing where friends had saved a place for us. More introductions were made, but as I responded, my mind was on Millie and Anne. Sadness pricked at my excitement as I thought of their disappointment if Bruiser won the cup.

The blare of trumpets called the crowd to attention for the singing of "God Save the Queen." As the closing strains faded, the horses entered the arena. Hooves prancing, they made a slow circuit around the racetrack while the crowd cheered approval.

"Which is Bruiser?" I asked.

"The third one," Neville replied, pointing to a bay gelding ridden by a man dressed in a green uniform.

"And Night Flyer?"

"Number six."

At that distance, I could only tell that the horse was black and that the rider wore red. As they drew closer, the fluid motion of the black horse's gait caught my attention. My gaze shifted to the jockey.

A tiny gasp escaped my lips when I recognized the wiry man I'd seen talking to Jeremy Moulton.

"Who's Night Flyer's rider?"

Neville was slow to answer. "One of the jockeys. Ned Krueger, I think."

"Why not Brock McKade?"

"McKade's too large. Owners look for small men or older boys to ride the horses."

Only half hearing his reply, I remembered the wad of bills I'd seen the jockey counting—money given to him by Jeremy Moulton. I didn't know what the exchange of bills meant, but it was enough to make my eyes follow Night Flyer's progress to the starting line.

The crack of a pistol signaled the start of the race. Fifteen horses broke away from the gate and hurtled down the track. The roar from the crowd was deafening. As the horses thundered toward us, I closed my eyes and turned my face into Robert's shoulder. Although he and Neville were cheering, Robert put his arm around me. "It's all right, Jessa."

Even with my eyes tightly closed, the pounding hooves stirred up waves of fear that kept my face buried in Robert's shoulder. Only after they were well past did I raise it and look. "Who's ahead?"

"Some cob that doesn't stand a chance. Firebrand, I think. He'll fall off, mark my word. Bruiser's not far behind."

"And Night Flyer?"

"Just behind Bruiser, but the race has just started. A lot will happen before it's over."

I hoped so, for I suspected that much of the McKades' future hung on the outcome of the race, while Robert's . . . My mouth tightened. Robert, like me, would be fine regardless of the outcome.

By now the horses had completed their first circuit and were thundering toward us again. Neville and Robert both cheered loudly as Bruiser began to gain on Firebrand. My attention was nailed to the black horse and red-clad jockey, who were also gaining. I closed my eyes as the horses dashed past, the heavy drum of hooves making the ground tremble.

"He's making his move!" Neville cried. "Just like I told him."

"Firebrand is slowing," Robert cried. "I knew he would."

I kept my gaze on Night Flyer. Like Bruiser, he was narrowing the distance to Firebrand. Then he was past, Night Flyer and Bruiser running neck and neck.

"Come on, Bruiser." Olivia's voice was a tense whisper.

"Bruiser!" Robert yelled.

My voice joined the cheers, though my companions could not know for which horse I rooted. "Come on! Oh, come on!"

Mine was not the only voice lifted for Night Flyer. My excitement soared when he pulled ahead. The two horses raced toward the finish line with Night Flyer almost a neck ahead.

"Faster!" I cried.

As the word left my mouth, Night Flyer faltered, the pause no more than a second before his pounding gait flew toward the finish line. But now Bruiser led by a nose—the two horses rushing, jockeys' whips flailing, the crowd hysterical. When they streaked across the finish line, Bruiser still led.

The air erupted into a cacophony of exuberant cheers and disappointed groans, the hats of Robert and Neville thrown into the air in a jubilant celebration like those of a hundred others.

Speechless, I watched the lathered horses slow to a walk, my mouth opening in astonishment as Brock McKade leapt over the railing and onto the track.

"You no good, dirty bounder!" he shouted. In three quick strides he grabbed Night Flyer's jockey and hurled him to the ground. When the little man hit the turf, his attacker lifted him to his feet and pitched him over the fence. "That'll teach you to throw a race."

Others poured onto the track and more blows were exchanged. Robert looked ready to join them, but Neville put out a restraining hand. "No," he said and shook his head.

By now the police had joined the melee, while jockeys urged their mounts out of the way. Someone caught Night Flyer's bridle and led him in a slow walk around the track.

My gaze remained fixed on Brock McKade, my mind still reeling as I caught a glimpse of dark brown hair and angry features. "Why?"

"He's a poor loser and claims the jockey threw the race."

By now the police had the crowd on the racetrack under control. Most left peaceably, but a few were escorted away, Brock McKade among them. My heart went out to Anne and Millie as I imagined their embarrassment—one made more intense by the disappointment in Night Flyer's loss.

When the area had been cleared of all but Bruiser and his rider, Neville left me to join his horse and jockey and to accept the prize. The crowd cheered as a wreath of flowers was placed around Bruiser's neck and the Melbourne Cup presented to Neville. Discordant boos mingled with the cheers.

"The jockey threw the race. Didn't you see how Night Flyer faltered?" a man near us yelled. Some tried to shout him down, but others shouted agreement.

"I told you Bruiser would win." Robert squeezed my arm. "Aren't you glad I placed a good-size bet for you?"

"I'm not sure, especially if the jockey made him lose."

"That's poppycock. No one threw the race."

I remembered the exchange of money between Jeremy Moulton and the jockey. As I started to tell Robert, instinct closed my mouth. It would be better to wait until we returned home.

* * *

It was almost evening before I had a chance to be alone with my brother. Robert still glowed from the outcome of the race, his smile wide as he invited me into his study.

"Your winnings are considerably less than mine," he said when he handed me a fifty-pound note. "But now you'll have spending money of your own . . . Enough to buy a new hat or a few trinkets, though I hope you know I plan to pay for anything larger."

I stood on tiptoe and kissed his cheek. "It's good to know I have you to look after me. Thank you, Robbie."

"It's my pleasure. Having you here is like a breath of fresh air." He gave me a hug in return.

Had the circumstances been different, I would have welcomed having my own spending money, but the knowledge that the jockey and the man I'd seen with Jeremy Moulton were one and the same eroded any pleasure. The smile I gave Robert was strained and faded altogether when I looked down at the bills he'd given me. "Robert?"

"Yes?"

"I think the McKade jockey really did throw the race."

Robert looked at me as if I'd taken leave of my senses. "What are you talking about?"

"I recognized the jockey. He's the same man I saw three days ago counting a large sum of money."

Robert looked even more baffled, but as I told him about my walk in the woods his face grew still. "The man who gave the jockey the money is someone I met aboard ship. He said his name was Jeremy Moulton, but it might be a lie, for he struck me as an unsavory person."

"Jeremy Moulton." Robert repeated the name in a half whisper.

"Yes, I've been wanting to tell you since the race. I know it should be reported, but whom do I tell?"

"You don't tell anyone. Egad, Jessa. Do you know who Jeremy Moulton is? Believe me, he's not anyone you want to cross. In fact, if you were to report what you saw, you might well end up . . . dead." Robert's tongue stumbled on the word, and for a fleeting second I saw fear. "You must never tell anyone what you saw."

My heart gave a frightened leap. "Is he that ruthless?"

"He is."

"Then why did I see him leaving your study last week?"

Robert's face paled, and for a second his features looked frozen. "What . . . ?" he began.

I heard his loud swallow, and when he failed to go on, I stepped closer. "Robbie?"

My voice bought no response. After a long moment, his tongue flicked over his lips.

"Why was he here, Robert?"

His voice when he finally spoke was unsteady. "Look, some of Mr. Moulton's dealings are perfectly legitimate. Yes, legitimate," he added. "From time to time I've employed him to check on certain land deals, but it would be the end of my political hopes if any of this came to light." He paused and took my hands. "Please, Jessa, forget you ever saw it. All of it."

"I can't, and neither can you. We must make this right."

Robert's eyes hardened and his hands tightened on mine. "I meant what I said, Jessamyne. Don't tell anyone. Do you understand me?"

The coldness in his voice filled me with sickness. This was my beloved brother. What was he saying and doing? I took a deep breath and strove to keep my voice impassive. "Yes, Robbie, I understand."

* * *

I lay awake long after I went to bed that night, my mind running down one path, then leaping without thought to another. Men like Jeremy Moulton and the jockey needed to be stopped, but if by doing so I put my brother and me in danger, then maybe Robert was right.

But it did not feel right, not when I recalled the sight of Brock McKade leaping over the railing to confront the jockey. Not when I realized that deceit had dashed Brock's hopes for bettering Tanybrae. They weren't just Brock's dreams, but his mother's and Millie's as well. I remembered the bright expectancy on their faces when they talked of the race—their expectancy erased by the duplicity of the jockey. I knew the McKades would have difficulty sleeping tonight as well, but unlike me, disappointment rather than indecision would be the culprit.

No! I sat up, knowing what I must do. I wouldn't let myself think of Robert. The revelation of what he had become was still too painful to explore. It must wait until later—until after I spoke to the McKades.

Shortly before dawn, I crept down the stairs and unbolted the front door, looking over my shoulder to make sure no one saw me. Breathing a sigh of relief, I quietly closed the door behind me. Mist shrouded the tops of the trees, and the breeze blowing off Prince Phillip Bay made me pull my shawl more closely about me in the half-light.

I set out at a brisk pace for Exhibition Street, knowing I must depend upon public conveyance to take me to the Grand Hotel. Luck was with me, and I was able to find a hackney on the next corner.

"The Grand Hotel," I told the driver.

He looked me over, my dress and demeanor seeming to tell him I had the price of the fare. The inside of the hackney smelled of tobacco and was none too clean. Instead of sitting back into the worn cushions, I sat on the edge of the seat, aware that despite the coolness of the spring morning, the palms of my hands were damp inside my gloves. The carriage moved at a steady pace toward the heart of the city and was soon joined by drays and other vehicles.

"Hurry, please hurry," I whispered when we were forced to wait for a cumbersome wagon. From there we rolled past Bourke and on to Collins Street and finally to the hotel.

I stepped out and, after paying the driver, looked up at the imposing edifice. Lifting my green skirt, I approached the entrance, at the same time recalling Millie's excited squeal when Brock told her where they'd be staying. A uniformed doorman greeted me, his brows lifting at my early arrival. My steps quickened as I crossed the thick-carpeted lobby. Pray to heaven the McKades were still in town. The clerk at the desk met my inquiry with a noncommittal expression.

"Miss Millie McKade?" he parroted back to me.

"Yes, she's here with her mother and brother. Perhaps the room is booked under her brother's name. Mr. Brock McKade."

I met the balding man's searching look with one of aloofness. Lowering his eyes, he consulted the register and directed me to room 212. "It's up the stairs and to your right, although considering the early hour you'll not likely find them risen."

Thanking him, I climbed the wide stairway, my heart jumping nervously as I neared their room. Like the clerk, I expected to find the McKades still in bed. Instead the door jerked opened in response to my first knock.

I stared at Brock and he at me, my eyes taking in his swollen lip and an ugly scrape on one cheek. Although he was fully dressed, his shirt was rumpled and splattered with drops of blood. By the looks of him, the jockey wasn't the only one injured in the row at the racetrack.

"Mr. McKade."

He nodded, his expression wary and puzzled.

"I doubt you remember me. I'm Jessamyne Clayborne and—"

"Miss Clayborne. I'm sorry, I didn't recognize you." Some of the wariness left Brock's face.

"It's not surprising. No doubt you find me greatly changed."

"Yes, though no more than you must find me." He raised a hand to his scraped cheek, shaking his head as if still not believing what had happened. "There was a fracas at the race."

"It's about the race that I came. Are your mother and Millie here?" I nervously glanced over my shoulder, half expecting to see Robert or Jeremy Moulton. "I need to talk to you."

Brock stepped aside and bowed. "Yes, of course. Please come in."

I felt relief when the door closed behind me, but that relief didn't last many seconds, for the eyes Brock turned on me were not friendly.

"Won't you be seated, Miss Clayborne?" With that he crossed the room and knocked on a door. "Mum, Miss Clayborne is here. She wishes to talk to us."

"Mercy . . . What can she be wantin'?" her groggy voice responded.

"I don't know." Brock's voice, like his expression, was noncommittal, but I could almost hear the questions rattle through his head. *What is Robert Clayborne's sister doing here? Didn't Millie say she was at the race with Neville Bromfield?* The unasked questions seemed to fill the space between us, removing Brock's usual friendliness and making me nervously play with the fringe of my paisley shawl. I was vaguely aware of the room's tasteful furnishing, the muted shade of green in the carpet accented by cabbage-size leaves in the pattern on the sofa.

"May I ring for some tea?" Brock asked. "Though, early as it is, it may take a few minutes."

"No, please. I didn't come for tea."

"Why did you come?" Although the room's width separated us, I felt as if Brock were standing over me, his dark eyes trying to fathom the answers without my speaking.

I rose to my feet and went to him, the tired lines around his eyes bespeaking the sleepless night he'd just passed. "I came to say I'm sorry Night Flyer lost and to tell you I think I have proof that the race was rigged."

"Rigged?" The word came in a rush of breath. "How?"

Before he could say more, the bedroom door opened and Anne and Millie hurried out. Neither had taken time to dress, and Millie was still tying the sash on her blue wrapper, her chestnut hair mussed and in its nighttime plait.

Millie's "Jessamyne" was drowned by Brock's deeper voice.

"Miss Clayborne thinks she has proof the race was rigged."

Anne's fingers closed around my arm. "If there's anything ye can tell us, we'll forever be in your debt." Her eyes filled with tears. "Anything," she whispered.

Brock cleared his throat and ran a restless hand through his thick hair. "Why don't we sit down and let Miss Clayborne tell us what she knows, Mum?"

"Yes, of course. What am I thinkin'? Sit down, lass. Millie, you too."

The three of us sat on the sofa, but Brock remained standing, his arms clasped behind his back as he gazed down at me. "Miss Clayborne?" he prompted.

"This will take a bit of explaining," I began. "When I sailed from England, I had the misfortune to meet an unsavory passenger by the name of Jeremy Moulton." Brock's dark brows lifted, but he remained silent while I revealed my thoughts on the man and the exchange of money I'd witnessed between Mr. Moulton and a man in the woods. "I thought no more about it until I saw the jockey riding Night Flyer. It was the same man. His sharp features are hard to forget. And then when Night Flyer faltered—"

"I knew it. The dirty—" Brock caught himself. "The dirty bounder," he amended. "I should have punched him harder."

"Brock." The censure in Anne's voice was lost in her next words. "I thought you said Ned Krueger was one of the best jockeys."

"He is. That's why I hired him. Moulton must have paid him enough to push him over the line." Brock shook his head and fixed me with a steady gaze. "Were you able to see the amount of the bills?"

I shook my head. "No, only that there were many."

"Blast," Brock growled, and in the next breath, "I wonder if Moulton was acting alone." He stopped and ran his hand through his hair, making the ends stand up in disarray. "Does your brother know you came here?"

"No. That's why I came so early and why I need to hurry home." I got to my feet. "I thought you'd know what to do and the names of the race officials to contact."

"I do, but none of this will do any good unless you are willing to tell them what you saw."

My heart plummeted even as my brain acknowledged that this was what I'd feared. A dozen pictures tumbled through my mind— Robert, Jeremy Moulton leaving the study, the ruthlessness I'd glimpsed in my brother's eyes. "I . . ." My voice refused to go on.

"Have you told your brother what you saw?"

I lifted my head and met Brock's gaze. "Yes."

"What did he say?"

"That Jeremy Moulton isn't a man to be crossed and that I must leave it alone."

Some of the rigidity left Brock's face. "Then why did you disobey?"

My answer came without thought. "Because men like the jockey and Jeremy Moulton shouldn't go unpunished." I wouldn't let myself think of Robert. Instead, my gaze went to Millie and Anne. "You're good, honest people, and I knew how tightly your hopes were pinned on Night Flyer winning the cup."

The sound of Brock clearing his throat sent my attention flying to Brock. As our eyes met, I became aware of the shadow of unshaved whiskers on his chin and upper lip, the ridge of his high cheekbones. Something passed between us, a feeling that was strangely unsettling and at the same time steadying.

After a moment, Brock spoke. "Then we must find a way to use what you've told us without giving away your identity." He nodded, and for the first time that morning he smiled. "If we put our minds to it, I'm certain we can figure a way." Despite his swollen lip, his smile widened. "Thank you, Miss Clayborne. A thousand times thank you."

Brock's fingers closed around my arm. "You need to be on your way. Let me see you to your carriage so you can return home before anyone notices you've been gone."

"Yes, do hurry, lass." Anne kissed me on the cheek, and Millie gave me a hug.

"You're so brave," she whispered. Tears shimmered in her eyes, but I saw hope too, its presence suddenly filling the room.

"Come," Brock prompted.

I stopped him when we reached the door. "It will be best if we're not seen together." Noting his frown, I hurried on. "Don't worry. I'll be fine." I opened the door and looked down the hall. Not seeing anyone, I smiled. "Good luck."

I was aware that Brock watched me as I hurried down the stairs and across the lobby. Seeing the doorman, I asked him to hail a passing hackney.

* * *

I remember little of my return to Rathdown Street, only my nervousness and whispered prayer that I'd be able to enter the house without being seen. Only firm control slowed my steps after I paid the driver and walked the two blocks to Robert's home. The pre-dawn mist had dissipated, and smoke rose from the chimneys of several homes. "Please, oh please," I whispered as I climbed the broad steps to the front door.

I cautiously turned the knob and eased the door open, silently blessing the servant who kept the hinges well oiled. The entrance hall was deserted, as were the stairs, although I could hear the clank of pans and the murmur of voices coming from the kitchen. Lifting my skirt, I tiptoed across the tile floor and up the stairs, breathing quick, my ears tuned for sound. When I reached the landing, I looked toward Robert's bedroom door. Nothing. No one. Taking a deep breath, I hurried down the hall and slipped into my room and closed the door. It was done. The McKades had been told. *Pray God Robert doesn't find out.*

Someone outside myself urged me to undress and don my nightgown. I followed the prompting, my fingers clumsy in their haste with the buttons. At last it was finished, my green skirt returned to the wardrobe and me in bed with the covers pulled over my shoulders. Now I could only wait and hope that when Polly came to waken me for breakfast, she would find nothing amiss.

* * *

Robert made no mention of our conversation when I joined him for breakfast that morning. Since Olivia was present, there was little opportunity for private talk. Even so, I was aware of a subtle change in our relationship, one signaled by currents of unease and the frequency with which Robert glanced at me.

As was his custom, Robert took opportunity to tease me, making much of my popularity at the race and the suitors who were certain to flock to my door. "Mark my words, Jessa, Rathdown Street will soon be Melbourne's most fashionable address." But the smile he gave me was stiff and failed to reach his eyes.

Robert didn't allude to the previous evening until he was leaving. It was no more than a whisper breathed into my ear as he bent to kiss my cheek. "Remember what I said, Jessamyne. Not one word. It could be the end of me. Perhaps you as well."

Tentacles of unease gripped me, and I prayed the smile I gave him passed as genuine. What had I done? Could my visit to the McKades truly put Robert and myself in danger? I shook my head as the enormity of my actions washed over me. Yet in my heart, I knew what I had done was right.

EIGHT

Unease followed me as I left the breakfast room. Although I knew I'd done the right thing, it didn't prevent me from worrying. If only I had someone with whom I could share my worries. In my longing I remembered the hours in which Sarah Hewitt and I had shared confidences while aboard ship. I wished many times over the next few days that she were in Melbourne instead of Geelong.

Two evenings later, Robert told me he needed to go out of town on business. Olivia had excused herself to see to Sophia, but Robert and I lingered, the meal cleared away and a plate of fruit and cheese brought for us to sample.

"Will you be gone long?" I asked. Although the atmosphere between us was still strained, I preferred Robert's company to Olivia's.

"Hopefully no more than a few days. Much will depend upon how long it takes me to settle things at Wooraronga"

"Wooraronga?" I looked up from the apple I was peeling. "Isn't that the property you own out by the McKades?"

"In partnership with Neville," Robert corrected. "It seemed a wise investment, one in which we had great hopes. But lately . . ." Robert's voice trailed away as he grimaced. "The man I hired to run the spread seems to court trouble. First it was problems with the McKades, now the couple who cook and look after the place have left." He sighed. "It looks like I'll have to find a new foreman. Neville is sending me out to put things back in order. Trouble at Wooraronga is the last thing we need right now."

He frowned and fell silent. Then seeming to want to change the subject, he attempted a smile. "Have I ever told you about my prospecting days?"

"You tried a few times, but each time you did, Olivia changed the subject."

"Olivia." Robert gave a harsh laugh. "She doesn't like to be reminded of where my money came from. Whereas I . . ." He smiled and seemed to relax. "I enjoyed those days. There was excitement and allure enough to make us forget our lack of comfort."

Robert had always been a great storyteller. In a few descriptive sentences, he took me to the Upper Yarra River, where he and Neville had dug for gold, recalling their disappointment and how they'd almost given up. "Then we met Jeremy Moulton."

My head jerked up, and for a second I thought I'd heard wrong.

"Yes," Robert said. "The very Jeremy Moulton you met on the ship." He reached into the inside pocket of his coat and pulled out a slender silver flask. Unscrewing the top, he poured a generous portion into his tea.

"There," he said with satisfaction, and without pause went on with his story. "Moulton told us in confidence that he knew where to find nuggets so big a man could scarce get his hand around one. Of course he exaggerated, but there was gold all right, but in a place so secret and dangerous he was afraid to go there alone. So the three of us struck a bargain—me, Neville, and Moulton. Two of us would dig, and one would stand watch for Abos, since the gold was on one of their sacred sites."

Robert's voice quickened with excitement as he recounted the day they reached the site. His description was so clear, I felt as if I were with them as they dug with pick and shovel into the wooded hillside, Robert pausing to sift through the red-brown rubble to extract his first nugget.

A smile crossed his features as the story progressed. "After all those months of nothing but dirt and rocks, I couldn't believe Lady Luck was finally with us. I wish you could have seen the size of some of the nuggets." He made a cup with his hand. "I can still remember the feel of the pouch, of hefting its weight and knowing it was all mine."

"What about Neville and Jeremy?" I asked, carried along by his story in spite of myself. "When it was my turn to stand watch, they were as busy filling their pouches as I'd been." He chuckled. "Neville wasn't the gentleman you see now, but then, neither was I. We lived rough and dirty, but it was worth it." He paused and stretched his long legs.

I tried to fit what he'd told me around the Neville Bromfield I knew. "When did the gold run out?"

"It didn't."

"Then why—"

"Abos. We were digging up their holy place." Pleasure fled his face. "Even though one of us always kept watch, they managed to creep up on us. They came like black fiends, spears and clubs flying. We were lucky to get away with the gold and our lives, I tell you. If it hadn't been for Moulton, I wouldn't be here."

Little beads of sweat sprinkled Robert's upper lip. Seeing it, I refrained from speaking. In the silence, without his voice to fill the room, I became aware of the hiss of the gaslit chandelier and of the unpleasant questions circling my mind. "Did he save your life?" I finally asked.

Robert nodded.

"How?"

Shutters seemed to shadow Robert's blue eyes. "It's not something I like to remember." His hand went to the scar on his cheek. "This is a little souvenir the Abos gave me. Suffice it to say I don't have any liking for blacks, and Jeremy downright hates them."

I stared at his scar with its tiny jagged edges, one I'd surmised he'd received in a fight, but never with Abos, and never with Jeremy Moulton saving his life. I searched for words to tell him that gratitude could only be carried so far, that Mr. Moulton's unsavory character had canceled the debt.

Before I could speak, Robert's voice slipped out of the silence, his tone as nonchalant as if we'd been discussing the weather. "Olivia said the two of you are planning a shopping excursion tomorrow."

I was too surprised to speak for a moment. "It . . . it seems that's the plan."

Robert raised his brows. "You don't seem overly enthusiastic at the prospect. Don't you enjoy having new clothes?"

"You know I do. It's just that—"

"You're not looking forward to shopping with Olivia," Robert finished for me.

"I . . ." I wanted to pull the conversation back to Jeremy Moulton, but Robert seemed bent on talking of frivolities.

"You don't have to explain," Robert hurried on. "I avoid shopping with Olivia whenever I can as well." He got up from the table and came around to help me from my chair. "Don't let Olivia force her opinion upon you. Buy only what you like." He smiled down at me. "Give no thought to the cost, either. Remember I can well afford it, especially after the killing I made at the races this week."

I stiffened, but Robert didn't seem to notice.

"By the by, I heard a bit of interesting news today."

My heart gave an uneasy lurch. Had he learned about my visit to the McKades?

"It seems McKade and his cohorts aren't willing to let the outcome of the race rest. They went to the racing commission and asked that Ned Krueger be questioned."

I gave Robert a quick glance. "Ned Krueger?"

"McKade's jockey. Unfortunately, Krueger is nowhere to be found. Rumor has it he's pocketed his earnings and left town."

I stared at Robert. "Then the jockey did throw the race."

"Pawsh! There could be a dozen good reasons for Ned to leave. The point's moot, and all the more reason for you to leave it alone." His eyes were no longer friendly. "Forget it, Jessa. Leave it alone."

With that, he turned and quit the room.

* * *

The next two days passed slowly. The unsettling fact that Jeremy Moulton had saved Robert's life wouldn't leave me. More than that, I wondered if he might have warned Ned Krueger to leave town. *Jeremy Moulton.* Just thinking his name sent my mind racing to Robert. There was much I didn't know about my brother, and the few things I'd discovered left me uneasy.

Such was my state of mind when Olivia and I set out for an afternoon of shopping. Pretty clothes had always been my weakness, and I entered the first shop with great anticipation. I was immediately drawn to a gown of sea-green crepe with yards of lace and ruching.

"Not quite the thing for you, my dear," Olivia said, noting my interest. "The white one in the window will be more suitable, especially if you wish to hold Mr. Bromfield's attention. I have it on good authority that he has a preference for women who wear white."

"I gave up wearing white the year I came out of the schoolroom, and as for Neville Bromfield, he isn't the reason I choose my clothes."

"Perhaps it might be wise to make it your reason."

I turned my attention from the gown to Olivia. The little smile she gave me rankled and smacked of petty satisfaction. "Why is that?" I asked in an unfriendly voice.

Olivia shrugged and continued to smile. "You are not getting any younger, you know, and since Robert feels it his responsibility to find a suitable husband for you, I must have the same concern."

"Please don't trouble yourself. I'm capable of attracting a husband without your help." Although I was drawn to the green dress, I had intended to look at several before making my choice. Perversity overrode good judgment and sent me to the proprietress who hovered close by. I was aware she'd heard our conversation, as had several others in the shop. I saw their covert glances, but rather than being embarrassed, I felt wry amusement.

Olivia continued to try to dissuade me while I discussed the dress with the proprietress, her voice rising as each word was spoken. "You are making a grave mistake, which is an injustice to Robert who must pay the bill. You should give more thought to how you spend his money."

I shook my head in frustration, my voice as loud as Olivia's when I spoke. "I don't wish to quarrel, but bear in mind that I've been choosing my clothes for the last three years. Since I don't try to tell you what to wear, I would appreciate the same consideration."

By now Olivia was aware that everyone in the shop had turned to listen. "Hush, Jessamyne. People can hear you."

I shrugged. "Then perhaps you should lower *your* voice." I turned to the proprietress. "I'm sorry for our rudeness. This could not have been pleasant for you. I'll come back another day."

Smiling at the other women, I left the shop. I assumed Olivia would not be far behind me, and in this I was correct.

"How could you?" she hissed. "I have never been so embarrassed in all my life."

I said nothing, concentrating instead on making my way through the throng of shoppers to our carriage. Seeing us, Walter jumped down to open the door. "Mrs. Clayborne. Miss Clayborne. Where can I be takin' ya?"

"Home." The tightness in Olivia's voice gave evidence of her mood. As soon as the carriage door closed, she turned on me. "You shall pay for this, young lady. Making me look the fool. Don't think you can run to Robert to wheedle him with your pretty charms, either." She took a deep breath, her sallow features mottled with spots of anger. "I was glad when I heard you'd been washed overboard. Glad, I tell you. You may be Robert's sister, but don't forget I'm his wife."

"I shan't forget, nor do I wish to quarrel." Although I managed to keep my voice steady, inside I was trembling. "Since all that you feel for me is reciprocated, I think it best that neither of us say anything more."

Fortunately, Olivia agreed, and the rest of the ride passed in uncomfortable silence, something that was becoming a habit. I made a pretense of looking out the window, the noise of passing carriages and the sight of storefronts and people hardly registering. All I could see and hear was Olivia's angry face and voice. To continue to live with Robert and Olivia was now impossible. I must find another home.

* * *

Neville Bromfield sent a bouquet of flowers accompanied by a note saying how much he'd enjoyed my company at the races. With it was an invitation to dine with him on Saturday evening. The act failed to raise my spirits, as did Chloe's invitation to join her and some friends for tea.

I couldn't get the quarrel with Olivia out of my mind. Not liking her company, I took my meals in my room. As I spent more time in my luxurious surroundings, a wave of homesickness washed over me. In my mind, I saw Father and Cook and Mrs. Woolsey. Each had cared for me, filling my life with warmth and love and laughter. Here there was only Robert, and given the glimpse I'd seen of his character, who knew where that would lead?

"Oh, Robert," I sighed to myself. Common sense told me I couldn't last many days in my present situation. But where could I go? What should I do? Recalling my answered prayers at the time of Father's death, I whispered a humble petition to God, asking Him to help me find a solution to my problems.

* * *

Shortly after breakfast the next morning, Polly tapped on my door. "Another letter for ya, miss. It's nice to see ya settlin' in and makin' so many new friends."

I thanked her and took the letter. The handwriting was unfamiliar, but since it bore no stamp, I assumed it came from one of my new acquaintances in the city. I opened the envelope and scanned the contents with interest.

Dear Jessamyne,

Mum and Brock join me in thanking you again for your kind act on Wednesday morning. It took great courage and we will forever be in your debt. Brock is pursuing the business and is hopeful that justice can be obtained. Since he must return to Tanybrae, he has put the matter in the hands of his solicitor. Mum and I will be returning with him and would like to invite you to come with us. PLEASE SAY YOU WILL! We leave tomorrow morning, which is short notice, but hopefully not too short for you to make arrangement to come. We are still in room 212 at the Grand Hotel.

Affectionately yours,

Millie McKade

The signatures of Anne and Brock followed Millie's—Anne's cramped and crooked as if she were not comfortable with a pen, Brock's large and bold, much like his character.

I scanned the missive a second time, my pulse quickening with excitement. A visit to the McKades seemed the perfect solution to my uncomfortable situation. More than that, I would be with people I respected and considered friends. I wouldn't let myself think overlong about Brock, but the fact that he would be at Tanybrae danced through my mind as I penned my reply.

Ringing for Polly, I handed her the note and a sixpence. "Will you see that this is delivered today?"

"Yes'm. I'll ask John to take it there himself."

As soon as Polly left, I walked over to the wardrobe. Which of my gowns should I take, and what must be left behind? More importantly, how long could I impose upon the McKades' hospitality? I rummaged through my clothes with but half a mind while the rest skipped to Olivia. I knew there would be another confrontation when she learned my plan. Robert wouldn't be pleased, either. Pray heaven I was safely ensconced at Tanybrae before he returned.

Too agitated to stay in my room, I sought relief in the back garden. Like everything at Robert's home, it was beautifully apportioned with immaculate beds of brightly colored flowers, beautiful shade trees, and two stone benches arranged by a fountain.

Despite the pleasantness of the garden, my mind was uneasy. What if Robert followed me to the McKades and demanded that I return? Even if I defied him and stayed, where would I go when my time at Tanybrae ended?

Not knowing the answers, I made my way across the lawn to the bench by the fountain. But sitting served me no better than walking. In the end, I returned to my room where a short time later Polly appeared with an answer from Millie.

Dear Jessamyne,

We are excited that you accepted our invitation to Tanybrae. I can't wait to see you. Since Brock wants to make an early start, we will pick you up at seven o'clock in the morning.

Until then,

Millie

Millie's enthusiasm cut through my worry. Things would work out. Hadn't I prayed for a solution to my problem, and hadn't the way been opened? In my mind, I could hear Sarah Hewitt's voice, *"Put yer trust in the good Lord."*

Holding tight to this thought, I asked Polly to retrieve my trunk from the attic. "I've been invited to visit friends who'll be here to pick me up in the morning."

Her pretty face registered surprise. "So soon, miss?" And in the next breath, "Do Mrs. Clayborne know 'bout this?" Seeing me raise my brows, she hastily stammered, "I'm sorry, miss. It's not my place to be questionin' ya. But the missus likes to know everthin' what goes on, and I'd not like to see ya get on her bad side."

"I'm already on Mrs. Clayborne's bad side. That's why I'm going." I paused and met her gaze. "It will be better for me if she doesn't find out. Can I rely on you to keep my secret?"

Polly's face turned serious, and I sensed her dilemma. What if Olivia found out and dismissed her? After a long moment, she nodded. "I'll see that it stays just our secret. There's all sorts of excuses I can invent."

And so it was done—my trunk brought to my room and packed, a note to be left for Robert in his study. I took much thought before I penned it.

Dear Robbie,

I hope you won't be too angry with me for leaving, but Olivia and I have quarreled AGAIN—the words spoken not easily taken back. Anne and Millie McKade are in town and have invited me to accompany them to Tanybrae for a visit. I know you're not fond of the family, but they have been very good to me. The length of my stay is uncertain, but I will keep in touch with you. Remember that I love you.

Always your sister,

Jessa

Sighing, I looked down at the words. Although I'd discovered unpleasant things about my brother's character, they didn't stop me from loving him. More than that, Robert was all I had left of my family.

Just before I went to bed, I took the note downstairs and placed it under the paperweight on his desk. *There, it's done.*

* * *

At seven o'clock the next morning, I waited on the front steps with portmanteau and parasol in hand. When I looked up the street, I was rewarded with the sight of the McKade vehicle.

Disappointment flicked through my smile when, instead of Brock, Henry and a young man jumped down to help me. The younger man doffed his hat before hoisting my trunk onto his muscular shoulder. After opening the carriage door and letting down the step, Henry turned to me with a wink and broad smile, his crooked teeth plainly visible.

"G'day, Miss Clayborne, and glad I am to see ya well and lookin' the tops."

Unbidden laughter struggled to escape. "Thank you, Henry."

"Ya recollect me name, do ya?"

"I do, and your kindness too. I shall always remember your help when you and the McKades came to the Aborigine camp."

Henry's ruddy face turned even redder. "'Wasn't nuttin, tho' I do try to be first in line to 'elp those what be needin' it." As he spoke, he took my portmanteau and parasol and stowed them inside the carriage. Stepping aside, he bowed. "Now for ya. Watch yer step, and 'Enry will be 'ere to catch ya should ya fall."

I suppressed a giggle and saw similar amusement dance in Millie's eyes as I stepped up.

"You mustn't mind Henry. He's a dear, but sometimes his tongue does run on," she whispered after he closed the door.

"Och, for sure, he's one what likes to blather," Anne agreed. She glanced significantly at the house. "And where might yer brother be on this bonny mornin'? I expected to find him here to see ye off."

I looked back at the house, breathing a sigh of relief as the horses and carriage navigated the turn and entered the street. "Robert is out of town. Actually, neither he nor his wife is aware I'm leaving."

Although Anne's gray eyes widened, she made no comment.

"Your kind invitation came like an answer to prayer, which it was, for I'd prayed for help to know what to do." I took a deep breath and hurried on, aware that both women listened closely. "Although I dearly love Robert, he's not the man I once idolized. I fear he's changed, and so have I. More than that, his wife and I have quarreled . . . not just once, but several times. She has made it very clear that she resents my being here."

My attempted smile fell into the silence. "So there you have the whole of it. If I can presume upon your kindness until I can make other arrangements . . ." Unexpected tears came to my eyes. "I know it's an imposition—"

Anne reached for my gloved hand and squeezed it. "'Tis no imposition, but the chance for us to enjoy yer company. Doona fash yerself, for ye can be stayin' with us for as long as ye find it to yer likin'."

"Oh, yes," Millie said. "We can pretend we're sisters and have the best of times."

I blinked at my tears. "Thank you, though I hate to impose."

"Dinna ye hear me, lass? There'll be no more talk of imposition. Millie and I are always wantin' company. Brock too, tho' he'd no' be admittin' to such."

"Where is Mr. McKade?"

"He'll be catchin' up with us shortly."

"Brock and Adam are riding Night Flyer and the filly," Millie explained. "Adam is one of the grooms and Brock's right-hand man with the horses. Since you'll be living with us, you'd best start learning everyone's name."

"I remember George and Henry."

"And Dan helped you with your trunk. He works with the horses too, rides them some. Dan and Adam even slept with the horses before the race to make sure nothing bad happened to Night Flyer and Flame."

"More like they should have been watchin' the jockey." Anne's wide mouth tightened. "Who would believe such shenanigans—bribes, the race fixed?"

By now we'd left the heart of the city and were crossing the bridge over the Yarra River. "Has your son made any progress in finding the jockey?" I asked when we reached the other side.

Anne shook her head. "Brock's no' one to give up. Like his father he is . . . no lettin' go till he succeeds." She shook her head a second time. "Such shenanigans."

At her second use of the word *shenanigans,* I recalled what Robert had said about Angus McKade. His description didn't fit what Anne had told me about her husband. Although the Scotsman might well have been hard-nosed and tenacious, I refused to think he'd been dishonest. Such a trait belonged to men like Jeremy Moulton.

"Brock's solicitor is helping," Millie said. "When he called on us yesterday, he expressed confidence in finding where Ned Krueger has gone."

"I hope they succeed, though if he hobnobs with the likes of Jeremy Moulton, who's to say where he may have gone? Did I tell you Mr. Moulton was a passenger on the ship I took from England?" Seeing Anne nod, I went on. "What if Ned Krueger booked passage on a ship and has left the country?"

"Brock and his friends wondered the same and checked with the port authorities. They have no record of anyone by that name or description. I try not to get discouraged, but . . ." Millie shook her head and sighed.

"Now, now, we'll have no more such talk," Anne scolded. "'Twill no' help a wee bit and only make us sad besides. Is no' the sun shinin' this bonny mornin'?"

Millie nodded.

"Then we have much to be thankin' the good Lord for."

With that, our talk turned to more cheerful matters—the play the McKades had attended the evening before the race, a boat ride they'd taken with friends on the Yarra River.

"Christopher Morgan went too. He's one of Brock's mates and ever so nice," Millie said.

"As ye can see, Millie is a wee bit taken with the laddie."

"Mum," Millie protested. "He's not a laddie, but very much a man."

"Och, that too." Anne laughed. Looking at me, she asked, "And how about ye, Jessamyne? Did ye find Melbourne and its folk to yer likin'?"

"I did, although the bruises kept me close to home for the first fortnight."

Anne clicked her tongue. "My heart aches thinkin' of yer poor face and the batterin' ye took. But now look at ye. Exceptin' for my Millie, I doot I ever laid eyes on a more bonnie lass." She studied me for a moment. "Aye, many would call ye a beauty."

Heat flooded my cheeks. "You are most kind."

"Truthful too, and I'm thinkin' I'm no' the first to be sayin' such aboot yer looks." Sensing my discomfort, she changed the subject. "So to continue with ye learnin' the names of our people, I think ye met Min and Callie the night yer brother dined with us."

Since being rescued by Sal and her family, I felt an interest and kinship with the Aborigines. "How long have Callie and Min worked for you?"

"Ye can't say they work for us exactly, for they come and go as they please. 'Tis the way of the Aborigines . . . listen to their own voice and hold to their old ways they do, but they're good workers." She paused and her brow furrowed. "As to how long they've been at Tanybrae, I think 'tis nigh on ten years. Min came first, no more than a wee lass when she come. Callie came a year or two later. Cousins I think they are, tho' 'tis hard to say, for the natives reckon families different than we do. They call their aunties mum whether she is or no', so 'tis a mass o' confusion. But they seem to know how they all fit together. The Abos are right strong when it comes to family."

"Didn't you say Min and Callie are related to Sal?"

"Aye, tho' who's to ken just how. I've a notion Parmee is Sal's brother and some kind of elder in their tribe, but he don't say much aboot such things. Right secretive they are."

I looked from Anne to Millie. "Who is Parmee?"

"One of the best blokes in Australia with horses. Talks to them, he does, with strange words that gentle even the most skittish stallion.

'Tis strange, almost spooky to watch him. My Angus considered himself an uncommon lucky man to find Parmee. So aye, we look t'other way when he and the girls leave. Walkaboot they call it."

Millie giggled. "Since they take off most of their clothes when they leave, I'd suggest you don't look too close if you see them slipping away."

I flushed at the memory of the scant covering Sal and her family had worn when they found me.

"'Twas after a walkaboot that Min came to us. Parmee appeared one afternoon, carryin' a long staff and with no' but a possum skin around his waist. The wee mite trailed at his heels and looked at us like she'd never seen anythin' so strange. 'Twas then Parmee told Angus he'd brought someone to help me. A year or so later, he came with Callie. The two of them live with Parmee in a cabin not far from the stable. Keep to themselves they do and are no' much at talkin' unless somethin' excites them. The most talk to pass their lips was when Sal told them aboot the dream she'd had."

"I shall always be grateful for Sal's goodness. Robert can't find much good to say about the Abos, though perhaps that's because he bears a scar from one of their spears."

"Really?"

At my nod, Anne hurried to reassure me. "Doona fash yerself aboot our Abos. They're peaceful and good to help. We count ourselves lucky to have Parmee and the girls . . . Mooney too when he comes to help. Some of the stations are not so lucky. Most claim the blacks steal them blind, tho' in their eyes they doona look on it as stealin'."

I gave Anne a puzzled look. "Why is that?"

"Blacks doona think of property like we do. To them the earth belongs to animals and humans alike. Ye take only what ye need, no more, and ye leave a water hole or hunting spot with enough for the next bloke to use. When an Abo feels hunger, he'll kill a roo or snake and share it with his family. Nowadays when they see a sheep or cow, they sometimes do the same. They believe the Great Spirit created animals for food and survival, no' like we do to be owned."

"Did you know that when a black kills an animal he asks its forgiveness?" Millie put in. Her voice trailed away as she glanced out the window. Her features lit up and she smiled. "Look, there's Brock and Adam."

I turned, my gaze noting the easy manner with which Brock sat on the black stallion and the way his moleskin-clad legs hugged the saddle. When he lifted his hat and returned my smile, I felt the force of his gaze, and something seemed to whisper that we'd known each other in some misty, forgotten time.

"I expected them to catch up with us before now," Millie said.

Anne leaned forward to better see her son. "No doot he had things to take care of in the city."

The miles rolled by, the jolt of the carriage becoming more pronounced as we passed through a belt of dense trees. I looked into the upper branches of the gum trees, hoping to spy a koala and was rewarded with the sight of a furry face gazing down at me.

"My favorite place for koalas is in the hills close to Tanybrae," Millie said, looking at her mother. "After Jessamyne gets settled in, can we pack a picnic and go there?"

Seeing Anne's nod, I thought of the days ahead. Despite her assurance that I wouldn't be an encumbrance, I knew I couldn't stay indefinitely. While I worried over the matter, I saw we had left the woods to travel over an undulating vista of grassland and rolling hills punctuated by occasional groves of white-trunked eucalyptus. The coolness of the morning had given way to the harsher light of noon, the sun beating down on the roof of the carriage and making me wish I had thought to bring my fan.

Millie, being better versed in the buildup of Australia's summer heat, reached into her reticule and took out a tortoiseshell fan, holding it so both of us could feel its breeze. Anne had closed her eyes, her head leaning back against the cushions, the relaxed state of her body telling me she'd drifted off to sleep.

"If you've a mind to join Mum in taking a nap, I shan't be offended," Millie said. "I might doze off for a while myself."

Despite the heat and jarring motion of the carriage, I fell asleep, trying to forget that by leaving Robert I'd cast away security and opened the door to uncertainty. Though my mind swam in lazy circles with worry niggling at the edge of my thoughts, assurance pulsed like a warm beacon at their center, whispering that everything would work out. Hadn't Sarah told me to pray and trust in the Lord?

NINE

The sound of tapping floated into my sleepy brain, incessant and buzzing like a pesky fly.

"'Tis Brock," I heard Anne say.

My eyes flew open. Through sleep-fogged eyes, I saw him lean close to the carriage and rap again with his riding crop.

"Kangaroos," he mouthed.

Lethargy fled as I looked past him. Rolling scrub was all I saw until movement by a grove of trees pulled my gaze to a herd of animals resting in the shade. While I watched, the carriage rolled to a halt.

"There they be," Henry said. "Let 'Enry 'elp ye down so ye can see the roos."

I hesitated, for the horse Brock rode was too close for my comfort.

"Miss Clayborne had an unfortunate experience with horses and doesn't like to get too close to them," Anne said in a quiet voice. "Tell Brock to keep his horse and Night Flyer away from her."

Henry's gaze flicked over me before he turned to Brock. "Ya 'ear that Mr. McKade? The young miss is shy o' 'orses."

Brock gave me a quick look as he urged the horse he rode away from the carriage. Night Flyer, who was on a leading rein, went with him. What Brock thought, I couldn't tell, for his expression showed no more concern than if he'd learned I preferred my tea with cream instead of sugar.

Anxious to see the kangaroos, I stepped down from the carriage. Despite pains to keep our voices low, the kangaroos were aware of our presence. Where but a moment before they'd been lying in the shade, now all were on their large hind feet, the smaller forelegs tucked close to their chests as if ready for flight.

"The three largest ones are the males, *boomers* we call them," Brock said after he dismounted and joined us. "If you look close, you can see a joey peeking out of its mother's pouch."

Following Brock's pointing riding crop, I was able to decipher the baby's dark head and nose silhouetted against the lighter fur of the mother's belly.

"Sometimes all you can see of the joeys are four little feet sticking out of the top," Millie whispered.

"How uncomfortable."

"I doubt they even notice," she giggled.

Her laugh sent the kangaroos bounding off through the trees, their leaping gait surprisingly fleet and agile. Swallowing my disappointment, I watched as they disappeared from view.

"There'll be others," Brock reassured me. "In a fortnight you'll have seen so many roos you won't think anything about them."

I looked up at him while my mind busily tucked away the terms *roo* and *joey* for future reference. Brock's gaze met mine, the blueness of his eyes seeming to gain color from the deep blue of his shirt. "Sometimes there're so many, they become a nuisance. Ask Mum what she thinks of the roos."

"Och, terrible pests they are," she said, rolling the *R*'s. "Especially when they take the notion to eat my garden."

"More than one roo has ended up in Mum's stew."

I wrinkled my nose, remembering the meat the Aborigines had fed me. "I knew Sal and her family ate them, but . . ." My voice trailed away when I saw mischief dance in Brock's eyes. "You're teasing," I accused.

Mischief transferred itself to his voice. "Millie will tell you I'm a tease, but it's the truth that Mum's more than a fair shot with a rifle."

I looked at Anne, recalling how she'd helped her husband and Henry fell trees and build a home in the wilderness.

"My Angus insisted I learn. Said knowin' such was necessary with us livin' so far from neighbors." She paused to remove the pins that held her stylish green hat in place. Reaching into the carriage, she set it on the seat and replaced it with a brown leather one. "I'm thinkin' the horses can use a rest, and so can we . . . not to mention I've a hankerin' for a spot o' tea," she said to Henry. "Will ye unload the hamper I packed at the hotel?"

Henry was quick to do her bidding, and in no time a quilt had been spread on the grass under a tree and the hamper opened. A loaf of bread, thick slices of cheese, and a carton of biscuits were nested between two containers of tepid tea.

"'Tis no' the same as dinin' in style at the Grand Hotel," Anne said when she, Millie, and I had settled on the quilt. "But I think a hearty appetite will make up the difference."

From the way the four men eyed the contents of the hamper, I suspected she spoke the truth. Henry and Dan found seats on a log while Brock and Adam lounged on the grass near the quilt. As Anne opened her mouth to take a bite of cheese, she stopped and looked nervously at the grass. "Did ye check good for snakes?"

"Yes'm," Henry replied. "Ya know I always keep a sharp eye out for the varmints."

I glanced around uneasily, recalling that Henry had run a stick through the grass before he spread the quilt. "Are there snakes?"

Anne grimaced. "Aye. Snakes are somethin' ye must keep in mind if ye live out in the country. Not that they're everywhere, but still—"

The memory of young Alice, who'd died from snakebite, crowded into my mind. Small wonder Anne checked for snakes.

"The big browns are what we mostly have to watch for, though we occasionally see tiger snakes," Brock said. "Besides a plentiful supply of flies, Australia is cursed with more than its share of poisonous snakes. Mum and Millie make it a habit to wear boots when they're away from the house. I don't want to alarm you, Miss Clayborne, but while you're staying with us, you'd be wise to do the same."

I took a mental inventory of my wardrobe and found it sadly lacking in boots, my only pair coming but an inch or two above my ankle.

Noting my uneasiness, Millie spoke. "Don't let Mum and Brock frighten you. I go weeks, sometimes months without seeing a snake. And if it's a lack of sturdy boots, I bought a new pair just yesterday that I'm sure will fit you." She smiled and leaned closer. "I'm so glad you'll be staying with us. Besides boots, I have dozens of things I want to share with you."

Millie's words did much to reassure and comfort me, and I bit with relish into a crusty piece of bread. From there the talk turned to more pleasant subjects—the number of new carriages seen on the streets of Melbourne, the band of Scottish bagpipes playing on the public green.

"'Twas grand . . . almost like being back home," Anne said. "Tho', of course, Australia's my home now."

No mention was made of the race, though it lay just under the surface, manifest in the frown on Brock's face as he stared off into the distance and the shake of Henry's head as he looked from Brock to Night Flyer. I studied the stallion as he grazed near the other horses, his long tail swishing flies as sunlight glinted off his ebony coat. At a distance, I thought him a magnificent beast and could admire the length of his long legs—legs that should have carried him across the finish line ahead of Bruiser. Small wonder Brock looked preoccupied and edgy.

Anne began to stow the remains of the meal back into the hamper. "Pleasant as it be to sit in the shade, such doona get us to Tanybrae."

Brock got to his feet and reached to help his mother, then Millie. When he extended his hand to me, I gratefully accepted it, aware of his touch as I gained my feet.

"I'm pleased you've come to visit us, Miss Clayborne. Your being here will do much to keep Mum and Millie pleasantly occupied." He cupped my elbow with his hand and escorted me toward the carriage. "Thank you again for telling me about the jockey. It was enough to start an investigation. Although we haven't discovered Krueger's whereabouts, good men are working on it."

"I hope you succeed."

His hand tightened on my elbow. "We will. I'm not one to give up easily."

I saw determination in his blue eyes and in the muscles of his square jaw. If anyone could succeed in finding the needed information, it would be Brock McKade.

* * *

We reached Tanybrae in the late afternoon.

"Isn't it beautiful?" Millie asked when the carriage entered the avenue of fig trees leading to the house. "Each time I see it, I think how fortunate I am."

I nodded as I looked out at the sprawling façade that was Tanybrae. Its whitewashed walls and shady veranda seemed to call a welcome, one voiced in the bark of the dog.

Anne ruffled the collie's head. "'Tis Dundee, another name ye'll want to add to yer collection."

Dundee nuzzled my hand with his long nose, his plumed tail wagging in acceptance. Brock and Adam rode the horses back to the stable while Henry and Dan carried our luggage into the house. With parasol and portmanteau in hand, I followed the two women across the wide veranda and into the coolness of the house, grateful I didn't have to be carried, as had been the case on my last visit.

Callie waited by the front door. "Good ya be home," she said. Her voice trailed off when she saw me.

"I doot ye recognize Miss Clayborne," Anne said, "as she's much changed from the last time ye saw her."

Something flicked through Callie's dark eyes, but her expression remained unchanged. "G'day, missy."

Anne removed her leather hat and hung it on a stand by the door. "Miss Clayborne will be stayin' with us, so I need ye and Min to ready the guest room." Glancing at Henry and Dan, she went on. "Ye know where to put Millie's case, mine too. For now ye can leave Miss Clayborne's trunk in the hall."

"You can come with me while Callie and Min get your room ready," Millie said. "I always like a washup to get rid of the dust and grime." Seeing that I still hesitated, she went on. "Remember, this is your home. At first our ways may seem strange, but before you know it, you'll feel like you've lived here forever."

"'Tis a truth," Anne put in. "Now off with ye. A good washup will be the very thing for ye both."

I gave Anne a quick hug, breathing in the faint aroma of tincture of roses mingled with perspiration and dust. Good smells, all of them—ones that bespoke the salt-of-the-earth woman that she was. "Thank you."

"Aye, and mine to ye for comin'." She gave me another hug. "I'll be in to ye in a minute. Millie's room is down that way."

Though Brock's room had been decorated in wood, accented with tones of deep blue, Millie's was a combination of frills and shades of pastel pink and yellow. "What a lovely room—soft and cheery, just like you are."

Millie laughed. "That's why I chose the colors—to remind me I'm a girl . . . a woman. Sometimes the long hours in the saddle with a dusty hat and drab, serviceable clothes make me forget. But here—" she ran her fingers along the length of the ruffled pink bed covering—"here I take leisurely baths and fuss with my hair and remember I'm a woman, not one of the stockmen."

I looked at Millie with new understanding, realizing there was much to be discovered about my new friend. I watched her graceful movements as she poured water from a flowered pitcher into the basin. In her white gown, sprigged with green and with a fetching hat perched on her head, she looked every inch a young lady of quality. And yet she had alluded to riding long hours with her brother and the stockmen. Yes, there was much to be discovered.

Washing my hands and face with Millie's perfumed soap was just as pleasant as she'd predicted. As I wiped my damp face, I became aware of Millie's gaze. What were her thoughts? Did I measure up? I hadn't cared two pence what Olivia and her Melbourne friends thought of me, but I very much wanted the McKades' approval. They were good, solid people, people I instinctively trusted. And I wanted them to feel the same about me.

Never shy about asking questions, I decided to voice my thoughts. "Do I meet with your approval?"

Millie gave a quick laugh. "You know you do."

"Yet I saw concern. What is it, Millie? If we're to be friends, sisters, then I hope we can always speak freely."

Millie nodded. "I want that too, not having to dance around what we really want to say." She smiled and took a deep breath. "I truly meant what I said about wanting us to be like sisters. As soon as we met, I felt admiration and liking for you. But it concerns me that you don't ride. In town it wouldn't be a problem, but here so much of what we do is on horseback." She reached for my hand. "Do you think you could try? Brock is wonderful with horses. Both of us will help you."

Fear licked at my middle. Just being near horses upset me, and to mount one . . . My mind shouted *No!* but the pleading look in Millie's hazel eyes stopped it. I swallowed, my throat dry and taut. "I'll try."

Millie hugged me the second time. "You're a dear. You don't need to start today. Give yourself a few days to settle in."

"That would be better," I agreed, while inside my mind was busy thinking of excuses.

* * *

The guest room at Tanybrae was every bit as nice as Millie's room, with a plumped bed, a tall wardrobe, and a small desk with carved legs that sat by a window looking out onto the veranda. The bed and windows were draped in shades of lilac, and a lovely painting of a bouquet of purple iris hung on the wall.

"It's one Mum painted," Millie said when she saw the direction of my gaze. "Since Da died, she's started painting again."

"Again?"

Millie nodded. "Mum would be the last to tell you of her talent, one exceptional enough that the Scottish laird in her village paid for her art lessons. According to Da, there were plans to send her to Edinburgh to study with a well-known artist."

Thoroughly intrigued, I stepped to examine the painting more closely. Although I was no judge of art, I thought it excellent. The shadings of purple were layered in such a way as to make the petals take on life and third dimension. "What happened?" I asked.

"Love . . . Da. When he left for Australia, Mum sold her paintings so she could buy passage and follow him. Have you ever heard anything more romantic?"

Before I could answer, Anne cleared her throat and entered the room. "Och, now, our Millie finds everthin' romantic . . . a sunset, moonlight. I fear she be an incurable case."

"Then I must be incurable as well. It is romantic."

Anne laughed. "'Tis the way of young lassies, always longin' for things of the heart. I must admit my Angus was a strappin' laddie, and right good in the face too, rather like our Brock." Her smile widened. "I was no' the only lass with my eye on him. He could have had his pick of any in the county. But 'twas me he chose, and I was not for takin' the chance of an Australian lassie catchin' his eye. Angus promised his undyin' love till he could save money for my passage, but still . . ."

"So you sold your paintings and joined him?"

"Aye, and never regretted it for a wee second." Her eyes clouded. "Angus was a good man, a good husband."

Millie put an arm around her mother. "I miss him too, Mum."

"Aye, we all do, but such canna bring him back. Instead, I paint and Millie rides horses or goes into the city. And Brock . . ." She paused. "Brock does any number o' things, but mostly he dreams of makin' Tanybrae the best station in the Gippsland." Shrugging, she looked around the room. "Such sentimental blather doona help Jessamyne settle in. Do ye find the room to yer likin'?"

"It's lovely."

"Och, a far cry from the wee hut we had when Brock was a bairn." A satisfied expression crossed her face. "Now we have a regular guest to use the room, tho' I hope ye'll come to consider us family, for already 'tis what I think of ye. Another sweet lass to spoil and count as my daughter."

* * *

I thought of her words over the days of settling in. With Mother taken from me at an early age, I'd never had a close relationship with another woman. Here I had two—each warm and loving in her own way, and neither giving indication that my presence was anything less than a treat. "I'm so glad you're here," was soon a phrase I heard each day. With so much affection, it was easy to count my good fortune.

Tanybrae itself was also to my liking. On the second day after my arrival, Anne and Millie invited me to go for a walk.

"There's more to Tanybrae than the house. We'll no' be goin' far . . . only to show ye the rest of those who live here, but ye'll be wantin' to wear a wide-brimmed hat, boots too, for ye no' can tell what ye'll meet up with when ye leave the house," Anne said as we prepared to leave. Millie supplied me with boots, and Anne offered me a floppy straw hat with a circle of faded silk flowers nestled above the brim.

"A parasol is such a nuisance," Millie said, "but sun here can be death to your skin and leave you looking old before your time. Some of the stockmen's wives have skin like old leather."

Knowing my fair skin would not take kindly to the harsh Australian sun, I donned the wide-brim hat without protest and tied it snuggly in place with its pink ribbons.

Anne excused herself shortly after we left the house. "I'll leave Millie to finish showin' ye around while I tend to my garden. It's been neglected for too many days."

Starting down the lane that dissected the property, Millie pointed out the stable—large and rising into the morning sun, the loft filled with hay for the horses. "Adam and Dan and Henry live in the bunkhouse behind the stable with the other single men," she explained. "I'd take you inside, but since you don't like horses, we'll wait for another time."

I nodded my appreciation and gave myself over to the beautiful spring morning. Colorful birds flitted through the thick branches of the fig trees, their happy songs mirroring my contentment. I saw a pasture close to the stable where more than a dozen horses grazed. Beyond it was a racetrack and training area.

Millie pointed to the oval. "That's where Brock spends most of his time. He and Adam are working with one of the yearlings this morning."

I'd also spied Brock, my eyes already trained to pick out his muscular form. He was dressed in his usual moleskin breeches and blue shirt with a brown leather hat covering his dark head. I watched as he used a long whip to take the horse through its paces, the yearling's head jerking on the leading rein as if it wished it were back in the pasture.

"Isn't Miranda a beautiful mare? Brock has high hopes for her."

I nodded, although my thoughts were more on Brock than on the chestnut mare. He seemed completely absorbed in what he was doing, the murmur of his voice and the touch of his whip keeping the mare in tight control. Even so, I sensed he was aware of our presence and that on some level it pleased him that I was there.

As if he had read my thoughts, Brock handed the mare's leading rein to Adam, vaulted the rail fence, and came to join us. He nodded to Millie and removed his hat as he spoke my name. His appraising glance made me glad I'd worn the light blue gown and paisley shawl. Blue had always complemented my features.

Before I could acknowledge his greeting, Millie spoke. "Miranda looks to be doing well."

Brock turned to watch Adam and the young mare. "She is. Mr. Dobson from Melbourne has already expressed interest in her." Glancing at me, he went on. "Are you and Millie out to see more of Tanybrae?"

I nodded, tilting my head to better see from under the wide brim of my hat. "I can see why I've heard good things about it. You are to be complimented, Mr. McKade."

I sensed that my words pleased him, but he passed them off with a shrug. "Most was accomplished by my father's hard work and good management, but the horses . . ." His gaze returned to the yearling. "The horses have largely been mine."

"It was Brock that built the racetrack and training arena," Millie said.

Brock's blue eyes narrowed against the glare of the sun. "The track's more than paid for itself. If Night Flyer had won the race—" His mouth tightened. "But that's water under the bridge, though with luck I'll be able to dam the flow and get back what should be mine." His voice held determination. "In the meantime, I've work to do with the filly, so if you'll excuse me, I'll leave Millie to show you around." He nodded, his features softening into a smile. "Miss Clayborne."

I returned his nod, watching as he walked back to the training area. When he reached it, he shot a glance in my direction before topping the fence. That's all it was—just a glance—but it was enough to make me hopeful.

After leaving the training area, Millie pointed out a chook coop, a pigsty, and the barn where cows were milked and the bullocks stabled. From there the lane curved south, revealing a cluster of small cottages and a blacksmith shop, all screened from the main house by a thriving orchard.

"The married stockmen and their families live here," Millie explained.

I looked past her to the whitewashed dwellings, noting a group of children playing in the shade of a tree and a woman weeding her garden.

"Elsie Callahan," Millie went on. "She and her husband have been with us for years, and their oldest boy helps George with the cattle."

Becoming aware of our presence, the woman straightened from her weeding and came to meet us, her billowy skirt of brown calico accenting her ample girth. Although her face was shaded by a shapeless hat, her skin was deeply tanned, as if she neglected to use it a good part of the time.

As introductions were made, I felt her gray eyes taking me in. *Quality,* they seemed to say as she self-consciously brushed dirt from her hands onto her skirt. Her countenance changed when she learned who I was.

"'Pon my soul! My James says yer a seven-day wonder and either uncommonly lucky or have angels watchin' over ya." Her work-worn hands made the sign of the cross. "I'm thinkin' the angels had a part in it, and right glad I am to be makin' yer acquaintance, Miss Clayborne."

I thanked her, but my mind had left Elsie Callahan, centering instead on the sensation that someone watched me closely. Looking across the lane, my gaze connected with that of a tall black man standing in front of a cabin, his stance so quiet and still, he seemed more tree than man.

"That's Parmee," Mille said. "He's not much for talking, but there's no one better with horses, not even Brock."

Parmee nodded his head, which was covered with gray curly hair and a beard. Although he was dressed in breeches topped with a shirt and vest, he retained the aura of someone who lived close to the earth. His appraisal of me was marked, but his expression remained noncommittal. After a moment, he turned and walked back into the hut.

"Like Sal, Parmee can be a little spooky," Millie said. "I'm never quite sure of what he thinks of us, but he keeps coming back. Most likely he's as enamored with horses as Brock."

I gave the hut a closer look. Although in good repair, it was small and crude. It was hard to imagine it as the McKades' first home, the log walls built from the trees Angus and Henry had felled, the roof thatched with the bark of the same trees.

"That's where I was born," Millie said as we passed a larger home, one almost double the size of the hut with a porch across the front and chimneys on either end. "Now George and his family live there."

As we retraced our steps, I learned that George was in charge of the cattle, while Brock gave the bulk of his attention to the horses. "Although there are times all of us are needed with the cattle," Millie concluded, "especially when they're calving. Dingoes can go through a herd and take down the new calves. Last year we lost almost a dozen."

My brows lifted. "Dingoes?"

"Wild dogs," she explained. "Alone they're too small to do much damage, but when they run in packs . . ." Millie paused and shook her head. "George and the stockmen try to keep them under control, but sometimes the dingoes get past." She gave me a speculative glance. "Would you be shocked if I told you I've shot more than one dingo?"

My eyes took in Millie's slender form, molded by the yards of edging and ruffles on her yellow dress. Trying to reconcile this modishly dressed young woman with one who rode with stockmen and shot wild dogs took some effort.

"I did shock you," Millie declared. "It's not something I enjoy. In fact, I avoid it if I can, but since our livelihood depends on the calves' survival," she shrugged, "I do what I have to do. The same as Mum did. In the early years, it was either shoot the dingoes or starve. Now it's not so drastic, but if we're to run Tanybrae at a profit we must—"

"Kill the dingoes," I finished for her. I put my arm around her waist. "I'm not shocked so much as amazed at your courage. You're truly amazing, Millicent McKade."

Color flooded Millie's cheeks, her pretty mouth lifting in a smile. "I suppose I am, though I doubt those in Melbourne would describe me as such." Laughing, she linked her arm through mine. "You're the only person I've told about the dingoes. Of course everyone at Tanybrae knows, but no one else." Her arm tightened on mine. "I knew we'd get on and that you'd understand." She gave a satisfied laugh. "I'm so glad you've come."

I smiled and gathered her words to my heart. My feeling of well-being increased when we entered the arbor gate to Anne's garden. It was like stepping into a miniature Eden. Roses clamored over the arbor and along a wooden fence, the riot of pink and red blooms calling a welcome, while more decorous spikes of lavender veronica added a muted greeting. Although I knew little about growing flowers, I sensed that what I saw was the result of hours of labor and love. A stone path wound among beds of Jupiter's beard and coral bells, while mounds of leafy shrubs added bold accents of green.

Anne straightened from weeding and leaned on her hoe. "Back are ye?" she asked. "And what might ye be thinkin' of Tanybrae now that ye've had a chance to look it over?"

"It's lovely. And this," I pointed to her garden, "is as much a work of art as your paintings."

"Thank ye." Satisfaction lifted the corners of Anne's mouth. "In the beginning 'twas only a place for my own pleasure, as Angus was not one to spare any thought for flowers and such. But when he saw the joy they gave me, he lent his hand." She touched the paving stones with the blade of her hoe. "The path was Angus's doing with a bit of help from Brock . . . the arbor too. Come see what else Angus made for me."

She led us past the colorful beds of flowers to a corner where a tree spread thick branches over a carved wooden bench. Ferns and low-growing plants carpeted the shady nook that housed an assortment of kangaroos, koalas, and birds all carved from wood and so lifelike I half expected to see them move. But it was the bench that drew the eye, the varnished back decorated with scrolls of flowers and filigrees entwined around a heart and the names of Angus and Anne.

"'Twas Angus's gift to me on our twentieth anniversary. No' the tree or the growin' things, mind. Those I planted myself, but the bench and animals . . ." Her hand touched the back of the bench, her fingers curving around the molding. "Carved them himself, he did, workin' at night or in the odd moments of the day when I thought him out with the cattle. Right deceitful he was and me not suspectin', though it took him most of a year." A smile curved her lips, and the lines in her face softened, giving me a glimpse of the pretty lass who'd caught Angus McKade's eyes. "I'll no' forget when he brought me to see his surprise, for surprise it was, with me laughin' and cryin' and completely taken aback." Her fingers traced the chiseled outline of Angus's name. "Now I canna do naught but wax and polish the wood, or sit here of an evening and remember. 'Twas a good marriage we had, one the likes of which I want for my children, though I'd as soon Millie waited a year or two, but Brock . . ." Her head turned in the direction of the horse paddock. "If Brock but can find a lass to love and make him as happy as Angus did me, I'll no' be askin' more of the good Lord or His angels."

In my mind I saw Brock as he worked with the yearling, his hat pulled low over his brow, his long, booted legs following the mare as she went through her paces. Did Brock have his mind set on any particular lass? The animated faces of Chloe and her friends niggled at the corner of my mind to remind me that, like Angus McKade, Brock could likely have his pick of the lasses.

Ten

The time at Tanybrae slipped by in a pleasant ribbon of days. I tried not to think of Robert, for each time I did, snippets of unease filled me with worry. What if he followed me to Tanybrae and demanded that I return to Melbourne? What would I do, and what, if any, were my rights? Shoving the thoughts to the back of my mind, I concentrated instead on my good fortune in having found such a pleasant refuge with the McKades.

Only one thing scratched at my contentment, and its source came from Brock McKade. It wasn't anything I could actually put my finger on. He was all a gentleman should be—kind, charming—but all was done when someone else was present, and even then I felt that everything I said and did was carefully weighed and pondered, as if he sought for a double meaning. Did he distrust me, even after I'd told him about the jockey? Or did the fact that I was Robert's sister always lurk in his mind? His quiet appraisal of me was unsettling. Besides making me self-conscious, it ate at my confidence and caused my words to be stilted.

"Don't you like Brock?" Millie asked one afternoon as we sat on the veranda.

My heart bumped against my ribs, for at that precise moment I saw him make his way into the stable. "Of course I like him. Why do you ask?"

Millie shrugged. "You seem to act differently when he's around . . . quieter and not yourself."

It was my turn to shrug. "I think I'm not yet used to Australian men. They're not the same as those I knew in England."

"Really?"

I nodded, knowing full well such was not the reason for my constraint.

"Maybe your being English is why Brock is not himself around you."

"Does he treat me differently?"

"My, yes. Usually, Brock is a terrible flirt. Half the girls in the city are in love with him."

I thought of Chloe and her friends. "Yes, I met some who expressed interest in him."

"See what I mean? He's always teasing and flirting." A little frown ruffled her forehead. "But with you he's . . ." she shrugged.

"Maybe he's not sure how to treat another sister," I suggested.

"Maybe." The look Mille gave me said she wasn't totally convinced.

* * *

Later that afternoon, I went to the sitting room to take another look at the painting that hung there. It was a landscape, a lovely garden scene I'd admired. But after hearing about Angus's gift to his wife, I wanted to look at it again. Anne had captured the vivid color of her flowers in all their glory, and there amid a froth of leaves and ferns was the bench, the heart and names depicted in flowing detail. But it was the shadowy figure of a man standing half hidden by tree branches that I'd come to see. Before I'd paid him little attention, my main focus on the bench and the riot of colorful flowers. Now I studied him carefully, knowing without question who he was. Although in shadows, Angus's craggy features spoke of quiet determination, as did his stance and the half-raised arm resting on a branch. I saw confidence as well, the essence of the man who'd carved both a home and a bench for his wife—all captured in the loving, talented strokes of Anne's brush.

A wave of longing washed through me, one so intense it made me turn away from the painting. Would it ever come to me, the bond of friendship and love that Angus and Anne had known and shared? I closed my eyes, aware of hollow loneliness that gaped like a jagged hole in the fabric of my life. *Where? When?* I wondered, while my heart whispered, *Soon, oh soon.*

With a sigh, I walked to the door. When I opened it, I became aware of voices—one Brock's, the quieter that of his mother.

Not wanting to intrude, I started to close the door, but the angry tone in Brock's voice stopped me.

"I shouldn't have to do this. Tell Adam we must wait until next year to enlarge the stable and buy another brood mare. It was there, the win so close I could taste it . . . The money stolen from under my nose."

I heard Brock's boots as he paced the veranda. "I try to follow your advice and not think about it, but most times the anger's too strong to be buried. If I had my way, I'd gallop into Melbourne and beat Jeremy Moulton to a pulp." The smack of Brock's fist against his palm made me flinch. Although they were outside my range of vision, I could feel his wrath.

"Ye know such would be foolish," Anne remonstrated. "'Twasn't just Jessamyne's brother who said Mr. Moulton was not a man ye should be messin' with. Yer solicitor said the same."

"Aye," Brock said. "As Da would say, leave it be, laddie. But doing such is hard, especially when I'm as mad at myself as I am with Moulton and the jockey. I shouldn't have placed such a large bet on Night Flyer, but I was so sure he would win."

I heard the rasp of Brock's footsteps and saw his hand strike the veranda post as he came into my line of vision.

"Yer no' the only one certain Night Flyer would win. Ye dinna ken it, son, but I put a wee bit of me own money on the horse."

Brock swung to face her. "Mum!"

"Oh, aye . . . it seems foolishness runs in the blood. But doona be fashin' yerself on my account, for 'twas only a wee bit. Still and all, I've no' seen a more likely horse, or one with more heart, either. 'Tis his speed and heart ye must think on. Remember there's always next year."

Brock grimaced. "It should have been this year." He was quiet for a moment, looking down at his feet, the afternoon light a soft glow behind him.

Afraid of discovery, I tried not to move, one hand on the edge of the door and my body filling the narrow opening. Where before I'd felt Brock's anger, now I sensed a change, one manifest in the firm line of his mouth when he raised his head and in the resonance of his voice when he spoke.

"I'm going to make sure Jeremy Moulton pays for this. And while I'm at it, I mean to dig deeper into the matter. It doesn't make sense that no one else was involved. I've a feeling other hands besides Moulton's were involved . . . hands that might well belong to Neville Bromfield or Robert Clayborne."

I wanted to fly out the door and tell Brock he was mistaken, but the impulse was swept away by the image of Jeremy Moulton leaving Robert's study. Following it was the memory of Robert's certainty that Bruiser would win and the quick look he and Neville had exchanged when he said it. Sickness like a heavy lump of congealed porridge slid into my stomach and forced me to lean against the door for support. What if Brock were right?

* * *

I didn't have much appetite for dinner, nor did I sleep well that night. Each time I roused, I remembered Brock's words, "Perhaps Neville Bromfield or Robert Clayborne." *No!* I thought, and then just as quickly, *Yes!* But more often my thoughts swam in the gray area of indecision. In the end, my need to believe in my brother won out. Until I learned otherwise, I would endeavor to keep an open mind.

Such was my attitude when I joined the McKades for breakfast the following morning.

After grace was said, Millie began to chatter about an unusual dream she'd had. I listened with but half a mind until she stopped and looked at me in concern. "Are you unwell? You don't seem yourself this morning, and I noticed you didn't finish your tea last night."

Brock looked up from the scone he was buttering, and Anne stopped eating.

"I'm fine . . . just tired from not sleeping well." Putting on a bright smile, I encouraged Millie to tell me more about her dream.

Anne also made an effort at conversation, though I sensed that, like me, her thoughts were elsewhere. Brock said little, but his lack of conversation didn't interfere with his appetite. Even so, he was the first to push back his chair and ask to be excused. Instead of working attire, Brock was dressed in black trousers and a white shirt; the rich texture of his damp hair still showed the marks of the comb.

"Remember 'tis the Sabbath, and we'll be meetin' in the sittin' room to read from the Bible."

Brock nodded. "I'll be there as soon as I've spoken to Henry."

After watching Brock leave the room, I gave Anne a puzzled look.

"'Tis the way of the McKades. Though we live too far from a kirk to worship as others do, Angus and I didn't want our bairns growin' up like heathens." She paused and gave me a measured look. "The truth is, I doona hold with organized religion. Too much of what they preach isn't to my way of thinkin'. Such doona mean I've given up on God and prayin' tho'. At least once a month, sometimes oftener, we hold a wee church service in the sittin' room. We'd be pleased to have you join us if ye'd like."

I hadn't been inside a church since Father's funeral, and, sad to say, my attendance before that had been sporadic. It wasn't that I hadn't wanted to attend, but rather that Father preferred to spend his Sunday mornings reading the newspaper or stopping in at his club. Cook and Mrs. Woolsey had often been too busy to accompany me, and rather than attend by myself, I usually joined Father in his study. As a result, I was more familiar with the names of political candidates or why the prime minister was opposed to the latest tariff than I was with the books of the New Testament. But Father's death and my friendship with the Hewitts had sparked my interest in religion, while my terrifying ordeal in the heaving waves had solidified my belief in prayer. Smiling, I met Anne's gaze. "Thank you. I'd like to."

As Anne left the table, I noted that instead of a dress of practical cotton, she wore one of black satin, the bodice piped with circlets of gray and a gold broach nested under the high collar. Although it wasn't as flattering as the burgundy gown she'd worn at the race, Anne was nonetheless well turned out. As was Millie, her usual morning dress of pastel cotton had been replaced by one of mauve silk.

Millie looped her arm through mine as we left the kitchen. "I'm sorry I forgot to tell you about our Sabbath service. What you're wearing will do nicely, but it won't do to come without hat and gloves."

A half hour later, I joined the McKades in the sitting room. Chairs had been brought from the parlor to make enough places. Several of the stockmen's wives were there with their children, and Min and Callie stood at the back with Adam and Dan. Though the well-furnished room with flowered burgundy carpet and matching velvet drapery still seemed more sitting room than church, our slightly off-key singing made it seem like the Sabbath, as did Brock's reading of a prayer. I bowed my head and listened to the deep tone of his voice, the words read with calmness instead of the anger I'd heard the day before.

As I listened, I wondered if Brock had ever voiced a personal prayer, perhaps one driven by fear or concern as mine had been. Did men ever pray? Were they ever fearful and unsure of themselves as women were? The idea posed new questions that set me to wondering if God placed a distinction between read prayers and those that were pleas from the heart. But my mind returned to the service when I heard Millie's amen.

Raising my bowed head, I caught the edge of Brock's glance as he settled back onto his chair. Color rose to my cheeks when I realized it was his face I'd pictured as I wondered about men.

Holding her Bible, Anne got to her feet and asked us to turn to the beginning of Psalm 37. Since I was without a Bible, Millie and I shared hers, the pages rustling as her mother's voice took up the words. "Fret not thyself because of evildoers, neither be thou envious against the workers of iniquity. For they shall soon be cut down like the grass, and wither as the green herb."

Anne paused, and her gaze rested on her son, the expression on her face brimming with love and softness. Although Brock's gaze remained on his Bible, I knew he was aware that his mother's gray eyes rested on him. After a moment she went on. "Trust in the Lord, and do good; so thou shalt dwell in the land, and verily thou shalt be fed. Delight thyself also in the Lord; and he shall give thee the desires of thine heart."

Love and pleading were braided through the words, a mother's prayer for a son, imploring him not to let anger and lust for revenge eat at what was good. "Cease from anger, and forsake wrath . . . For evildoers shall be cut off: but those that wait upon the Lord, they shall inherit the earth."

Bowing her chestnut head, she added, "Please Lord, help us to let go of anger and wait on Thee."

Millie and others in the room added their quiet amens, but the deeper tone of Brock's voice was sadly lacking, as was mine. Not because I didn't agree, but because I wondered what Brock McKade thought and felt. Did he resent his mother for preaching to him in public, or had he taken King David's words to heart, knowing that letting God deal with those who sinned was the greater part of wisdom.

Please help him to understand and let go, my mind whispered. Only then did I realize that, like Anne, I too was praying.

* * *

Millie and I spent the rest of the morning on the back veranda, embroidery in hand as we chatted and stitched. It was a lovely day, with a light breeze blowing the leaves and painting shifting patterns against a shimmering sun. Carrying a book, Anne joined us, but we saw nothing of Brock.

"Off with the horses he is," Anne said when Millie enquired about her brother. "'Tis well that he has the steadiness of work to occupy his mind. Otherwise, who's to say what he might do." Anne sighed and looked past us to her garden. "I worry aboot him. He's far too much like his da."

Millie glanced up from the blood-red poppy she'd fashioned with needle and silken thread. "I should think you'd like Brock's resemblance to Da."

"Most times I do, but ye ken yer da's temper put him in more'n one spot of trouble. I'd no' like to see the same happen to Brock. Ye saw what he did at the race. We can thank our stars he didn't land in jail. Had it not been for his solicitor, he would have."

Millie giggled. "Tell me truthfully, Mum. Aren't you glad Brock landed a blow to the jockey? It's exactly what the bloke deserved."

The rich texture of Anne's laugh spilled around us. "Och, lass, ye ken yer mum too well. 'Twas exactly what the blighter deserved, but still and all, ye ken what the Savior said aboot turnin' the other cheek."

Millie pursed her lips. "I know, but still . . ."

No one spoke in the comfortable silence. The only sound to break the stillness was the whisper of needles pulling strands of bright thread through linen. Anne opened her book and removed the ribbon that marked her place.

"Since yer new to Australia, would ye like to hear a bit of our poetry and tales? There's much inside this book that's to my likin'."

·I nodded, and while bees droned and flitted from bloom to bloom in Anne's garden, I learned of "boomers," and "billabongs," and "The Tale of the Dying Drover."

The loud barking of the dog and Min's voice from the back door broke into the tale. "Excuse me missus, someone comin'."

Anne closed her book and got up. "I wonder who." Nodding her thanks to Min, Anne hurried into the house.

Millie was quick to follow. "Company's an occasion at Tanybrae, especially company that's unexpected."

I put down my embroidery, unsure of whether to go or stay. Perhaps now I would have opportunity to meet some of the McKades' neighbors.

In no time, Millie was back, her slender figure framed in the open doorway. "It's . . . it's your brother!" she gasped.

My heart gave a jerk. "Robert?"

Millie nodded. "I hope he doesn't plan to take you away." She paused when I joined her, reaching to take my hand. "Can he do that . . . tell you to pack your trunk and leave?"

"No," I answered, though in truth I didn't know. Although Father had allowed me to speak my mind, in the end I'd known that my rights as a woman were limited, and so it would be with Robert. Pray he'd listen to reason.

By the time Robert dismounted, Millie and I had joined Anne at the front door. We were not the only ones aware of his arrival. Adam had come to take his horse while Henry called off the dogs. Remembering Brock's feelings about my brother, I was glad he wasn't present.

Robert was dressed for riding, the legs of his brown riding breeches tucked into expensive boots, his white shirt topped by a waistcoat. Removing his hat, Robert walked in purposeful strides toward the front steps, the hard set of his mouth telling me he wasn't happy.

Motioning for us to wait in the entryway, Anne stepped onto the veranda and greeted him. "Mr. Clayborne. How nice to see you again."

Robert gave a curt nod, clearly not in the mood for pleasantries. "Is my sister here?"

"She is." Anne hesitated, her black-clad figure like a sentinel at the door. "Won't you come in?"

I would be speaking an untruth if I said I was glad to see my brother, yet as soon as he crossed the room to take my hands, my feelings softened.

"Jessa, thank heaven you're all right."

"Of course I'm all right. How could you think otherwise?"

Relief and displeasure warred for position on his flushed face. "The letter I received from Olivia left me unsure of what to think. What's this nonsense about a silly quarrel?"

"Did Olivia enclose the note I left for you?"

Robert's mouth tightened. "No . . . only a hurried letter filled with crossed-out words and hysterics. I could hardly make heads or tails of it." Shooting an impatient look at Anne, he asked, "Is there a room where Miss Clayborne and I can speak in private?"

"Certainly." With a nod, Anne led the way to the sitting room.

As Robert took my arm, I glanced at Millie. Although she attempted a smile, her gray eyes looked uncertain and a little afraid. I wondered if mine looked the same. Brave though I pretended to be, inside I trembled.

Robert closed the door and turned to face me as soon as we entered the room. His voice sounded pleasant enough, but his attitude was that of one who intended to have his way. "I'd appreciate it if you gave me your version of what happened between you and my wife."

I did not tell him all that was said, but enough to let him know the relationship between Olivia and me was irreconcilable. "When

Olivia said she was secretly glad when she heard I'd been washed overboard, it did not leave any room for friendship," I concluded.

Robert swore under his breath. "Stupid woman."

"But one who is nonetheless your wife and the mother of your
children. As such, your first loyalty is to her, not me."

"Poppycock! You know blood runs thicker than water. Besides, I
want you in my home . . . need you. Since you came, I can look
forward again to sitting down to tea and having a sensible conversation. Do you have any notion how boring and tedious Olivia can be?"

"Then why did you marry her? Surely you weren't so blinded by
her beauty that you couldn't see how it would be."

Hands in his pockets, Robert walked to the window. "You know
full well why I married her. Money, position . . . maybe too so I could
prove to Father that I'd finally arrived."

Seemingly not to want to talk further of Father, he turned and
looked me hard in the face. "Such has no bearing on why I came.
You're to come home with me. This foolishness has got to stop."

Since I'd anticipated Robert's edict, I was prepared with my reply.
"It's not foolishness, and my answer is no. The McKades have invited
me to stay with them and that's what I intend to do."

"McKades!" Robert's voice was a snarl. "And what do you intend
to do when you've worn out your welcome? Or have you even
thought of that? You know you can't stay here forever."

"I'm aware of that." I couldn't believe what I was saying, knowing
full well the doors my words would close. Then I recalled what Anne
had read that morning, *Wait upon the Lord and don't fret about those
who indulge in evil.* That was what I must do—trust in a higher
power and wait for answers to my prayers.

"I haven't yet made up my mind what I'll do," I said after a
moment. "Since I've had a good education, perhaps I can find a position as a governess."

Robert's mouth dropped open. "Have you lost your mind? Egad,
Jessa, what will my friends think?"

Perhaps I shouldn't have been surprised by Robert's reaction, for
I'd seen signs of his selfishness. Even so, it gave me a turn. I strove to
push back anger, but my voice was taut when I spoke. "This whole

thing is about you, isn't it, Robert? *You* want me to come back because *you* find Olivia's company tedious, and *you* don't want me to do anything that might cause *you* embarrassment."

Robert didn't seem to know how to answer. I watched as he attempted to smile. "That's not true. I act only out of love and the fear that something unpleasant might happen to you. Everything can turn out nicely if you'll just come back. Neville has asked about you several times. I'm sure it wouldn't take much to make him consider marriage. Think of it, Jessa—married to a man of substance and position. Such would be far better than being a governess or wasting away in the back of nowhere with the McKades."

"I'm not wasting away. And for your information, the McKades are pleasant company." Knowing we were about to start down the same path again, I reached up and touched his cheek. "I love you, Robbie, but all of your talk won't change my answer. I'm not coming back with you."

"Jessa."

"No, Robert."

He pushed my hand away. "You always were a stubborn thing. Spoiled too. Father was far too indulgent with you."

"And he wasn't with you?"

Robert stiffened, and I knew I had struck a nerve. His voice when he spoke was imperious. "You know nothing about the matter. Olivia warned me not to try to persuade you to change your mind. I see she was right."

He moved to leave, then changing his mind, he grasped my shoulders. "Whatever you do, Jessamyne, you're not to say one word to the McKades about Jeremy Moulton and the jockey. Do you hear me?"

"I hear you." Though I pretended calmness, my heart pounded erratically. "Unfortunately, it's too late."

"What do you mean?"

"I mean I already told them."

"Told—" The air seemed to evaporate from Robert's lungs, leaving him pale and speechless. "Why?" he hissed when he'd regained his breath. "You knew it was dangerous. If Jeremy finds out . . ." His hands tightened, and he gave me a little shake. "Didn't I tell you if word got out it could be my downfall?"

"How, Robert? The only two people I saw were the jockey and Jeremy Moulton. How can that affect you?"

Robert's swallow was audible. "It—" Seeming to think better of what he'd been about to say, he released my shoulders. "I wash my hands of you." He started for the door.

"I'm sorry you feel that way, Robbie. Even though we've quarreled, I'll always love you."

Robert bowed his head. "I love you too, Jessa," he said after a moment, "but I wish to heaven you'd kept your mouth shut."

With that he left, his boots echoing loudly in the entryway. When the front door closed, I went to the window to watch him make his way to the barn. A moment later he reappeared with his horse. Sorrow tugged at my heart as I watched him mount and the horse canter down the avenue of fig trees. He was gone, and so was my pleasure in the day.

ELEVEN

Neither Anne nor Millie asked what transpired between Robert and me. I'm sure if Millie had had her way she would have done so, just as I'm certain that Anne had forbidden it. Drained and unsettled from Robert's visit, I retreated to my room. Only then did the tears come—a quiet mourning for the brother I adored but could no longer admire. *What changed you? Oh, Robbie, can't you see what you've become?* My questions went unanswered and it was some time before my tears were spent and I'd repaired their damage. Finally, in late afternoon I went to the open window hoping for a breeze. Looking out on the pasture, I heard the distant low of cattle, and, from the fig trees, the song of a magpie, which unlike that of his raucous English cousins was low and melodious.

I took a long, steadying breath and told myself I'd be all right, but Robert's words had reopened concern. Though I'd spoken of becoming a governess, I cringed at the thought. I'd seen too much of my governess's life to want it for myself. As for marrying Neville Bromfield . . . I shook my head. He might be handsome and charming, but something in his character told me I couldn't be happy with such a man.

Lost in troubling thoughts, I was unaware of the approach of Brock and Millie until I heard an exasperated voice.

"Why didn't you tell me Robert Clayborne was here?"

"I didn't know where you were."

I watched them come across the yard, Millie still in her Sunday dress and Brock in work clothes.

"You should have guessed I was out with the yearlings. Egad, Millie, even Min and Callie know that."

Millie put her hand on his arm. "I wanted to, truly I did, but it happened so fast. Besides, Mum told me not to."

"Mum?" Brock's voice cracked.

"She . . . she was afraid you might try to hit Mr. Clayborne like you did the jockey."

Brock's laugh was unpleasant. "I hope Mum knows I have better manners than that. Though you have to admit, it wouldn't be a bad idea. It's not just that the bloke's sheep keep coming onto our land. There's something more, something that tells me he's up to no good. And then the race." Brock paused and looked across the pasture. "If the race hadn't been rigged, I would be negotiating with Carlson for his tract of land. Instead . . ." He shook his head and gave another harsh chuckle. "Mum sure knew how to hit a mate between the ears with the scriptures she read this morning. And I mean to try, I really do."

Millie stood on tiptoe to kiss his cheek. "I know you're trying. We all are."

Brock put his arm around her shoulder. By now they were so close I feared they might see me at the window. I stepped away, but not before I heard Brock ask, "And you say Miss Clayborne is staying?"

"Thankfully, yes."

"Good," Brock said. "Good."

* * *

Later that week, Millie suggested we go on a picnic. "Remember the koala bears?" she'd asked. "Well, the place where they live isn't far, and I'm sure Hilda will pack a special tea for us."

The next day Anne, Millie, and I climbed into the front of a cart with Min and Callie in back with a hamper of food. Min and Callie seemed as excited at the prospect of a picnic as Millie. I heard their whispers and giggles as they dangled their bare feet from the back of the cart.

Our destination was surprisingly close and just as enchanting as Millie had said. After passing the rolling pastureland, we followed a stream into the hills. Thick foliage studded the slopes—wide-trunked gum trees and slender mountain ash rising amidst a luxurious tangle of large frond ferns and lush plants. As our cart climbed, the somnolent sounds of the stream turned exuberant, skipping and tumbling over stones and boulders. Even the air felt cooler as the warmth of the valley gave way to dewy moistness.

When I craned my head to look at a mossy grotto nestled in the uprooted trunk of an ancient tree, Millie laughed. "Didn't I say it was lovely?"

"It's like the corner of your garden, only bigger and more lush," I said to Anne as we rolled along.

"And where do ye think I got my idea?" Holding to the reins, she clucked to the horse. "The spot for our picnic is just ahead."

When we stopped, Millie jumped down and offered her hand to me and her mother. Min and Callie lifted the hamper and carried it between them. Reaching a grassy area, Callie probed it with a stick, her actions reminding me of the need to watch for snakes.

In no time, Callie had spread a flowered cloth on the grass and Min had unpacked the hamper. I wondered again at their ages—Min more angular with straight dark hair caught back with a leather string, Callie prettier-featured with wavy hair. Although their dresses were loose-fitting, such didn't conceal that they were young women.

After grace had been said and our plates filled with chicken and flaky scones, I asked Callie her age.

She dropped her eyes and shrugged as if unsure. Min wasn't quite so shy. "I have eighteen summers," she said proudly. "Callie sixteen."

"I have twenty-one summers, and Millie almost nineteen." My words were greeted with silence, as both girls now looked stoically at their plates. I supposed that answering questions was different from making conversation. Fearing I'd been too forward, I turned to Millie. "Thank you for suggesting a picnic. It's beautiful here."

Millie smiled. "I thought you'd like it. We've been coming here for years, though it was Da who first found it."

Anne nodded. "Discovered the stream and forest when he and Henry came lookin' for a place to attach the McKade name. Angus said 'twas as bonny as anything he'd seen in Scotland, though bein' more rugged and untamed 'twould take hard work to make it pay."

She paused and took a bite of scone, her mouth curving in satisfaction. "This part, of course, was too steep and tangled to tame, but Angus wanted it just the same, and no' just because the stream gives water. Though he was a brawny man, my Angus had an eye for wild beauty." Her eyes traveled over the ferns and lush undergrowth. "After seein' this, he would no' settle for anythin' less for me."

"How fortunate that he didn't."

As I spoke, the horse nickered, and a moment later a man on horseback emerged from the trees.

"Over here, Brock," Millie called, waving her hand.

Brock dismounted and tethered his horse. I felt a pulse of excitement as he walked toward us, glad I'd worn a dress that became me. Although I'd chosen it because it had no bustle, I knew the bodice, trimmed with pleated red grosgrain and tiny red flowers, added color to my cheeks.

"What are you doing here?" Millie asked when Brock joined us.

"Hilda told me the best of the chicken had gone on the picnic, so I thought to join you."

Millie laughed up at him. "Trust you to look out for your stomach." She lifted the cloth covering the chicken. "You're lucky there's any left."

"I wasn't worried since Hilda said she'd sent extra just in case."

"In case what?"

"In case I joined you. Hilda knows I like to raid your picnics."

"Perhaps when you were younger, but the last time you joined us was a good three years ago."

Brock shrugged and settled himself on the grass between me and Callie. "No one forgets good food, do they Callie?"

She ducked her head and giggled. "That right, Mister McKade."

Brock shot a challenging look at his sister. "See, even Callie agrees. Now, if you'd be so good as to pass me some of that chicken."

Millie complied with an exaggerated sigh, and I forgot to eat when Brock leaned past me to reach the plate. The sleeves of his blue chambray shirt were rolled to expose the tanned skin of his forearms. I stared in fascination at the dark hair growing above his wrist, saw the play of muscles when he took the chicken in his long fingers.

Brock directed his gaze at me. "What do you think of our wilderness?"

For a second, I couldn't think or do anything except stare at his deeply tanned features. "It's—it's lovely . . . Unlike anything I've seen before," I stammered.

"I thought you'd like it."

Did that mean he'd given some thought to me as well? Perhaps so much it had spurred him to seek us out at the picnic? *Stop being so vain,* a tiny voice whispered, but the rest of me gave myself over to seeing what else Brock would say and do.

He said quite a lot, teasing Millie and Anne and managing to elicit a few words or shy smiles from Min and Callie. I smiled at his teasing banter just as they did. Even so, I was curiously tongue-tied, which was unlike me. Had I been in England conversing with Bertram Higgins or any other of my numerous suitors, I would have flirted and responded in kind. But with Brock, it was strangely different—as if seeing him in my dream had imbued me with fear of saying or doing something wrong. Instead of flirting, I watched sunlight dapple his dark hair with shafts of gold. My gaze was just as often on his eyes. Anne's and Millie's were a lovely shade of gray, but Brock's were indigo blue, their hue so deep that at times they appeared almost black.

Brock's voice intruded into my thoughts. "What do you think about it, Miss Clayborne?"

My mind scrambled to recall what they'd been talking about, and I could do nothing but stammer. "I . . . I . . ."

Someone laughed, the raucous tone filling the air. I glanced at Millie, then at Min, but neither was laughing. The sound came again, rolling and joyful like someone enjoying a good joke.

Brock leaned close and pointed to a branch in the gum tree. "It's the kookaburras—Australia's famous laughing birds."

Looking up, I saw two long-billed birds with puffy white heads perched just above us. Like a performer who knows he has an audience, one of the birds opened his bill, laughter rolling out. It was so contagious that we joined him.

"How delightful," I said, not minding that the joke had been on me, an untried English girl caught unawares.

"When we've finished eating, I'll take you to look for koalas," Brock said.

"But I'd planned to show them—" Millie began. A quelling look from her brother stopped the protest, and my enjoyment of the picnic increased.

When the last of the chicken had been eaten and Hilda's short-bread sampled, Brock got to his feet and offered me his hand. "Miss Clayborne."

Only Millie chose to accompany us. Anne stayed to sketch, and Min and Callie went for a walk of their own.

"The place where the koalas like to feed is farther up the slope," Millie explained.

The quiet of the forest closed around us as we climbed, the crunch of feet on the leafy path mingling with the distant sound of tumbling water. Brock led the way, with Millie and me following. Since the path was moist and uneven, I was glad for the loan of Millie's sturdy boots. We walked for several moments among ferns and tumbled logs, pausing from time to time to look up at the lofty branches of the gum trees.

"The koalas spend most of their time in the trees," Millie whispered.

A few steps more and Brock stopped and drew me to his side. "There," he said, his voice low in my ear. "See the mother and cub?"

For a second I forgot to breathe, my senses aware of his closeness. Even so, my gaze followed his pointing finger, though I remained keenly aware that his other hand still curled around my arm. When I saw the furry, dark-fringed face of the mother looking down at us, I almost forgot the touch of Brock's hand. The bear was eating a cluster of eucalyptus leaves, some protruding from her mouth. A dark button nose and round ears made up the rest of her face. She was unlike anything I'd ever seen—a delightful mixture of bear and raccoon. Her cub clung to the same branch, its face a lighter minia-ture of its mother.

"The eucalyptus leaves contain a mild opiate," Brock explained, his hand still on my arm. "It makes the koalas drowsy, so they do little besides eat and sleep."

"How do they keep from falling?" As I spoke, I realized the answer, for the koalas were wedged firmly into the space where limb met trunk.

While Brock explained, I listened with only half a mind, the rest of me enjoying his closeness. I wasn't sure what had caused his aloofness to melt into warmth and charm. Perhaps the reason lay in the fact that my refusal to leave with Robert placed me squarely on the side of the McKades.

We continued up the slope, Brock slowing so that we often walked together, the red fringe around the bottom of my skirt brushing against his moleskin breeches. What Millie thought of Brock's actions she didn't say, but she seemed to take them in stride. She was as pleased as I was when we came upon a large male koala and later another mother and cub.

"Do people ever keep koalas as pets?" I asked, quite taken by the furry face of a cub peering down at me.

"We had one once," Millie began.

"Who had one?" Brock corrected.

Millie shot him an exasperated look. "You're right . . . I had one." She turned to me. "I wanted a koala, but Brock told me they needed to live in trees, not on the ground. But my heart was set, and I wouldn't give in."

Brock grinned and leaned against a tree. "Do you get the notion that our sweet Millie was a wee bit spoiled as a child?"

"Brock!" She gave him an impish grin and slipped into a Scottish brogue. "I fear the laddie's a wee addled, for he canna tell a corkscrew from a hammer." I laughed at her antics. "Now as I was saying," she continued, "since Brock was slow to comply, I was forced to cry and wheedle, as any little sister knows she must do."

Brock was clearly enjoying the banter, as was I, entranced by this side of his nature. "And sweet Millie was not a pretty sight when she wheedled and cried—more like a howling dingo."

Millie shrugged. "You must do what you must, as I'm sure Jessamyne knows. My asking went on for weeks, and it was almost my birthday. By now it wasn't just Brock who said a koala wouldn't make a proper pet. Mum and Da agreed. In fact, Da was so tired of hearing me carry on that he told me he didn't want to hear another word about it." Millie's shoulders slumped and her face turned woebegone. "Our da didn't often get angry, but when he did, we knew better than to argue."

Brock took up the story. I knew he played to me, wanting my smile and approval. "Although I was still set against Millie having a koala, I was a bit of a softie when it came to my sister. When I saw her sadness and noticed she didn't eat her breckie the next morning, I decided to help her."

"What about your father?" Having glimpsed Brock's temper, I suspected his father had the same.

"Da was a bit of a problem, but I was as determined as he. 'Tis a trait of the McKades, as Mum would say." Humor danced in his blue eyes, and I smiled, totally enchanted.

Millie and I found a log to use for a chair. We sat, faces tilted and smiling as Brock went on.

"I knew the only way to get around Da was to build a pen well away from the house. It took me a day to build it, though despite what Millie says, I'm quite handy with a hammer." He paused and looked up at the tall branches of the giant gum tree. "My next task was to find a koala cub and get it away from its mum. My heart didn't take to the idea, for I don't hold with separating babes from their mums. Koalas are like roos and carry their young in a pouch."

His eyes rested on me, not Millie, making my heart warm. "My idea was to find a cub who'd left its mum's pouch but was small enough for a boy to handle. Of course, this was nigh on impossible, for no mum was about to let an impudent boy kidnap her cub. Several unsuccessful attempts and a jarring fall from a tree all but convinced me it couldn't be done."

In my mind, I tried to picture Brock as he'd been—gangly but determined, with a smudge of dirt on his youthful face.

Brock stepped away from the tree, his muscular body a far cry from the boy I'd conjured up. "On my way home, I heard a cry and rustle in the undergrowth. Being a brave Australian bloke, I picked up a stick and began my hunt. What I found was a dead mother koala with her cub clinging to her and mewling." He paused and pursed his lips. "I couldn't believe my luck, though I felt bad for the cub. Despite my best efforts, it didn't take kindly to being picked up, but I'd come prepared with a burlap sack, and I finally managed to stuff him inside."

Millie giggled. "I couldn't believe it when Brock told me he had a surprise for me. Since he and Da had been so forceful about me not having a koala, it never once entered my mind."

"I got several excited hugs when she saw it," Brock put in.

I felt a twinge of regret as Millie continued with the story, breaking my connection to Brock.

"Even I could see that the cub was terribly unhappy. Instead of eating, he whimpered and curled up in the corner of the pen. We tried everything—a teat Da used for the orphaned calves, even fresh eucalyptus leaves." Millie's voice softened. "When I ran out to see the cub the next morning he was dead, his little body curled up in exactly the same place I'd left him." Millie got to her feet. "Brock dug a grave and helped me fix a cross and scatter the mound with flowers." Her expression turned tender. "Remember how you read one of the prayers from Mum's missal?"

"You were quite inconsolable."

"And you were the best of brothers." Millie hugged him. "As you still are."

Brock returned her embrace, his arms holding her close while his chin rested on her head. At that moment, I wished it were me in his arms. Then I felt the force of Brock's cobalt eyes, read the message of a similar longing, and I wished for nothing more.

Twelve

Near the end of the week, Millie tapped on my bedroom door. When I opened it, I saw she was dressed for riding, the loose gown she'd worn for breakfast exchanged for a cream-colored top and what looked to be a divided brown riding skirt.

When Millie saw my interest in her unusual attire, she smiled. "I know those in polite society would censure me for wearing such a skirt, but as isolated as we are, both Da and Brock thought it too dangerous for me to ride sidesaddle. When I was younger, I wore a pair of Brock's outgrown breeches, but now that I'm a 'young lady'"— she winked and struck a pose that showed off the division of her skirt—"I wear this. It's wonderfully comfortable and ever so convenient. Mrs. Morrison, one of Mum's good friends, found a seamstress to make it for me."

"It seems the very thing," I said, though my dislike of horses prevented any show of enthusiasm.

"I've been itching to go for a ride, but before I do, I hoped you'd come to the stable with me—not to ride, just to look," she added hastily. "Perhaps little by little, you'll see that you needn't be afraid of horses."

My first instinct was to tell her I wasn't feeling well, but the bright expectancy on Millie's face made me put the excuse aside. She and her mother had been so kind.

I reluctantly followed her out to the stable where I stopped at the door, my hand reaching for the sturdy doorframe in an effort to bolster my flagging courage. The smell brought back frightening memories of my terrified screams when Father and Robert tried to entice me into the stable after Mother's death. Today, although no scream passed my lips, the palms of my hands grew clammy.

Millie gave me a questioning look. "Would it make it easier if I bring my horse outside to you?"

I nodded, my throat so compressed with fear that I couldn't speak. Needing no further encouragement, I hastily sought refuge in the shade of a tree. From there I listened to Millie speak to her horse, heard the animal's soft nicker and the jangle of bridle and saddle. Those sounds mingled with my weak attempt to bolster my courage. *You're not a child anymore. Didn't you survive the ocean? A horse can't be any worse than heaving waves.*

Despite my brave thoughts, when Millie and the horse came through the stable door, I shrank back against the solid trunk of the tree.

"This is Nimble. Isn't she a beauty?" Not waiting for an answer, Millie went on. "Da gave her to me when she was just a foal—let me train her to halter, then to bridle. Nimble and I have a long history together. More than six years."

I tried to look at the mare through Millie's eyes, noting her rich, chestnut coat and how she affectionately nuzzled her mistress's shoulder.

Millie pushed the horse's head. "None of that my fine lady. You're here to show Jessamyne what a sweet mare you are. Only your best manners for company." She brought the mare a step nearer. When she did, the mare snorted and lifted her head.

My heart leapt and only tight control kept me in my place.

"Easy, girl." Millie stroked the mare's neck in an effort to calm her. "Why are you so skittish?" she asked, even as her eyes sought mine. "Sometimes the stallions can be high-spirited, but Nimble is usually as gentle as a lamb. Mum says it's because I spent so much time with her, but Brock says it's a matter of breeding. Her dam was gentle, and Nimble's foals are too. Did you know she's a dam twice over? Brock sold both of her colts to a man from Melbourne."

I knew Millie used her chatter to reassure me, even as I noted her frown as she jerked on the mare's rein. Nimble tossed her head again, her eyes suddenly wild. The sight took me back to the terrified look I'd glimpsed in my pony's eyes just before he bolted. My fingers pressed into the tree's rough bark, its hardness all that kept me there. Breathing in quick gulps of air, I managed to hold fear at bay until Nimble suddenly snorted and pranced sideways.

My control snapped, devoured by mindless terror that pushed me away from the tree and across the yard, my shoes digging into the sod, arms and hands flailing blindly at the morning air. In my fear, I scarcely saw Brock as he reached to stop me, his presence but a blurred obstacle as I thrust past him, escape my only thought. Stumbling, I scrambled up the back steps and across the veranda.

I heard Brock and Millie call, but my frenzied mind paid them no heed as I flung open the door and darted through the kitchen toward the sanctuary of my room.

A dark form moved to block my way, Callie's mahogany figure filling the passageway, her voice an urgent whisper. "No, missy. Be brave."

Shoving past her, I ran into my bedroom and slammed the door. The solid *thunk* as latch connected with notch brought a vestige of safety. Breathing in wild gulps, I leaned my face against the door, its firmness like a buttress to my tear-slicked cheeks. Through it all, I was aware of someone wailing, the high-pitched keening sending shivers down my spine.

"Jessamyne . . . are ye all right, lass?"

At the sound of Anne's voice, the wailing ebbed. Only then did I realize the strangled cry came from my throat and trembling mouth. Striving for control, I took a steadying breath as my hand closed around the doorknob to prevent it from turning.

"Jessamyne!" Millie's voice came high and unnatural. "I'm so sorry. Please forgive me."

Unable to speak, I clung to the knob, my body pressed hard against the door. Fear slowly abated, replaced by anger and burning humiliation. *Why had Millie insisted that I look at her stupid horse? Why had I lost my head? What must Millie and Anne think of me? And Brock?* I stiffened when someone tried the doorknob.

"Leave her be, Millie. The poor lass needs time alone to collect herself."

Silently blessing Anne, I listened as they moved away, Millie's voice crowded with tears as she repeated, "I'm sorry, Mum. I didn't know this would happen."

"She'll come around. The sweet lass just needs time to herself."

Their retreating footsteps melded into the clatter of pans from the kitchen and a raucous cry from a galah. Wiping my tears, I left the door and searched the dresser for a handkerchief. As I did, I saw the bouquet of fresh roses Anne had picked for me. The sight of them brought a fresh spate of tears. What a dear, sweet woman, and Millie wasn't far behind, her warmth and impulsive chatter making me wish she truly were my sister.

My cheeks burned with mortification as I imagined what they must think of the wild, hysterical woman who'd taken possession of my body. *Coward* and *spineless* were words that filled my mind. Why hadn't I stood my ground? Why? Why?

I threw myself onto the bed, my face pillowed on the softness of the lilac-sprigged covering. The softness brought fresh tears and an even greater lowering of spirits. *Ninny. Goose.* The words circled through the memory of the shocked expression on Brock's face as I'd rushed past him, pushing wildly as he attempted to stop me. I knew Anne and Millie, being women, would try to understand and find excuses for my uncontrollable terror and hysterics, but Brock was all male strength, his lean, muscled body honed by long hours of work in the outdoors. Coupled with his father's tenacity, I doubted he would have much tolerance or understanding for a woman who turned tail and ran at the mere sight of a horse.

Sighing, I rolled over and stared up at the ceiling, its pristine whiteness offering nothing to lift my spirits. Instead I was left to my previous thoughts, none of them pleasant. "So," I finally whispered after some time, "are you going to mope in your room for the rest of the day, or are you going to try to undo some of the damage?"

It took me a moment to gather myself. With a shaky hand, I poured water into the basin and splashed it over my face. I grimaced when I saw the blotched cheeks and red-rimmed eyes that stared back at me from the mirror. Wringing out a wet cloth, I lay down on the bed and placed the cool covering over my face. This did much to revive me, and a short time later, with hair and face tidied, I went in search of Anne and Millie.

I found them sitting at a table on the veranda, Millie's shoulders slumped and Anne's chin cupped in her hands.

"May I join you?" I asked.

Millie jumped to her feet. "Are you all right?" Before I could answer, she added, "I'm so sorry. I shouldn't have been in such a hurry, but Nimble's never acted that way before. Brock said she must have picked up on your fear—animals do that sometimes. But still—" Tears prevented her from saying more.

I reached for her hands, the sight of her own blotched face telling me I wasn't the only one who'd given way to emotion. "I'm fine, Millie. Truly I am. It wasn't your fault . . . Please don't blame yourself."

"Well, Brock does. He says I'm the greatest dunderhead there ever was and that I should have known better."

"I was the dunderhead," I countered. "I can't believe I acted so wild. It was inexcusable, and I'm terribly ashamed."

"Now doona fash yerself. 'Twas no one's fault, and such was I tellin' Millie. 'Tis just a bit o' time ye need to recover yerself." Anne paused and directed her gaze at her daughter. "Just the same, I'm thinkin' a spot o' tea might settle us and put things back to right. Would ye be so good, Millie, as to run ask Min to bring fresh tea?"

After Millie left, Anne invited me to sit down. "I've a wee bit ta say to ye before Millie gets back." She patted my hand. "Like I said, I doona want ye to fret. We all have our demons. With me 'tis snakes, and with Millie 'tis fear of heights and lightning. Even Brock is no' without a fear or two, tho' he'd no' be admittin' to such." Her voice stilled as she looked out over the rolling green of Tanybrae. "My Angus had his demon too. 'Twas fear of failure, and no one saw it better than I. He woke with it each morn and it dogged his steps each day. So," her fingers tightened on my hand, "know that yer among those what ken aboot demons. The McKades'll no' think less of ye because of yer own."

I thought of Anne's words after Millie rejoined us—thought of them again when Callie rather than Min came with the tea, her light footsteps like the whisper of leaves in a soft breeze, the glance she gave me quick before it retreated. I felt no censure during the brief second our eyes met, but rather a quiet call for courage, coming like an echo to the words she'd spoken in the passageway. *No, missy, be brave.*

So it was that I was able to stand on the veranda and wave to Millie as she cantered her mare down the lane between the fig trees. For the first time since early childhood, I felt envy for one who rode a horse, wished it were I instead of Millie who sat straight and secure in the saddle, she and the chestnut mare moving as if they were one.

This startling revelation followed me into the dining room that evening and sat on my shoulder like an invisible guest, causing me to look at Millie in a new light, seeing a young woman who was terrified of heights, but who could ride a horse with expertise and zest. If Millie could do it, was there hope for me?

I continued to think of this while I watched Callie and Min place bowls of food onto the table, the grace and silence with which they moved both fascinating and a little unnerving. Where had they learned to walk and move in such a way? Was it ingrained along with their dark skin, or was it something they'd been carefully taught?

Callie's gaze darted over me as she set down a bowl of early peas, her glance telling me she wondered about me as well.

Before constraint could build a barrier to conversation, Millie asked me to tell them about the people I'd met on the voyage from England. This was easy to do, for with the exception of Jeremy Moulton, I'd enjoyed the company of the other passengers. My description of the Hewitts took up most of the talk, my voice filling with warmth as I related their kindness and told of Jamie's adoration of the captain.

"Mormons ye say?" Anne asked. "I doona recall hearin' of such a religion." She turned to Brock. "What aboot ye?"

Brock shook his head. "When I'm with my mates, our talk is on horses, not religion."

"Not girls?" Millie teased.

Brock laughed. "Trust you to bring up the subject."

"I just want to know if there's any hope of you marrying."

Although Millie teased, I sensed there was purpose in her words. Brock seemed to feel it too, his tanned cheeks taking on a slight flush in the lamplight and his lips tightening.

"How come you're blushing?" Millie giggled.

Brock ignored her question, but I could tell he was a little disconcerted. "I've told you that when I find the right one, I'll not waste any time tying the knot." For a fleeting second, his blue eyes rested on me, making my heart thump against my ribs. Then so quick I couldn't be sure of his purpose, he looked at his mother. "Besides, Mum may not like it if I marry. You know bairns usually follow and that will make you a grandma . . . an old woman."

Anne laughed. "Doona be tryin' to shift the blame for no' marryin' on me. Ye ken I've a soft spot for bairns. Ye'll no' find me complainin' should ye give me a dozen to coddle and love."

Brock held up his hands. "You do plan big, Mum. First I'd better find the right woman."

From there the conversation turned to the numerous grandchildren belonging to one of their neighbors. As I listened to the easy talk and banter, I contrasted it to the dutiful talk that had surrounded Robert and Olivia's table and to the long silences that often accompanied the meals with only Father and me sitting at the table. It wasn't just my attraction to Brock that made me wish I could always stay at Tanybrae. The love that abounded there appealed to me as well.

Brock made no mention of the episode with Nimble. Even so, I felt his gaze upon me more frequently than usual, as if he were trying to discover the answer to a puzzling question. Under ordinary circumstances I might have met his gaze, but the memory of my humiliating actions made me pretend not to notice. His actions didn't prevent me from suspecting that Brock thought me the silliest of women. As enamored as he was with horses, how could he be expected to understand my fear?

These unsatisfying thoughts filled my mind until shortly after dinner when we retired to our rooms. As was my custom, I undressed and picked up a book, intending to read it in bed. As I turned back the covers, the sight of a bug with bright colored legs and wings made me gasp and jump away. Heart pounding, I studied it from a safe distance, slowly realizing that like Sal's butterfly, it was an ornament, the legs and wings fashioned of green and blue feathers fastened around a slender spine of a white bone. Even so, the sight unnerved me, although I sensed it had been placed on my bed as a gift. But from whom?

I carefully picked up the creature, the tiny knots of dark hair that held the puffs of feather to the bone making me suspect it had come from Callie or Min. It was slightly different from the one I'd seen earlier. I tried to remember what Sal had told me about her butterfly. Something about courage.

I opened the top drawer of the tallboy and placed the charm on top of a folded handkerchief. I would wait until morning to try to discover who'd given it to me.

* * *

In my dream I was a child again, the day cloudy and overcast as I rode my pony across the meadow. Mother was just ahead on her mare, a spirited animal named Dancer.

In my childish eyes my mother was the most beautiful of women, the most caring too, for in addition to teaching me to ride, she let me know in a dozen other ways that I was the center of her life.

That morning she looked especially pretty in a blue riding habit with a matching hat set at a jaunty angle on her dark head. As was her custom, she set the pace for our ride, holding in the mare so my pony could keep up.

At five, I was proud of my riding ability and thought myself almost as competent as Mother. I set the pony to a gallop, urging him with my little whip, hoping to close the space between Mother and me. I felt the rush of the wind on my face as I leaned close to the pony's neck. Faster. Faster.

Trees and a fence rushed by, a sudden swirling mist making them seem like shadows. "Faster!" No matter how hard the pony galloped, Mother and her mare remained ahead. I called, asking her to wait, but the rumble of thunder covered my voice and sent her mare to a faster gait.

"Mother . . . wait!" Wind threw the words back into my mouth, damming my throat and making my eyes run with water. "Wait . . . Please, wait." My cry meshed with the headlong rhythm of the pony's hooves, the pounding staccato becoming one with the crack of thunder and pelting rain.

Lightning spit through the dark clouds in jagged fingers and fiery bolts of light. Earsplitting thunder followed. The crack jerked me awake. Heart pounding, I peered through the darkness for Mother.

A mirror caught a flash of lightning as it fleshed out the outline of the bed and my upright figure sitting amid a tangle of sheets. My breathing was uneven, and I was aware of the dampness of tears on my cheeks. "Mother?" I called her name softly, even as I realized that only the storm and my tears were real.

Slipping from the bed, I walked to the window, a hand to my damp cheek as I pulled back the curtain and looked out at a wild night filled with wind and rain and flashes of lightning.

Thunder rumbled through the darkness. *Boom-booms* Mother and I had called them. The almost forgotten phrase took me back to an afternoon when I'd run to Mother in fear, felt the haven of her softness and heard her reassuring voice as she told me of a kindly giant who lived in the clouds.

He's taking his wife and children for a ride in their carriage. Each time the wheel strikes a stone, it gives off sparks and makes a loud rumble.

Her words banished my fear, and thereafter I often sat by the window with nose pressed against glass, hoping to catch a glimpse of the kindly giant and his family riding through the dark clouds in their carriage.

Since then, storms held no menace. Instead, the wind and thunder and lightning invigorated me. Tonight they sent me to the veranda, the cool dampness of the wood a pleasant sensation on my feet, the few drops of rain that blew past the railing a welcome respite from my dream and the heat.

Tongues of lightning darted in the distance, sending patterns of flickering light through dancing tree branches. A breeze laced with the acrid scent of eucalyptus ruffled the edge of my nightgown around my legs and feet. Leaning against one of the columns, I looked up at the sky and imagined a colossal carriage bumping along a rocky thoroughfare.

A deep voice spoke from the shadows of the veranda. "I see that you enjoy storms too."

The sound of Brock's voice jerked my head toward him, my eyes deciphering his outline in one of the chairs.

"The . . . the thunder wakened me," I replied in a voice not altogether steady. "And yes, I like storms."

Brock didn't say anything for a moment, his silence making me conscious of my bare feet and that I wore only a thin cotton nightgown. Thank heaven for clouds and shadows.

When Brock finally spoke, his voice was tinged with amusement. "I imagine the thunder woke Millie as well, and that she probably covered her ears and pulled the quilt up over her head."

"Millie doesn't seem the type of woman to be afraid of anything."

"Neither do you, Miss Clayborne. It took uncommon presence of mind and courage to survive the ocean . . . and courage of a different sort to ignore your brother's warning and tell me about the jockey."

I leaned my back against the wooden column, the strands of hair pulled from my nighttime plait blown by gusts of wind skittering into the veranda. Seeing the silhouette of Brock's dark figure did something to my breathing. "That was—" I began, intending to downplay his words.

"That was courage," Brock finished for me. "Da always said that 'Courage dinna mean a bloke was no' afraid, but that he dinna let fear stand in the way.'" Darkness prevented me from seeing Brock's face, but I sensed he studied me and that his eyes held a challenge.

"What are you trying to say, Mr. McKade?"

"That a woman with your strength and courage shouldn't let fear of horses keep her from learning to ride." Brock got to his feet, his tall form a shadow against the house. "Should you ever change your mind about riding, I would count myself fortunate to be a part of it." He crossed the distance between us. "If I were to teach you, I'd go slow, not rush into it like Millie did. I was thinking tonight that I'd start you with one of the foals, same as Da did with Millie and me. Let you come to see that a foal can be yours as surely as a pet dog or cat."

For a second I pictured Brock standing next to me as I cared for a foal, his tanned hands showing me how to groom it, perhaps even touching mine. A flash of lightning brought me back to myself, its illumination playing over Brock's tall frame, flickering over his dressing gown and showing that his feet, like mine, were bare. For a moment I couldn't think of anything but his closeness. "Such a plan could take weeks, months," I managed to get out. "I can't impose upon your family's hospitality indefinitely."

"Why not?"

"Because . . ." A gust of showery rain drove me away from the edge of the veranda and toward Brock.

"Mum said you'd quarreled with your family. Where else do you have to stay if not at Tanybrae?"

"I'm not . . ." I licked my lips, unsure of what to say. "Perhaps the situation with my brother will change," I finished.

"From what I've observed of your brother, I doubt such will happen, though if gossip is correct, you could always marry Neville Bromfield."

My chin lifted while my mind whirled, aware of his nearness. I fought the impulse to touch him. What was I thinking? "Perhaps you put too much credence to gossip." I took a steadying breath. "Regardless, what if I don't wish to marry Mr. Bromfield?"

A chuckle rumbled through the rich timbre of his voice. "Then I'd say you're a woman with uncommon brains as well as courage." A tiny silence followed, and I knew in some unfathomable way that Brock was as acutely aware of me as I of him. A sudden gust of wind blew tendrils of hair against my face. He reached and gently brushed them away, his voice unsteady as he spoke. "Know, too, that I'd like it if you chose to make your stay at Tanybrae indefinite." Brock's fingers lingered on my cheek, his touch gentle as his eyes looked deeply into mine. "Don't be afraid, Jessamyne. With me to help you . . ." His thumb moved to cup my chin, and for a glorious moment I thought he would kiss me. Clearing his throat, he dropped his hand and stepped back.

Silence stretched between us, neither of us knowing what to say. Flashes of lightning and the rumble of thunder seemed to echo my clamoring emotions. After a long moment, Brock turned and walked away.

Loathe to see him go, I spoke. "Bro—" I cleared my throat. "Mr. McKade?"

Brock turned, a hand on the door, his head at an attentive angle.
"Thank you," I said.

"You are welcome . . . more than welcome." I heard the smile in his voice, and then, it seemed reluctantly, he entered the house.

* * *

I found sleep difficult, my mind replaying each word Brock had spoken. With a hand to my cheek, I strove to cling onto the memory of his touch. Hadn't the man in my dream brushed my cheek as well? What did it mean? My mind was too full of what had happened to fathom it out. Brock McKade was attracted to me, and I to him. I smiled, scarcely believing it was finally happening. "At last," I whispered. "He's come at last." The thoughts lulled me into hopes of more dreams.

I awoke the next morning still imbued with euphoria, my hysterical actions on the previous day all but forgotten. The heart-stopping moment when Brock had touched my cheek danced through my thoughts, along with his wish for me to stay at Tanybrae. He even wanted to help me overcome my fear of horses. I shook my head, scarce believing what had happened on the veranda. Humming a tune, I arranged my hair. When I finished, I stepped back to view the result in the mirror. The young woman who gazed back at me appeared inordinately pleased with herself. Her eyes shone, and the pink hue of her gown added color to her fair cheeks. All in all, the mirror reflected the picture of a fetching young lady.

Pleased with the results, I entered the kitchen with a quick step. The McKades used a table in a cheery nook of the kitchen to eat breakfast, the dining room reserved for the evening meal. I suffered a twinge of disappointment when instead of Brock, only Anne sat at the table.

"There ye be, and lookin' the top of the mornin'," she said in greeting.

"Thank you." I looked at the empty places at the table. "Am I late?"

"No, tho' ye would have to be up before the sun to break bread with Brock. Off to see to some o' the cattle he is. As for Millie, I've a notion she dinna sleep well last night. Poor mite never does when there's thunder crackin'." She paused and gave me a measured look. "By the looks of ye, the storm dinna interfere with yer sleep."

"Only a little," I hedged, not thinking it prudent to tell her I'd spent time on the veranda with her son.

"'Tis no' like a storm to clear the air . . . right good for the cattle too. Goin' too long without rain takes a terrible toll on the poor beasties. Since yer city bred, I doot ye ken how dependent we are on the weather." She shook her head. "A drought year can well nigh wipe us out, and too much rain can wreak havoc as well. Three years past, the creek flooded, and we lost more'n a score of cattle."

"I didn't realize weather played such an important part in your life."

"Oh aye. Life's a gamble as they say, but 'tis no' my way to fret afore 'tis time. Like the good book says, 'Sufficient unto the day is the evil thereof.'" Anne's hands had been as busy as her tongue, as she'd filled an enameled tray with plates and cups and a chafing dish of food. "'Tis too fine a morn to be stayin' inside. I thought to take our breakfast out to the veranda."

Welcoming her suggestion, I added the teapot and a container of cream to the tray. I paused as I stepped out onto the veranda. The morning was unusually fine, the air rain-washed and cool. A chorus of birds added joyful songs to the day.

"'Tis a lovely morn—just too bonny," she reiterated.

I nodded and spooned a generous portion of eggs onto my plate. As I took my first bite, a multicolored lorikeet flew from a tree and landed on the railing. The bird's bright plumage reminded me of the token I'd found on my pillow. My first instinct was to tell Anne, but caution closed my mouth. What if Anne scolded the girls for their actions? "Do Abos have a religion?" I asked instead.

"Aye, tho' exactly what I canna tell ye. Somethin' to do with the dreamin', which is their version of the creation. And I've heard of corroborees—secret ceremonies that none but the Abos are allowed to see. Some say they dabble in powerful magic, but I think," she frowned and took a sip of tea, "I think 'tis just their way of worshippin' God."

"Do they ever make or wear ornaments or jewelry?"

Anne nodded. "I've seen some . . . little stones and sometimes feathers and such. I think 'tis their way of bringin' good luck or to ward off evil."

As she spoke, I saw Min leave the stable, her walk graceful and upright, the morning sun glinting off the rich mahogany tones of her hair.

Anne noticed the direction of my gaze. "Speaking of Abos, I've a notion our Min is with child."

I looked more closely at Min's slender figure, but her loose-fitting gown hid most of her form. Embarrassed to be caught studying her, I dropped my gaze.

"I doona mean to make ye blush by mentionin' Min's condition," Anne chuckled. "Since the birth of a new foal is talked aboot freely, I see no need for actin' shy aboot one of our own." She paused and nodded. "Ye'll soon see that country ways are not those of the city."

Anne's words would have shocked my governess. "Who's . . . the father?" I asked in embarrassment, for like it or not, old teachings weren't easily put aside.

"Most likely Nerong, the young black who followed Min home from the last walkaboot. A right strappin' laddie, if I remember correctly, tho' he dinna stay long. But Henry says he sees him skulkin' aboot from time to time. I've a notion Nerong prefers the old ways over those of a stockman."

"Are Min and Nerong married?"

Anne frowned. "Likely a ceremony of some sort was performed, tho' not like ours, mind. According to Angus, the Abos mostly stay faithful. Like I said, they're strong on family."

"Will Min go back to her people for the birth of her baby?"

"Aye . . . and likely stay with them so the bairn can learn the old ways. Maybe later she'll come back." Anne made a regretful sound with her tongue. "I'll miss her, for I'm right fond of both her and Callie."

Almost as if she'd heard us talking, Min's silent form appeared at the edge of the veranda. Was it only my imagination that she watched me more closely than usual, perhaps looking to see if I wore the gift?

"Ya need me, missus?" she asked after a long moment.

"Not now, Min. Perhaps later."

As Min walked away, Anne gave me a searching look. "What would ye say to helpin' me teach Callie and Min their letters?" She hurried on. "I've been thinkin' to start a school for the stockmen's children as well. 'Tis no' right that the lads and lassies grow up without learnin', tho' some of their mums try the best they can." She paused, her gaze steady. "I need more'n my paintin' to fill my time, and Millie canna be spendin' all her days ridin' with the stockmen." She shook her head. "No, 'tis time to be makin' some changes, and I've a notion yer bein' here will be the very thing we need. What do ye say?"

"Yes . . . though I've never tried to teach before."

Anne patted my hand. "Ye'll do just fine."

I hoped so, for I was anxious to find a way to repay her in some small way for the kindness she and Millie had shown me, Brock too—although my eagerness to please him came from a different source. Glancing toward the stable, I impatiently counted the hours until I'd see him again.

THIRTEEN

When I saw Brock at dinner that evening, he acted just as he always did, his banter and smile no more intimate than they'd been in the past. Masking my disappointment, I strove to do the same, even as my mind clamored for an explanation. Had I mistaken his emotion? Generous by nature, perhaps Brock had extended his offer only because I was homeless? *Surely not,* my heart cried, yet I realized that the night and the storm might have caused Brock to act in a manner that he now regretted. Spooning a helping of peas onto my plate, I chided myself for foolishly trying to pin my own emotions onto him. *Foolish, foolish!* But when next I looked up and encountered Brock's gaze, I saw a look of tenderness in his face. Not knowing what to think, I concentrated on my meal.

It was well that I had the reading lessons with Min and Callie to put my mind on, and I concentrated on such topics the remainder of the evening. The following afternoon, Anne invited Min and Callie to join us on the veranda. "We'll see how it goes. If we're successful, we can include the stockmen's children."

Although Min and Callie had agreed to the lessons, I sensed their nervousness. Oddly enough, it was Min who seemed most uneasy, her hands tightly clasped in the cup of her lap and her bare feet poised as if ready for flight. Did she worry what Nerong might say, or fear that the strange markings we made on paper could harm her unborn child?

Millie had found two worn slates in a closet. I took one and suggested that Callie join me on a chair a little apart from her cousin. I'd asked to teach Callie because she seemed to watch me more closely than Min, her fleeting gaze showing both interest and shyness. Picking up the chalk, I printed her name on the slate, my strokes slow and deliberate.

"This says Callie." I pointed to each letter and said its name.

Although Callie sat stiffly in her chair, her hands hovered above the gray fabric of her skirt as if they could hardly wait to hold the chalk.

I went over the letters several times, Callie repeating them with me as I pointed. Each time my voice grew softer and Callie's louder until she recited the letters herself.

"Good. Very good."

Callie ducked her head, but not before I saw her smile. The smile widened when I offered her the chalk. "Now, try to copy the letters."

She shot me a quick look before her fingers curled around the piece of chalk, her expression one of delight, the light in her dark eyes an extension of her smile. I expected Callie's attempt to be uncertain and crude, but her movement was surprisingly deft—the *C* clearly recognizable, as was the *A*.

"Wonderful, Callie."

She looked at the letters with pride and started on the *L*. How could she manage the chalk so well without practice? The image of the feathered amulet flashed through my mind. I remembered the tiny knots and the intricate placement of the feathers and suspected that Callie's deft fingers had fashioned it.

* * *

The next day I tucked the feathered ornament into my pocket. When Min and Callie had finished with their letters, I asked Callie to stay. She gave me an uneasy look, as if she expected a scolding.

Taking the amulet from my pocket, I smiled. "Thank you for your gift. It's beautiful."

Callie made a small sound and nodded.

"Did you make it?"

She shook her head, a bare foot rubbing nervously at her leg. "Sal make it."

"Sal?" In my mind, I felt the leathery touch of Sal's hand when she'd taken mine and saw the tears pooled in her dark eyes when we'd said good-bye.

"Sal say give to missy."

Not knowing what to say, I looked down at the insect's delicate wings. What did it mean? Aware that Callie watched me, I asked, "Why did Sal give it to me?"

For a moment Callie didn't speak. Finally, she touched the insect. "Bone pull strength from earth." Her finger moved to the feathers. "Wings take courage from sky. This bring missy strength from earth . . . courage from sky." For a brief moment her brown eyes met and held mine. "Sal say fish people carry you out of water from the dreaming. Now we help you . . . Sal . . . all us."

Emotion tightened my throat, and for a moment I was with Sal again, seeing her hair like a halo as she looked down at me, feeling her love and concern. "Thank you, Callie. Tell Sal thank you too."

Her answer was a quick nod before she slipped from the veranda to join Min. I watched them leave, Min taking the lead and Callie a step or two behind. I expected to see Min ply Callie with questions. Instead they silently made their way down the lane to their home, just as they did each afternoon. They seemed to communicate without speaking—Min asking and Callie responding, their silence a whispering of spirits.

I looked down at the delicately fashioned insect, saw strength in its back, courage in its multicolored wings. I would need both if I intended to learn to ride, for strange as it seemed, that was what I had determined to do.

* * *

The next evening when I saw Brock leave the house, I hurried after him. "Mr. McKade."

He turned, his expression showing both surprise and pleasure. "Jessamyne . . . I mean Miss Clayborne."

"Please, since we see each other every day, wouldn't it be easier to call me Jessamyne?"

He nodded. "Then you must call me Brock."

"All right." An awkward silence fell between us. Not wanting him to think my only purpose in coming was to ask him to call me Jessamyne, I hurried on. "On . . . on the night of the storm you said you'd like to help me learn to ride. Is that still your wish?"

I had Brock's full attention now, his deep blue eyes studying me as if trying to fathom what had happened. "It is. Like I said, I've had some thoughts about it. But what made you change your mind?"

"Being at Tanybrae. In the city there are buggies and carriages and even the new railcar for me to use. But here . . ." I lifted my head to meet his gaze and found that he watched me closely. "Here a horse is the most practical way to get around. It would be selfish to expect you to supply me with some other form of conveyance. But more than that . . ." I paused and the muscles in my stomach tightened. "It's not pleasant being afraid . . . being . . . well, you saw how I was. Not only is it upsetting, it's demeaning, and I don't like—" The need to cry closed my throat. After pausing, I went on with effort. "I don't like being like that." Swallowing, I raised my eyes to meet his. "Please, would you help me?"

Something warm and indefinable softened Brock's handsome features, but he was slow to answer. "Only you can conquer your fear, Miss . . . uh . . . Jessamyne, but I have no doubt you can do it. If you'd like me to help . . ." He grinned suddenly, the act making me catch my breath. Small wonder the young women in Melbourne talked about Brock McKade. "Meet me here after breakfast in the morning. Be sure to wear your boots and . . ." He paused to survey my mauve dress with its nipped-in waist and fashionable bustle. "Although your gown is most becoming, it would be wise to ask Millie for more practical attire. I'm certain she has something she can lend you. And one other thing . . ." He paused. Even as I wondered what other instructions he would give, my mind held to what he had said about my gown—"most becoming." I smiled to myself—Jessamyne Clayborne, who'd received more than her share of compliments, in raptures because Brock McKade had admired her dress.

"What makes you smile?" he asked.

"Smile?" I feigned puzzlement, even as my lips widened. His chuckle warmed my heart, and for a second I forgot where we were in our conversation. "What . . . what was it you were about to say?"

"Oh . . ." A slight flush crept to his cheeks. "When you borrow Millie's dress, tell her she can't come with us in the morning. Better yet, I'll tell her myself. Much as I love my sister, she rushes at life with too much verve." His face sobered. "I want to go slowly with you and the horses . . . and that's exactly what we'll do."

* * *

Shortly after breakfast the following morning, I walked with Brock to the paddock where the yearlings and some of the older foals were kept. Since Brock had spoken to Millie the night before, she showed no surprise when I asked to borrow one of her gowns.

"I have the very thing for you, though it's a little worn."

The "very thing" was a plain black skirt and tailored white bodice. "Will it do?" I asked after I'd changed.

Millie nodded and handed me Anne's old hat, her expression unhappy. "I wish Brock weren't so adamant about me staying away. I know I did wrong by rushing things, but I promised just to watch." She sighed. "He won't budge, and I've learned that Brock can be as stubborn as Da."

Although I was very fond of Millie, I was secretly pleased to have Brock all to myself.

She gave me a tentative look. "Would you see if you can make him change his mind?"

I gave her a questioning look. "I doubt I have much influence with your brother."

"You have more than you think," Millie countered. "Please, will you try?"

"I'll see what I can do," I replied, although I didn't intend to exert much effort.

* * *

My promise was quickly forgotten, for having Brock's full attention was a little overpowering. Just remembering to strive for nonchalance when his gaze met mine took effort. *Don't be such a ninny,* I told myself. After that, I concentrated on listening to Brock and tried to keep nervousness at bay. Although the yearlings were not full grown, they were nonetheless horses and much bigger than me. I was grateful for the fence and the few yards of pasture that separated us.

Brock had given my skirt and floppy hat an approving nod when I joined him, but unfortunately he hadn't described either as becoming. "I thought to have you look over the horses and see which one you like. Some choose their mounts by color or stance, but I've learned that horses are much like people. They have their own personalities, and it's what's inside that counts." He paused and pointed across the pasture. "See that black colt in the far corner?"

I noted the animal and wondered if it might be related to Night Flyer.

"He has fine lines and coloring," Brock went on, "but he shows signs of temper . . . something Adam and I are trying to curb." His gaze moved to a horse closer to the fence. "That brown colt is a bit of a bully. As you watch and come to know the horses, you'll begin to notice their different natures."

I looked over the rest of the horses. They numbered over a dozen, the majority almost grown, a few leggy and still coltish in appearance. Blacks and browns were the predominant colors, with a sprinkling of bay and roan. Spying Brock, the chestnut mare he and Adam had been training nickered and came at a trot toward us.

I grasped Brock's arms and backed away, placing him between us. I half expected Brock to encourage me to move back to the fence.

"Do only what you feel comfortable doing," he said.

I swallowed and slowly released my hold on his arms before focusing my attention back on the mare. Watching Brock with the yearling was a lesson in patience. She stopped a few feet from the fence, her head bobbing nervously. Brock remained still, one hand resting on the top fence rail, his voice his only overture of friendship. "Easy, Miranda. It's all right."

The mare studied us, her nostrils flaring. I was glad for the fence, glad too that Brock stood between us. I willed myself to look at her, noting a lighter marking above one eye and the way her ears pricked as if she sensed danger. Brock had told me to try to discover the horses' traits. The only words that came to mind were skittish and distrusting.

She took a nervous step closer while Brock continued to speak encouragement. "If I were Millie, I'd move my hand about now, and off Miranda would gallop, the chance to woo her spoiled by impatience."

Woo her? I wanted to ask, but fortunately I had enough presence of mind to know my unfamiliar voice would spook her.

"Aye, woo her, Jessamyne," Brock went on in a soothing voice, as if he had read my thoughts. "You like being wooed, don't you, girl? Both horses and people enjoy knowing they're sought after and admired."

As if to verify his words, Miranda took a cautious step, then another.

"That's the way. You're a beauty, just like your mother. Her mum was one of our first brood mares and is dam to several of our best horses."

Giving a soft nicker, Miranda took the final step, her head but inches from Brock's hand on the fence. She snuffled at his fingers, and for a second I feared she would bite them. Closing my eyes, I willed myself not to run, my heart accelerating and the palms of my hands clammy.

"You want your treat, don't you, girl. You'll get it, but first you need to learn it's enough just to come."

I opened my eyes and watched Brock stroke her nose, his voice dropping so low I only caught "my beauty." Continuing his croon, his other hand stole to his pocket and extracted a wedge of apple. "Here's your reward . . . one you've well earned."

Miranda's lips seemed to inhale the apple. As soon as it was gone, her head snaked across the fence as she searched for more. Brock slipped her another wedge, then gave her a little pat. "Now, off with you."

The mare set off at a trot. As the distance widened between us, I gained courage enough to move back to the fence. "I was sure she was going to bite you."

"No fear of that," he chuckled, "though I've been bitten a time or two. There's a knack to how you do it—one I'll show you when it's time."

I stifled a shudder. "I could never let a horse eat out of my hand."

"You can and you will." Brock turned to meet my gaze. "Just as you stood your ground just now. I thought only to bring you out to the paddock. What you saw with Miranda was something I hadn't planned." A satisfied smile creased his tanned features. "The filly wasn't the only one who passed her test. You're to be congratulated Miss . . ." He grinned. "Sorry, I'm not used to calling you Jessamyne."

I liked the way he said my name, liked even more the admiration in his cobalt eyes.

He turned back to the paddock. "Do you see one that catches your eye?" When I shook my head, he went on. "Don't forget the foals. There are some likely prospects there as well."

I looked to the far end of the paddock where two of the foals frisked about. Leggy and still a little awkward, their lack of size made them less intimidating. "If I should choose a foal, how long before it's big enough to ride?"

"At least two years . . . though slight as you are, perhaps less."

My eyes shifted back to the yearlings. "The foals will take too long."

"And what have you got, if not time?" His brows lifted and he gave me a teasing grin. "Unless you have a pressing dinner engagement with Neville Bromfield."

I laughed. "You know I haven't."

"And glad I am that you don't." Like his smile, his gaze was warm. "We both have time, and so do the horses. And takin' it slow, as me Da used to say, can bring miracles that make the waitin' all the more sweet."

* * *

Each morning Brock and I walked down to the paddock. Sometimes we stayed for only a few minutes, other times as long as an hour, all the while watching the horses and talking. At first I kept my distance from the fence, but as the days passed, I became bold enough to rest my arms on the top rail like Brock.

"The black I pointed out to you the first morning shows the most speed," Brock told me. "As I mentioned, Jet Star has a bit of a temper, but so did Night Flyer when he was young. With patience I managed to break him of it."

"Are Jet Star and Night Flyer brothers?"

"They share the same sire, but different dams."

"I think I'd prefer a horse that isn't so fast." I purposely kept my gaze on the yearling, not wanting Brock to read the fear that the image of me astride a fast-paced horse conjured up.

"Like Millie, you'll probably do best with a mare, though my sister's an excellent rider and does well on anything she decides to ride."

"I had a pony once."

"Did you now?"

"His name was Prince. I loved him dearly and brought him lumps of sugar each time Mother and I went for our ride." My words surprised me. The fear and trauma of the runaway horse had erased the memory of earlier days. "I think I rode well. At least Mother said I did. Like Millie, she was excellent with horses. That's why—" My voice could not push past the tightness in my throat.

"Mum told me how your mother died."

Although I continued to watch the horses, my mind was flooded with the image of the runaway horse and pony and me scrabbling to retain my seat in the saddle. "It was long ago, and yet in ways it seems like it happened just yesterday."

"A bairn learning to walk doesn't let his first fall stop him," Brock said in a quiet voice.

"I know, but—" I bit my lips and searched for a way to change the subject. "Is the bay horse next to Miranda a filly or a . . . a male?" My tongue slid over the word in embarrassment.

"She's a filly. And just so you know, we call them colts or stallions, not males." I could tell that Brock was hard-pressed not to laugh.

"Since you're staying at Tanybrae, you'd best get over your city ways and learn to call the animals by their proper names. We have heifers and bulls, mares and stallions . . . sows and boars too."

I felt my cheeks warm. Scrambling for something to say, I asked, "What do you think of the filly?"

"She'll do you quite well, but the important thing is what you think of her." There was a tiny pause. "And don't forget the foals."

This was the second time Brock had mentioned the foals. Did he have a favorite in mind, one he hoped I would choose? He left me wondering.

* * *

Stubbornness kept me from going to inspect the foals. In fact, I ignored them for two days. Then on Friday, as we picked our way through the tall grass to the area where the foals tended to congregate, I turned to Brock. "Tell me about the foals. How old are they?"

"These three were born about five months ago. Two are fillies, and the black one is a colt." He paused and looked pleased. "Our foaling went well this year. Besides these three, we have two others still too young to be separated from their dams."

I remembered Millie mentioning the brood mares. "How many dams do you have? Just the five?"

Brock nodded. "When my father got the idea to raise horses, we only had the one. Since his death, I've managed to buy a new brood mare each year." Brock paused and looked with satisfaction at the horses. "All the yearlings and foals show promise. All in all, I'm pleased with how well things are going."

Aware of our approach, the foals ceased grazing, their ears pricked and their stances alert. They had gangly legs and heads slightly out of proportion to their bodies, and I wondered with amusement if one would someday be mine.

Recalling how much Mother had loved her mare, I realized that on some level I'd already determined that the horse I chose would be either a filly or a mare. *Will it be one of you?* I wondered, and suddenly knew it would. They were no bigger than my pony had been. By starting with one so small, perhaps the filly and my courage could join hands and grow together.

As the thought formed, the icy circle of fear that encased my chest loosened slightly. Yes . . . perhaps I could do this. I doubt Brock knew a tiny milestone had been passed, or that in doing so, it had freed me enough of fear to look at the two fillies with a measure of objectivity. Which would it be?

As if my question had conveyed itself to the foals, one of the fillies lifted her head and nickered. Giving a snort, she galloped to the far side of the paddock, coming to a stiff-legged halt, then turning to trot back. *Look at me,* her antics said. *Aren't I wonderful?*

"That one," I said as she came to a jolting halt a few steps from the fence. "That's the one I want."

Brock's eyebrows lifted. "But you've scarcely looked at her."

"That's the one," I said firmly, at the same time taking note that one ear was darker than the other and that she had a blaze of white across her chest.

"All right." I heard both surprise and humor in his voice, and I suspected he thought my quick decision was but further evidence that a woman's actions could never be fully explained.

I didn't understand my decision either, but it had come so strongly that I didn't question it. I only knew the choice had been made and that a subtle easing of my fear had occurred. Now the only thing I needed to do was decide what to name her.

* * *

I thought that as soon as I'd selected the filly, Brock would introduce her to me on closer terms. In this I was mistaken.

"Continue to watch her for a few days," Brock had told me one morning. "There's much you can learn about an animal by watching it." Sensing my surprise, he added, "Watching her will help you decide upon a name as well."

With that he'd tipped his leather hat and excused himself to get on with Miranda's training. *You'll do fine,* his expression told me.

My newfound confidence had ebbed as soon as he'd walked away. I hadn't realized how much his solid presence by my side had meant to me. With Brock's departure the horses seemed larger, the fence less sturdy. It was several moments before I could force my feet to take me to the fence, and even longer before I could gather the courage to touch it. *There, Jessa. See, you can do it.*

With that hurdle passed, I concentrated on the foals, taking satisfaction in being able to quickly pick my filly from the others. I watched them play a form of tag, and noted with pride that mine seemed cleverest as she dodged and kicked up her heels. But what would I name her? The matter would take some thought.

My time at the paddock only took up a small part of each day. The rest was spent helping Anne with her garden or other duties, tasks that brought surprising pleasure. After noon tea each day, Anne had made a practice of reading aloud to Min and Callie. The stories and poetry were so interesting that I frequently joined them. Lessons followed. I soon realized that Min didn't care for them and only complied out of duty. On the other hand, Callie enjoyed both using the chalk and learning her letters. The rest of each afternoon was ours to do as we pleased—even for Min and Callie. Millie usually went for a ride, and Anne used this time for her painting.

I dabbled at my embroidery and sometimes read, but since I'd begun spending time with the horses, an unsettling restlessness wouldn't let me do either with my usual enjoyment. Frustrated one afternoon, I donned boots and hat and set off across the meadow with a sturdy stick in hand, as Anne's fear of snakes had made me skittish as well. I followed the stream that wound through the meadow up into the nearby hills, its course a meandering path, the sound of water harmonizing with bird song. By now I was familiar enough with the songs of lorikeets and magpies to pick them out from those of the more mournful doves.

After leaving the meadow, the path became steeper and made me glad for my stick. The lush tangle of undergrowth and the flashy color of hibiscus made the effort worthwhile. Moreover, I felt a renewal of energy, one I hadn't experienced for several days.

The picnic spot was closer than I expected, the grassy knoll where Min and Callie had spread the quilt my destination. I heard the cackling laughter of the kookaburras, greeting me like an old friend. "Ta-ta to you, as well," I called, and laughed when one cocked its feathery head at my rejoinder.

Instead of exploring, I sat down on a log to enjoy the beauty. A profusion of ferns and mosses clothed the lower trunks of the trees, the mixture of mountain ash and gray gums a pleasing contrast. The tumble of water on stone added a soothing music. Small wonder the McKades sought this paradise for their picnics.

I lazed away the afternoon, the tenseness built up from being around horses tumbling away like water in the stream. After a while, I took Anne's slender volume of Australian poetry from my pocket; while sun-dappled patterns played across the pages, I read "The Lay of the Last Squatter."

This is Australia, I thought, and for the first time I felt a sense of kinship with the strange land. Perhaps in the future I could even come to think of it as home.

Realizing the afternoon had slipped away, I closed the book and put it into my pocket. As I got to my feet, I saw a small, strange-looking kangaroo leap across the grassy knoll and disappear into the trees. Excited to see a joey, I followed, the path and animal taking me higher up the hill.

My steps became more labored as I strove to keep the animal in sight. Then with a bound, it disappeared into a thicket of trees and undergrowth so dense I knew I couldn't follow. Leaning against a tree to catch my breath, I was startled to see a man and woman standing in a nearby clearing. I recognized Min, her head lifted to the bronzed young man who spoke to her.

He was tall and muscular with curly dark hair and a broad nose. The fact that his lithe brown body was unclothed except for a loincloth girdled around his waist caused me to look away. I felt heat rise to my cheeks, even as I reminded myself that the Aborigine must be Min's husband and the father of her child. His actions seemed to bear this out as he pulled Min to him, his head bent to hers, their lips and bodies meshing.

An ache of yearning struck me and erased my embarrassment. I suddenly wished it were I, not Min, who had found a man to love— one who would hold me with tenderness and caring. I painfully wondered what had gone wrong with my life. I'd had my share of suitors and been considered a social success by everyone except myself. How could I explain my own lack of response to their overtures? None had held my interest for more than a few days, their words seeming hollow and without depth. *Where are you?* I asked, and before the question had fully formed, my mind filled with the image of the man on horseback and Brock McKade.

* * *

We lingered over tea that evening. Of late, instead of excusing himself to check on the horses, Brock often stayed too, his deep voice and laughing quips adding an exciting dimension to our conversation. As I joined in the talk, I realized that the constraint between Brock and me had wholly disappeared.

I had changed out of my black skirt and white bodice into something more feminine, not unmindful that the deep teal of my gown made my eyes take on luster. After Millie told us about her outing on Nimble, she asked what I had done.

As I told them of my walk and described the kangaroo I'd seen, Anne exchanged a quick glance with Brock. "'Twas a wallaby ye saw, not a joey . . . a wee relative of their bigger cousins. Though wallabies are appealing, they can do damage to the garden. I've taken my rifle to them more than once." Seeing my expression change, she explained. "In our early years at Tanybrae, there was no' enough food for them and us too." She shrugged, her face showing neither apology nor embarrassment.

"I think it would be wise to teach Jessamyne to shoot a rifle," Brock said.

I opened my mouth to protest, but before I could speak, Anne cut in.

"I doot ye'll ever have need to use it, but like Brock, I think 'tis a skill every lass in the bush should learn, especially if ye plan to go for long walks. I taught Millie, ye know."

Millie nodded. "Shooting a gun isn't as intimidating as you might suppose, and it makes me feel safer when I ride Nimble."

Even as I recalled the rifle ensconced in her saddle holster, I pointed out that I probably wouldn't be riding.

"Not at first," Brock agreed, his eyes a warm challenge in the lamplight. "Just the same, I'll rest easier knowing you are able to handle a gun. Will you let Mum teach you?"

Because Brock asked, of course my answer was yes.

* * *

As Millie had said, shooting a gun was not as threatening as I'd imagined. The following afternoon, instead of going for a walk, I followed Anne to an open area well away from the house.

"'Tis the corn the roos and wallabies like to eat. A herd of either can nigh wipe out a crop, and even one or two can do a fair amount of damage."

We skirted the vegetable garden. I carried a stout stick, and Anne carried a rifle. Several rows of corn followed by trellises of beans and rows of cabbages spoke of the garden's success.

Anne was a competent teacher, her voice as calm and matter-of-fact as when she taught me a new embroidery stitch. The parts of the gun were explained, along with its workings. "For like bakin' a cake, ye have need to be familiar with both the recipe and the ingredients," she went on with a grin. Next I was shown the proper way to hold it and aim, the need for steadiness repeatedly stressed. "Tho' I have no concern for yer steadiness as yer a lass with plenty of pluck," she finished with a wink.

Armed with her encouraging words and my promise to Brock, I cocked the rifle and fired at a makeshift target Millie had nailed to a tree. The kick and loud burst from the rifle made me flinch. My first attempt went wide, but by the fifth shot, the bullets began to connect with the target.

"Good lass . . . very good." Anne's praise was like the taste of sweet honey. Not wanting me to feel self-conscious, she'd forbidden Millie to accompany us. I knew she wouldn't be long in sharing my success with her daughter—Brock too, as I found out at evening tea.

I tried not to preen like the colorful parrots about my success, but a similar emotion filled me along with the satisfaction of knowing that, should the need arise, I could protect myself. Images of snakes and dingoes flitted through my mind along with the more menacing specter of bushrangers and the isolation of Tanybrae.

Although I had no intention of carrying a rifle each time I left the confines of the yard, I went several times with Anne to practice shooting. Imbued with the power of knowing I could protect myself, I took additional satisfaction when Anne pronounced me a competent marksman.

"The poor roos won't stand a chance now that you've joined forces with Mum and Millie," Brock teased later that day.

Although I was now the recipient of his playful friendship and sometimes an admiring glance, since the night on the veranda there'd been no other overtures from Brock. But his feelings for me were there, the tenderness in his eyes glimpsed in unguarded minutes. But I was impatient for something stronger and found it difficult to wait. When would his feelings manifest themselves more forcefully?

FOURTEEN

I looked back on my first few weeks at Tanybrae with satisfaction. Not only could I now shoot a rifle, I was able to approach and lean on the fence of the paddock without trepidation. A scant six months before, I couldn't have imagined doing either.

There were other signs of change in Miss Jessamyne Clayborne as well. My former attire of silks and satins had been replaced by simple muslin gowns, and thanks to Millie, I now had boots, a black skirt, and a white bodice to wear when out with the horses.

After almost two weeks of watching my foal, I still felt satisfaction in my selection. The filly seemed pleasant-natured, and in my eyes she outshone the other foals, but try as I might, I couldn't settle on her name.

"It will come," Brock assured me. He had joined me at the fence, his absence for the past two days keenly noticed. Slipping a quick glance at his handsome features, I pretended interest in the horse as I pointed out her good points to Brock.

"I think she'll do very well for you," he agreed. "I knew she was a likely filly as soon as she was born." He turned to me, his gaze both direct and challenging. "How would you like to offer her a piece of apple?"

I felt the familiar surge of unease and was about to offer an excuse when Brock went on. "Think of her as a babe no bigger than your pony. I know you can do it."

Both his eyes and voice were challenging, and because I wanted to please him, I swallowed and nodded.

Brock gave me one of his heart-melting grins. "Good. I knew you would." Tightening his lips, he emitted a sharp whistle. The three foals looked up. "Like people, horses are curious. Now that we have their attention, we need something to entice them over." Brock grabbed a handful of grass and held it out to the horses. Following his example, I did the same.

"None of the foals have tasted apples, so we'll start with something they know and like." His voice changed to a croon. "Come, that's the way."

The colt responded first, but both fillies were quick to follow.

"Call her," Brock instructed. "She's grown used to seeing you at the fence. Now she needs to learn your voice."

I nervously wet my lips and called. "Come, girl. See what I have." All of the foals responded, but I concentrated on my filly. I felt confident she would come to me and not Brock—knew it as certainly as I'd known she was my choice. "Come, girl," and in that moment I knew her name. "Come, Lass."

Knowing her name imbued me with greater confidence. *Lass.* What a wonderful name, and she would grow up to be a wonderful mare—one I would love as dearly as I'd loved Prince. But first I needed to muster the courage to let her come close enough to eat from my hand. "That's a girl," I crooned. "What a beauty, my Lass."

Although Brock continued to talk and call to the foals, I was aware that he watched me closely, his grin telling me he was pleased. I was pleased too, my need to succeed stronger than my fear. I opened my hand and flattened my palm so the grass lay across its table.

The foals stopped and watched us, wanting the grass, but suspicious of the way it was offered. I wanted to speak and encourage, but Brock's stillness told me it would be a mistake. *Patience,* he seemed to say.

After a long moment, the colt took a cautious step. Lass followed, ears pricked as if she might run. *Come, my lass, I won't hurt you,* while inside a more subtle voice cautioned, *What if she bites you?* As the thought formed, the foals spooked and bolted.

I lowered my arm in disappointment, letting the grass slide to the ground.

"It's rare for them to eat from a hand the first time it's offered. Pick more and we'll try again."

Twice more we offered it. The third time Lass led the foals, her tail swishing as she came at a trot. She halted a few steps from the fence.

"Come, Lass," I crooned. "It's all right."

She took a step, then another, her friends standing a little apart and watching. "You can do it." By now my desire to feel her velvety lips against my palm overcame fear. Trauma had buried the memory of Prince's mouth on my childish hand, muted the sound of my giggle. When at last Lass took the bait, her touch brought exhilaration and made me want to laugh.

"Good." Brock's voice was low. "Now carefully take mine and offer her that."

My second offering disappeared as quickly as the first. As soon as it was gone, Lass nickered and looked expectantly for more.

"Here," Brock said, slipping a slice of apple into my hand.

Lass's quickness in taking it made me giggle. "Hungry are you?"

By now the other foals clustered around, and some of the yearlings came from the other end of the paddock.

"The word is out," Brock said, "but I only brought one apple."

I laughed for no other reason than that I was happy. I'd done it. Dear heaven, I'd done it!

"Off with you," Brock said when the last of the apple was gone. The horses were slow to comply. "Off," he repeated. To give finality to his words, he turned from the fence and let the full force of his gaze fall upon me. "Who would have thought?" he asked.

"I can't believe I did it either." My laughter was that of pure joy— one that enfolded Brock, who looked as pleased as I felt, his grin sending shafts of light to his blue eyes.

"Och, I'm thinking we must all take on a Scottish brogue now that ye've decided to call her Lass." Both his eyes and smile were warm. "Lass . . . the very name for her. I think you've chosen well."

I was so happy, I took all he said as a compliment. We turned as one and looked at the foals, our elbows resting on the top rail, the warmth of success and the morning sun surrounding us. "So . . . what comes next?"

"More of the same for a few days. Then when you feel it's right, try to touch her."

The idea of touching the foal dragged at my euphoria. "I . . ."

"You can do it. When the time is right, you'll do it. See how well you did today. Hold your success close and your confidence will grow."

"How will I know when the time is right?"

"You'll know. Now if you were Millie, I'd have to warn you not to be in a rush. But with you—" he paused, the depth of his blue eyes warming. "I think without knowing it, you have a way with horses."

I stared at him. Could it be true? Like Mother, did I have a way with horses? "I hope so," I said. Happy tears and laughter warred for position. Without thinking, I gathered Brock's hand in mine. "Thank you," I whispered. "Oh, thank you."

"You're very welcome."

Tears quivered on my lashes, and I saw tenderness and something I had never seen before fill Brock's blue eyes. I stared, aware of the warmth of his tanned skin on my fingers, the calluses across the palm of his hand. Unable to tear my eyes away, I felt his hand tighten on mine, the pressure telling me that the tumbling emotions I experienced were reciprocated by this man who was as enchanted as I. Neither of us spoke until I reluctantly released his hands and stepped away. "I . . . I must tell your mum and Millie about feeding Lass." Not waiting for an answer, I rushed away.

For a second, the rashness of my impulsive gesture consumed my mind and sent a surge of heat to my face. Then I heard a laugh of surprise and wonder. "Miracles do happen." Then so soft I couldn't be certain I heard it, "Thank you, sweet Jessa."

* * *

I worried that what had transpired would cause constraint between us, but when Brock greeted me at dinner in his usual friendly manner, I was able to respond in kind. With Anne and Millie to fill in the gaps of conversation with chatter of their own, I told myself that taking Brock's hand had been a natural gesture. If Robert had been there instead of Brock, I would not only have taken his hand, but kissed him on the cheek as well. But Brock was not Robert, and well I knew it. Instead of chastising myself for boldness, I pulled the words "sweet Jessa" closer to my heart and let myself just enjoy his company. My enjoyment increased when I noticed that his gaze kept flitting to me and that he smiled as often as I did.

That evening, the four of us gathered in the sitting room for a final cup of tea before retiring. After Anne had poured the steaming beverage into dainty china cups, Brock reached into his pocket and extracted a letter.

"I received a letter from my solicitor today."

Anne looked up from her pouring. "Does he have good news?"

"If you mean has he been able to find Ned Krueger, the answer is no. Nor has he or the race commission been able to locate Jeremy Moulton." Opening the letter, Brock began to read.

Mr. Moulton told his landlady he had urgent business in Sydney, but all enquiries with port and railroad authorities have led to nothing. We continue to search for both men, and in time we hope to be rewarded for our efforts. I am happy, however, to be able to convey one spot of good news. Despite Neville Bromfield's formal protest, the race commission continues to hold the purse. They believe the disappearance of both Mr. Moulton and Mr. Krueger is suspicious enough to warrant their retaining the prize money.

"Good," Anne breathed. "Then there's still hope that ye'll get the purse."

Brock nodded. "But only if Jeremy Moulton or Ned Krueger are found." He grimaced. "Getting them to confess will be another matter."

"Where could they be?" Millie asked.

Brock shook his head. "I wish I knew."

I wished it too—wished also that my mind hadn't jumped so quickly to Robert. Could he and Neville Bromfield truly have been involved in rigging the race? I remembered how badly Robert said Neville wanted to win and the large amounts of money both men had put on the outcome. Had greed and the desire for prestige lowered them to dishonesty?

Although I'd refrained from telling the McKades that I'd seen Jeremy Moulton leave Robert's study two days before I witnessed the exchange of money, I thought of it now. The memory brought a wave of sickness. Then, hearing my name, my mind jerked back to the conversation.

"Thanks to Jessamyne, even if they canna find the jockey or that terrible Mr. Moulton, Mr. Bromfield canna lay his hands on the prize," Anne concluded.

I shifted uncomfortably. "I wonder if the two men left together or went their separate ways."

"Maybe they've headed for the outback," Millie put in. "Christopher said all sorts of unsavory men and bushrangers head there when they don't want to be found."

"'Tis true," Anne sighed. "I'm thinkin' the only thing we can do is to pray and rely on the Lord. In time, I'm sure He'll tell us what we must do."

I saw Brock's mouth tighten, but he refrained from saying anything. Did he agree with his mother, or did he think that those who sat around expecting God to intervene might have a very long wait?

* * *

Later that week the weather turned rainy, forcing us to stay inside or risk a drenching. The rain was welcome, for it cleared the dust from the air and gave some respite from the heat. By the third day, only clouds remained. After Millie and I finished with Callie and Min's lessons, Millie donned her riding skirt and went for a ride on Nimble.

Restless, I gave the sullen sky a questioning glance. A seam of blue sliced the gray, its breadth giving hope that the afternoon would clear and turn sunny. My optimism was such that, after stopping to watch the foals, I set out for the hills. By the time I reached the picnic spot, the clouds had diminished enough to allow intermittent glimpses of the sun. I had come there so often that I claimed the secluded knoll and leafy bower as my own—an idyllic hideaway to drink in beauty and be alone. As I admired the tangle of ferns and tiny lavender orchids, I wished I had Anne's talent to capture them with paintbrush and oils. Lacking this, I searched for words to describe the lovely spot. Quickly moving past *captivating* and *beautiful,* I had progressed to *exquisite* when I felt a drop of rain.

I glanced up and saw the sun obscured by dark clouds and more hurrying to join them. Not wanting a drenching, I hurried too, glad for my stick to add balance and for my hat with its wide floppy brim to keep the rain off my face.

By now the drops were coming more often, spotting my black skirt and sprinkling the sleeves of my bodice. I paused to see how far I still had to go and saw the house and tumble of outbuildings in the misty distance. If I left the stream and crossed the grassy expanse where the cattle grazed, I could get home much faster.

The shortcut was indeed quicker, the grass cropped short by the cattle, the terrain less rocky. Despite the wide brim of my hat, occasional droplets blew onto my face and wet the fabric of my sleeves.

"Coo-ee!" a male voice called.

Heart pounding from exertion, I looked up and saw two men on horseback cantering toward me.

"Jessamyne," the voice called again.

I recognized Brock and one of the stockmen. Gladness and chagrin joined in a contest, for I knew I must look a sight. I wiped a hand across my damp face and waited.

Brock reined in his horse before he reached me, and after dismounting handed the reins to his companion. The stockman lifted his hat and cantered off with Brock's horse in tow.

"Take this," Brock said, shrugging out of his mackintosh. "More rain is coming, and you'll be soaked before we get home."

"What about you?"

"I've been caught in enough rainstorms to think nothing of a wetting." He draped the slicker around my shoulders and waited for me to slip my arms into the sleeves.

I brushed a lock of damp hair away from my face. "Thank you."

He nodded, his eyes holding warmth.

Entranced by his close proximity, I was loathe to move away. Instead, I took in the sharp angles of his cheekbones and noted a tiny knick on his chin from shaving. Suddenly remembering myself, I gave a nervous giggle. "You must think me a terrible dunderhead . . . having hysterics over Millie's horse and now having no more sense than to get caught in the rain."

Brock chuckled, and his indigo eyes remained warm. "Dunderhead is not a term I'd use to describe you. Lovely, yes . . . delightful too. Actually, I can think of any number of flattering terms, but now is neither the time nor place." Giving a wry grin, he took my arm and started across the pasture. "As for having hysterics, given your past it was entirely understandable. Likewise today. Since you're newly arrived, you don't know how fickle our Gippsland weather can be. Sunshine one moment, rain the next. As I said, I've been tricked more times than I can count."

"You're too kind, but I thank you just the same for trying to make me feel less the fool."

"Never a fool," Brock countered. "As for me being kind, when you know me better you'll discover there are times when I lack the trait. I fear there's too much of my father in me. Perhaps you've heard that the McKades have a reputation for being scrappers."

He shot me a quick glance from under the brim of his hat, a look that seemed to assess my reaction. When I smiled, his own came quickly, warming my heart as the now-wet mackintosh slapped against my boots, my hands hidden in the slicker's long sleeves.

"You forget that I was at the race and saw a display of your scrappiness."

Brock sighed. "That was not one of my finer moments."

"Nor was mine with Millie's horse."

Heads bent against the sprinkles, we walked without speaking. Where before I'd run in my eagerness to reach home, now I was content to match my step with Brock's slower stride, even more content to feel his fingers as they held my arm through the slicker.

"Speaking of the race," Brock went on. "The society column of the Melbourne newspapers made much of you being escorted by Neville Bromfield. One even hinted marriage might be in the offing."

I shook my head. "Mr. Bromfield is handsome and possesses considerable charm, but the two occasions I was in his company failed to ignite my desire to be his wife." It was my turn to give him a sideways glance. "I believe I told you this previously."

"You did." His tilted head revealed an expression that was not altogether composed. "In addition to having a bit of a temper, I've been known to request that important facts be repeated."

Important facts. Neither my mind nor tongue knew how to respond, but my heart did, its impromptu dance making me want to sing.

Unfortunately, Dougal chose that moment to run out to meet us, his bark and wagging tail expressing his happiness in seeing Brock. My own heart slowed in disappointment.

"Hey there, Dougal. Did Mum send you to rescue us?" He bent and patted the sheepdog, releasing his hold on my arm as he ruffled the dog's fur. "Wet," he grumbled, "just like Miss Clayborne."

"Jessamyne," I corrected. "And I think one time I heard you call me Jessa."

It was Brock's turn to look disconcerted. "Now who's repeating the facts?"

"Me," I laughed. "You."

Our laughter meshing, he put an affectionate arm around my shoulder. I wanted it to remain there, my head fitting naturally against his shoulder, floppy hat and all.

"Jessa. Yes, I like that very much."

Feeling left out, Dougal nuzzled Brock's side, then ran ahead in an invitation to play.

"Sorry, mate, you'll have to find someone else to play with." Dougal continued to try, running ahead, then returning to circle us. So it was that we reached the lane, the three of us damp and a little bedraggled.

Millie came to meet us. "There you are. I was stabling Nimble when Will rode in and said you'd stayed behind with Jessamyne." Her expression showed concern as she looked me over. "I hope you didn't get too wet."

"Since Brock loaned me his slicker, he's the one who got the wetting." I paused to look him over. "You don't look very wet."

Brock held out his arm. "You're right."

Millie giggled. "In case you didn't notice, it stopped raining several minutes ago."

"We noticed. I was only teasing," Brock said quickly.

Before Millie could ask more revealing questions, I shrugged out of the slicker. "Thanks for the use of your mac."

"You're welcome." His voice still held warmth. Glancing at his sister, he went on. "When the weather clears, why don't you and Jessamyne plan another picnic?" With a nod, he draped the mackintosh over his shoulder and walked to the stable.

I knew better than to stand and look after him, though it was what I wanted to do. Instead, I linked my arm through Millie's and started for the house. "How was your ride? Did the rain catch you unawares too?"

I'm ashamed to say I scarcely listened to Millie's answer, my mind occupied instead with the thought that Brock and I had been so caught up in ourselves that we hadn't noticed when the rain stopped. Other thoughts danced through my mind—thoughts filled with *important facts* and *Jessa* tumbling among them. All in all, it had been a most satisfying day.

* * *

The lessons with Min and Callie continued to go well. After teaching them to write their names, we started with the alphabet, taking one new letter a day. Min was able to form the new letters on her slate but encountered difficulty when it came to connecting the letters with sound. Callie had no difficulty with either, and I hoped that before long she could begin reading. My hope to break past her reticence and talk as friends had, as yet, not borne fruit. Most of my questions were answered with yes or no, and despite many attempts, she wouldn't be drawn into conversation.

"Don't they like us?" I asked one evening after Min and Callie left the house.

"I doona think 'tis exactly that . . . tho' who could blame them if they don't? Dinna we take their land and are we no' changin' their ways?"

Anne, Millie, and I had gathered in the sitting room, embroidery in hand. Anne shifted in her chair. "I think 'tis that they feel uncomfortable with us and are no' much at makin' conversation, even with their own." She looked up from her sewing. "Of course, I could just as easily be wrong. Since I've always tried to be kind, I think in their way they like us."

I thought of the amulet Sal had given me. Several times I'd taken it out of the drawer with the intent of wearing it, but each time I did, something stopped me. If Sal had intended me to wear it, wouldn't she have attached it to a leather thong?

When I frowned, Anne patted my arm. "Doona worry, lass. I'm sure Min and Callie like ye, just as we do. I was tellin' Millie just yesterday that havin' ye here is the best Christmas present we could have."

"Thank you." I was surprised at her reference to Christmas. Caught up in Brock and the filly, I'd lost track of the passing days. Summer and Christmas didn't seem to go together. "How far into December are we? How long until Christmas?"

"Less than a fortnight," Millie said. She looked to her mother. "Remember how Brock and I used to pester you to know how many days until Christmas? Though we're not as bad now, I do look forward to the parties in Melbourne."

My needle stilled. "Parties?"

Millie nodded. "Since Da died, we go into Melbourne for Christmas. Mum's good friend, Mrs. Morrison, is widowed too. She's alone in a big house in the city and is as hungry for company as we are. We have wonderful times . . . parties, dances, and lots of people. My favorite is the ball on New Year's night." She quickly added, "Of course, you're invited too. This will be a wonderful chance for you to meet my friends."

While Millie described their last Christmas, my mind jumped to Brock. By now it was a habit, my thoughts wrapping around him without conscious intent. I'd never seen Brock in formal wear, nor had I danced with him. How would it feel to be taken into his arms for a waltz?

Millie's next words brought my mind away from my daydream. "Was it last year we thought Brock would ask Daria Somerset to marry him or the year before?"

"Last year." Anne paused to knot her thread. "Sometimes I still think he'll ask her. Dinna he dance two times with her at Dolly Morrison's wedding and ride in the same boat with her the day before the race?"

"Who's Daria Somerset?" I asked, trying to keep my voice nonchalant.

"She's a lovely lass," Anne began.

"Not half as lovely as you," Millie interrupted. "She and Brock have been friends forever. Pretty as she is, she's had several offers for marriage, but my friend Victoria says Daria turned them down. We both think she's waiting for Brock to propose."

Her words struck at my confidence. Although I was well aware that Brock had numerous admirers, none had borne a name. Somehow just having a name gave this one more substance. Daria Somerset. I wrapped my tongue around it, disliking the taste, even as I tried to picture this faceless young woman. Lovely, Millie had said, then pretty. The hope I'd gathered in the rainstorm dried like dust around my heart.

Not wanting my concern to be noticed, I questioned Millie about the New Year's dance.

"It's a wonderful affair with a full orchestra and everyone dressed in their best. All the prominent people are there with enough of the rest of us to make a large crowd."

"Will Robert and Olivia be there?"

Millie pursed her pretty lips. "They always have been in the past." A delightful giggle escaped her mouth. "Your sister-in-law is such a snob. I had no liking for her before, and after hearing about her from you, I have even less. You're well rid of the bluenose, and with so many people, I doubt you'll even have to speak to her."

Instead of fretting about Daria Somerset or Olivia, I set my mind down more pleasant paths as Millie and I discussed ball gowns and the latest fashions.

"It will be such fun," she assured me.

Imbued with her optimism, I determined to enjoy myself. If Brock's feeling for Daria Somerset were taken seriously, wouldn't he have proposed marriage before now? *Yes,* I told myself. Then yes again.

* * *

Now that summer was fully upon us, Anne limited the time she spent working in her garden to those hours of earliest morning or after the sun went down.

Lured by her pleasant company and the beauty of the little Eden, I often joined her, learning how to snip off the flowers' spent blooms and sometimes weeding. I came to look forward to the pleasant interlude of fresh cool air and the songs of colorful birds. Millie studiously avoided the garden, preferring to be out with the horses, but Callie often accompanied us, her neat rows of vegetables separated from the formal garden by a wooden fence. We worked together, the scrape of hoe and snip of scissors blending with cheerful bird songs. Sometimes Anne and I became so engrossed in our work that we forgot to stop for breakfast. Not Callie. She knew exactly when breakfast was on the table.

One such morning, I glanced up and saw Callie lean her hoe against the fence and come through the gate. Nearing me, she suddenly stopped. "Snake, missy. Don't move!"

I shrank instinctively into myself, my eyes searching wildly for the snake. At first I saw nothing except the green leaves of the Jupiter's beard and the red-brown soil where I'd been weeding. A slight movement drew my gaze to the ground where I'd bent to pull a weed just seconds before—the slithery brown color of the serpent blending with the dirt, the leaves a patchwork of shadows over a coiled body.

I swallowed a strangled lump of fear, wanting to turn and run when I saw its dark eyes and flickering tongue, but Callie's, "Don't move," which she'd repeated a second time, won out.

Like me, Callie hadn't moved, both of us watching the reptile in fascinated horror. Anne had frozen, her arms and the raised hoe like statues against the rays of morning sun. Callie began a chant, the words unintelligible, her tone low and singsong.

The brown, coiled snake moved, its darker head lifted and alert. Shivers pricked my skin and raised the hair on my arms and neck. I was certain the snake would strike. *Please, God, help!*

The snake seemed to be listening to Callie's chant, head raised, its tongue darting in and out. Then slowly, the ropelike body uncoiled and slithered away, a leaf quivering as the snake passed. Its long, unwound length both surprised and terrified me. I jumped back as soon as the snake's tail disappeared into the foliage.

Anne remained where she was. Then like a caged beast suddenly freed, she slashed with the hoe at the snake, the strokes a frantic chopping.

"Devil!" she cried. "Horrid devil! Ye'll no' be killin' any I love ever again." The frenzied chopping continued long after the snake was dead, as if a festering hatred had been loosed, the anger too volatile to be quickly contained.

"Missus," Callie's voice interjected. "Snake dead now. Snake dead."

Anne slowly lowered her arms, her body convulsing in shudders as she turned away. "I hate them . . . hate them," she sobbed. Then in a quieter voice, "Dear heaven, what have I done?"

I went to her, trying not to look at the blood and bits of flesh that clung to the hoe and the fragmented pieces of the snake that lay near her feet. I gathered Anne's trembling body into my arms and pulled her close while Callie took the hoe from her hands. "You've done what any woman who's lost a child to snakebite would do. You've killed it, and glad I am that you did."

Anne shuddered again.

"You be all right. Soon Missus be all right," Callie reassured.

I reached for Callie's hand. "Thank you, Callie. Your warning . . . the chant." I swallowed through my shock. "You saved my life."

Callie nodded, the expression in her dark eyes telling me that despite her calmness, she'd been frightened too.

Putting my arm around Anne's waist, we slowly made our way to the house. "Thank heaven for Callie," I whispered, "and what you did too."

Anne shuddered again. "If only I'd gotten there in time to save little Alice." She began to cry in harsh, wracking sobs, tears running down her cheeks. Until then I'd never thought of Anne as anything but a capable, vital woman, but the way she leaned on me and the uncertainty of her steps told me she was more upset and vulnerable than I'd supposed.

Min and Millie quickly took over. Anne was made to sit with her feet up, and both of us were offered cups of strong tea. I pulled my chair next to Anne's, taking her cold hand in mine so I could rub it. Little by little, she ceased to tremble, and the color came back into her cheeks. Even so, the frightening events of the morning never went far from our minds.

Callie returned to the kitchen after disposing of all signs of the snake. Despite this, it was several days before I could make myself go to the garden, and even longer before I felt comfortable enough to search among the flowers for weeds and spent blooms. A serpent had invaded our little Eden and left marks of unease on the women who'd been there.

FIFTEEN

The time before Christmas passed more quickly than expected, for there was much to fill my hours. Each morning I went to the paddock to visit Lass. She now came as soon as I called her, liking the slices of apple I brought and growing used to my voice. As I watched her, I wondered if Daria Somerset owned a horse and if she enjoyed riding. The question acted as a further goad, and I realized my desire to overcome fear was balanced by an equal need to win Brock's admiration.

* * *

The Sunday before we left for Melbourne, another church service was called. As before, we met in the sitting room with the chairs arranged in a circle and all of us dressed in Sunday attire.

When Brock said a prayer, my mind was more on him than on his words. Of late, my mind seemed always to be on the man who stood before me, wondering if the warmth I glimpsed in his eyes would ever materialize into words. While we made a quavering attempt at a hymn, his gaze met and held mine. He cared. I knew he cared. Too distracted to think, I stumbled through the words, aware that Millie watched us and smiled.

When Anne stood to read from the Bible, I listened with interest, wondering if more verses would be aimed at Brock's ears. Instead, Anne chose a text from 2 Timothy 1:7. "For God hath not given us the spirit of fear; but of power, and of love, and of a sound mind."

While her Scottish brogue rolled over the comforting words, I realized the text had been chosen for me. What a dear, sweet woman. As I listened, her brogue seemed to change to the rounder accent of my mother. In my mind I heard her voice reassuring me when I'd been frightened by thunder. Tears stung my eyes, and I blinked to clear them. How peaceful and nice. Afterwards I thanked Anne.

"Ye are welcome." She paused and gave me a thoughtful look. "Would ye like to pick the text for one of our services? 'Tis Millie's turn next, so ye'll have plenty of time." Seeing me hesitate, she hurried on. "You won't need to read them—I always do. But we all take turns. Last time was mine. Today was Brock's. Ye needn't worry aboot choosin' wrong, for all God's words are good."

Put that way, I could hardly refuse. But it was today's scripture, not the one I would choose, that filled my mind as I returned to my room. Brock had chosen it. Surely that meant something.

I entered my room in a reflective mood. What Anne didn't know was that the only Bible I possessed had been my mother's. I'd seen her read it on numerous occasions, often doing so as she sat by my bed at night, the soft rustle as she turned the pages the last thing I heard before drifting off to sleep. She'd left her Bible on the table by my bed the night before her accident. Still dazed with grief and uncontrollable tears, I'd found the leather volume the next night and had fallen asleep with it tightly clasped to my chest, taking scraps of comfort from the lingering scent of Mother's perfume.

It had taken all of Mrs. Woolsey's persuasion to pry the Bible from my hands long enough to wrap it in one of Mother's gauzy shawls. "There now, love. Ya wouldn't want no harm to come to her Bible, now would ya? See, her shawl will keep it safe and cozy for ya. 'Tis what I'm thinkin' she'd like ya to do, keep it safe till yer old enough to read it yerself."

In the years since, I'd never opened her Bible. I'd unwrapped it often enough, but in my childish mind the essence of Mother had been trapped between the fragile pages. If I opened them, the last touch of her fingers would be lost forever, vanishing just as she had, never to return.

Wrapped in her pink shawl, the Bible had made the voyage to Australia and now lay in the bottom drawer of the tallboy at Tanybrae. After removing my gloves, I slowly opened the drawer and took it out. Closing my eyes, I held the soft bundle against my cheek. *Are you there, Mama? Do you still watch over me?*

I listened, longing for a reply. When none came, I sat down on the bed and unwrapped the book. As an only child, Mother had been pampered and made much of, according to Mrs. Woolsey. The rich leather binding and gilt lettering on the spine and cover gave evidence of her family's indulgence.

With reverent fingers I opened the cover, saw her name written in fine spidery swirls—*Charlotte Wycliffe,* which had been her maiden name. A slender piece of blue ribbon marked her place. Was it there she'd left off reading? Opening the book to the marker, I lifted it to my face and breathed in deeply. Mother's faint scent was suddenly there along with the curve of her smile and the sheen of black hair. Closing my eyes, I felt the touch of her lips on my cheek as she kissed me good night, heard the whisper of her skirt in gentle farewell. Tears misted my eyes, and I silently wept for the child bereft, the young woman now alone.

It was some moments before the words on the page ceased to swim before my eyes. Wiping my tears, I discovered that the ribbon marked a place in Matthew 7. Several verses had been underlined. I read the words aloud; then after a moment I read them again. "Ask, and it shall be given you; seek, and ye shall find; knock, and it shall be opened unto you: For every one that asketh receiveth; and he that seeketh findeth; and to him that knocketh it shall be opened." Why were the words familiar? Had Mother sometimes read them aloud as well? I closed my eyes while half-forgotten memories swirled through my mind—Mother reading from her Bible, then pausing to stare out the window, a soft smile on her face. "Yes," she'd whispered, "that's what I must do—Ask . . . knock." On another occasion I'd peeked in her sitting room from behind the door and found her kneeling in prayer. What answers had she sought?

I sat for several moments, remembering my mother's faith. Each night she'd helped me with my childish prayers, stressing their importance and admonishing me to trust God's love. After her death, I'd not only forgotten to pray, but I'd failed to turn to His book for guidance. Not once had I opened what had been precious to her, nor had I prayed except in moments of crisis.

Shame washed over me, and I knew that if God had granted Mother a chance to watch me from the vastness of heaven, she would be disappointed at my lack of piety. *I'm sorry, Mama.* I carefully set the Bible on the table. Starting tonight, I would read from it before I retired. I would pray too, not just when desperate, but on a regular basis like Sarah Hewitt and Anne McKade—and most of all like Mother.

* * *

Two days later we set out for Melbourne. The journey went well, and Millie's eyes were bright with expectancy as she stepped out of the carriage after Henry brought the horses to a halt at Mrs. Morrison's door. Anne was in fine spirits as well. I hadn't decided how I felt. Although I looked forward to the parties and ball, the news about Brock and Daria Somerset had dampened my enthusiasm, as did dread of accidentally meeting Robert and Olivia. *All will work out,* I told myself, and with Millie's bright chatter and Mrs. Morrison's warm welcome, it was easy to hope my stay in Melbourne would prove enjoyable.

Harriet Morrison was a heavyset woman, her steps slow and her voice a little wheezy. After embracing Anne and Millie, she turned to me with a smile, her plump hands reaching for mine. "Anne wrote of you, Miss Clayborne. I'm happy to have you join our little party."

"Thank you." I could see why Anne liked her, for everything about the woman spoke of kindness and caring, the trait further evidenced when she turned to Brock. "Don't think you can get away with just my hand to your lips," she said, and with that she enfolded him in a hug. "There, that's better." Stepping back, she looked him over. "I don't know what's wrong with young women nowadays. Why hasn't one snapped you up and attached her name with yours? If my Elizabeth weren't already settled with a husband and baby, I'd suggest she take a long look at you."

Brock laughed. "Elizabeth had ten years to look me over. Fortunately for us both, she saw that we didn't suit."

Harriet Morrison gave an exaggerated sigh. "Silly girl, but you can't blame a mother for trying." Turning to Anne, she linked an arm through hers. "Come see the new sofa I purchased last month . . . Millie, you and Miss Clayborne too. Brock and Henry can see to your luggage."

She led us into a white clapboard home trimmed with salmon-colored brick. Although smaller than Robert's home, it was comfortable and spacious. After the new sofa had been duly admired, she took us upstairs.

"I thought to put you in your usual rooms," Mrs. Morrison said, the wheeze in her voice more pronounced as we climbed the stairs. "Miss Clayborne, I hope you don't mind sharing a room with Millie."

The bedroom was as comfortable and spacious as the downstairs rooms. In no time we had unpacked and settled in. Since Brock had ridden horseback, there hadn't been opportunity for conversation with him on the trip from Tanybrae. I looked forward to seeing him at dinner and took extra pains with my appearance before I went downstairs.

"Brock asked me to make his excuses," Mrs. Morrison explained as we took chairs around her table. "Off to see some of his mates, he said, and that we're not to wait up for him."

I swallowed my disappointment. Did that mean Brock enjoyed being with his mates more than me? At least it was better than being with Daria, I supposed.

Millie grimaced. "In other words he's with Kip and Dennis. The three of them never know when to call it a night."

"Don't you like Brock's friends?" I asked.

"Well enough, but . . ."

"Yer wishin' Brock was with Christopher and that they'd decided to stay here instead of going out," Anne finished for her.

"Yes . . . no." Millie's protest ended in a giggle. "You know me too well, Mum. But I was hoping Chris would come by. Maybe he'll be at Victoria's party tomorrow night," she added hopefully.

* * *

Millie's wish came true. Not only was Christopher present, but he sought her out as his partner at charades. Millie was obviously taken with the young man. Although I thought him less handsome than Brock, he was attractive in a rugged way, with thick blond hair and eyes so light a shade of blue they appeared gray. I thought they made an attractive couple—Millie small and vivacious, Christopher tall and sure of himself.

As had been the case the night before, Brock wasn't present at the party. Although I was frustrated by his absence, I made a show of enjoying the evening. Thanks to Millie and her friend Victoria, I was introduced to many, included in conversations, and was not without a partner for refreshments and charades.

As soon as we arrived, several of the young women asked about Brock, their faces falling when they learned he was off with his mates. One in particular held Millie in conversation, plying her with questions, some concerning me. Not as slender as Millie, the young woman was nonetheless attractive, with pretty features and large hazel eyes. Her most striking feature was her hair—a mass of russet curls that glowed like copper in the lamplight. I suspected who she was even before we were introduced.

"This is my friend Jessamyne Clayborne," Millie said, making the introductions. "She's been staying with us the past month." Millie reached for my hand. "Jessamyne, this is Daria Somerset."

"It's nice to meet you," I said, making an effort to put warmth into both my voice and smile.

Daria's answering smile was stiff, but she made a show of saying all the correct things. I was conscious of her appraising look, as I'm sure she was of mine.

"Brock and I have been friends for ever so long," she said as if I'd voiced questions about their history. "We have a close relationship."

"How nice." I didn't want to spar with her or engage in much conversation, but neither did I wish to be impolite. I settled on what I thought was a neutral subject. "Do you live in Melbourne?"

Daria nodded. "For the last two years. Before that we lived on a spread not far from Tanybrae. Wooraronga. Perhaps you've heard of it since your brother and his partner purchased it from my father." The look she gave me was challenging, as if she waited to pounce upon my answer.

"I've heard of it," was all I said as I wondered if she'd been a frequent visitor at Tanybrae and if she and Brock had often gone riding.

Daria's eyes were full of questions too, but before they could be voiced, Millie took me off to be introduced to more of her friends. The rest of the evening passed pleasantly, but I wasn't disappointed to see it end. Since Brock had chosen not to attend, I found the company lacking. The only crumb of comfort I found in his absence was that he hadn't sought out Daria. But where did that leave me?

* * *

The next day Millie invited me to go shopping. "I need to buy new gloves for the ball, and with Christmas almost here, there are one or two things I wish to purchase."

Since Harriet Morrison's home was within walking distance of the shops, we chose not to take the carriage. It was a lovely summer day, with a soft breeze blowing inland from the bay to temper the heat. In such weather it was hard to remember it was Christmas. Where were boughs of evergreens and the crispness of snow?

The streets were crowded with carriages, and the shops did a brisk business. After helping Millie decide on a pair of gloves, she suggested we separate. "I want my next purchase to be a surprise," she teased.

Left to myself, I crossed the street and looked in the shop windows. Fortunately, I still had money left from my winnings at the race. I'd already embroidered Anne's initials onto two lacy handkerchiefs, and knowing of Millie's liking for ribbons, I'd selected several yards of grosgrain from the array of ribbon I'd brought from England. But for Brock I had nothing, and there was money in my pocket.

I wandered in and out of several shops. Unfortunately all that I saw was either too expensive or not to my liking. Only when I spied a bookstore did I take heart. Recalling the books I'd seen in Brock's bedroom, I went inside, immediately becoming aware of the faint scent of leather and pipe tobacco. Tall shelves of books stretched from floor to ceiling, the vast array a little daunting. After browsing for several moments, a journal with plaid binding caught my eye. How appropriate for a Scotsman. I opened it slowly, imagining Brock writing across the blank pages in a bold, flowing hand. It was the very thing for this man I adored.

After the journal had been wrapped in brown paper, I went in search of Millie, feeling extremely pleased with myself.

The next morning we gathered around the table for Christmas breakfast. Everyone was in a festive mood, and since Brock joined us, I felt a special surge of happiness.

"Merry Christmas," he said, looking at me instead of the others.

I smiled, savoring the moment while his eyes held mine.

He dropped a kiss onto his mother's cheek and did the same for Millie, taking her hands as she stood on tiptoes to receive his kiss. I wondered if he'd follow suit with me, but Mrs. Morrison and I only received an affectionate smile and a Christmas wish before he took his chair.

Instead of disappointment, I concentrated on the happy fact that he was with us instead of rushing off to be with his mates.

I wondered where they went, whom they visited, what they talked about so late at night. I didn't think Brock had a weakness for drink, but could he truly spend so much time talking about horses? While I filled my plate with scones spread with butter and marmalade as well as slices of ham, I remembered snippets of gossip about certain types of women whom men wined and dined in hope of sampling more of their favors. My heart sank. Surely not Brock.

Lifting my head, I encountered his gaze, one that conveyed happiness in seeing me across from him at the table. I gathered this warmth and held it close, giggling as often as Millie in response to Brock's teasing.

After breakfast, Harriet excused herself to attend church. "Are you certain you don't wish to accompany me?" she asked Anne.

"You know how we McKades are when it comes to attending church," Anne replied. She turned to me. "But Jessamyne is free to go with you if she'd like."

I shook my head. Although I'd looked forward to attending a Christmas church service, loyalty to the McKades kept me at their side. More than that, I was curious to see how they celebrated Christmas.

I followed them into the parlor. Instead of gathering around a cozy fire for the reading of Christmas scriptures, we sat with the windows opened, a chorus of birds from Harriet's garden our choir, and instead of a minister, Brock's deep voice reading the words from Luke. My eyes remained on him as he read, admiring the strongly defined planes of his handsome features, the ease with which his deep voice formed the words. "And she brought forth her firstborn son, and wrapped him in swaddling clothes, and laid him in a manger; because there was no room for them in the inn."

Brock's voice slowed when he finished reading. "May we remember our Lord and feel of His love on this day that we celebrate His birth."

My amen joined the others, and a feeling of peace stole over me. Was this not the day we honored Christ? Instead of worrying and fretting about Brock, I needed to concentrate on the true meaning of Christmas.

"I'm afraid Harriet thinks we're nae better than heathens for staying away from church." Anne sighed and looked at me. "'Tis no' that we doona believe in Christ, but only that some of the preachin' is such that we canna hold to it. The churches have all gone astray . . . fallen away." She leaned forward and fixed me with her gaze. "Ye must'na think ye must hold to us though. Yer free to choose yer own church, just as Harriet does. I should have told ye sooner so ye could have gone with her if 'twas yer wish."

"It was not my wish. Like you, I am searching." In saying the words, I realized their truth. Until I knew more of organized religions, I felt no desire to place one above the other.

A glimmer of something passed between us that drew me more firmly into the family circle. "Good," she said. Animation lifted her lips as she looked around the circle we'd formed with our chairs. "I have a Christmas remembrance for ye. One I hope 'tis to yer likin'." She reached into her reticule and withdrew three small parcels wrapped in tissue paper. "Open them together, for they're all alike."

I opened mine amid a rustle of paper. Like Brock's and Millie's, it was a bookmark trimmed with ribbon, my name embroidered in pastel silk down the linen center.

"Since yer all readers I thought to make ye somethin' ye could use and remember me by."

"Thank you." I took Anne's hand and squeezed it. "I have a present for you in my room."

Excusing myself, I ran upstairs to get my parcels. By the time I returned, Brock and Millie had exchanged presents with each other and their mother—brushes and pots of paint for Anne, a fan for Millie. The sudden manner with which they broke off talking when I entered the room made me suspect I'd been the subject of their conversation. Did they pity me for being estranged from Robert, or was it something else?

Feeling awkward, my voice came out stiff and unnatural when I spoke. "What I have for you is insignificant when compared to all you've given me these past weeks, but I hope you know they come with affection and deep appreciation."

Anne exclaimed over the handkerchiefs, and Millie did the same with the nest of gaily colored ribbon. "You are a dear," she declared. "How well you know my weakness for pretty things."

I could hardly wait for Brock to open the journal. I watched him unwrap the paper, his tanned fingers blending with the brown paper—watched his brows lift when he saw the plaid cover, then raise again when he opened it and saw the pages were blank.

I read his question when his eyes met mine. "You live a very interesting life at Tanybrae. Now you'll have something to record it in."

"You think my life is interesting, do you?" Both his smile and voice were warm.

"I do."

His smile stretched wide. "Thank you. I've never thought to record my days. But this . . ." He nodded. "What a splendid idea. Thank you."

His words and the way he looked at me made the color rise to my cheeks. The color came again when Brock reached behind the door to retrieve a long parcel. "Merry Christmas," he said, handing it to me.

At the same time, Millie offered me her gift.

"Which shall I open first?" I asked, though my fingers itched to tear the paper away from Brock's

"Mine, of course," Millie said.

I sat down on the sofa, Brock's parcel propped against the gathers of my burgundy skirt while I pulled the wrappings from Millie's present. Inside I found a hair ornament made up of a cluster of claret flowers. "It's lovely."

"Now you see why I asked you to wear your burgundy skirt. Here, let me fasten it in your hair." I sat while her fingers worked to secure it around the upsweep of my curls. "There," she breathed, stepping back to admire the results. "I knew you'd look lovely."

I glanced at Brock who watched with amusement. "Will it do?" I asked.

"Most certainly. Our Millie doesn't lack in taste." The softness in his eyes told me he found more to admire than the cluster of claret roses, however. "Now mine," he prompted.

Excitement warred with curiosity as I unfolded the wrapping and found a pair of kid gloves nested around a riding crop. "Oh," I whispered.

"Do you like them?" A hint of worry edged his voice.

"Yes . . . very much." Too overwhelmed for speech, I slipped my hand into one of the riding gloves, felt the richness of the leather as I pulled it more snuggly around my fingers. It fit perfectly, as if Brock had memorized the size of my hand.

Brock leaned forward and touched my gloved hand, the pressure of his touch pulsing through the leather. "Yes . . . I felt sure they'd fit."

When I raised my eyes to meet his, the shimmer in their blue depths obscured Anne's and Millie's faces and tangled with the gossamer threads of love around my heart.

Millie's hand and voice intruded into the fragile moment as she lifted the riding crop out of the wrappings. "Look, Brock gave you this too."

I took the whip from her to admire the intricately carved handle, but it was to Brock that I spoke. "The gloves . . . the whip, they're both lovely. Thank you." Then, in an attempt to put things back on a more comfortable course for the onlookers, I added, "You don't seem to have any doubt that I'll ride, do you?"

"No." But his eyes said more, their steadiness burrowing deeply into the threads around my heart to whisper that I mustn't doubt his feelings either.

* * *

Brock remained at home for the remainder of Christmas day—a fact that brought everyone pleasure. This was something I'd never noticed before, the way a man's presence adds spark and verve to an occasion. As for me, I felt as if I danced through the rest of the day, my feet scarcely touching the floor, my heart as light as the rolls we ate at Christmas dinner.

I'm certain my giddiness showed, but on that wonderful afternoon I had no thought for discretion, wanting instead to bask in the fact that Brock addressed most of his remarks to me over dinner and made certain it was me, not Millie, who sat next to him when we retired to the sitting room.

"It's so good to have you home," Millie declared as we joined Harriet around her piano for singing carols. Our pleasure in the day was such that it didn't matter that our singing was mediocre or that Harriet's fingers stumbled as she pressed the keys.

That night, although I supressed the impulse to tuck the riding crop under my pillow, I tried on the gloves for the second time.

Watching me admire their fit, Millie spoke in a quiet voice. "You like them, don't you?"

"Yes . . . very much."

The smile she gave me hinted of a secret, but instead of revealing it she gave me a quick hug. "I'm glad. Glad, too, that you and Brock have become friends. For a while I feared you didn't like him."

"It just took us a while to grow used to each other," I hedged.

Millie laughed and gave me another hug. When she released me, her eyes were full of questions—ones I was grateful she didn't ask.

* * *

Brock was preparing to leave when Millie and I went down to the breakfast room the next morning. He paused when he saw us, his eyes on me, not his sister.

"You're looking lovely today, ladies," he said.

"Thank you," I said.

Millie smiled her appreciation, but then realizing Brock was leaving, frowned. "Surely you're not off already. Have you forgotten it's Boxing Day?"

"No." Brock picked up his hat, his eyes still on me. "I'd like very much to stay, but I have business that can't wait."

"Business?" My voice mirrored my disappointment even as I wondered how he could have business when all the establishments were closed for the holiday.

Millie was bold enough to ask.

"Those are not the businesses I need to visit." Grimness edged his voice and made me wonder again where he was going. Then he gave me a regretful smile, one that made me forget everything except that I was in his presence. "I'm truly sorry. I'd much sooner stay." With that he put on his hat and quit the room, taking much of my happiness with him.

Millie turned disappointed eyes to her mother. "What would take Brock away on Boxing Day? You don't think it's some woman, do you?"

"No." Anne's voice, like Millie's, held regret. "'Tis no' a woman but the need to find Jeremy Moulton or the jockey that takes him away. He means to spend his time in Melbourne lookin' and askin' questions. Kit and Dennis are goin' with him . . . as will Chris after he pays ye a visit." Anne's voice turned more cheerful. "See, 'tis not all lost. According to Brock, Chris is right eager to see ye again."

This news cheered Millie, and hearing that Brock was looking for Jeremy Moulton, not chasing after an admirer, made me feel better as well. I spent a pleasant hour helping Millie decide what to wear. Her steps were quick when she went downstairs in response to Christopher's knock, her gray eyes bright when she saw he'd brought a nosegay of flowers.

Anne and I pretended interest in a magazine while Millie and Chris talked in low voices at the other end of the sitting room. When Chris prepared to leave, he made Millie's day complete by asking Anne if he could call on Millie again.

"Ye know yer always welcome," Anne responded, the expression on her face as pleased as Millie's.

The door had scarcely closed before Millie turned to us. "Besides wanting to call again, Chris asked me to save all the waltzes for him at the New Year's Ball. Oh, Mum!" For a moment Millie seemed at a loss for words. "Can you believe I finally have a beau?"

"And all this time I've been worryin' ye would end up on the shelf with the old maids." Anne chuckled. "If ye believe that, yer denser than I thought. There's no' a prettier nor sweeter lass and 'tis more'n yer mum who think so."

I was pleased for Millie, but a part of me worried for myself. At twenty-one I was neither married nor did I have an official suitor. Then I recalled the look in Brock's eyes as he'd gazed at me on Christmas morning. *Patience,* a voice whispered.

Happiness took me through Boxing Day visits to the McKades' friends, making it possible for me to converse with and listen to Daria Somerset with scarcely a twinge of annoyance as she talked endlessly of Brock. Part of my happiness came from the fact that, as yet, Brock hadn't called upon Daria, nor had he given her a beautiful pair of kid leather gloves.

* * *

The following day I asked Millie if Henry could drive me in the carriage on an errand.

"Yes . . . of course." Her expression burst with unasked questions.

"Please don't think me rude for not inviting you to go with me, but this is something I must do alone."

"Of course," she repeated and immediately called for the carriage.

It wasn't until I was in the vehicle that I let myself think of what I intended to do. "Rathdown Street," I instructed as Henry prepared to close the door. His brow lifted when he recognized the address where he'd gone to tell Robert that I hadn't drowned.

The desire to look beautiful for Brock sent me to Robert's home. Before Father's death I'd been fitted for a new ball gown, one I'd only worn once. Its striking peacock color and sweeping style had made me stand out. Wishing to gain Brock's admiration at the New Year's Ball, I wanted to wear it again.

Since I'd left the gown at Robert's, I was unsure of how things would be, especially when going there put me at risk of meeting Olivia.

Determination sat beside me in the carriage and followed me to the front door. Polly had been my accomplice when I'd left, but who would help me now?

Taking a deep breath, I lifted the knocker. *Olivia can't eat you,* I assured myself, but another voice reminded me she could refuse to admit me to her home.

The door opened at my second knock, Polly's dark eyes widening in surprise. "Miss Clayborne. How nice to se ya. Won't ya come in?"

"Thank you, Polly, but it might be better if I wait outside. That is, if I could persuade you to help me?"

"I will if I can, but—" She threw a quick look over her shoulder, and when she spoke her voice came low. "Mrs. Clayborne was right angry at me when ya left. 'Twern't pleasant for any of us for a few days. Now with Christmas and all, she's nicer." Polly giggled. "That is if ya could ever call the woman nice." Moving so she and the door prevented those inside from seeing me, she asked in a conspiratorial tone, "What's it ya want me to do?"

"Do you remember the blue ball gown you admired?"

"How could a body forget somethin' that lovely?"

"Exactly. Could you get it from the wardrobe?"

Concern filled Polly's eyes "'Tain't in the wardrobe for me to bring. Like I said, Mrs. Clayborne was fit to be tied when ya left . . . so mad she ordered everything of yers to be throwd out in the dust bin."

My hopes plunged. "No."

"She was somethin' else, I tell ya. Scared me and Dot half to death." Polly paused and threw a nervous look over her shoulder. "Of course, we had to do what the missus said, but—" Another nervous giggle escaped her lips. "All except for yer ball gown, that is. There were no way I was agoin' to let somepin' that pretty end up in the dust bin."

I leaned close. "Where is it?"

"Wrapped in a sheet and under me bed. Dot knows about it, but I swore her to secrecy."

I laughed and gave her a quick hug.

Olivia's voice cut through my laughter. "Who's at the door, Polly?"

"It . . . it's only—"

Olivia was at the door. "What are you doing here?" she demanded.

Polly's unease jumped to my shoulder. I made an effort to quell it. "Good day, Olivia." The coolness in my voice surprised me. "I've come to retrieve some of my things."

Polly edged away from the door, her eyes sending a silent appeal.

"What nerve," Olivia responded. "Nerve won't get you anywhere with me, however. As for your belongings, I told the maids to throw them out." Olivia flicked her hand for emphasis. "Gone they are, and I advise you to do the same. You're no longer welcome in my home, Jessamyne. Not only have I washed my hands of you, but so has your adoring brother." She gave a contemptuous laugh. "You would be wise to think before you burn your bridges next time, young lady. Even Neville Bromfield thinks you acted imprudently. Unfortunately for you, I took pains to make sure that bridge has been burned as well."

Rather than respond, I watched Polly hurry toward the back stairs. Suddenly, I understood her silent message. She'd gone to retrieve my gown. Knowing the errand would take a few minutes, I stalled for time. "Did you and the children have a happy Christmas?"

"What?" Olivia looked at me as if I'd taken leave of my senses. "Oh . . . I see. Well, being pleasant won't get you any further than your nerve did. Didn't you hear me say you are no longer welcome? No chit of a young thing is going to invade my home and try to tell me what to do. Oh no. I've had quite enough of that."

"Then I will bid you a good day." With head held high, I lifted my skirt and went down the front steps.

The sound of Olivia's "Good riddance" followed me as the door slammed shut. Taking a long, steadying breath, I strove for composure in case Olivia watched from the window. If the truth be told, I was more upset by her spiteful attitude than I cared to admit. "Burned bridges" and her contemptuous "adoring brother" had struck close to my heart. *Dear Robbie, I never wanted it to end like this.*

Swallowing the need to cry, I made my way toward the carriage where Henry waited by the horses. "I'll only be a few minutes more," I explained, for as yet there was no sign of Polly.

"No worries." Henry's cheerful voice lifted me, and as if his voice had conjured up Polly, she came around from the back of the house.

"Here it is, Miss. Just like I told ya, wrapped up all nice and tidy in one of the sheets."

I took the gown from her arms. "Thank you, Polly. I shan't forget your kindness and help."

"Wasn't nothin', and I'd do it again should the need come."

"You're a dear." I gave her a quick hug. "Hurry back before you're missed."

"Yes'm." Nodding, she smiled and hurried back to the house.

Lifting the bulky wrapping of my gown, I was glad for Henry's helpful hand as I climbed into the carriage. Settling back into the soft cushions, I gave a satisfied sigh. "I did it!"

Sixteen

I didn't take the gown from the protection of the pinned sheet until I reached the bedroom. I'd seen no sign of Millie when I came through the house, and I was glad for a few minutes to look at the ball gown alone. Was it as lovely as I remembered? And more importantly, would it hold Brock's eyes on the night of the ball?

Removing the sheet, I laid it on the bed to admire. Despite wrinkles, the peacock blue satin with alternating ruffles of lighter *crêpe de chine* was lovely. I ran my fingers over the bows that cascaded down the back of the skirt, the peacock satin a perfect foil for the lighter *crêpe de chine*. Tucked into the bottom fold of the sheet were long white gloves, satin slippers, and a hairpiece of flowers and feathers. Bless Polly. She'd thought of everything.

Thinking of Brock, I held the dress against me and studied myself in the mirror. Smiling at what I saw, I heard the door open.

"Oh," Millie whispered. "It's lovely, Jessa . . . the most beautiful gown I've ever seen. Wherever did you get it?"

While I told her about the dress and Olivia, Millie moved to touch the row of *crêpe de chine* that outlined the low-cut bodice, and she gazed in wonder at the cascade of bows down the back.

"It's truly beautiful. No wonder you risked seeing your sister-in-law." The smile she offered me seemed a little forced. "You'll be the talk of the ball. Everyone else will hardly be noticed."

"You know that won't be true. Look at you, Miss Millicent McKade. There's no one more fetching than you—your friend Victoria, too. There will be dozens of pretty young women to catch the eye."

Hoping that my words reassured her, I laid the ball gown back onto the bed. "I can't wait until tomorrow night. We can help each other with our hair and—" Millie's still-tight smile stopped me. "What's wrong? Did I do wrong to get my gown?"

She sighed. "Of course not." Her hug brought a return of her usual self. "If I had a dress as lovely as yours, I'd want to wear it too." With a shrug, she hurried to tell me that Brock and Christopher would be accompanying us to the dance. "They'll be going ahead in Chris's carriage. I think Chris arranged it."

"Now see who's going to be the talk of the ball," I teased.

Millie's giggle was so spontaneous and bright that I ceased to worry about my ball gown.

* * *

The night of the ball finally arrived. Mrs. Morrison's two maids were kept busy with four women to wait upon. Fortunately, Millie and I both had a talent for arranging hair. With an occasional sugges-tion from Anne, we were soon beautifully coiffed. Millie finished dressing first. Her gown, a soft shade of yellow, enhanced her rich chestnut hair.

Anne nodded in satisfaction. "Aye, I've always thought ye bonny, but tonight . . ." She stepped back. "There's the look of my mother in ye . . . a rare beauty she was and ye no' one whit less." She started from the room. "I've something for ye to wear tonight," she called over her shoulder.

Millie peeked at herself in the mirror. "Mum's a little free with her praise, but I suppose I'll do."

I stood beside her in my corset and chemise. "You'll do very well. More than well. Your gown is the very color for you, and I'm sure Chris will be more than impressed."

"I hope so." A mischievous smile touched her lips. Cocking her head to one side, she gave her reflection a wink. "Aye, a right bonny lass ye are, Miss McKade."

"What's that yer sayin'?" Anne asked as she came back into the room.

Millie blushed. "I was just talking nonsense."

"'Twas no nonsense if 'twas about ye being bonny." She stepped behind her daughter and draped a necklace around Millie's throat. "There," she said, fastening the clasp. "'Tis the very thing for ye."

A circlet of delicate topaz graced the gold links of the chain, their amber light catching the rays from the lamp.

"Mum . . . this was your mother's."

"Aye, and now 'tis yers. I know she'd want part of herself passed on to one who's so very like her." Anne turned Millie around and gently kissed her cheek.

"Oh, Mum—" Millie's voice caught as she embraced her mother.

"Now, none of that," Anne protested in an unsteady voice. "Ye'll muss yerself before the ball."

Millie touched the delicate strands of topaz. "Thank you, Mum. I'll cherish it always."

"I know ye will." Anne cleared her throat and turned her attention to me. "Now 'tis Jessamyne's turn. With two of us to help ye into yer gown, we'll have ye ready in no time."

Taking pains that the fabric didn't spoil the arrangement of my hair, they slipped it over my head. While Millie worked with the fastenings, Anne arranged the rows of gathers that edged the low neckline so the ruffles would cap my upper arms like little sleeves.

Anne stepped back to inspect their work. "Perfect. Yer gown looks as if 'twas made for a queen, and yer as lovely as any princess." Anne kissed me on the cheek. "I've nay to give ye but my love. I hope ye know 'tis given wholeheartedly."

The muscles in my throat tightened as I returned Anne's embrace. "Thank you . . . not only for tonight but for all of your love and kindness."

Only then did I look at myself in the mirror. I was excited at what I saw, for the peacock blue *crêpe de chine* seemed to add brightness to my eyes and luster to my hair, which was arranged in soft curls around my face. The nipped-in waist set off my figure to advantage as well. Surely it would be enough to make Brock forget all about Daria Somerset.

I turned to loop my arm through Millie's, but the wilted look on her face stopped me; the vivacity that had lighted her face just a moment before dimmed as if by a sudden cloud. Even to my eyes, her yellow gown had diminished, its simple lines and soft hue overshadowed by the vivid color and elegance of my own. *What have I done?* But it was too late to change. Subdued, I pulled on my gloves and picked up my fan.

Mrs. Morrison called up the stairs for the second time. "The carriage is waiting, and two handsome young gentlemen grow impatient."

Anne led the way downstairs, her erect form in a full-skirted gown of dove-gray satin giving her the appearance of a much younger woman. Millie followed, her head high as if she didn't care two pins that her gown wasn't stunning, for Chris was smiling up at her with a worshipful look on his face.

My awareness of Chris and Millie receded when Brock stepped from the shadows. For a moment he stared, his expression one of wonder and admiration.

"Two lovely young ladies," Harriet Morrison exclaimed.

"Yes indeed," Brock agreed, his eyes remaining on me.

I returned his smile, my gaze as admiring as his when I took in his broad shoulders fitted into a black coat with tails. The high white collar of his shirt tied with a dark cravat complemented his deeply tanned skin. I was clearly entranced, and so was Brock, his eyes continuing to hold mine.

The soft clearing of Anne's throat reminded us we weren't alone. Brock kissed his mother's cheek and lifted Millie's hand to his lips while telling Chris he'd be lucky to have so much as a waltz with Millie.

My heart gave a happy leap when Brock lifted my gloved hand and kissed it, his eyes looking deeply into mine before he released it. "What must I do to ensure that I have claim to most of your waltzes?"

"You have only to ask," I responded.

Brock tucked my hand into the crook of his arm to escort me to the waiting carriages. What else was said as Anne, Harriett, and Millie chatted excitedly, I can't recall. My mind and heart were tuned only to his touch and the pleasure I felt in being by his side as he helped me into my seat and smiled as he left for his own carriage.

* * *

The way to the premier's mansion was crowded with conveyances, the congestion and excitement much like the morning of the Melbourne Cup. When our carriage drew up in front of the imposing edifice, Brock and Christopher, who had ridden ahead, were waiting for us.

"What a lovely night for a ball," I said as Brock helped me down. "It's been more than a year since I've danced, and I'm looking forward to it."

"Remember you promised to save the waltzes for me."

I smiled up at him. "I could never forget."

We made our way up broad marble steps to tall double doors where colorful moths flitted around two enormous gaslights. Many guests had arrived before us—men in formal black tails escorting women in silks and satins with colorful ornaments in their coiffed hair.

The premier of Victoria and his wife stood at the entrance to the ballroom to greet the guests. While we waited in line, I saw Brock nod to some of the younger gentlemen and ladies. Although I saw no one who looked familiar, I was aware of the whispers and admiring glances sent in my direction. I met them with a polite half-smile, aware that Brock still kept my hand on his arm, and that, like me, he was aware of the interest and speculation. His arm tightened when a nearby woman spoke in a hushed tone.

"She's Robert Clayborne's sister. Don't you remember seeing her at the Melbourne Cup with Neville Bromfield?"

"Ah, yes. That's why she looks familiar, though if Olivia is to be believed, the chit takes on airs and can be shockingly rude. Olivia told me—" The woman put a fan to her face and whispered the rest to her friend.

My chin lifted, and I gave the women a cool glance.

By now we'd arrived at the arched entrance to the ballroom where the premier stood with his attractive middle-aged wife, a red ornamental sash outlining his slightly rotund form.

"McKade," he said. "That's a fine stallion you've got. I saw him at the Melbourne Cup." Our host turned a balding head to me, his mustached lips lifting appreciatively as his pale eyes looked me over. "Miss Clayborne, how nice to have you in our fair city. Perhaps if you're not otherwise occupied, you'll give me the honor of dancing with you later this evening."

Surprised, I murmured, "Yes," aware that Brock's arm had tightened again. When I gave him a reassuring smile, he relaxed, but my smile didn't prevent him from noting that I'd gained the attention of several other gentlemen as well.

I would be speaking less than truth if I said I didn't enjoy the attention. I'd known for some years that I was attractive, but that night in my peacock gown I felt stunning. Riding a cloud of elation, I laughed and talked to Brock and Millie with more vivacity than usual, not noticing that the more I did, the quieter Brock became, especially when two gentlemen approached and asked to be introduced.

Others followed, and before the music even began, my dance card was almost filled. After adding another name to it, I glanced up at Brock, intending to say I would save the rest of the waltzes for him. I found him looking toward the ballroom door with a scowl on his face.

Following the direction of his gaze, I saw the premier leading a dandified young man toward me.

"This is my son, Randolph," our host said when they'd reached us.

The son bowed low over my hand, giving me opportunity to see that his thick blond hair was beginning to thin at the crown.

"Miss Clayborne." His voice lingered over my name as his blue eyes admired me. Although not handsome, his bearing was confident and his thin lips smiled warmly. "Would you do me the honor of being my partner for the first dance?"

I looked for Brock, having purposely kept the first dance blank so he could fill it with his name. He'd turned and appeared to be enthralled with a young woman who'd joined him. Not wanting to appear rude, I murmured a soft acceptance.

After he'd signed my card with a flourish, the premier's son tucked my hand into the curve of his arm and followed his father, who, with a lift of his hand to the orchestra, led his wife to the center of the ballroom.

Polite applause and the strains of a waltz accompanied the couple as they circled the floor—the premier stately in black tails and starched shirt, his wife in flowing purple satin with a long train draped over her arm.

At his father's nod, Randolph placed his hand on my waist to send us in a gliding circle behind them. Smiling, I matched my steps with his, conscious of the watchful gaze of many who'd crowded the edge of the dance floor. With another nod from our host, others joined us until the ballroom was filled with a crush of waltzing couples.

Still on a cloud of elation, I laughed and responded to Randolph's conversation as much as the exertion of dancing would permit. Through it all I scanned the faces of the crowd for Brock, wishing it were his hand on my waist, his tanned face smiling down at me.

The first dance was but a preamble to many that followed as attentive, admiring gentlemen partnered me in graceful steps around the room. At first I enjoyed myself. What woman wouldn't, knowing she was one of the evening's brightest stars and that many vied for her attention? But where was Brock? Why hadn't he come to place his name on my dance card?

When I voiced the question to Anne, who sat with Harriet and some of her friends under the balcony, she shook her head. "I was but askin' Harriet the same. Usually by now he comes to partner me for a dance." She gave me a long, searching look. "For sure, ye haven't lacked for partners."

"I know, but I wanted to save—"

A male voice skillfully inserted itself into the conversation. "You wanted to save the next dance for me."

I turned and found Neville Bromfield standing behind me. The smile he gave me was engaging, and despite Olivia's claim that he had changed his mind concerning me, he seemed genuinely pleased to have found me. "I began to think I would never see you again. You have a way of disappearing . . . first from the ship, then from Melbourne. I believe we were to have dinner together before you so suddenly disappeared. That being the case, I think it warrants that my name is put next on your dance card."

I lifted my head and, uncertain of how to reply, merely nodded.

Those around us made way as Neville led me to the dance floor. Many were curious, for Neville Bromfield was well known. More than that, he was said to have the ear of the premier.

Putting my features into a semblance of enjoyment, I rested a gloved hand on Neville's shoulder and felt his own touch my waist. Then we were circling the floor, our steps matched, Neville's deft touch on my hand and waist confidently leading. He was an accomplished dancer, and under better circumstances I could have enjoyed myself. But all I could think was that he and Robert had probably caused Night Flyer to lose the race.

"Relax, Miss Clayborne. I promise not to scold you further about leaving Melbourne."

Only then did I meet his gaze. "Circumstances dictated that I leave on short notice."

"Circumstances in the form of Olivia?"

I nodded, relieved to find the smile he offered me held no censure.

"I suspected as much. One does not have to be long in your sister-in-law's company to realize she would be difficult to live with."

Remembering what Olivia had said about burned bridges, I thought it prudent to make no reply.

Looking pleased, Neville continued to guide us around the floor. As we passed one end of the ballroom, I met Brock's startled gaze. His eyes held mine for a fraught-filled second before his handsome features furrowed into a scowl.

His scowl gave me hope that was quickly smothered by guilt.

Neville had also seen Brock, and his next words referred to him. "Although I sympathize with your need to leave Olivia, I think your choice of destination was unwise. Brock McKade has a reputation for temper and rude behavior . . . not to mention that of a poor loser. Are you aware that he and his solicitor are trying to keep me from receiving the purse from the Melbourne Cup?"

I made a point of meeting Neville's gaze. "I am."

Hearing the coldness of my tone, Neville turned our conversation to the warmth of the evening and the number of people who attended the ball. Neville spoke some minutes on this last subject, concluding with, "Sometimes I think the premier grows careless in those he chooses to invite."

As he spoke, Neville glanced significantly to our left. Following his gaze, I saw Brock waltz past with a comely young woman in a pale blue gown. Fair in coloring, she laughed at something Brock said, her manner open and adoring.

Jealousy squeezed my heart, even as I wondered if the sight of me dancing with Neville had caused Brock a similar pain.

Not wanting Brock to read my jealousy, I turned my attention to Neville. "Tell me, do you have other horses besides Bruiser?"

"No, I leave the breeding of horses to the likes of McKade." Amusement and a hint of superiority threaded through his voice. "Bruiser is but a business investment like my speculation in land." He glanced significantly at Brock who was still in our area. "I'm not a man who takes kindly to being thwarted in my endeavors. Those who stand in my way soon wish they hadn't."

I realized his words had been spoken in the hope I would convey them to Brock. We were saved from further sparring with the ending of the waltz. As Neville was about to escort me back to Anne, I saw Robert and Olivia. It was useless to pretend I hadn't noticed them, for they were already upon us.

"Jessamyne, I didn't expect to see you here," Robert said. His manner was friendly, a sharp contrast to Olivia's stiff coldness. Without her telling me, I knew she wasn't pleased to find me with Neville. More than that, I knew she hadn't told Robert about my visit. Despite her claim that Robert had washed his hands of me, his warm greeting said otherwise.

Aware of it, Olivia cut in. "Where did you get that dress? Didn't I tell you—?" Realizing the hole she was about to step into, Olivia stopped.

"The dress is mine," I answered. "I brought it with me from England." Dismissing Olivia, I turned to Robert. "I'm in town with friends."

Robert nodded, and I sensed that seeing me with Neville pleased him.

I think Olivia sensed it too and looked for a way to destroy his pleasure. "I suppose by friends you refer to the McKades? Are you aware of the grief Brock McKade is causing Robert and Mr. Bromfield? Sticking his nose in their affairs and casting untrue aspersions about their character. How can you have the audacity to call them friends?"

My anger rose. "I don't think my choice of friends is any of your concern, Olivia." Not wanting to cause a scene, I glanced at Neville.

"I promised the next dance to Mr. Harper. Would you kindly take me back to those I came with?"

"My pleasure."

I smiled up at my brother. "Robbie."

Robert nodded, his manner and expression neutral.

When we reached the chairs where Anne and Harriet sat, Neville bowed over my hand. "Perhaps later this evening you'll find your dance card empty enough to allow me another dance."

"Perhaps." My tone, like Robert's, was noncommittal.

I didn't notice Millie until she whispered in my ear. "Was that not Neville Bromfield?" And before I could answer she warned, "Do have a care, Jessa. Remember Brock's temper."

"Brock." I gave a heavy sigh. "What happened, Millie? I thought he would ask me to dance."

"Sometimes his pride stands in the way of good sense."

"Pride?" I gave her a questioning glance.

"Aye," Anne said, getting up from her chair. Taking my arm she went on. "It's terribly warm in here. Why doona we step outside for a wee breath of fresh air?"

The crush of people was more than the ballroom could comfortably hold. Such didn't seem to deter anyone's enthusiasm. Nor did the heat, which, despite open windows and a surfeit of ladies' fans, was warm and uncomfortable. Punch bowls were placed in numerous places, and the press of people around them made it difficult for us to navigate the ballroom.

Once we were outside where flaming torches lit the terrace and grounds, Anne stopped and turned to face me. "Pride," she repeated. "'Tis a weakness of the McKades, one that's more curse than blessing." She grimaced. "His da was just as bad and sometimes did things he later regretted. Ye must have patience with Brock, lass."

I looked from Anne to Millie. "That's all very well to know, but I have no notion of what I've done to put such distance between us."

"As Millie said, 'tis his pride. When ye were at Tanybrae, ye were one of us. Tho' Brock's worked hard to make something of our name, the McKades are at heart but simple folk, ones who doona care overmuch for trappin's or society. But tonight—"

"Mum calls us 'fringe folk,'" Millie put in. "Those content to stay on the fringe of society. We dress well enough, and we like to think we behave well enough, but we're nowhere near the top of the heap. Not like your brother and his wife . . . not like you."

"I'm not—" I began.

Anne's voice cut past mine. "For sure yer not, and thankful we are. But the gown yer wearin' says otherwise. Top of the heap it cries, and ye like a princess with even the premier and his son falling at yer feet. Brock seein' it thinks ye've changed and remembers only that he's but the son of a poor Scottish crofter."

Suddenly everything was clear, Brock's reaction understood. Watching me respond to admiration, he'd mistaken my actions for other than they were. "How foolish of me." The words slipped out, my voice scarcely more than a whisper. "I wanted to catch Brock's eye. Instead—"

Millie laughed and took my hand. "There, you've finally admitted it. You do care for Brock . . . and any fool can tell he's head over heels for you."

"But you spoke as if Daria and Brock might be getting married."

"Only because I hoped you'd give some sign of how you felt."

Warmth came to my cheeks. "Did . . . did he put you up to it?"

"Goodness no. Brock keeps to himself when it comes to women. I can only tease him and hope he lets something slip."

"And he hasn't." My voice was both question and statement.

Millie's hand tightened on mine. "Not in so many words, but I know he's never given Daria more than an occasional box of bonbons, but with you . . ."

"Did ye not ken Brock carved the handle of the whip he gave ye?" Anne asked. "Just like his da he is with carvin' and surprises . . . pride and temper too, sad to say. But I've a notion ye'll find ways of handlin' them both." She fixed me with a smile. "'Tisn't just Millie that's put her hopes on ye and Brock. I've had my heart on it this past month or more."

I kissed Anne on the cheek. "I couldn't ask for dearer friends and allies. Thank you."

* * *

The ball continued with more dances and music. Although I didn't lack for partners, neither did Brock. As if that weren't enough, I spied him with Daria Somerset.

"There you are," Daria said to Millie. I knew it was me who'd caused her to join us, her happiness in at last having Brock by her side something she wanted me to witness.

Instead of meeting my gaze, Brock kept his eyes pinned on Daria. Only the knot of muscle in his tightly clenched jaw gave clue to his inner tension.

Although I had no interest in Geoffrey Maxfield, my next dance partner, I welcomed him when he came to claim me just as Brock led Daria onto the floor.

I pretended to enjoy myself, laughing at Geoffrey's humorous quips and making a valiant effort to keep my mind on him instead of Brock.

The hour grew late, and some of the dancers were flagging. Each time the orchestra struck up a new tune, I looked for Brock. Not once did he make his way in my direction. Anger pricked my emotions with such force that when I saw Neville Bromfield watching me, I didn't look away. I wasn't proud of my actions—encouraging a man I didn't like, but hurt and anger overrode good sense. I wasn't disappointed when Neville came to put his name on my dance card.

I pretended not to notice Anne's concerned look when he led me away. The night had taken me in a direction I hadn't planned, and although caution urged me to take care, the new role I'd accepted left me unsure of how to make a dignified exit. Instead, I smiled and chatted with Neville while we waltzed.

Then without warning, he swung me into an alcove with a punch bowl. "I prefer refreshment and conversation to dancing just now," he said by way of explanation. Taking a glass of punch from an attendant, he handed it to me and asked, "How long will you be staying in Melbourne?"

"The McKades plan to leave tomorrow."

"And you go with them?"

I nodded, not sure where the conversation was leading.

"Is there no way I can persuade you to stay longer? A fine dining establishment has recently opened on Collins Street. I would count it a favor if you'd be my guest there for an evening."

"I'm afraid the situation with Robert and Olivia precludes me from staying with them."

"I could put you up in the Grand Hotel," he countered. "I assure you that your acceptance of my offer will not compromise your reputation in any way. I seek only the opportunity to become better acquainted and enjoy the pleasure of your company over tea and a late dinner."

My heart gave a nervous bump. In a bid for time, I pretended interest in one of the dancing couples. "You are most kind, but I think we both know it would not do. It's best that I leave with the McKades."

Neville's mouth formed a hard line. "It seems I misjudged you. I thought you a woman of better sense than to be taken in by Brock McKade's supposed charm."

As if he had planned it, Brock danced into my line of vision, his arm on the waist of the same slender blond he'd been with earlier. Although he didn't acknowledge me, his anger was apparent when he saw me at the punch bowl with Neville.

"Anyone observing Mr. McKade tonight should realize he considers me as no more than his sister's friend. But even if I'd been taken in, as you say, I fail to see how that concerns you."

Neville laughed, the hardness leaving his mouth. "You have spirit, Miss Clayborne, something I admire as much as your beauty. Soft and pliant women have never been to my liking."

"Really?" I hoped the coldness in my voice conveyed my feelings.

Neville hurried on. "Jealousy isn't all that prompts my remark about McKade. Concern for your welfare plays a part in it too. It's well known that his father gained Tanybrae by questionable means, and Brock is known to be a fair copy of his father."

Anger rose in my throat. "I hadn't thought gentlemen put much credence in gossip, but since you do, you must be aware there's ample supply about you as well."

My thrust struck a nerve and set Neville's lips into a thin line.

"I appreciate your warning," I went on more gently. "It's a comfort to know there are those who feel concern for my safety and well-being."

My soft voice left Neville at a loss for words, and he made no protest when I suggested we return to Anne and Millie.

"That man can be insufferable," I whispered when Millie joined me.

"Then why in heaven's name did you consent to dance with him?"

Before I could answer, Brock was at my elbow. My heart gave a bump of pleasure and unease. Had my plan worked?

"I believe you promised to save some dances for me," he stated in a voice unlike himself.

"I did, but unfortunately you never came to claim them."

He held my eyes in a steady gaze, their expression a mixture of anger and purpose. "Are there any left?

"Only this one," I lied, for I'd given the last unclaimed one to Neville. Fearful that the gentleman who'd placed his name on my card would come to claim me, I suggested we go in search of refreshment. An uncomfortable silence tightened around us as we walked amid the crush of people. Thankfully, the orchestra struck up the first bars of a waltz before we reached the punch bowl.

Brock led me to the dance floor. My eyes lifted briefly when his hand reached for mine. Something shifted in their blue depths as my fingers rested on his shoulder, and his own touched my waist to lead me into the waltz. My heart vibrated with awareness of his closeness as I matched my steps with his.

Happiness lifted my eyes to his face. "I've waited all evening to dance with you."

"One wouldn't guess it from watching. You appear to have enjoyed yourself immensely and haven't sat out so much as one dance."

Laughter threatened to replace my smile. "Much as you did," I countered.

His lips twitched as if he wanted to do the same. "You noticed, did you?"

"Of course . . . just as you did." Laughter was now a fact. Taking courage, I hurried to add, "I think we'll both enjoy the evening more if we cease to play games."

"Was it a game you played when you danced with Mr. Bromfield?"

"It was." Tipping my head, I asked, "Didn't you guess I would much rather be dancing with you?"

"No." His voice was a growl and his hand on my waist pulled me closer. "Do you know how devilish tonight has been for me?"

"I saved five dances for you. Why did you stay away?"

"Because." His jaw clamped down, and for a second I feared he wouldn't go on. I waited, silently praying as he expertly led us past another couple. "Can we talk of this another time? Perhaps when half of Melbourne isn't watching?"

Having noted that both Millie and Chris were doing exactly that, I nodded. "Like you, I would welcome a bit of privacy."

The words had scarcely left my mouth when Brock swung me into an alcove. Making no pretense of needing refreshment, he simply gazed down at me.

Disconcerted by his closeness, I struggled to find something to say. "What would you deem an appropriate subject to discuss while others watch?"

"I can think of several . . . your beauty, for one. Have I told you that I admire your looks?"

I laughed. "You know you haven't. The highest compliment you've paid me was to say the roos and wallabies must now take cover since I've learned to shoot a rifle."

The rich timbre of Brock's laughter dissolved the last barrier between us. "I admire that as well, but I see that I make you blush, so perhaps we had best change the subject."

Though I would gladly have borne the embarrassment, the sight of Daria dancing with Geoffrey gave me pause. "Miss Somerset told me you and she have been friends for much of your lives."

"Since we were children," Brock replied. "And if you're going to next ask if I plan to marry her, the answer is no."

Mischief jumped to his eyes when I smiled. "What?" I asked, as if he had posed a question.

"Are you not going to commend me for my good sense as I did when you told me you didn't wish to marry Neville Bromfield?"

"Did I tell you that?" I asked with feigned seriousness.

"You most certainly did, although when I saw you twice dance with him I wondered if my memory failed."

"Had you but asked me to dance sooner, you wouldn't have needed to wonder."

His only reply was to take me into his arms and resume waltzing. What else was said, I don't recall—only the touch of Brock's hand on my waist as he pulled me a trifle closer, my fingers aware of him through the dark fabric of his coat. When I lifted my eyes to meet his, I read love in their blue depths. When my own answered in kind, his lips curved in a tender smile.

"Jessa." Never had my name been spoken with such sweetness, the sound like a soft echo to what I saw in his face. In that moment it was as if we were alone, the other dancers fading to fleeting shadows, the lilting music but a song sung by our hearts. Caught up in what eyes and touch conveyed, we continued to dance a few steps after the music stopped. Only then did Brock release my hand, but his hold remained on my waist, its pressure like a long, sought-after gift as we made our way through the throng to Anne and Harriet.

The two women had already risen in preparation to leave. Others were doing the same, lacy shawls arranged around bare shoulders, promises to write or visit exchanged between friends. Being with Brock had made me forget it was the last dance.

"I must say the two of ye looked well together," Anne remarked. "Like ye were meant for each other."

"My, yes," Harriet agreed, "and we weren't the only ones to notice."

Brock's only response was to grin and make a point of keeping his hand on my waist.

Just then, Millie and Christopher joined us. "Wasn't this a lovely evening? I don't know when I've enjoyed a ball so much." She arched her brows significantly at Brock. "By the looks of you and Jessa, we're not the only ones who enjoyed the last dance."

Brock chuckled in my ear as we began our slow progress toward the ballroom door. "Trust our Millie."

Most of those we moved among were strangers to me, but Brock nodded and spoke to several while keeping his hand on my waist. As we neared the door, a man bumped against him. Unease shot through me when I recognized Neville, his face scowling and unfriendly.

"If you know what's good for you, McKade, you'll keep your nose out of my affairs."

I felt the muscles in Brock's arm tighten, and when he spoke his voice was as taut as they were. "I'll do what's necessary to get to the bottom of that farce at the race. If such entails sticking my nose into your affairs, then you'd best get used to it."

"Have a care, McKade, and don't forget who you're dealing with. If your meddling doesn't stop, you'll soon wish it had." Although Neville kept his voice low, his barely suppressed anger made it possible for me to hear all he said.

"Is that a threat, Bromfield?" Brock's voice was as icy as Neville's.

"Take it any way you wish, but remember you've been warned." Neville's brown eyes flicked to me, their coldness like that of an arctic wind.

Tension vibrated around us, and I felt Brock's hand clench into a fist on my waist. For a second I feared he would plant it into Neville's scowling face. A taut second pulsed while the men measured each other, Neville looking ready to spring at Brock should the opportunity arise.

I heard the release of Brock's indrawn breath and felt his muscles relax. "You'd best take care as well," he said. "I'm not a man to give up easily." With that, Brock moved past Neville, Chris and Millie behind us, Anne and Harriet at my side. I caught a glimpse of Robert and Olivia standing next to Neville, my brother's expression as icy as Neville's. In that moment I realized that any reconciliation between Robert and me had forever passed. In allying myself with the McKades that evening, I'd built a final barrier between us.

Good-bye, Robbie, my heart cried, and I linked my arm through Anne's to keep her close to my side.

SEVENTEEN

The journey home in the carriage was strangely quiet; Harriet Morrison sat upright in the seat she shared with Anne while Millie fidgeted with her fan beside me. Even Millie's exuberance had been dampened by the exchange between Brock and Neville.

"At least we can be grateful Brock dinna lose his temper and hit the bloke," Anne sighed. "I think 'twas only ye being there that held him back."

Like Anne, I was grateful for Brock's control, though I knew it had not come easily, his natural instinct to fight tempered by the wish to please me. *Dear Brock.* I could hardly wait to have a private moment with him.

Arranging this didn't come easily, for Christopher and Brock were waiting to help us from the carriage, and Chris was in no hurry to leave Millie once he gained the sitting room. Anne and Harriet were no better and seemed bent on discussing every inflection of Neville's voice and what should be done about it.

"I think we'd best leave it until morning," Brock interrupted. "A good night's rest will give us a clearer mind."

After allowing Millie and Chris a moment alone on the doorstep, Anne started upstairs, yawning and saying she looked forward to bed.

When I looked at Brock, I was rewarded by his teasing smile. "I'm in need of some fresh air to settle my mind. Would you care to join me for a walk about the garden, Jessamyne?"

"What a lovely idea." I was hard put not to smile when Anne hesitated on the stairs, but the look she shot us held pleasure rather than censure.

Brock opened the door to a small walled garden. The night had cooled, and a slight breeze ruffled the branches of a tree. We walked without speaking until we reached a stone bench at the far end of the garden. The air was soft with the scent of creepers cascading over the wall, their bright pink blooms without color in the moonlight. The twisted branches of the old fig tree arched in a canopy over the bench, the leaves a dark pattern against the moon-washed sky.

All of my romantic feelings surfaced, making me aware of Brock's tall figure and the increased tempo of my pulse. Still not speaking, he turned to face me, his white shirt catching the soft glow from the moon. When his fingers brushed my cheek, I didn't move or breathe, my senses tuned to his touch.

Slowly cupping my chin, his face moved close to mine. "Do you know how many times I've regretted not kissing you that night on the veranda?"

"No." My voice was low and unsteady as my nerves stretched, my fingers longing to reach him.

"Often . . . so often." He bent his head, lips soft on mine, his movements deliberate, as if he wanted to prolong and savor the kiss, just as I did.

I gathered his closeness to my heart as his lips moved to my cheek, then my eyelids, his voice a soft whisper of love.

"There," he whispered in an unsteady voice, "This is where I want you to be . . . to stay, but—"

"But what?" I asked, my head pillowed against his shoulder.

"I'm sorry about tonight . . . the way I acted. But the sight of you looking like a princess with the premier and all those men wanting to dance with you made me think I'd misjudged you . . . that in your heart you longed for wealth and the trappings of society."

I shook my head, wondering how he could think I could prefer such things to him. "No . . . only you."

Moonlight bathed the sharp angles of his handsome features as they softened with love. "You're certain?"

"Very certain. The fact that I'm unwed doesn't come from lack of opportunity but because my heart was never touched." I ran my fingers along his cheek, felt the firmness of his jaw, not quite believing I was able to touch him. "Until I found you," I added.

I was caught again in his arms, felt the pressure of his lips on mine, their tenderness saying what he hadn't yet spoken, but hoped he soon would—that he loved me dearly and wanted me for his bride.

Later we talked of other things, asking questions and receiving answers to puzzles we'd wondered about. My relationship with Neville had to be examined again, along with his with Daria Somerset.

"In all the years I've known Daria, I felt nothing stronger than friendship. Once or twice I tried to pretend it was more, for everyone was anxious for me to tie the knot." His lips lifted in a smile as we sat, shoulders touching and his fingers wrapped tightly around mine. "Each time that I thought perhaps friendship in marriage could be enough, something stopped me."

He paused and gathered me into his arms so that my head rested against his. "I've thanked God many times that I listened to my heart instead of others. I began to think I'd never find someone to love until you walked into our room at the Grand Hotel and I realized who you were."

I remembered that morning and my awareness of him.

"The rest is history," he went on, "though tonight I almost let my pride make a mess of things."

"Hush." I lifted my head and kissed his cheek. "It's enough that we're finally together."

His lips told me that he agreed, as did the quickened rhythm of his heart as he held me close and whispered his love.

* * *

It was late when I slipped into the bedroom. The room was filled with shadows interspersed with shafts of moonlight filtering through thin curtains. I leaned against the door, clinging to the memory of Brock's lips on mine, the feel of his arms as he held me.

Millie's voice brought me back to my surroundings. "I'm not asleep, so don't think you must tiptoe around. Besides, I knew you'd need help getting out of your gown."

"You're a dear. I was afraid I might have to sit in a chair and wait until morning."

Millie giggled. "It would serve you right for staying out so late." She left the bed, a gray outline as she struck match to wick and lit the lamp. In its yellow glow I saw the questions dance in her eyes, her cheeks pink with excitement. "You and Brock must have needed a generous amount of fresh air. Only my high regard for you kept me from peeking out the window."

"You wouldn't!" I protested, not wanting to share the tender moments with Brock with anyone, not even Millie.

"I promise I didn't, though I was sorely tempted. Did you know curiosity is the bane of the McKade women?"

"No, but I sincerely thank you for not giving in to it."

Millie began to unfasten the hooks on my gown. "Your dress was the envy of every woman at the ball. Mum said she even heard the premier's wife comment on it."

"It is lovely, but I would gladly have exchanged it to have Brock dance with me as often as Chris danced with you."

"I still can't believe it happened . . . me with a beau." Millie hung my ball gown in the wardrobe and pirouetted in a circle around me. "Such a lovely, lovely evening," she exalted. Coming up behind me she whispered, "Tell me, did Brock kiss you when you were in the garden?"

"Millie!"

Her laughter floated around us. "I only asked because Chris—" Fingers flew to her mouth. "There . . . I almost told you." As if she feared she'd confide something she'd later regret, she danced to the lamp and blew out the flame. After we settled in bed, Millie gave a long sigh. "How will I ever sleep?"

I wondered the same, my mind eager to recall each word and emotion I'd felt in Brock's arms.

Giggling, Millie turned onto her side. "You still haven't told me if Brock kissed you."

"And I won't. You'll have to be content in knowing your brother has made me gloriously happy."

* * *

I awoke early, my mind no longer satisfied with dreams when reality was so much nicer. I touched my lips, thinking that only a few hours before, Brock's kiss had warmed them. I wanted to savor the memory of our time in the garden, even as the need to see Brock urged me to hurry and dress. I quietly slipped out of bed.

Despite my care, Millie stirred and stretched. "Was it a dream, or did Chris truly dance most of the night with me?"

"It wasn't a dream," I laughed. "He was far more attentive than Brock was with me." I paused and poured water into the flowered basin. "Until later, that is."

Millie giggled as I washed my face. "And now you can't wait to see him again." At my nod, she left the bed to hug me. "You know it pleases me . . . you and Brock. I've wished it for weeks. Mum too. There's no one we'd sooner he marry."

"You do have a way of trying to rush things."

"True." She paused to empty the basin and pour fresh water into it. "Even so, I'm usually right. I saw the way Brock looked at you when he thought no one was watching. And you were just as bad. It took great control not to march Brock up to you and demand that he say what he felt."

I reached into the wardrobe for my pink dress. "I'm very glad you didn't. Brock's way was much more satisfying."

The talk went on in similar fashion while we dressed and arranged each other's hair. "There," Millie declared when we'd finished. "Brock will be hard-pressed not to kiss you as soon as he sees you."

Wrapping her words around my happiness, I hurried downstairs with Millie. We found Brock and Anne at the breakfast table, their faces serious. When Brock saw me, he pushed back his chair and came to me.

"You look very fetching, Jessa. Did you sleep well?" He took both my hands in his, his eyes and smile warm as he looked me over.

At his touch, my heart gave a happy jump, my smile stretching wide at the sight of his handsome face so near that I could reach up and touch it if I took the notion. His nearness coupled with love made my breathing quicken. "Yes . . . I mean no. I was—"

"Like me," he chuckled.

A tiny noise from Anne reminded us we were not alone. "It seems none of us slept well, and glad I am that some of ye slept with smiles on yer faces, for my own was creased with worry. As I was but sayin' to Brock, I have serious misgivings about Mr. Bromfield and the threats he was makin'. From gossip I heard last night, he has powerful friends and—"

"You're not to worry, Mum. I plan to meet with Mr. Whitney-Smyth this morning to let him know what Mr. Bromfield said." Dropping my hands, Brock guided me to my chair, his hand lingering on my waist as if loathe to leave and take his place on the other side of the table. "For now, let's enjoy each other and our breakfast."

It wasn't difficult to do, for Millie was in high spirits too. Smiling fondly at us, Anne apologized. "Forgive an old woman for givin' in to worry. 'Tis better to concentrate on all that's good, which by the look of yer faces there's more'n plenty of this mornin'."

The rest of the meal passed pleasantly, though I have no notion of what I ate. I only knew that I was happier than I'd ever hoped to be, the sight of Brock's warm gaze making me aware of how much I loved him.

The pleasant interlude ended all too soon, with Brock leaving to meet his solicitor and Millie and me returning to our room to pack. By ten o'clock we were on our way back to Tanybrae, Henry driving the team and Dan on the seat beside him. Unfortunately, the business with the solicitor had proven lengthy, and Brock and Adam would have to catch up on horseback later.

This information was conveyed in a note addressed to me instead of Anne. I shared his news with the others, but the final lines I kept for myself, holding the words of his love close to my heart while I accustomed myself to the bold roundness of his writing, the strokes firm and purposeful like the man who'd formed them.

"'Tis as it should be," Anne said when she saw me reread Brock's note as we left the city. "The transfer of his love to ye. Oh, not that he'll love me any the less, only that 'tis time for him to feel a different kind of love." She reached and took my hand. "Know that there's none I'd sooner my son give his heart to. I felt great affection for ye when I nursed ye after yer ordeal in the ocean. Now 'tis grown to a love that wants to claim ye as my daughter."

Tears constricted my throat, and my words came out in a quaver. "Thank you. Know too that I feel love for you and Millie. It's like God heard my prayers for a family and led me to you."

Anne patted my hand. "Aye, 'tis the way of the good Lord, givin' us trials so we can grow, then surprisin' us with gifts we never thought to own. Tho' I lost my Angus and the bairn and sweet Alice, God left me with Brock and Millie to fill my life with their love." She paused, her smile tender. "And now He's sent us ye."

Although Millie said little during the exchange, her affection was obvious, as was her enthusiasm about our time in Melbourne. She had much to say about the wonderful parties and ball, and Anne and I were quick to agree. Our talk filled the first hours as the carriage bumped and swayed through wide vistas of grass and scrub and belts of trees. Once we came upon a family of kangaroos resting in the shade on a nearby knoll, but even our enjoyment of the sight couldn't prick the lethargy caused by the heavy combination of heat and lack of sleep. Tongues slowed and heads nodded as the jostling lulled us to sleep.

The tap of Brock's riding whip on the side of the carriage roused me. I gave him a sleepy smile, saw him laugh as if, like me, he had only to fill his eyes with the one he loved to know happiness.

"Look," Millie said after a few minutes. "There are the McKade cattle. I can't believe we're so close to home."

Less than an hour later, the carriage turned into the tree-lined approach to the house and stable. Dougal and Shep ran out to greet us, their barks and wagging tails signaling their gladness. Min and Callie stood by the steps to the veranda. When Min's hand rose to shade her eyes from the lowering sun, the swell of her advanced pregnancy became more obvious. I felt a pang of regret when I realized she would soon return to her people.

Instead of riding back to the stable, Brock handed the reins of the bay gelding to Adam and helped his mother and Millie from the carriage. Leaving Henry and Dan to carry our trunks, he helped me down and slipped his arm around my waist.

"Miss me?" At my smile and nod, his hold on my waist tightened. "Good, because I've been counting the hours until I could see you again."

I laughed up at his handsome features and wished we could be alone. Instead, I was aware of Min and Callie as they exchanged quick glances and of Hilda standing in the doorway, her mouth slightly agape.

"They'd best get used to this and more," Brock said in a mock whisper. "I've had my fill of acting like you're my sister, and I mean to let everyone know how I feel. Unless . . ." He stopped and turned me to face him. "Unless you have objections."

"You know I haven't."

"Good." With his arm firmly on my waist, we approached the veranda. What Henry and the others thought of the display of affection I can't say, but I was deliciously happy and couldn't wait to see what lay ahead.

* * *

Each morning after breakfast, Brock and I went to the pasture to watch the colts and yearlings. Lass now came as soon as I called to her, lifting her head and nickering in anticipation of a treat. My confidence and hers grew until, on the third morning, my tentative hand reached to touch her cautious nose. Lass's head bucked against my hand when I attempted to stroke it, but Brock's solid presence leant me courage and kept my hand in place. I felt warmth through the short bristles of hair, saw wariness in her brown eyes. Gradually we both relaxed, and she allowed me to stroke her with a light touch—my breath, like my fingers, a little unsteady.

"Good," Brock said when I stroked her the second time. "Didn't I tell you that, like women, horses like to be wooed?"

I smiled at him. "You did, though I believe you said people, not women."

"Only because I didn't want you to think I was wooing you, though the intent was never far from my mind."

"Why didn't you want me to know?"

"I was afraid you might spurn me."

"Spurn you?" I turned to face him, Lass and the colts forgotten.

"Aye. Several in Melbourne have made it a point to remind me that my father was no more than a poor Scottish crofter—one whose business practices weren't always honorable." The lines around Brock's mouth tightened. "Being poor is true, but my da was a hard worker and a man of high principles. Did you know Olivia's father had his eye on what is now Tanybrae? When Da filed his claim first, Mr. Griffith put it out that Angus McKade had cheated. Since my da's concentration and energy were spent keeping Tanybrae afloat, he had no time for squelching the rumors. On the other hand, Mr. Griffith was fast making a name for himself in banking and in Melbourne social circles, and so . . ."

Brock shrugged, his smile a little forced. "You know my pride and temper. They've landed me in more than one spot of trouble. Since Robert is your brother, I thought he'd prejudiced you against me."

"He did say a thing or two, but I paid it no mind." I placed my hand on his cheek. "My father taught me not to place credence in gossip. More than that, I'm a woman who likes to make her own decisions."

"Are you now?" Brock's eyes, like his voice, were tender. "And what would you think of gossip that says Brock McKade is deeply in love with Jessamyne Clayborne and that his greatest desire is to have her as his wife?"

"I'd hope the gossip were true." Happy tears made my voice tremble.

He pulled me into his arms, Anne's floppy hat pushed back so his finger could run more freely over my face and hair. His lips were warm on my mouth.

When the kiss ended, he set me away from him, his eyes dark and serious as he looked into my face. "Will you marry me, sweet Jessa?"

"Yes." My lips sought his, and my arms pulled his face more closely to mine. In my happiness I thought the bright Australian sun more romantic than dappled moonlight, the soft snuffle of the colts a melody sweeter than a chorus of angels. It was enough to know Brock loved me and that he wanted me as his bride.

EIGHTEEN

Later we walked to the house to tell Anne and Millie about our plans. Millie was ecstatic as she and Anne hugged us. "At last I'll have a sister," she cried.

"Aye, 'tis what we've both been prayin' for." Anne turned to Brock and tenderly touched his cheek. "Yer da would be pleased too."

Although no date had been set, everyone agreed it would be better to wait until fall when the weather was cooler.

Over the next days, I went about with a perpetual smile on my face. My confidence around horses also increased. The need to be near Brock took me often to the training area where he, Adam, and Parmee worked with the yearlings. Where before I'd avoided both the training area and race track, I now went there daily, leaning my arms on the fence rail, my eyes as often on Brock as they were on the horses. Sometimes Millie came with me, but more often I went alone, preferring to concentrate on Brock without the interference of her cheerful chatter. Perhaps it was shameful to be so besotted, my thoughts and interests now focused solely on Brock, but in those early days of love, being near him was as essential to me as breathing.

By now I'd grown familiar with the lunge whip and rein the men used to train the yearlings. At first the whip and rein looked cruel, but when I understood their use, I quickly came to see they were an important part of training—the tap of the lunge whip a reminder of lessons taught, the lunge rein a check to keep the yearlings in line.

Watching Brock with the horses was a lesson in patience and stamina. To my inexperienced eye, the tug of rein seemed a constant battle, Brock's muscled frame inconsequential against the strength and size of the yearlings.

Although my interest was mainly on Brock, it sometimes strayed to Parmee. I soon saw why Millie claimed he had a way with horses. Although he used the lunging whip and rein, he seemed to communicate with the horses on a higher level, his eyes locked with theirs as he called instructions in strange, singsong words. When a horse had difficulty learning, sometimes Parmee whispered in its ear, the movement of his grizzled beard the only evidence that he spoke.

When Parmee wasn't working with the horses, he often watched me from his precarious perch atop the fence. Although the brim of his hat prevented me from seeing much of his face, something in his stillness told me he watched and assessed. What conclusion he came to I couldn't tell, but I sensed that his stillness was as much a part of him as his curly beard and bronzed skin. Snippets of information I'd heard about the Aborigines flitted through my mind, and for an instant it wasn't Parmee who sat on the fence, but a hunter—boomerang in hand, arm poised to hurl his weapon, the old ways of his people superceding the borrowed garb of a stockman. This image didn't frighten me. Instead, just as Sal had, his quiet watchfulness conveyed a tacit promise of protection.

More than a week after our return from Melbourne, a stockman rode at a gallop to the training area, his pace and the grim expression on his face like an alarm clanging.

"What is it?" Brock called.

"Some of the cattle have been shot. I found more'n a dozen of 'em lying dead in the north section."

I heard an expletive as Brock handed the lunge rein to Parmee. "Bromfield . . . and probably Wooraronga men." He glanced at Parmee. "After you put the horses back into the paddock, keep a sharp eye out for strangers."

Brock vaulted the fence and took my arm. "Go tell Mum and Millie. They'll want to ride out with me." Anger tightened his features.

"How can you be sure it's Bromfield?"

"After what he said, who else would do it?"

"I'm sorry," I said. Then quickly, "I'll tell your mum."

I set out for the house at a run, my divided skirt lifted, aware that Brock hurried to the stable. By the time I reached the house, Anne and Millie had come out on the veranda.

"What's wrong?"

Anne's expression turned grim as I explained. "Dear heaven," she whispered, untying her apron. "Tell Min to fill the water bags," she went on. "In this heat we'll be needin' them."

While Anne and Millie hurried to change, I went in search of Min and found her dusting the sitting room.

"Yes'm," she said when I gave her Anne's instructions.

Wanting to help, I followed her to a room off the kitchen where several burlap bags hung on wooden pegs. Grabbing two, Min hurried to the pump in the kitchen. "Min pump, you hold bags," she said.

My frustration with my slowness to ride built as I placed a bag under the spout. I should be preparing to ride out with Brock. Instead I was left to carry bags out to the stable, water dripping through the burlap and onto my skirt.

Brock and several men waited with saddled horses. As soon as he saw me, he came for my water bag.

"How long will you be gone?" I asked, my thoughts a bit panicked.

"I don't know. If I ever catch the blokes who did this . . ." His voice trailed away.

Anne and Millie had joined us. Unlike her daughter, Anne wore men's breeches, the long legs tucked into her boots and the band gathered by a belt at her waist. Without asking, I knew the breeches had belonged to Angus. Most likely the gun she carried too. Millie also carried a rifle, as did Henry and Adam.

"Do you expect trouble?"

Brock slipped his arm around my waist. "Probably not, but we can't be sure the ones who killed the cattle aren't still skulking around." He turned to his mother. "Are you sure you're up to this?"

Anne snorted. "There's still pluck in these old bones, so don't think ye must baby yer mother."

Brock's grin erased the harsh lines on his face. "I knew you'd say that. Just the same, I felt I must ask."

Anne gave him a steady look. "I'll be fine."

Brock nodded and pulled me close. "Don't worry. Like mum said, we'll be fine."

"Take care," I whispered.

I stood with Min and Callie as Brock and the others rode through the gate and across the pasture. In addition to rifles, all of the men carried water bags. Even in my inexperience, I knew they faced a long ride under a sun that blazed without mercy from a cloudless sky. Anger caught in my throat at the unseen man or men who'd killed Brock's cattle. *Our cattle.*

Watching the riders grow small against the horizon, I resolved to put fear aside so that by the time Brock and I married, it would be me, instead of his mother and Millie, who rode by his side.

* * *

Millie and Anne returned two hours later, their grim, sweat-streaked faces a testament to what they'd witnessed.

"'Twas terrible," Anne replied to my questions. "The poor beasties lyin' hurt or dead, vultures and flies thick as grass. Two were still alive but so badly hurt there was no hope to save them." She stripped her brown hat from her head and flung it against the wall. "I ken God says to forgive, but 'twill be hard to do such with those who slaughtered our cattle."

"The cattle they shot were in their prime," Millie put in. "Brock's fit to be tied."

I shook my head, as upset by the wanton act as they were. My stomach tightened when I recalled the coldness in Neville's eyes when he'd warned Brock to stay out of his affairs. The slaughter of Tanybrae cattle gave evidence that the threat hadn't been idle.

It was evening before Brock and the men returned. Although he gave me a quick hug when he gained the veranda, I was wise enough to realize that his barely suppressed anger must be dealt with before I could offer any comfort.

Tea was delayed until Brock had bathed and changed from his grimy clothes. We were subdued as grace was said, the meal served by Min and Callie who were equally solemn. I scarcely tasted the cold beef and fresh vegetables as my mind slid in desultory circles around the deliberate slaughter of the cattle.

"Our stockmen will be staying out with the cattle tonight," Brock said through the silence. "I doubt they'll strike again so soon, but we can't be sure."

"Do you think Mr. Bromfield ordered it?" I asked.

"We can't know for certain, but who else would do such a vicious thing? You heard him. We all heard him."

I swallowed uncomfortably and wished I'd remained silent.

"I'm sorry," Brock apologized. "Since Bromfield is close with your brother, I understand your reluctance to think the worst of him." He looked across the table at me, his eyes softening. "One thing I'm sure of is that my time in Melbourne wasn't wasted. What happened to my cattle proves that what I unearthed about Bromfield has made him nervous."

Brock paused while Callie carried in a bowl of the first apricots of the season.

"What did you discover in Melbourne?" Millie asked when Callie left the room.

Instead of answering, Brock looked at me. "Didn't you say you met Jeremy Moulton aboard the ship from England?" At my nod, he went on. "From what Dennis and I were able to learn, Mr. Moulton was sent to England to transact some business for Mr. Bromfield. Just what it entailed isn't important, but it does prove that the two of them have had previous business dealings."

I recalled Mr. Moulton's boast to me on the ship. "He had business with my brother too. I didn't want to believe it at first . . . that Robert would deal with such an unsavory man. But later—" I looked down at my tightly clasped hands. "Later, I saw Jeremy leaving Robert's study."

I had their undivided attention—Millie's face full of questions, Anne's solemn. But it was Brock whose gaze I met and held. "I'm sorry for not telling you sooner. I almost did on the morning I came

to the hotel, but the truth was"—the look I gave him pled for understanding—"I didn't want to admit the truth to myself . . . let alone
anyone else . . . that . . . Robert was not the brother I'd believed in
and longed to see."

"There's nae need for ye to be lookin' so guilty," Anne reassured.
"We can all understand yer feelin's."

"Even when I tell you that the morning Moulton visited my
brother was just two days before he bribed the jockey?"

There was a tiny moment of shocked silence, one that left me
unable to breathe while I continued to hold Brock's gaze. I feared I'd
find signs of censure and distrust. Instead I saw only acceptance and
understanding.

Brock rose and came around to the back of my chair, his fingers
on my shoulders as he bent to kiss my cheek. "Your loyalty to
Robert should be commended, not criticized. It's what I hope Millie
feels for me."

"Thank you." Tears pooled in my eyes as I covered his hand with
mine. "It's been a difficult truth to face, but after today . . ." I swallowed before going on. "Perhaps it was Robert who ordered the cattle
killed. Remember his reputation and money are as much at stake as
Neville's."

Brock's fingers tightened on mine. "I didn't want to be the one to
say that about your brother."

"I know you didn't." I looked up into his eyes. "Since I'm soon to
take your name, I want you to know both my loyalty and heart are
yours."

* * *

The next few days passed in somewhat normal fashion, although
the specter of the dead cattle was never far from our minds. George
rode out each morning with fresh men to replace those who'd kept
watch during the night, and a single gunshot was agreed upon as a
signal should more trouble arise.

Only then did we learn that Henry had been wakened by the
sound of gunfire on the night the cattle were killed, but he'd thought

the sound too distant to be of concern, and he'd rolled over and gone back to sleep.

Now everyone listened for the sound and slept with ears turned for unfamiliar sounds. The dogs picked up on the tension as well and barked more often than usual. After much debate and discussion, Brock decided that confronting the foreman at Wooraronga would be futile. He was sure to deny involvement, and until proof was found, nothing could be done. Even so, a gauntlet had been thrown down, and Brock and the men at Tanybrae were not ones to ignore it.

Just what was discussed in the bunkhouse and stable, I couldn't know, but Brock did all he could to reassure us. "Stop your worrying," he protested after Millie asked his plans for the third time. "Things are under control. The men know what to do."

I was content with this, knowing that the problem was in capable hands. Just as Anne had trusted Angus, I trusted Brock.

Each morning we went out to see the horses. Our enjoyment of being together made it easy to forget the need to worry. The third day after the loss of the cattle, I asked Brock if I could go into the paddock.

"You're ready, are you?"

At my nod, he grinned, the expression still having the power to steal my breath. We walked arm in arm through the gate and into the pasture. At first the foals were a little skittish, for until now the fence had always been between us. But with apples and encouragement, Lass was soon enticed to approach. I stood my ground, wanting us both to pass the test.

"Well done, Mrs. McKade."

"Is that what you plan to call me after we're married?"

"Never that." He lifted my floppy hat so his lips could make a trail across my cheek. "I'm thinkin' Jessa is what I'll call you. My darling Jessa."

I raised my fingers to touch his tanned cheek. "Darling Jessa. Yes, I'll like that." But I wanted more. I wanted to be with him in all aspects of our lives. Taking a deep breath, I spoke again. "Now to the yearlings."

Brock gave me a measured look. "You're sure?"

I nodded, sensing both his happiness and concern.

We walked over the uneven terrain of the paddock to the end where the yearlings usually congregated. Brock's solid presence at my side and his arm around my waist filled the gaps in my erratic confidence. *You can do it, Jessa* was my steady incantation.

Most of the horses were too busy grazing to pay us much attention, but some watched—Miranda among them. At Brock's whistle, the chestnut filly started toward us, her skittish hooves hesitant. Although the mare was used to Brock and the stockmen, she seemed unsure of my skirt as it swished around my legs. Stopping, Brock and I waited for Miranda to approach, her russet coat gleaming in the sunshine. Almost fully grown, she was a good deal bigger than the colts, her head on a level with mine.

"That's a girl," Brock said.

Miranda was only a step or two away, ears pricked and her liquid brown eyes watchful. Mine were just as wary, though I tried to make them otherwise. *She won't hurt you. Not with Brock here.* The pressure of his arm reinforced the words and imbued me with courage. Even so, I was aware of my quickened breathing and the unnatural skip of my heart.

Courage, Brock seemed to say.

My tension slowly dissipated, replaced by tentative confidence. *She's as nervous as you are. You must let her understand there's nothing to fear.* The words tumbling through my mind were my own, but I felt that Mother had placed them there. In my mind I was with her in the stable, her hand guiding mine on the brush as I groomed Prince, her voice reminding me that my pony looked to me for care and confidence. *In return Prince will be your friend and carry you wherever you wish to go. It's all very simple.*

Suddenly it was simple, fear shrinking in the bright light of Mother's assurance and the warmth of Brock's arm. I smiled at Miranda and offered her the last of the apple. When she stepped close to take it, I neither flinched nor blinked, but thought instead of her fine lines and of me astride her back as we rode across the pasture. Neither she nor I was ready yet, but it would come. It would come.

Clinging to this thought, I was able to stroke Miranda's nose after she finished the apple, ask Brock about her training, and walk with him among the horses—their size not so overwhelming with him by my side. Like Mother had said, it was simple.

* * *

The following week, Brock and Adam left Tanybrae, leading two of the horses. One was Nugget, the other a likely two-year-old. Although it was never mentioned, I suspected Brock would also have another meeting with his solicitor.

After our private good-bye, I stood on the veranda with Anne and Millie, calling good wishes and waving. His mother and sister were used to Brock's horse-selling trips, but to me it seemed the light and strength of Tanybrae left with the man I loved.

Determined not to spend the time while he was gone pining and sighing, I looked for ways to keep busy. After helping Anne in her garden, I went out to the paddock. Not confident enough to enter it alone, I contented myself with feeding and talking to the horses through the fence.

I was grateful for Min and Callie's lessons to keep me occupied as well. Min's lack of enthusiasm was still often evident. Not so Callie. Her eagerness to learn was almost palpable, and I planned soon to start her in one of the readers.

One particularly fine day after a rainstorm had cooled the air, I decided to walk to the picnic area in the hills. My close call with the big brown had left me cautious of snakes, and I never left Tanybrae without a sturdy stick—always keeping a sharp lookout for sudden movement among the grass along the way. As I walked beside the stream and into the hills, the cool air brought a lift to my step.

Once there, I sat down on a log and extracted two golden apricots from my pocket. Biting into the sun-warmed fruit, I leaned back against a gnarled branch. *What a lovely day.* If Brock had been with me, I would have counted the afternoon perfect. Although I realized that many in England and Melbourne might consider Tanybrae life boring, with Brock it held everything I desired.

A piercing scream sliced through my thoughts. I jumped to my feet when the scream came again, muffled as if a hand smothered it. Grabbing my stick, I scrambled up the path, ears straining for another cry to lead me to its source.

Lungs heaving, I leaned against a tree to catch my breath and recognized the clearing where Min had met her husband some weeks before. Was it Min I'd heard? But why had she screamed?

Movement drew my eyes to a horse tethered to a tree. Curious, I moved toward it, caution keeping me to the cover of the thicket. The horse pricked its ears and watched, but as yet there was no sign of its rider. Questions skittered through my mind, pushing caution more forcefully to the forefront. I gave the horse a wide berth and moved closer to the clearing, my heart jerking when I heard a muffled cry and sounds of struggle. Muscles taut, I slipped forward, my hand going to my mouth to cut off a horrified cry when I saw Callie struggling with a burly man who'd wrestled her to the ground. For a second I could only stare, knowing the stick I carried would be useless against her attacker. *What to do? Dear heaven, what can I do?*

A movement from the horse reminded me of the rifle I'd glimpsed in the saddle holster. Anger kicked past fear and sent me hurrying back to the horse to carefully slide the gun from the holster and extract four bullets from the outer pocket.

Callie's frightened cries and the man's growled curses goaded my shaky fingers to shove a bullet into the gun's chamber. Swallowing hard at fear, I crept forward until I had them clearly in sight. Callie fought like a tiger, writhing and flailing as the man tried to straddle her.

"Get off or I'll shoot!"

Eyes wide, the man half turned, his broad features showing surprise and frustration. My own surprise was almost as great when I recognized Jeremy Moulton, his face flushed and mottled and with bloody scratches streaking his face.

Shock caused my hold on the rifle to waver. "Get off," I repeated, my voice and the gun unsteady.

Instead of responding, Mr. Moulton gave an ugly snort and slammed his fist into Callie's face.

"Do you want to be shot?"

Mr. Moulton snorted again. "Ya think to scare me with a gun? I doubt ya ever held one before . . . let alone shot it."

Taking aim at his fallen hat, I pulled the trigger. The loud explosion and the kick of the rifle came simultaneously. Mr. Moulton's surprised curse and the skip of the hat lifted by the bullet quickly followed.

"I can both hold and shoot a gun." The firmness of my voice surprised me, for it had taken all of my control to keep my hands steady. "Now get off!"

Attempting to laugh, he rose, his beefy legs splayed wide above Callie.

My unsteady fingers slipped a fresh bullet into the chamber. "Put your hands above your head and turn around," I ordered, my voice like one I'd never heard before.

Mr. Moulton slowly complied, the front flap of his breeches partially unfastened, his fleshy face a sneer. "Ya think yer quite the fancy lady, don't ya, Miss Clayborne. But I can tell ya some things about yer brother that ain't fancy . . . yes, indeed."

I ignored his remarks and concentrated on Callie, who'd recovered enough to crawl to her feet. Her gray dress was grass-stained and torn, and her nose and cut lip were bloody. "Are you all right, Callie?"

Callie wiped her face and nodded. "Ya . . . missy."

I kept the rifle trained on Mr. Moulton. "Go to the horse," I told her.

Badly shaken, she moved toward the horse on unsteady legs. Somehow, I managed to appear calm. "Leave," I ordered Mr. Moulton. "Get off Tanybrae land and don't come back."

He bent to pick up his hat. "Think yer somthin', don't ya?"

"Leave the hat. It and the horse stay here."

Mr. Moulton's blotched face turned incredulous. "But—" he began.

"They stay here," I repeated.

"How do ya expect me to go anywhere?" he sputtered.

Someone outside myself put steel in my back and firmness in my voice. "Walk . . . and keep your hands above your head."

Mr. Moulton's eyes narrowed. "Ya'll be sorry for this," he snarled. "What I done with that black gin ain't nothin' to what I'll do to you."

The hatred in his eyes sent cold tendrils of fear through my insides. "Go!" I ordered.

He shot me another hateful look before he set off across the uneven ground. His progress was awkward. Without his arms for balance, he looked like a man who'd had too much to drink. Had it not been for his threat, his undignified gait might have amused me. Instead my brain absorbed the icy knowledge that I'd made a deadly enemy.

*　*　*

Most young women would have had an attack of vapors after the rough treatment and near rape Callie had suffered. But Callie bore it stoically, although she was shaken enough to agree to ride the horse.

After watching Mr. Moulton's awkward form grow small in the distance, we made a hurried procession down the hill and across the pasture, Callie riding the horse, me following on foot and carrying the gun. I kept a wary eye on our surroundings, fearful that Mr. Moulton might double back through the trees and try to overpower me. But God and good fortune were with us, and when the house and barn were clearly in sight I told Callie to hurry ahead and alert Henry and George.

Henry and Millie were waiting by the time I reached the gate.

"Thank heaven you're safe," Millie cried. "I can't believe such a terrible thing could happen so close to Tanybrae."

Instead of answering, I leaned into her embrace, aware that my legs were unsteady.

"The dirty bounder," Henry muttered, taking Mr. Moulton's rifle from my hands. "We'll make 'im pay for this—see that we don't. Dan and George be saddlin' up this very minute to find the scum."

"Did Callie tell you he's on foot?"

Henry nodded. "She did. Without a 'at too." A wry smile curled his little mouth. "Such'll make the 'untin' of 'im all the more inter-estin' in all this 'eat."

"It was Jeremy Moulton," I said in an unsteady voice.

Henry stared and Millie seemed too surprised to speak. "Jeremy Moulton?" Henry panted. "'Im what bribed the jockey?"

"Yes."

"Yer sure?"

"I know the man. It was definitely him."

Henry hurried to spread the news, his short bandy legs moving surprisingly fast.

Millie gave me another hug. "What a fright you've had," she said. Then quickly added, "If only Brock were here."

It was a wish my heart echoed, one I'd carried all the way home. With a shake of my head, I put my mind on more pressing matters. "How's Callie?"

"Mum and Min are with her. She's in good hands."

Sensing that I was anxious to see her, Millie led me to the little house Callie shared with Min and Parmee. I paused at the closed door. Millie knocked until Anne opened it.

"How is she?" I asked, looking past Anne to Min's dark silhouette.

"Aboot as ye'd expect after what the poor lass's been through." Anger tangled with concern in her voice. "There's no words bad enough for the likes of him who did this."

"Did he—?" I began.

"Thank the good Lord, no, but 'twern't from lack of tryin'." Anne's lips trembled. "The poor mite don't say much, but ye can tell she's badly upset."

"Can I come in?" I asked, relieved to hear Mr. Moulton hadn't succeeded in his intent.

After giving me a searching look, she nodded. "'Twill be better if Millie waits outside. Ye know how private Callie and Min are."

As my eyes adjusted to the room's dimness, I saw Callie lying on a pallet on the floor. Min had moved from the window to bathe Callie's cuts with a cloth dipped in water.

I knelt on the floor next to Min and took Callie's hand, wanting to cry when I saw blood oozing from her cut lip and badly swollen eye. "I'm so sorry." Tears came to my eyes, and I saw answering moisture pool in Callie's. Neither of us spoke as barriers of culture and color melted to nothing. In that moment we were sisters, Callie's pain and degradation my own.

Callie gently laid my hand against her cheek. "Thank you, missy. All time ever Callie thank you."

"As I've thanked you for saving me from the snake."

A tiny smile curved her cut lip. "Now Callie and missy same." She looked at me for a long moment before she released my hand, the meshing of souls put away but not forgotten.

Loathe to leave Callie, I slowly got to my feet. The surprise on Anne's face was evident. The doorway into the young woman's heart had been opened a small crack, and I'd been allowed inside.

* * *

Parmee didn't learn about Callie until he returned from herding cattle that evening. By then George and those he'd taken to look for Jeremy Moulton had ridden back as well.

Hearing the horses, we hurried outside, disappointment knifing through me when I saw Mr. Moulton wasn't with them. "Didn't you find him?"

"No ma'am." George slowly dismounted and handed his horse's reins to one of the stockmen. "We looked everywhere for him. Either he had a mate what gave him a lift on his horse, or the bas—" George swallowed what he'd intended to say and turned red. "Sorry, ma'am . . . or he sprouted wings."

George looked at Anne, obviously upset at the failure. "I'm right sorry, ma'am. We was sure we'd find him."

Anne frowned. "Ye must try again tomorrow."

"Right-o." George made to leave, then turned back. "Until the scoundrel's found, ya ladies best stick close to the house." He looked significantly at Millie. "No ridin' out on yer mare. Yer brother left me in charge, and I know it's what he'd want."

"'Tis good advice, and we'll be takin' it," Anne said. When George was out of earshot, she added, "I wish to heaven they'd found him." The wish was never far from our minds and was discussed over the evening meal.

It was brought up again before we went to bed. "Do you think Moulton's been out here since the race?" Millie asked when we'd gathered in the sitting room over cups of tea. "Chris says the outback is full of men trying to escape the law."

"Tanybrae isn't the outback," Anne pointed out. I knew she hoped her words would lessen our unease, but no amount of talking could change the fact that he'd been here.

Unlike Millie, I thought it more likely he'd been hiding at Wooraronga. Didn't the property belong to Robert and Neville? Its isolation made it an ideal place for a man who didn't want to be found. Reluctantly, I spoke. "Have you thought he might be staying at Wooraronga?"

Anne and Millie exchanged glances. "Aye, lass, but we dinna want to cause ye pain by mentionin' it, what with yer brother and all."

"You're my family now. It's true that Robert will always be my brother, but his lack of scruples has killed my loyalty."

Reassured by my words, Millie lost no time in expressing her feelings on the matter. "Both George and Henry say Wooraronga stockmen are the kind that no one else will hire. Such men would gladly help someone of their same kind."

"Maybe Moulton is the one who shot our poor cattle," Anne put in, though she was kind enough not to add, *at yer brother's orders.* Sighing, she got to her feet. "Such doona help find the man." She paused and wearily shook her head. "I do wish Brock were here."

Gathering up our cups and blowing out the lamp, we quit the sitting room. After I'd prepared for bed, I went to stand at the open window. The night was calm and held remnants of coolness from the earlier rainstorm. Looking up at a pale moon, I assured myself there was no need to worry. Weren't Henry and Dan out in the bunkhouse?

But the fact that Mr. Moulton hadn't been found interfered with my sleep. Twice, small noises jerked me awake, and in the darkness I was reminded again of Mr. Moulton's snarling threat and the hatred I'd seen in his eyes.

Nineteen

Sunlight spilling through the window wakened me the next morning. Relief at having passed a night without incident penetrated the room along with the sunshine. Everything seemed less threatening in the morning light, the menace of Jeremy Moulton shrinking to a size that was not so frightening, the loss of the cattle a hurdle Tanybrae could surmount.

Millie and Anne awoke in a cheerful mood as well, and we all made a show of normalcy as Anne and I went to the garden while Millie went out to the stable.

A few minutes later Millie hurried back. "Henry says one of the stockmen's horses came up missing this morning."

I straightened from snipping off the spent blooms of the veronica to give her my full attention.

"He was on night guard with the cattle. When he woke up to take his turn on patrol, his horse was gone. He and Levi have looked everywhere for it. Henry thinks Jeremy Moulton probably took it . . . that he hid someplace yesterday and watched for his chance and—"

Anne's harsh voice cut through Millie's. "Is there no end to this? The race thrown . . . cattle shot . . . and now this with Jeremy Moulton. Why was the stockman sleepin' instead of watchin'? Times like this make me wish I was a man!" She threw down the hoe and strode from the garden, the morning's peace shattered by the news and its effect on Anne.

Millie sighed. "I didn't have a chance to tell Mum Parmee's gone too."

"On a walkabout?"

She shook her head. "Min said he left to track down Jeremy Moulton." Her pretty face creased with worry. "We're not the only ones who want to find him." Although the morning was warm, Millie shivered and wrapped her arms around herself. "I wouldn't want to be Jeremy when Parmee finishes with him."

"Why?"

Millie's face was grim. "You don't want to know."

The harshness in her voice told me not to inquire further. Instead I picked up the hoe and returned it and my scissors to the shed. Then we went to look for Anne.

We didn't find her until she came in for breakfast. By then she was more herself, though she still showed signs of being upset. "We've not had so much trouble since the early days at Tanybrae. Then 'twas Mr. Griffith who tried to scare us away. Now 'tis Bromfield and Jessamyne's brother. But they'll find the McKades doona scare easily. 'Tis what I was tellin' George and Henry. If we're to win the battle we must be more watchful instead of hurryin' to pick up the pieces after harm's already come." She moved a chair and sat down. "'Tis what Angus and Brock would be sayin' if they was here. Since they're not"—her mouth pulled into a thin line—"we must carry on until Brock gets back."

Pausing for breath, she attempted a smile. "Millie, would ye be so kind as to say grace so we can get on with our breakfast? 'Twouldn't hurt none to ask for God's blessin' of wisdom as well."

Millie's voice was soft and sincere as she asked a blessing on the food and the household. I wasn't aware of Callie's quiet presence until she moved from the shadows to set a plate of freshly baked oatcakes onto the table. Her lip and eye were still swollen, but she appeared composed, a clean dress replacing the torn one, her dark hair braided and neat.

"How are you feeling?" I asked, her injured face tearing at my heart.

"Better, missy." As usual her words were brief, but the look she gave me held gratitude.

"Henry said Parmee went to find the man who attacked you," Anne interjected.

Callie nodded, and when she spoke her voice held conviction. "Parmee find him."

"I don't blame Parmee for bein' angry," Anne said after Callie left the kitchen. "But we need the scoundrel alive. How else can we learn what he knows about the race?"

"Most likely he's been hiding at Wooraronga all this time," Millie said.

Anne nodded. "'Tis as likely a hidin' place as the outback."

I refrained from taking part in their conversation, remembering instead how Robert had said he must go to Wooraronga just two days after the race. Had he been the one to spirit Mr. Moulton away from Melbourne?

Not liking the unpleasant journey my thoughts had taken, I attempted to fill the rest of the day with activities to keep my mind on other paths. But even Lass and the horses failed to divert me. Anne and Millie were no better. The hours dragged. Where was Parmee? When would Brock return?

It was late afternoon before Parmee rode his horse into the yard. Millie and I were sitting on the veranda, our attempts at conversation and embroidery unsuccessful. Millie hurried to the stable as soon as she saw him, and I wasn't far behind.

"Did you find him?"

Parmee dismounted and looked at us for a long moment. "Find where man hide after hurt Callie . . . then where he steal horse. Tracks led to Wooraronga. Men there won't listen. Tell Parmee get off land." He paused and removed his hat, the late afternoon sunshine reflecting off his dark features to reveal the anger in his eyes. "Him not there, but Parmee find soon."

Anne joined us as we gathered around him. "You mustn't kill him, Parmee. He's the man who made Night Flyer lose the race. Mr. Brock needs him alive so the police can question him."

Parmee's expression changed slightly, his dark eyes locking with mine. "Missy see what man do to Callie. He must pay."

"He should pay," Anne agreed, "but if you hurt or kill a white man, the police will come after you instead of him."

Parmee shrugged, the mention of the police seeming not to affect him.

Anne stepped closer. "Please, Parmee, let Mr. Brock take care of Jeremy Moulton."

Instead of answering, Parmee tugged on his horse's reins and led him into the stable. As I watched them go, I realized he was not as tall as I'd first believed. The lack of stature didn't lessen the impression of strength. He was of a world that was one with nature, and I knew, like the trunk of an ancient gum tree, he wouldn't be turned from his path.

* * *

Although Parmee didn't leave Tanybrae, fear that he might act rashly was never far from our minds. It was discussed each morning over breakfast and again at evening tea. "Surely he must realize how badly Brock needs Moulton alive," was repeated several times a day.

On the following Friday, Brock and Adam returned from Melbourne. I flew down the steps to meet him, the sight of his blue chambray shirt and dark hat changing from a blur to the substance of the man I loved. Brock's pleasure in seeing me lit his eyes as he dismounted and pulled me into his arms. I savored his closeness and solid strength, needing it to gladden my heart and blow away the fear that had surrounded it since Mr. Moulton's threat.

Not wanting the unsettling news about Mr. Moulton to detract from Brock's homecoming, I drank in the sound of his voice.

"Jessa . . . Jessa, how I've missed you."

"As I've missed you." To prove the point I raised my lips to meet his.

Only then did we start down the tree-lined lane to the house. Thankfully Adam possessed enough tact to take Brock's horse to the stable, and Millie and Anne were kind enough to wait on the veranda. Wanting to postpone the bad news, I asked about the sale of the horses. "How did it go?"

"Good. Enough to cover the loss of the cattle and with some left over."

"Did you talk to Mr. Whitney-Smyth?"

Some of the pleasure fled his face. "Yes, though he told me what I expected . . . that without proof we have no recourse."

We walked without speaking, arms joined as we neared the house. Only then did Anne and Millie join us.

"Did you tell him?" Millie asked.

"Tell me what?"

We continued up the steps. "We had some unpleasantness while you were away, but I thought I'd let you catch your breath before I told you."

Brock stopped. "I'd sooner hear it now."

Between the three of us, we told him. As the story reached the part about Mr. Moulton and the gun, Brock's arm tightened around my waist. "If he'd hurt you too . . ."

"He didn't." I attempted a smile. "You can't know the number of times I've wished I'd been brave enough to bring Jeremy back with me and Callie, but we were both so shaken I was afraid he might overpower us."

Brock's arm pulled even tighter. "You did right."

Each sentence spoken after that seemed to pile more concern onto Brock's shoulders, especially when he heard about Parmee. "I'll make sure I have a word with him." In a try at optimism, he added, "I'll ride over to Wooraronga first thing in the morning and talk to the foreman. We need to let the race commission know Jeremy Moulton's been seen too."

Brock's return imbued all of us with a renewed sense of well-being, and for the first time in several evenings, laughter was heard around the dining room table. Even Callie and Min seemed less quiet and ghostlike as they carried bowls of food to the table.

That night, when Brock left me at my bedroom door with a lingering kiss, I felt that life was warm and good again. "Thank you, Father," I whispered as I knelt in prayer. After climbing into bed, I snuggled into my pillow and fell into a deep and restful sleep.

* * *

Shortly after breakfast, Brock left for Wooraronga. Although he assured me he didn't expect trouble, the fact that Adam and two of the stockmen rode with him told me otherwise, especially when I noticed that all four men were armed.

"'Tis but a precaution," Anne assured when I commented on the matter. "'Tis better to be prepared for trouble than caught unaware."

Despite her optimistic words, I sensed her unease. It settled like flies just before a rainstorm, permeating the house and spreading to those who worked outside. Even the weather added to our discomfort as sullen, gray clouds, instead of bringing moisture, held in the heat until we felt as if we were swathed in a hot, sticky blanket. Tempers stretched thin, and to escape the rasp of Hilda's strident voice scolding Min, I went to the paddock to watch Parmee and Dan work with the horses. But today, even Parmee's skill with a recalcitrant horse failed to hold my attention. Along with the heat, my mind seemed saturated with worry that things weren't going well with Brock. Twice I walked to the end of the lane to look for them, and twice I was disappointed.

"How long does it take to ride to Wooraronga?" I asked Millie, who fidgeted restlessly.

"Less than two hours."

I sighed and returned to sorting linen—anything to take my mind away from discomfort and worry.

It was well into the afternoon before Brock and the men returned. I knew at once things hadn't gone well. The men looked as lethargic as their horses, and the smile Brock offered me was halfhearted.

"How—?" I began.

"Not good." Brock removed his hat and wiped the perspiration that had beaded on his forehead. "Schuler claimed he'd never heard of Jeremy Moulton, which is likely true. I doubt Moulton used his real name."

"What about the scar on Jeremy's face?"

"He denied seeing that too. Of course he was lying, and itching for me to say as much so he'd have an excuse to pick a fight."

I quickly inspected Brock for sign of a scuffle and was relieved to find none.

His chuckle was rueful. "You don't know how close I came to wiping the smirk from his face." He put his arm around my shoulder and started for the veranda where Anne and Millie waited. "See . . . you've already reformed me, though the fact that we were outnumbered might have played a part in it."

I smiled up at him. "You'll find him. In time, I know you'll find him."

"I will." His mouth was firm as he pulled me against him. The gesture told me more than he might have suspected—that the burden of recent events weighed heavily on his shoulders and that my confidence in him eased some of the burden.

Matching my steps with his, we reached the veranda where Anne and Millie plied Brock with more questions.

"The man was lying," he concluded. "More than that, Schuler was enjoying himself." He frowned and pursed his lips. "It wasn't just that he knows where Moulton's hiding. It's something more . . . like he has a trick up his sleeve."

No one spoke for a moment, Brock dusty and sweaty, Millie's yellow gown drooping in the sultry heat. I absently swatted a fly that buzzed in lazy fashion near my head, its pesky presence scarcely noticed. I wished I could wipe the lines of worry away from Brock's face.

"What can it be?" Millie asked in response to Brock's information.

"I don't know," he answered, "but I mean to find out."

* * *

Brock had bathed and changed into a clean white shirt when he joined us for the evening meal. The sight of him looking more like himself gladdened my heart and made me believe everything would work out.

Anne seemed to be of a similar opinion, though she drew her optimism from the Bible instead of Brock's smile. "I've been readin' and thinkin'," she said after Brock had helped her into her chair, "and I've found the very verse for us."

She paused and opened her Bible, which she had brought with her into the dining room.

"'Tis a verse I turn to often . . . one I hold to when life tries to make me doubt." Clearing her throat, she began to read from Proverbs 3:5–6. "Trust in the Lord with all thine heart; and lean not unto thine own understanding. In all thy ways acknowledge him, and he shall direct thy paths."

The pleasant cadence of Anne's lilt surrounded the words as they poured into my heart. "Yes," I breathed, making a mental note of the chapter and verse so I could read the words again. Trust and let God direct us. How very right.

Brock seemed to be similarly affected as he led us in grace, his voice resonant and trusting as if he'd taken the verse to heart.

"Henry should be in Melbourne by now," he said after grace. "He'll go first to Mr. Whitney-Smyth to let him know Moulton's been seen here. I also sent a letter to alert the race commission." Satisfaction edged his voice as he speared a piece of beef from the platter Callie handed him. "Although Schuler wouldn't admit that Jeremy's hiding at Wooraronga, I'm certain he's there." He smiled across the table at me. "Today wasn't a total loss. Now that we know where Moulton is, Parmee and the men of his family are committed to tracking him down."

"Wong and Mooney?" I asked, remembering the tall, silent men who'd carried me to their camp.

Brock nodded. "Callie is one of their women, and she's been shamed. They're anxious to see Moulton punished."

The knowledge that the Aborigines would be helping Brock look for Mr. Moulton gave a much needed boost to our confidence, especially after Anne related how Wong had helped find a neighbor's lost child. "The Abos are wonderful at trackin' those that are lost or canna be found. I'm thinkin' 'twill be the same with findin' Jeremy Moulton."

Her words followed me as I prepared for bed. In my mind I pictured Parmee and Wong moving like dark shadows across the great tract of land that made up Wooraronga, spears or perhaps rifles in hand, their eyes intent on finding the man who'd injured Callie.

Opening Mother's Bible, I turned to Proverbs. *Trust in the Lord . . . and lean not unto thine own understanding.* Perhaps this meant relying on dark-skinned men whose ways and understanding weren't ours but who were nonetheless a part of God's plan.

* * *

With Brock back home, life resumed a more normal rhythm. Despite the flies and heat, I welcomed each day, my happiness in being with him making the season's discomfort more bearable. Nature added to my satisfaction by sending showers of rain to freshen the air and break the worst of the heat.

As happy as I was, I could tell Brock was frustrated at his lack of success in finding Mr. Moulton. Although Henry had retuned with the news that both Mr. Whitney-Smyth and the race commission had been notified, nothing had as yet transpired. It was the same with the Aborigines. Three days had passed since Parmee's departure. Why hadn't they found him?

Life at Tanybrae went on as always. Cattle grazed over the tracts of grass, and the training of the yearlings continued. Early in the mornings while the air was still cool, Brock or Dan raced Night Flyer and Flame around the oval track. Only at night did the routine change. No longer did the cattle go unattended, and Brock started sleeping in the bunkhouse with Henry and the stockmen. The memory of Schuler's smirk wouldn't leave him, and he feared further trouble was planned.

On Wednesday, Callie and Min failed to come to the house. Anne frowned when Hilda informed her. "'Tis likely they've left on walka-boot, but still . . ."

The memory of what had happened to Callie sent me from the garden with Anne, unease our silent companion as we hurried down the lane to the little house.

"Do they usually tell you before they leave?"

"Sometimes." Lines of worry creased Anne's brow when we failed to see smoke coming from the chimney. Our concern increased when no one responded to her knock. "I doona like to go inside when they're not home, but after what happened . . ." Her voice trailed away. "Since Parmee's not here to offer protection, we need to know if they left of their own accord."

Silence met us when she opened the door. Although they'd only been gone a few hours, the house had an unlived-in feeling. Thankfully, there were no signs of a struggle—the few pieces of furniture were in place, and their dresses hung on pegs.

"Walkaboot," Anne said with relief. "They never take their clothes when they leave."

"Since Parmee and Wong are gone, who did they go with?"

"Most likely Narong came for them. Tho' 'tis still some time before Min's baby is due, I'm thinkin' he wants it born away from here." Anne closed the door and squinted up at the sun that shone hard upon us. "Their people ken what happened to Callie, and they want her away from Tanybrae until it's safe."

Knowing that the young women hadn't left against their will put things back to rights. Even so, the kitchen seemed less cheery without their quiet presence, as did the veranda when it was time for afternoon lessons.

Having been waited upon all my life, I was surprised at the amount of cleaning and straightening that needed to be done that day. Hilda grumbled to herself at the thoughtlessness of "those gels" for "takin' off without warnin'" and leaving her to cope in the kitchen by herself. Although she enjoyed cooking, she had no liking for dirty dishes.

"Mrs. Turpin's oldest daughter has promised to help us next week," Anne reminded her. "Till then we must make do the best we can. Millie and Jessamyne can help you today. We've done it afore and 'twill likely happen again."

Thus both Millie and I were pressed into sweeping floors and dusting, and instead of helping Anne with her flower garden that morning, I took over the care of the vegetables.

"When do you think they'll come back?" I asked Millie as we gathered up the slates and chalk later in the day.

"We never know. Sometimes just a few weeks, sometimes longer."

I heard her with only half a mind, the rest focused on a leather necklace that hung from the corner of Callie's slate. "What's this?" I asked. Slender strips of leather had been braided into a pendant. Interspersed through the plaiting were dainty knots of flowers, the petals formed from minute tufts of green and blue feathers.

"Sal," I whispered, remembering the colored feathers on the butterfly she'd given me. It was Sal who'd come for Min and Callie. Leaving Millie with the slates, I hurried to my room for the amulet.

I'd just finished fastening it to the leather necklace now around my neck when Millie joined me. The white bodice of my blouse was a perfect background for the ornament. "How does it look?"

"Very nice, but . . ." She shook her head, clearly puzzled. "Why did Sal give you such a strange thing? I know you saved Callie from Jeremy Moulton, but still . . ."

Looking down at the necklace, I explained how Callie had brought Sal's gift to me on the day I'd had hysterics. "She told me the bone brings strength from the ground and the feathers draw courage from the sky."

Millie gently touched the ornament. "How nice. How very nice." Giggling, she went on. "All this time I've thought you so brave to want to learn to ride, when in truth it was the charm that did it."

"Maybe," I laughed. "Whatever the case, I'm very grateful." With that, I hurried to show Sal's gift to Brock, knowing that, like me, he would be pleased.

* * *

Two nights later, shouting voices jerked me awake. The sound tumbled through my mind as I jolted more fully awake, heart pounding while I scrambled out of bed. Snatching my wrapper from the bedpost, I pushed my feet into slippers and ran out on the veranda.

Millie was already there, the outline of her white nightgown a blur in the uncertain light, the quick pounding of her running feet an echo to my pounding heart.

"What is it?" I asked, running after her.

We stopped when we reached the end of the veranda where the tall gable of the stable loomed against a midnight sky. Slits of light pricked through cracks in the stable door.

"Fire!" Millie cried. She flew down the steps with me just a step behind. Muffled oaths, thuds, and a cry of pain pierced the night air as Millie reached the stable door and struggled to pull the pin from the hasp. I joined her, breath coming in gasps as I lent my weight to hers, pulling hard to swing the heavy door open.

Light, rather than fire, lit the stable, the lantern held by Henry, its glow outlining Brock and Adam standing with a struggling man between them. Anger as viable as the lantern light pulsed through the night air.

"Tie him up," Brock ordered, his voice unsteady from the struggle. Before he could say more, the captive's boot connected with Brock's shin. Anger blazed across Brock's face as he grabbed the man's throat and pulled him tight against his chest. "That's better," he growled when the man went limp against him.

Dan quickly wrapped rope around the stranger's legs and wrists and shoved him against the snubbing post. Although Brock and Adam were fully dressed, Henry and Dan only wore breeches.

Still unnoticed, I watched at the door with Millie, my stomach tightening when Brock's handsome features pulled into an ugly grimace.

"What are you doing in my stable, Tucker? Weren't you told to leave and never come back?"

Tucker shrugged.

Frustrated, Brock kicked him. "I want answers. What are you doing here?"

Silence permeated the circle of men who scowled down at Tucker. The pulsing light from the lantern flickered over their harsh features, changing those I knew and trusted into cold, unfeeling strangers.

I was vaguely aware that Anne had joined us, a rifle clutched tightly in her hands, but most of my attention was focused on Brock and the man who'd slipped past the dogs and reached the stable.

Another hard jab from Brock's boot encouraged Tucker to speak. "Someone promised me a lot of money to pizon yer mares."

Brock drew in his breath. "Who?"

Something cunning and animal-like crept over the man's battered features. One eye was already swelling, and blood trickled from his nose. "What's it worth to ya if I give ya his name?"

"I don't play games. The time you worked here should have shown you that." Brock nudged Tucker's leg with the toe of his boot. "I want his name."

"And I need money . . . 'specially since I can't collect none now for pizonin' yer mares." He spat contemptuously into the straw. "I shoulda knowd ya'd be keepin' watch, but I figured if I drew off the dogs with some meat, I'd be able to slip inside, dose the mares' water, and be gone afore ya knowd I was here."

Brock's voice was hard. "You figured wrong."

"So I did." Tucker scratched his back against the snubbing post. "Was worth a try, seein' as how the fine gentleman offered me enough to make it worth my while."

"Probably Bromfield . . . or was it Clayborne?"

Although the night was warm, I shivered, unable to believe Robert would stoop so low.

"Don't rightly recall." Tucker's face was set, and even I could tell he wasn't going to divulge any more information. At least not now.

"Where's the poison?" Brock asked, changing tactics.

"In my pocket." His stubble-covered chin indicated the right pocket of his skirt.

Brock unbuttoned the flap, extracted a folded packet, and sniffed it.

"Rat pizon," Tucker said before Brock could ask. "Works the same with horses if ya give 'em a big enough dose."

I thought of the gentle brood mares writhing in agony from the poison. I saw Brock's fist clench, and I heard him swear. "You'd do that to Beauty after you helped deliver her foal?"

Tucker shrugged. "Can't afford ta be soft when money's to be made."

"You're dirt, Tuck. Nothing but dirt." He nodded at Adam. "Keep a close watch on him." With that he walked to the door where the three of us waited—Millie with bare feet and in her nightgown, Anne fully dressed and holding a gun. As intent as Brock had been with Tucker, I hadn't thought he'd been aware of us, but perhaps, like me with him, he always sensed when I was near.

None of us spoke as we made our way carefully back to the house. Without a lantern, the yard was dim and fraught with shadows. I was glad for the light color of Millie's nightgown to lead the way, even more glad for Brock's hand on my back to lend assurance and balance. Another shiver ran down my back as the shock of what I'd seen washed over me again—Brock and Adam struggling to subdue a writhing figure who fought like a man possessed—Adam's blow to his body and the coldness on Brock's face as he'd choked the air from Tucker's throat.

Feeling me shiver, Brock put his arm around my shoulder. "You all right?" and before I could answer, "I'm sorry you had to see this."

The soft concern in his voice changed Brock into a warm, caring man instead of an angry combatant who'd looked as if he might kill. Was this what was required of men to build and hold onto their homes in the harsh environs of Australia? Was the same required of its women?

Millie reached the kitchen first. I heard her fumble for the matches in the box above the stove and saw the spark of its flame wave like a tiny beacon as she lifted the chimney and lit the wick. The glow was welcome as the dancing flame replaced the scene in the stable with the solid shape of table and chairs and the feeling of home.

Anne sighed and slowly lowered herself into one of the chairs. "Merciful heaven." Like mine, her hair was still in its bedtime plait with scraggly wisps curling around her pale face.

Brock touched his mother's chair. "Are you all right, Mum?

"Oh, aye . . . as right as a woman of me age can be when she's jerked out of bed in the middle of the night. With such a ruckus, I thought sure 'twas Abos raidin' Tanybrae."

"Mum," Millie giggled. "You know it wasn't as bad as that, though I could do with a cup of strong tea."

Wanting tea and a sense of normalcy, I lifted the lid of the stove to stoke up the fire, Hilda's lesson from the day before still fresh in my mind. In hardly any time, the tea was ready and poured, the four of us sitting around the kitchen table, the comfortable clink of cup on saucer as welcome as the lamplight.

Over tea, Brock told us he'd half expected something like this to happen. "Bromfield knows the horses are our main source of income. That's why I've been sleeping in the bunkhouse . . . the stable actually . . . though sleeping's difficult when you do it with one eye and ear opened."

I pictured Brock in the stable—a place I hadn't entered until tonight. Had he bedded down in the loft or stretched a blanket on the straw near one of the mares' stalls?

"Tho' I had no likin' for ye sleepin' there, 'tis well that ye did. 'Twas somethin' yer da would o' done." Anne suddenly laughed, the sound dancing in circles around the table. "No doot he'd a taken' pleasure in poundin' Tucker too. Who'da thought the man would sink so low as to try to poison the mares?"

"Who's Tucker, and why did you tell him to leave Tanybrae?" I asked.

Brock paused to swallow his tea. "He was a fair enough bloke . . . or so I thought. Used to work for my da and then for me. Right good with horses, especially the brood mares. Unfortunately, he had a weakness for the bottle, and one night when he was the worse for drink he knocked over a lantern and set fire to the stable."

Brock's mouth pulled into a line. "Luckily Henry and Adam were awake and able to put out the fire before it did much damage. Otherwise—" He shrugged and took another swallow of tea. "He'd been warned, for it wasn't the first time he'd drunk himself into a stupor." Setting down his cup, he added, "So I let him go . . . none too kindly I might add, for the thought of losing the stable shook me up. The last I heard he was working at odd jobs."

"So . . . 'tis back to Wooaronga is it?" Anne cut in.

"I'm afraid so." No one seemed inclined to speak; the length to which Neville and Robert were prepared to go was beyond our comprehension. Then I remembered the cunning in Tucker's face, his greed when he'd spoken of the money he'd been offered. Greed was the motivator, be it Neville, Robert, or their hired goon.

Millie's voice broke into my thoughts. "Remember how Tucker used to sit under the fig tree with Dougal? Shep too. He was real fond of the dogs."

"And used it to his advantage," Brock quipped. "His familiar voice and the meat did the rest." He got to his feet, the act bringing an end to our time around the table. "There are ways to make a man talk. Much as I hate to use them, I will unless he changes his mind and opens up on his own."

Aware of my concern, he placed a reassuring hand on my shoulder. "A few hours of being trussed up might do the trick. In the meantime, I suggest we all try to get some sleep."

* * *

I gave the stable a wide berth the following morning, the knowledge that Tucker was being held there keeping me away. I tried not to think about what he'd planned to do with the mares or that Robert or Neville had been the impetus behind the act.

Unfortunately, being tied to the post overnight hadn't broken Tucker's stubbornness. "'When ya'll give me sumpin' to make it worth ma while, I'll tell ya what ya want to know,'" Brock said, quoting the man as we sat at breakfast. He growled in frustration and added, "Then the man laughed and said, 'Perhaps I'll tell ya that and a bit more, for ya'd be surprised at all the fine gentleman had to say.'"

"Do you think he actually knows, or is he trying to lead you on?" Millie asked.

Brock shook his head. "For all his faults, Mack Tucker has a talent for ferreting things out . . . a 'secret gatherer' he likes to call himself." He rubbed his hand across his chin in a gesture of further frustration. "I'm giving him until morning. After that . . ." Brock shrugged.

Later that day, Brock entered the kitchen with a smile on his face. The sight of his solid presence filled both my heart and the kitchen.

"Tucker talked," he announced with satisfaction.

"Did you have to—"

"I did no more than make him an offer," Brock cut in smoothly. "A right good offer . . . one Mack Tucker was smart enough to accept."

"What was it?" I asked, relieved that force hadn't been used.

"Either he talked or I turned him over to the Aborigines."

Millie stared. "Brock, you know you can't do that."

"Tucker doesn't know it." Brock turned to me. "He's terrified of Abos. His parents were burned out by them, and the memory of it left a mark."

My mind lept past the talk of Abos. "Who hired him to poison the mares?"

"A man in Melbourne who called himself Mr. Kingsley, but Tucker said he heard one of the men with him say Bromfield."

A wave of relief washed over me. Thank heaven it was Neville, not Robert. Looking at Brock, I saw similar relief in his eyes.

"How do you know he was telling the truth? Remember you mentioned Bromfield to him last night."

"I did." He quirked his dark brow at his sister. "But Mack described him to a tee. . . slender build, dark hair, and a mustache. He said he offered him ten pounds to do the dirty work . . . one pound at the time they made the deal, the rest when the mares were dead."

I felt slightly sick when I recalled the evening when Neville had kissed my hand. "So it was Neville," I breathed.

Brock nodded. "I'm surprised he approached Tucker himself. He'd have been smarter if he'd used one of his men."

"Maybe Mr. Bromfield planned to murder the poor man instead of payin' him the rest of the money," Anne observed.

"That's probably true. Thanks to Bromfield's mistake, we now have his name and Tucker's confession." Brock smiled, his expression clearly satisfied. "Now all I have to do is take Tucker into Melbourne and turn him over to the police. Brock put his arm around my shoulder. "If I leave now, I can be in Melbourne by evening and home before tomorrow night."

Soon after, I helped Anne pack food and a container of tea. Then I went with Brock to the stable where Dan and Adam had loaded Tucker into the wagon.

"Dan's going with me." Brock bent his head to mine and kissed me. "Don't worry. Things are about to take a turn for the better."

I held his words close as I watched him ride down the lane. Then turning with a sigh, I returned to the house to retrieve my hat and go out to Lass and the foals. *A turn for the better* tripped through the rhythm of my steps and lifted my lips into a smile when I saw Lass. Yes, it was time for our luck to change.

* * *

Shortly after ten o'clock the next morning, a small wagon with a fringed covering for shade rattled up the long drive between the fig trees. Dougal's bark alerted us to the arrival, and I stepped out onto the veranda to watch the approach.

A dark-skinned man drove the team and a woman sat on the seat beside him.

"Abos," Millie said when she joined me. "What can they want?" She squinted against the bright sun. "It's not anyone I know."

Alerted by Dougal, Adam hurried from the training area. Remaining in the wagon, the occupants watched his approach.

"Letter," the Abo said in a loud voice. "I bring letter for missy."

"What missy?" Adam asked.

The man shrugged and extracted a piece of paper from his shirt pocket. Handing it to Adam he added, "Letter say."

After giving it a quick glance, Adam started for the veranda, his expression mirroring his puzzlement.

Unable to contain her curiosity, Millie ran down the steps. "Who's it for?"

"Miss Clayborne."

My surprise was as great as theirs. Why would strange Aborigines bring a letter for me? Curiosity impelled me down the steps to take the paper. As soon as I saw my name scrawled across the front, I knew who'd written. "Robert . . . it's from Robert." With unsteady hands, I unfolded the letter and read aloud.

Dear Jessamyne,

I had not expected to write to you, but the problems that have arisen with Brock McKade warrant that I try to intervene before they accelerate more. I don't approve of what's transpired and I will do all in my power to prevent further trouble. Can we talk? I feel confident that after you hear me out, you can be a valuable intermediary. I don't deem it wise to come for you myself. Instead I have sent Jiki and his wife to bring you to Wooraronga where we can talk and end the problems. Please know that I cherish tender feelings for you. In the meantime, I remain your affectionate brother.

Robert Clayborne

"Well," Millie breathed.

But it was Anne to whom I looked. She stood without speaking, her gaze on the cattle cropping the grass in the far pasture.

"What do you think?" I asked.

Anne was slow to answer. "Maybe he writes the truth, but after all that's happened . . . especially with Tucker's confession, it makes me wonder whether 'tis but a ploy to put us off our guard."

"I know." Like Anne, I felt torn. If only Brock were here. I looked for Adam, but he'd left as soon as I took the letter. He'd leaned against the shady side of the stable and was keeping an eye on the Abos. My gaze went back to Robert's letter and lingered on certain phrases: *I don't approve,* and *before things accelerate further,* and finally, *you can be a valuable intermediary.*

The unsettling events of the past weeks had cast a pall over Tanybrae. If by working with Robert I could help bring the trouble to an end . . . I looked at Anne, who watched me closely.

"I must go," I said, surprised at the firmness in my tone. "Even though I'm unsure of what Robert has in mind, I can't let the opportunity to help pass."

Anne's gray eyes held both concern and trepidation. "I doona know, lass." Then quickly, "If only Brock were here."

"But he's not." I held her gaze. "You've never stinted on your love and caring for me. Neither has Millie. Now is my chance to do something for you . . . for all of us. It's what I must do."

"I suppose yer right."

Seeing Anne's misgivings, my mind clapped hold of trust. "Despite Robert's weaknesses, I know he loves me and would never put my life in danger." Reaching for her hand, I added, "I must at least meet with him."

Anne sighed. "All right."

So it was that a few minutes later Adam helped me up into the wagon. The backseat looked to have been hastily improvised, the board rough and uneven. Still, it was better than bouncing loose in the back of the wagon.

Millie handed me a quilt and Anne gave me a hamper of food. "'Twill give ye paddin' for the seat, and who's to say when ye'll be eatin' again."

"Thank you." Feeling the weight of what I was doing, I added, "Please pray for me."

Anne's eyes brightened with tears. "I will . . . Millie and Hilda too. We'll all be prayin' for ye."

The driver slapped the reins and started the team and wagon back down the lane. I turned to wave, the love and concern on their faces as they called good-bye bringing a lump to my throat. It continued to grow when I spied Hilda wave with her apron from the kitchen door.

"Good-bye," I whispered, my throat too constricted for speech. Taking a deep breath, I scolded myself for being such a ninny. It wasn't as if I'd never see them again. Even with the distance between Tanybrae and Wooraronga, I would be home before evening. With this thought to brace my sagging spirits, I turned my attention to the man and woman sitting on the front seat. They looked older than Min, probably close to middle age.

"Do you know Parmee or Sal?" I asked, hoping to fill the long miles with something besides the creak of the wagon and worry about my meeting with Robert.

The woman turned and gave me a shy smile, showing a missing top tooth as she did. "Yes, missy. Parmee uncle."

"And Sal?"

"She mother . . . grandmother, a wise woman."

I remember what Anne had said about their concept of family, but hearing that they were related to Sal helped.

"I know about you," she went on. "Sal all time talk of missy . . . how storm and waves bring you."

Her words and English surprised me as much as her willingness to talk. Since she wasn't averse to conversation, I pressed her further. "What's your name and how long have you worked at Wooraronga?"

"All time call me Galla, and he Jiki. Wooraronga . . ." She paused as if unsure of her answer. "We come . . . go. Not all time at Wooraronga."

Pleased at her friendliness and the potential of further conversation, I concentrated on the passing scenery. The cattle grazing on the grassland told me we were still on McKade property. Summer heat had browned the vegetation, so it wasn't as lush and green as when I'd first arrived in Australia. I turned for a last look at Tanybrae, but the house and barns had disappeared behind the fold of a hill. The way ahead was more open and flat, the grass sparser. No wonder Angus McKade had chosen the rolling hill country.

As the miles slipped by, the sight of sheep told me we were now on Wooraronga land. It was strange to think that I traversed my brother's property and that the sheep grazing on the close-cropped tussocks of grass belonged to Neville and him.

From time to time Galla pointed to kangaroos bounding across the scrubland in great leaps or to a spiny echidna trundling through low-growing grass next to the rutted track.

I remembered that Daria Somerset had once lived at Wooraronga and that she and Brock and Millie had probably often ridden their horses along the track we now followed. Few made the journey between the two stations anymore. I suddenly wished Robert lived there with a wife who could be my friend—their children, though older, fond cousins to the children Brock and I would one day have.

From time to time we passed a solitary windmill with a water trough. We were closer to the sheep now, their plaintive bleating coming in a steady cadence, each bleat echoed by a chorus of others. I looked curiously at their woolly bodies and dark faces, never having been this close to so many sheep before. They seemed to stretch without end. Instead of a few hundred animals like Brock's cattle, the sheep must have numbered into the thousands. Robert and Neville were doing very well for themselves.

This set my mind down another path, one I'd been trying to avoid since leaving Anne and Millie. There was no longer any doubt that Neville Bromfield intended to ruin Brock and Tanybrae. Bribing the jockey so he could win the race said much about his character, but to send Tucker to poison the mares painted an even blacker picture. And what did this say about Robert?

Love and loyalty attempted to build a dam against images of Robert providing the money to bribe the jockey, but stopped abruptly before I could pin the slaughter of the cattle onto him too. *No, not Robert.*

From there I fell to wondering what my meeting with him would reveal and how I could help stop further damage. The uncertainty of what I would find grew like wildfire fanned by a strong breeze. I had asked Anne and Millie to pray for me. I must turn to God as well.

* * *

The barking of dogs announced our arrival at Wooraronga. A moment later, Galla jumped down from the wagon to open a hinged gate marking the confines of the station. I thought Jiki would wait for

Galla to close it and get back on the wagon, but he kept the team at a steady pace and left the woman to follow on foot.

My attention was immediately pinned on the yard and buildings. A wooden house surrounded by a veranda sat beneath the shelter of several tall gum trees. Off to the side were a stable and two long shearing sheds. Both the house and stable were smaller than those at Tanybrae and badly needed a whitewash.

Robert came to help me down before the wagon rolled to a stop. "Jessa." His smile was wide and welcoming. "I'm sorry I couldn't send a carriage, but as you can see, Wooraronga is a little lacking in the conveniences of Melbourne."

Before I could respond, he wrapped me in his arms and hugged me. "Ah . . . it's good to have you here. I've missed you."

I felt as if I were two different people as I smiled up at him—a child looking at her older brother with adoring eyes, a woman noting tenseness and that his blue eyes didn't quite meet mine. I was immediately aware that there was a strange air about him, coupled with the faint smell of liquor on his breath.

"It's good to see you too," I responded, wanting to keep things on a cordial note. "Wooraronga is larger than I thought. It seems like we rode for miles. And all the sheep . . ."

Robert beamed, clearly pleased that I'd noticed. "We run more than two thousand, and I mean to buy more. Wool has made many a squatter a rich man, and I mean to do the same."

I gave him a questioning look. "I thought Neville Bromfield was part owner of Wooraronga."

"He is," Robert said quickly, "but he leaves the business end of it to me." Clearly not comfortable with the direction our conversation had taken, he put his arm around my shoulder and steered me toward the house. "It's far too hot to stand outside talking. The house is cooler, and I asked Mrs. Newell to fix some tea."

The coolness of the house was welcome, though it took my eyes a few seconds to respond to the dimness and make out the room's sparse furnishings.

"The place is short on comfort since I don't spend much time here," he explained before he left me to go in search of Mrs. Newell.

While he was gone, I inspected my surroundings, noting the pale outlines on the flowery wallpaper where pictures had once hung. The only words that came to mind as I looked around were *drab* and *forlorn.*

The sound of Robert's footsteps reminded me of the purpose of my visit. *You must be on your guard, or he will soften you with sentimentality.* Lifting my head, I watched my brother with more critical eyes, noting his thinning hair and forced smile. In a sudden flash of insight, I realized Robert was as nervous about our visit as I was. Sensing this gave a much-needed boost to my confidence.

"Here it is," Robert said, stepping aside so Mrs. Newell could carry in the tea tray. She was a large woman with dark brown hair pulled tightly into a bun. Despite her size, she was surprisingly deft in her movements, the tray and its contents set without spilling onto the room's only table.

"Would ya like me to stay and pour?" she asked.

Robert shook his head. "Miss Clayborne will see to it." He waited until she left the room, then he closed the door. "There," he said, rubbing his hands together. "Now we can talk without listening ears."

My heart gave a start, and despite my show of nonchalance, my hand wasn't altogether steady as I poured tea into mismatched cups. Even so, the thought of what Olivia would say to the spartan arrangement made me want to smile.

As if he guessed my thought, Robert chuckled. "Can you imagine Olivia at Wooraronga?" Before I could answer, he hurried on. "Years of prospecting taught me a man can get by on less than he might suppose." He paused and fixed me with an affable smile as I handed him his cup. "Did I ever tell you about my prospecting days?"

I nodded. "On a day when Olivia wasn't there."

"Olivia," Robert snorted. "Men grubbing in the dirt aren't to Olivia's liking. Whereas me . . ."

Watching Robert pour whiskey from a flask into his tea made me wonder if he'd been drinking all morning. The thought surprised me, for he'd never been one to indulge in heavy drinking, especially in the middle of the day. He frowned as he fingered the jagged edges of his scar, one put there by Aborigines.

"If you don't like the blacks, why do you keep them at Woo-raronga?"

"Because they're dumb enough to work for almost nothing . . . food, a place to sleep, and a few trinkets keep them happy. Whisky too, though they don't know when to stop drinking."

I thought of the generous serving Robert had just poured into his tea but refrained from mentioning it.

"I mean to run Wooraronga at a big profit. Cheap labor helps keep costs down."

How like Robert. With him, money would always come before people. The thought acted like a catapult to the purpose of my visit. Clearing my throat, I set down my empty teacup. "I don't think you asked me here so you could talk about cheap labor. I want to know why Jeremy Moulton bribed the jockey. And if he hates blacks, why did he try to rape one of the Aborigine women at Tanybrae?"

Robert's head jerked up. "Jeremy tried to—?"

"He did."

Robert swore under his breath, any pretense at making small talk forgotten. "Fool," he muttered in a louder voice, "though he said when he left for Wooraronga that being without a woman would be hard." The fact that Robert would speak of such things to me increased my suspicions that the flask had been in use before I'd arrived.

"So you've known all this time that Jeremy was hiding here?"

"Yes." His lips tightened. "Remember, he helped us find gold and saved my life. Besides that—" Robert shut his mouth and looked past me to the window.

"Besides, since you gave him the money to bribe the jockey, he has a hold over you," I finished for him.

Surprise and dismay warred for position before merging into an expression of indignation. "What a thing to say. Really, Jessa."

His tone was a fair imitation of Olivia's, which rather than cowing me served to get my back up. "You asked me to come to Wooraronga so we could talk . . . and talk we will, but only if you promise to be honest. If we're to succeed in putting an end to the trouble, there can be no more lies."

"Playing the high-and-mighty are you?" A heavy sigh covered the anger that flicked through his eyes. "All right. No more lies."

Before he could say more, Galla knocked on the door and came in to clear away the tea tray. "Missy like the scones?" she asked.

"Yes, they were delicious."

Robert got to his feet so quickly his chair almost toppled. "Get out of here," he shouted. "You know better than to talk when we're eating."

Though she waited until she was well out of Robert's reach, she retorted, "You not eating."

"Impudent," he muttered. "If I had my way, there'd be no blacks in my house. But every time I say they must go, Mrs. Newell threatens to quit. Says there's too much for her to do alone."

Seeing my disgust, his voice turned conciliatory. "Come now, sis. Surely you haven't turned into an Abo lover."

I gave him a cool look. "If *Abo lover* means I treat them the same as anyone else, then I suppose I am."

"They're little better than animals. Look at the way they live . . . sleeping on the dirt and digging for grubs." He scowled down at me. "Animals is what they are, and that's how we must treat them."

"Not me." I moved impatiently in my chair. "Tell me what you wanted to speak to me about. What can I do to help?"

He gave a rueful shrug. "Not a great deal, I fear."

"Then why—?" I began.

"Because I hoped that between us we could find a way to stop things before they get uglier." His face grew solemn. "Neville is determined to shut McKade up . . . if not by ruining him, then more permanently."

Coldness clutched at my middle. "No," I whispered.

"Yes." Robert nodded for emphasis. "Now do you see my dilemma?" He began to pace the floor, four steps to the window then back again, his footsteps the only sound in the hollow room. "You asked for honesty, so I might as well say that, in the past, I haven't been above the law in some of my business dealings. That's why I was disinherited. But I've never stooped to murder." He licked his lips and began to pace again. "Never murder," he repeated.

I stared at him in horror as I realized that Neville or someone else planned to kill Brock. "Please, you must do something."

"Don't you think I've tried? It's no use. Neville is set on it."

"Then tell him you won't be a part of it anymore."

"No!" His sharp tone cut through my words. Shaking his head, he went on in a softer tone. "I can't."

"Why not?"

"Because—" He rubbed a palm across his chin. "Because Neville's threatened me . . . said he'd tell the race commission I gave Moulton the money to throw the race."

There, it was said, the words hanging heavy in the somnolent air, my suspicion made fact by his words. Sickness settled into my stomach, the small hope I'd cherished that I might be wrong blighted by reality. "Why?" I asked. "Why on earth did you do it?"

Robert sighed. "It was such an easy way to make money. Do you have any idea the amount I won? Neville too, but he made sure he kept his nose clean." His mouth pulled into a grimace. "He's clever that way and always makes sure he keeps the upper hand."

Seeing Robert's bitterness gave me hope. Maybe he wasn't so firmly ensconced on Neville's side after all. "There must be things you can hold over his head."

"Several. But what's the sense if I'm disgraced and sitting in prison myself?" He commenced his nervous pacing. "Don't think I haven't thought of it all . . . gone over it piece by piece. It's no use. Neville will always come out on top."

I absorbed his words and frustration as I got to my feet. "What about Brock's cattle? Who gave the order to kill them?"

Robert's blue eyes slid away from mine. "I did . . . though Jeremy was part of it too. It was something we hatched up together."

Anger put a bite to my words. "Just like that . . . a dozen beefs shot and a big hole cut into Brock's income."

"We needed to stop him sniffing around. Because of him, the race commission and now the police are breathing down our necks."

My eyes locked with his. "Who started it? You, Robert. And now you're trying to ruin a man who's only fault was to own a fast horse. He's a good man too . . . good and honest." My voice broke on this last.

"Spare me the tears, Jessamyne. Why don't you admit that you've been taken in by the bloke? Don't think I haven't heard the rumors . . . my sister staying at Tanybrae, and who's to say what else she's doing?"

Before I could think, my hand shot out and struck his cheek, the sound vibrating through the room. "Don't ever talk that way about me again," I hissed.

Robert put an unsteady hand to his cheek. "Egad, Jessa. What's come over you?"

Afraid of what I might say, I willed myself to control. "What you hinted at isn't true, and you know it."

"All right," he said, though he continued to rub his cheek. But the narrowness of his eyes put an uneasy silence between us, one that gave me time to realize that no amount of talking could change the situation. He and Neville had woven a terrible web of deceit, their ruthlessness threatening to harm those I loved. Grasping at straws, I tried to make my voice more pleasant. "Why don't you just tell the authorities the truth?"

Robert stared, the slap and now my question seeming to put him off balance. "Are . . . are you crazy?"

"Far from it." Choosing my words carefully, I went on. "Can't you see it's the only way . . . not just for yourself, but for everyone? Like it or not, Robert, one of these days you're going to be caught in your lies and brought down. How much better to be man enough to confess than to be forced into it by Neville or the police?"

Robert backed away, his loud swallow showing his dismay. "No," he whispered. "I'll be disgraced."

"You should have thought of that years ago."

"I won't. I can't. Neville and Jeremy have told me what they'll do to me if I . . ." He shook his head and made an effort at calmness. "It's out of the question."

Realizing I battered at a door that wouldn't open, I tried another tactic. "Where's Neville now?"

Robert was clearly relieved at the change in my questions. "In Melbourne."

"And Jeremy Moulton?"

"I don't know." Returning confidence spilled onto his face. "He left several days ago . . . said he had some business to see to."

Schuler, I thought. Schuler must have alerted Mr. Moulton about Brock's visit. But what neither man knew was that Parmee and Mooney were on his trail, and that they wouldn't give up until they found him.

I stared past Robert, knowing nothing more could be gained by staying at Wooraronga.

Seeming to sense the change in my thinking, Robert put his hands on my shoulder. "I'm sorry, sis."

"No you're not. You'll allow men like Neville and Jeremy Moulton to determine your path instead of being man enough to speak the truth." I closed my eyes against a headache building between them. "Please, will you ask Jiki to bring the wagon around? I want to go home."

"I'm afraid I can't do that."

"What do you mean?"

"I mean, you can't go back to Tanybrae just yet."

I stared at him in astonishment, my mind unable to absorb the full implication of his words. "Robert . . ." Something urged me to run, but before I could move, Robert grabbed me around the waist and forced me down the hall and into a room.

Struggling fiercely, I kicked and tried to free myself, but I was no match for Robert's greater size and strength. With a final shove, he thrust me from him and slammed the door.

"Robert!"

The sound of a key turning in the lock was his answer.

"Robert . . . let me out!"

"It's for your own good."

I yanked on the doorknob.

"You can yank and pull all you like, but it won't do any good. I made sure the lock was strong."

"Why are you doing this?"

"Because it's too dangerous for you at Tanybrae."

His words seemed to echo through the room. *Dangerous!* If it wasn't safe for me, then it wasn't safe for Brock . . . or Anne and

Millie. Desperate, I glanced around the sparsely furnished room for means of escape. The window. I must get to Tanybrae and warn them.

Robert's voice stopped me before I could reach it.

"Don't think you can climb out the window. I told Toby to watch and stop you if you tried."

Looking out the window, I saw an Aborigine sitting in the shade of a nearby gum tree, his dark face and form a contrast to the whiteness of the tree trunk. With my body still poised for flight, I leaned out the half opened window to gauge the short drop to the veranda.

Seeing me, the man got to his feet and brandished a long knife, his expression menacing.

I backed away, knowing it would be useless to call for help. *How can I get away?*

My mind darted and jumped like a caged creature looking for escape, my thoughts so fleeting and erratic they had no direction. Twice I retried the doorknob, knowing before I did that my effort was futile. Still I tried. *Fool!* I'd been such a fool to think I could end the strife and friction between Robert and Brock.

By now I realized the note had been part of the plot, just as killing the cattle and attempting to poison the mares. Robert wanted me away from Tanybrae to protect me. But from what?

Nerves on edge, I paced the room, the sound of my boots on the bare floor forlorn and devoid of purpose. Looking out the window, I saw the guard sitting under the tree, and beyond him a tabby cat on an over-turned wooden crate. Chickens clucked contentedly and scratched in the dirt. All was quiet and serene, a sharp contrast to my fear and frustration.

While I continued to pace the room, I noticed long shadows laying across the yard. Soon it would be dark. My mind fastened onto this, knowing that what was planned for Tanybrae would take place under cover of darkness. But what? How could I warn them?

In my mind I pictured Brock as he'd ridden off to Melbourne with Tucker, confident that things were about to change for the better. *Brock!* I closed my heart against the thought of never again feeling his arms around me or savoring his tender kisses.

"Please, God." Speaking the words, I knelt beside the bed, my mind and soul centered on the only one who could help me. Tears mingled with my fervent plea for direction. A God who loved me and knew of my love for Brock and Anne and Millie would surely answer. "Please show me the way, Father."

After some moments of pleading, my faith grew stronger and I asked more calmly for direction. I thought of Mother's trust in the Lord. Anne and Sarah's too. Peace stole over me, a feeling so strong I couldn't mistake the sensation. With the peace came calmness that smothered my erratic, useless thoughts and replaced them with purpose. I knew without doubt that my prayer had been heard. Now I must open my mind to receive direction.

Getting to my feet, I returned to the window. Both the cat and the chickens were gone, but my guard still sat under the tree. *Courage. Be brave,* the breeze rustling the eucalyptus leaves seemed to say. *Yes,* I answered. Unfastening the top button on my white blouse, I extracted the necklace Sal had given me. Fingering the feathers and bone, courage melded with peace and calmness. If I trusted, answers would come.

I remained at the window, watching while the sky changed from vibrant pinks to soft yellow before fading slowly into dusk. Time was passing. How much longer until answers came?

I continued to stand at the window until a knock sounded on the door. "Yes," I called, wondering if Robert had returned.

"Food, missy. Galla bring food." As she spoke, the key turned in the lock.

I reached the door as Robert opened it for Galla to carry a tray into the room. Standing so his body blocked the opening, he waited without speaking while she placed the tray on the table. Knowing it would be useless to try to dissuade him from his intent, I silently watched Galla remove the napkin covering the tray.

"Food ready," she said with a shy smile. For a second her gaze fastened on Sal's necklace, surprise registering in her large dark eyes. When they raised to meet mine, they filled with a silent message. *Courage. Be brave.*

"Get out, woman," Robert growled.

Fearing he would see the hope Galla's message had generated in my heart, I kept my eyes on the tray. When the door latched and locked, I felt hope rather than despair. If I kept my heart and mind opened to God, a way to escape would come.

Twenty-One

Escape came at midnight with a whisper at the window and a shadowy face at the opening.

"Come quick, missy. Galla help."

I tiptoed to the window, knowing stealth was of the essence. Putting a booted leg out the window, I ducked my head under the half-raised sash and with Galla's help climbed awkwardly through the opening.

"Quiet," Galla breathed, putting a finger to her lips.

We kept to the dark shadows as I carefully followed Galla down the veranda steps and past the tree where the guard had kept watch. Now, like the cat and chickens, he was gone.

Heart quickening, I copied Galla's quick steps as best I could, resisting the impulse to look back while prickles of nervousness ran along my spine. Had someone seen us?

Like Callie and Min, Galla walked quietly, her steps like whispers, while mine were awkward and stumbling as I tried to keep up. Where she was taking me, I didn't know, but I trusted she was part of God's answer and followed her without hesitation.

When we reached the first shearing shed, Galla stopped and took off the shirt she wore over her dress. "Put on," she instructed. "Make missy dark."

Only then did I realize that my white blouse stood out like a shaft of light in the darkness. As I slipped my arms into the shirt, I smelled the sharp scent of eucalyptus and suspected it belonged to the man who'd kept guard by the gum tree.

Many questions crowded my mind as I followed Galla past the shearing shed and across an open area to a copse of trees, but fear of discovery was uppermost in my mind. Twice I looked back, expecting someone to step out of the shadows and order us to stop. When a silent form stole out of the trees, a tiny cry escaped my lips.

Galla's arm shot out. "Koko," she whispered. "Him help, not hurt."

My heart beat a frightened dance against my ribs as Koko beckoned to us.

"Hurry," Galla whispered.

I stretched my legs to match hers, grateful for my divided riding skirt that allowed me to move more easily than a dress. Nerves swallowed calmness, pushing my breathing and pulse to an erratic pitch by the time we reached the sheltering trees.

Koko waited for me to catch my breath. "Sal send me. Have dream that bad soon come to Tanybrae."

"Sal?" In my mind I remembered the touch of her hand in farewell.

"Missy need warn Tanybrae." Koko went on. "Horse ready. Ride fast!"

My gaze jumped to a horse tethered to a tree, its dark form filling me with fear that clutched my middle. *Ride!* The word grew until it verged on panic. No! Without Brock beside me, I could never do it.

"Men soon go burn missy's home," Galla whispered. "Go quick. Warn ladies."

Urgency jumped from Galla to me, but I couldn't move.

As if she felt my fear, Galla gently touched the winged insect nestled against my blouse. "Courage. Be brave," she said. "Sal say all time our people take care of missy."

Her calmness cut through my fear and reminded me of Callie's belief that the water people had brought me from the ocean and assigned her family to help me until I grew strong enough to care for myself. Now was the time.

I closed my eyes and willed myself to absorb Galla's calmness. God had sent these good people so I could escape and warn Brock. Now I must have the courage to mount the unfamiliar horse and ride. I reached for Galla's hand and squeezed it. "Thank you," I whispered.

As my feet crossed the distance to the horse, the memory of walking among the yearlings poured into my mind. *You can do it, Jessa.* I placed my hand on the mare's neck and stroked her, hoping the gesture would make her my friend. *Like Lass,* I told myself. *Pretend she's Lass grown up.* The thought settled around me like a comforting quilt.

I hadn't noticed that Jiki waited in the shadows. Now he led the mare to a log and motioned for me to use it for a mounting block. I awkwardly placed my boot into the stirrup and swung my leg over the saddle. Panic and exhilaration meshed as I settled myself in the saddle and Jiki shortened the stirrups. I'd done it! Dear heaven, I'd done it.

From my vantage point, I looked past the trees to the open expanse of Wooraronga. How would I ever find my way to Tanybrae in the darkness? But if I waited for daylight, it would be too late.

"I don't know how to get back to Tanybrae."

Jiki shot me a quick glance, and I could almost hear his thoughts. *Silly white woman. Even a child should know such a simple thing.* "Follow the track," he said instead. "Here . . . Jiki show missy."

He left the trees, indicating with his arm that I follow him. At first the horse wouldn't budge, but with encouragement from my heels she set off at a walk after Jiki. Unease flicked and was subdued by confidence as I realized that such things as balance and the correct way to hold the reins came back like trusted but neglected friends. A bolt of excitement shot through me. It wasn't nearly as frightening as I'd imagined.

Jiki had eyes like a cat and walked without hesitation to an area well past the shearing shed. "Here track. Follow." He stepped closer. "Jiki hear stockmen say soon burn Tanybrae."

His words brought a return of unease and the need to hurry. "Thank you," I whispered, relieved to discover that even in the darkness the outline of the track was faintly visible. Turning for a last look at Galla and Koko, I waved. Then taking a deep breath, I set the horse to a faster walk, the pale outline of a half moon my only light.

The need to hurry made me want to set the horse to a faster pace, but caution warned that Robert and the stockmen would hear her galloping hooves. More than that, I needed time to get used to the saddle. We had gone some distance before I judged we were far enough away to urge her to a faster pace. I clung to the saddle as I adjusted to the mare's rhythm when she passed from a jarring trot to a gentler lope.

"Good girl." Exuberance filled my voice and heart. I'd done it! Now I must get to Tanybrae before Wooraronga's stockmen.

I leaned low over the saddle, the lessons Mother had taught returning as if I'd never forgotten them. *I think you have a way with horses,* Brock had said. Although I longed to set the horse to a gallop, I knew that in the darkness it would be unwise. *Steady,* I told myself.

My thoughts flew to Brock. By now he should have returned from Melbourne. Was he in bed or outside in the stable keeping watch? And what of Anne and Millie? I looked back over my shoulder, grateful to see nothing but darkness. When I turned back, the dim outline of a windmill loomed before me. Startled, I reined in the mare. Had we passed this close to a windmill on the trip to Wooraronga, or had the mare and I veered off the track?

Peering down at shadowy grass tufts and low-growing foliage, I knew panic. Where was the track? Then I saw it, the outlined ruts a few yards to the left. Relief washed over me, along with a stern admonition to keep my mind on where we were going. I couldn't risk being too late to warn Brock.

Brock . . . Brock. His name joined the steady rhythm of the mare's hooves. Coupled with it was the need for speed. *Hurry . . . hurry.* Against my better judgment, I set the mare to a gallop. She stumbled, and for a frantic second I scrambled to stay in the saddle, blind panic coursing through me until she righted herself and slowed to a safer pace. Swallowing hard against the racing beat of my heart, I patted the mare's neck and tried not to think of her writhing on the ground with a broken leg and me in a senseless heap beside her.

Too shaken to continue, I pulled the horse to a halt and looked back over the way we'd come, my ears tuned for pursuit. Relief washed over me when the only sounds were those of night creatures and the distant bleating of sheep.

Taking heart, I set the horse to a walk, then a trot, and finally back to a lope. *How much farther?* By now both the mare and I were tiring, but I couldn't stop. *Hurry!*

Not seeing any more windmills, I took this as a good sign. We must be on Tanybrae land. Soon I'd see the house and stable rising through the fig trees. On I rode, the moon lighting our way while the dark outline of the hills grew closer.

A horse and rider suddenly loomed out of the shadows. Fear's sharp teeth ran up my spine while thoughts of Jeremy Moulton flashed through my mind. *No . . . oh, no!*

"Stop!" a male voice shouted. "Stay right where ya are."

Heart pounding, I drew in the mare. "George . . . is that you?"

Startled silence filled the night, followed by an astonished, "Miss Clayborne?"

"Yes, George." Urging the mare forward, I closed the distance between us, my voice high and unnatural when I spoke. "Wooraronga stockmen are on their way to burn Tanybrae."

"The dirty—" he muttered. Without another word he set his horse to a gallop, leaving me to follow as best I could. Rather than being upset, I was thankful for his speed and quick response.

Encouraged by George's horse, the mare responded as well, her gait quickening as we followed the shadowy outline of horse and rider galloping across the grassland.

"Cooee!" George shouted. "Cooee the house!"

By the time I reached the avenue of fig trees, lights shone from the house and bunkhouse, and men milled around the stable. Which one was Brock?

As I cantered the horse into the yard, a man detached himself from the others and hurried to meet me.

"Jessa!" In three quick steps Brock reached me and lifted me down from the saddle. "I can't believe you rode all that way." I slid into his embrace, my legs unsteady and without strength. My greatest desire was to stay safe and warm in his arms, but the press of fear wouldn't let me.

"Did George—?"

"Yes." Brock set me away from him, his arm still offering support. "Have they left yet?"

"I don't know." Brock listened while I explained about being locked in the bedroom and how the Aborigines had helped me escape. "Jiki only said the stockmen would leave soon and for me to hurry."

Several had joined us—Henry taking the mare into the stable for a rubdown while Anne and Millie and several men I didn't recognize gathered close.

"The police from Melbourne," Millie whispered as Brock left me to talk to the men.

The sight of so many filled me with comfort—men alert and ready to save Tanybrae.

It was decided that Henry and four men would stay behind while the rest rode to intercept the stockmen before they reached Tanybrae. Before the men mounted their horses, Brock pulled me close and kissed me on the mouth, then my cheek. Lifting his head he whispered, "My brave Jessa."

"I love you," I said.

"And I you."

His love pulsed like a heartbeat between us, making it difficult to leave the security of his embrace and watch as he and the men rode away.

"Douse the lamps," he cautioned as they started down the lane. He looked at Henry. "Remember, you're in charge of those I love."

"Right-o." Henry's reply was as normal as if he'd been admonished to water one of the horses.

His cheery tone did much to buoy my spirits as I walked to the house with Anne and Millie. As soon as we entered the kitchen, Anne lifted the lamp and blew out the flame.

"There, though I doona ken as I like to sit and wait in the dark."

Millie pulled a chair to the window. "I'm glad for the darkness. We can see outside without being seen."

Anne led me to another chair. "You must be tired after all you've been through."

I gave her a weak smile, not wanting them to know how shaken and drained the last twelve hours had left me. I'd left for Wooraronga filled with optimism and hope and returned disheartened by the duplicity of my brother. Gratefully, I sank down on the chair, my legs still feeling like they belonged to someone else. I again thanked God the mare and I had arrived in time to sound the alarm. With so many to help, surely Brock could intercept the stockmen in time.

I clung to this thought as I sat with Anne and Millie by the open window. The moon had now reached its zenith and bathed the yard and buildings in dusky shadows. The chirp of crickets mingled with the sound of Henry's soft footsteps as he patrolled the veranda. The knowledge that he and others kept watch was comforting, as were the sympathetic comments from Anne and Millie as I recounted what had happened at Wooraronga.

"The very idea," Millie exclaimed when she learned what Robert had said, while Anne murmured sympathetically from time to time. Their voices and the reassuring pressure of Millie's fingers on mine warmed like sunshine after a dismal week of rain.

Through it all, my ears listened for the sound of hoofbeats and my eyes searched the horizon for movement. Had they been able to stop the stockmen?

I tried not to think of what would happen if the raiders approached Tanybrae from several directions—one to set fire to the stable, another the house, while others darted between shrouded buildings to enflame the barn and cottages. I closed my eyes, forcing my mind to block the thoughts. *Brock will stop them.* I held hard to that.

The sound of gunfire jerked me to my feet.

"They've found them," Millie cried.

She and I ran outside to Henry who peered through the shadows in the direction of the gunfire.

"Where are they?" I asked. "Can you see anything?"

"Nary a thing, but ya can count on Tanybrae winnin' the match."

More gunshots rang out, their distant report loud and quick.

"Dear Father," Anne whispered as she joined us, and I knew that, like me, she was praying for Brock.

We stood together on the veranda, our hands and hearts entwined. If only we could see what was going on.

Like the shadows, silence gathered around us. Unable to bear the suspense any longer, I went to the edge of the veranda for a better view.

"Nothin'," Henry said, though I hadn't asked.

Nerves taut with trying to see past the darkness, I willed myself to be calm. Instead, my mind kept flying back to the gunshots. Were Brock and the others safe?

Just when I thought I couldn't bear the waiting any longer, I heard the distant pounding of hooves.

Henry ran past me to the edge of the lane, gun in hand as he kept to the shadows. "There's four of 'em."

My voice came low and unsteady as I ran after him. "Are they Tanybrae men?"

"Get back," Henry hissed. "Brock'll 'ave my skin if anythin' 'appins to ya."

Ignoring him, I crouched in the shadows as four horsemen rode across the far pasture, the rough bark of a tree biting into my fingers as I clutched its branch.

A deep voice penetrated the night. "Cooee, the house!"

"George?" Henry called.

"Right-o . . . all went well."

My pent-up breath released in a sigh even as I wondered why only four had come back. Where were Brock and the others?

We watched the riders' silhouettes grow larger and more distinct.

Unable to wait any longer, I hurried with Henry to open the gate. "Where are the others?"

"On the way to Wooaronga."

"Was anyone hurt?"

George was close enough for me to distinguish his rugged features under the outline of his hat, but he waited until he was through the gate to dismount and answer. "None from Tanybrae. Thanks to yer warnin', we was able to ambush them . . . though not without a bit of a fight."

Relief washed over me. "Thank heaven."

"Aye, that too," George responded. He waited for the rest of the men to ride through the gate. "Dan here was able to pick off one of the scalawags, and a policeman got another. Soon as that happened, the rest couldn't wait to surrender."

"Were they killed?" Anne asked in a low voice.

"No ma'am . . . though the two that was shot will need some patchin' up." He paused and gave me a quick glance. "The police is anxious to get to Wooraronga and take . . . yer brother," he finished uncomfortably. "Mr. McKade and the rest rode along in case there's any trouble."

Anne took my hand as she addressed the men. "Thank ye, George . . . Henry . . . all of ye."

The men nodded and started in a quiet trail to the stable. Our return to the house was just as silent. I knew Anne and Millie weren't sure of what to say, just as I was unsure of what I felt. Relief and happiness that Brock was safe was paramount, yet sorrow for Robert dragged at my emotions, tempering them until they were a muddle of half-formed thoughts—my love for Robert battered down by the ugly realization of what he'd done. Although my brother deserved to be arrested, instead of satisfaction, I felt only a strange emptiness.

"I ken 'tis hard for ye, lass."

I nodded. "It's not pleasant to learn that someone you love is also your enemy. Hard as it is to believe he was part of shooting the cattle, the fact that he gave orders to burn Tanybrae—" I shook my head. "Brock . . . all of you could have been killed."

"But we weren't. Ye must hold tight to that thought."

When we reached the veranda, Millie hurried ahead to open the kitchen door. Once we were inside, Anne struck a match and lit the lamp.

The cheery light seemed to penetrate the darkness around my heart. Millie's smile and the clatter of the stove lid as she stoked the fire for tea brought further illumination. Brock and Tanybrae were safe, and I had the support of two wonderful friends. The thought shrank the lump of my feelings for Robert to a manageable size.

Lifting the teacup Millie set before me, I smiled at her. "We have so much to be thankful for, and in a few hours Brock will be home."

* * *

The rhythmic beat of hooves cantering up the avenue of fig trees wakened me the next morning. Climbing out of bed, I reached the window in time to see Brock and several men dismount by the stable.

I hastily donned clothes and shoes and hurried outside. Brock turned as soon as I reached the veranda, coming across the grass and up the steps to pull me into his arms.

"Jessa . . . Jessa." Then his lips were on mine in a wonderful melding of relief and joy.

I savored their pressure and the feel of his arms as they cradled me against him. Robert and fear were swallowed by touch and happiness. We were together. How good it felt.

Hearing a noise at the door, Brock reluctantly lifted his head.

"I . . . I'm sorry," Millie apologized, but it didn't prevent her from coming out onto the veranda or plying Brock with questions.

"The police have taken Schuler and Wooraronga's stockmen into Melbourne," Brock answered in response to her questions.

"And Robert?" I asked.

Brock sighed, and the lips that had so recently been on mine turned grim. "Robert wasn't there."

"Not there?" I echoed stupidly.

"The housekeeper—Mrs. Newell, I believe her name is—said he left shortly after he discovered you were gone." Seeing that his mother had come to the door, he suggested we go inside where we could sit down while he explained.

We gathered around the kitchen table, Hilda stoking the stove, the sound of her stirring scones and cracking eggs an accompaniment to Brock's voice as he recounted his frustration.

"Mrs. Newell said he stuffed food and a change of clothes into a pack and rode off. The Aborigines have left too . . . probably on a walkabout."

"But Robert . . ." I shook my head in disbelief. "Where could he go?"

"It's hard to say." Brock extracted a sheet of folded paper from his pocket. "Since this is addressed to you, I persuaded the police to let me keep it . . . though Captain Yates will be taking it back to Melbourne as evidence against Robert and Bromfield later today."

I glanced at Brock, not knowing what to expect. His expression was inscrutable, though I was certain he and the policemen had read the note. I carefully unfolded the paper, my emotions a tumble of confusion. Aware that Anne and Millie waited expectantly, I began to read the words Robert had scrawled in haphazard fashion across the page.

Jessa,

You called me a coward for not admitting what I've done. Now you'll think me a bigger coward for running away. I can't abide disgrace or sitting in prison for the rest of my life. I'm sorry, but maybe the things I write will make up for it. Please give this to the police who already suspect what you know, that I gave Jeremy Moulton the money to bribe Ned Krueger. I was also a part of killing McKade's cattle and sending men to burn him out. I'm not alone in my crimes. Neville Bromfield is partner in this too. He's been with me each step of the way. Tell the police to check into his dealings with Samuel Dunford in London. I don't regret leaving Olivia, but I'm fond of the children. Time doesn't allow me to say more except that I love you. Try to forgive me for all I've done. I remain your affectionate brother,

Robert Clayborne

No one spoke for a moment, the sound of Robert's words hollowly echoing around the homey sound of Hilda working in the kitchen. As I reread some of the hastily written sentences, I recalled the angry words I'd hurled at him. Not only had I called him a coward, but I'd also called him weak for allowing Neville and Mr. Moulton to dictate his conduct. Yet with all his faults, he'd tried to make amends.

"I wonder where he's gone?" I asked into the silence.

"Probably the outback. Once he disappears into the wilds, the police will have a hard time tracking him down."

I pictured Robert riding into the vastness of Australia's untamed land, a horse his only companion, the loneliness and endless tracts of desert a prison of his own making.

Tired of my unhappy thoughts, I smiled across at Brock, noting for the first time that the threads of worry that had clouded his blue eyes the past month were gone. "We have much to be happy for . . . so many good things to look forward to," I said.

Brock nodded. "It will feel good to walk around Tanybrae without half expecting a new crisis to occur. And to sleep," he chuckled. "It will be heaven to sleep with both eyes closed for a change."

Relief and happiness pushed the last dregs of Robert out the kitchen window and into the bright summer morning. I reached across the table and took Brock's hand, felt his long fingers curl around mine. "When the police finish their investigation, will the race commission give you the purse?"

"They should. And Captain Yates is confident that between Tucker's confession and Robert's letter he'll be able to bring charges against Bromfield. The ruffians he hired to set fire to Tanybrae are ready to talk too." Brock sighed and leaned back in his chair. "It's like I've wakened from a bad dream and found life as it should be . . . though I wouldn't turn down a bath and some of Hilda's scones."

We immediately set to work to see that Brock's needs were satisfied. Millie hurried to help Hilda with breakfast, and Anne went to retrieve a tub and carry it to Brock's bedroom. "Hilda's heating water for ye. 'Twill be ready before ye know it," I heard Anne say. I watched with a smile as she stood on tiptoe and kissed Brock's cheek. "God's been good to us . . . watched over us as well." She stepped back, a look of pride on her face framed by straggles of hair pulled loose from her plait. "I'm proud of ye, son, and I ken yer da would be too. More'n once these past days I've thought 'twas him, not ye, givin' orders and takin' charge." She nodded and looked at him with satisfaction. "Aye . . . 'tis right proud I am."

"Thank you, Mum. What you said means more than I can tell you." He gathered her into his arms and laid his chin on the top of her head—mother, son, and love melding with the embrace.

Not wanting to intrude on their private moment, I slipped away, savoring the knowledge that soon I would be part of the McKades' closeness.

Taking my floppy hat from the peg by the door, I went out to Anne's garden where colorful birds welcomed the day. I wandered dew-damp paths, pausing to cut choice blooms of pink roses and purple spikes of veronica. While Anne and Millie helped with bath and breakfast, I would gather nature's beauty to set on the kitchen table as a witness to Brock that life was indeed beautiful and good.

* * *

After breakfast Brock and I went to look at the horses, laughing at Lass's playful antics and talking of Miranda's training. Brock watched her for several minutes, his eyes narrowed against the sun. "She'll soon be old enough to sell. I'll get a good price for her too . . . especially after word gets out that the jockey was bribed and that Night Flyer did win the Melbourne Cup. All of our horses will now claim a better price." He put his arm around my shoulder. "Speaking of Night Flyer, how would you like to go for a ride?"

"On Night Flyer?" I teased.

Brock laughed. "Aren't you the cocky one? 'A wee bit full of yerself,' as my da would say."

"I'm a sad case," I admitted. Smiling up at him, I added, "Do you know how good it feels now that the fear's gone? Worried as I was that I might not get to Tanybrae in time, there were moments I wanted to laugh and shout and tell the moon to notice that I was actually on a horse."

Brock's fingers tilted my chin to kiss me, his lips making a soft trail across my cheeks and closed eyelids. "Have I told you how proud I am . . . and how much I love you?"

Before I could answer, Adam called to us. "Someone's comin'. Looks like Abos."

Stepping apart, we looked at Adam, who pointed to the north. In the distance I saw two dark figures carrying something on a pole between them. A third walked at the side, his loincloth and spear clearly visible. My first thought was that they'd killed a kangaroo. But why would Abos bring it to Tanybrae?

I lifted the brim of my hat and peered at the three men more closely. The realization that they carried a man, not a kangaroo, came with a jolt.

"Jeremy Moulton," I breathed. "They found him."

"Yes."

We watched the three men's progress, Parmee's stockman clothes and boots exchanged for loincloth and bare feet. But it was the man hanging from the pole by his trussed arms and legs that held most of my attention. He was without shirt and boots, and his body swayed in jerky rhythm to the men's stride. Any pity I felt for his discomfort was quickly swallowed by what he'd done to Callie. Half-forgotten words from the Bible poured into my mind. *As ye sow, so shall ye reap.*

Brock turned so that his body shielded me from seeing more. "Go to the house. This isn't something you should see."

"No." Lifting my head I met his eyes. "I need to see him for Callie . . . know that what he did to her . . . to all of us, hasn't gone unpunished."

Brock's jaw tensed, and his arm on my shoulder tightened. For a moment I thought he might argue, but something in my expression made him change his mind. Unpleasant as watching might be, it was what I must do.

After Dan opened the gate, he and Adam and Henry stood like sentinels as Parmee and Mooney carried Mr. Moulton past them.

The news of Moulton's capture passed on invisible wings around the station as George, the policemen, and Anne and Millie hurried to watch the procession.

The Abos stopped a few feet from us. "Here, boss," Parmee said. "Find man hurt Callie."

The crass, abrasive confidence that had once been so evident in Mr. Moulton had dissolved into the pathetic creature who dangled from the pole, eyes closed, mouth slack, his head hanging back. The sun had burned his face and torso into mottled red splotches, while scratches and blood streaked his skin.

Pity and distaste warred for position in my heart as a low moan escaped Mr. Moulton's cracked lips. When he made a feeble attempt to wrinkle the skin around his nose and mouth to rid them of crawling flies, I fanned the air to help him.

"Take him into the stable," Brock said. Like me, he sounded subdued, as if the pitiable sight had erased his need for revenge. "And get water."

We followed the Aborigines into the stable while Dan hurried to a horse trough and filled a battered pail with water. Mr. Moulton yelped when he and the pole were dropped to the stable floor, and Dan threw water onto his face. Sputtering, Mr. Moulton opened his bloodshot eyes and with thickened tongue licked the moisture that trickled from his nose and cheeks. "Water," he croaked. "More water."

Dan knelt and put the pail to Mr. Moulton's lips, Moulton's loud gulps and swallows clearly audible. When he'd drunk his fill, Captain Yates, one of the policemen, moved to take Dan's place, his long, thin legs a contrast to Mr. Moulton's thick form.

"Now would ya like to tell me what ya've been up to?"

"Abos." A shudder wracked Moulton's sunburned arms and body. "Black devils," he growled.

"I mean what ya've been up to with Robert Clayborne and Neville Bromfield."

Mr. Moulton blinked as if to clear his mind. "What d'ya mean?"

"I mean bribin' the jockey so Bromfield's horse could win the race."

Mr. Moulton's tongue flicked like a snake's across his lips as he stared up at Captain Yates. I'd had my fill of looking at him, and I returned to the stable door with Anne and Millie. From there I could see enough to know that Mr. Moulton was conscious and realized he was in serious trouble.

"We know ya've been hiding at Wooraronga since the Melbourne Cup. Schuler told us that." Captain Yates paused to let his words sink in. "By the way, did you know Schuler and the rest of the ruffians who pass for stockmen are in jail? In a couple of days Bromfield will join them."

Mr. Moulton's eyes made a wild sweep of the stable.

Seeing this, Parmee crouched down and moved Mr. Moulton's right leg. A guttural moan broke past Mr. Moulton's tightly compressed lips and his eyes rolled back into their sockets. Only then did I notice a large hole in the leg of his brown breeches and the blood oozing from an angry wound.

"Want me do more?" Parmee asked him.

"No . . . no!"

"Then answer."

Closing his eyes, Mr. Moulton began a slow, broken story of how, after Robert gave him the money, he'd bribed Ned Krueger to throw the race. From there he rambled on about shooting Brock's cattle and planning with Robert and Neville to burn Tanybrae if killing the cattle didn't work. His speech was weak, and each time he opened his eyes and saw Parmee, he shuddered. Through it all, I was aware of the soft sounds of the horses in the stalls, the distant song of a magpie, and the buzz of flies clustered on Mr. Moulton's damp face and red, splotched chest.

Captain Yates didn't speak until Mr. Moulton's low voice ran out. "Where's Ned Krueger?" he asked Mr. Moulton.

"What?"

"The jockey. Where is he? And if you don't tell the truth I'll let the black play with your leg again."

"No!" And then so quiet I had to strain to hear. "I killed him . . . dropped him in the bay with a weight round his neck."

Revolted by his chilling confession, I turned and made my way back to the house. Any pity I'd felt for the battered man lying like an animal in the dirt was swept away by what he'd done.

Anne and Millie went with me, none of us speaking until we reached chairs on the far side of the veranda.

After Anne settled herself, she spoke, her low tone an echo to my emotions. "Hell's too good for the likes of such a man. The devil himself could take a lesson from the scoundrel."

As I nodded agreement, my mind shifted to the Abos. Brutal as they'd been, their harsh form of justice came from a civilization probably more ancient than my own. Which way was best? Ours or theirs? Had God deemed it so, leaving His children to struggle and make their way alone, trying one way and then another? Or did He have a plan, one that included me?

My mind curled around the memory of the previous night. As clearly as if I were back at Wooraronga, I saw myself kneeling by the bed and asking God's guidance, felt His peace pour into me as I opened my heart to receive it. Hadn't His answer come as Galla whispered at the window and Jiki showed me the track to follow? I smiled at the zigzag path my mind had taken and wondered where in time it would take me.

"'Tis good to see one of us can smile," Anne said, "tho' I suspect that, like me, yer wishin' ye'd skipped watchin' Jeremy Moulton."

I nodded. "Awful as it was, I know God has been with us too.

Except when I was washed overboard, I've never prayed harder or felt God's warm peace more. If nothing more, the last two days have shown me He truly is mindful of us." I glanced at Anne, wondering what she and Millie thought of my little sermon.

Anne's response was a smile. "Spoken like a true McKade, and glad I am to hear yer searchin' like we are. Tho' we've no' found the answers yet, I've a feeling they're no' far away." She nodded and looked from me to Millie. "All we have to do is have enough pluck to walk out the door and find them."

* * *

That evening Brock asked me to go with him to the garden. "It's too fine an evening to spend inside." He pulled me close. "Besides, I want to be alone with you. We always seem to have an audience."

I was only too pleased to follow him outside where the last of the sunset painted the sky in a palette of pastel colors. Birds chirped sleepily as they roosted in the nearby branches, and the coolness of the air was pleasant on my skin.

I thought Brock wanted a leisurely stroll among the borders of shrubs and flowers, but he led me instead to the bench his father had carved for Anne. Dusk's grayness vied with occasional shafts of fading light through the thickness of the leaves.

"I come here often . . . especially when I need my da's advice. Somehow he seems closer when I sit on his bench."

"Are you in need of advice?"

"No . . . just a little privacy." With that he gathered me into his arms and kissed me, the heightened rhythm of his heart an echo to my own. "What would you say to getting married within the fortnight?"

I returned his kiss. "Yes," I breathed, "I'd like it very much." I sensed his happiness at my answer. "But can your mother be ready so quickly? I think she's written Mrs. Morrison and asked her to arrange a church for the ceremony. She said something about invitations."

Brock nuzzled my ear. "I'm sure the church and invitations can be arranged. Our friends in Melbourne aren't numerous. The important thing is for us to be together."

Looking earnestly into my face, he went on. "These last weeks have made me realize how uncertain life can be. My joy is with you, and I don't want to risk losing it. The sooner you can be my wife, the happier I'll be."

Twenty-Two

A week later we traveled to Melbourne. Brock rode ahead and was waiting to help me from the carriage when it came to a halt in front of Harriet Morrison's brick-trimmed home. The light in his eyes as he smiled down at me made me forget how tedious the long journey had been.

Tucking my hand into the bend of his arm, he leaned close and whispered, "Only four more days until you're mine."

Before he could say more, Mrs. Morrison bustled out to greet us. "There you are. I've been watching for you all afternoon." She paused and fixed Brock with her brown eyes. "I'm glad to see you've finally found a woman smart enough to snatch you up. And high time it is, for you know you're not getting any younger." Wheezing, she laughed at her joke.

After giving him an affectionate hug, she turned to me. "I can't think of a better catch for Brock. I was much taken with you at Christmas and think you'll do splendidly together."

She gave me a peck on the cheek before giving her attention to Anne and Millie. "Everything is ready for you . . . the church arranged and the invitations delivered. Elizabeth was a dear and helped me write them." The woman's mind hopped around like a plump robin in search of worms as she told Millie that Christopher had stopped by earlier to see if she'd arrived and asked if Anne knew Theda Hopkins had fallen and wouldn't be able to attend the wedding. "But I'm sure the others will be there," she concluded.

I glanced at Brock in time to see his amusement. "Now can you see why Mum says she can't do without Mrs. Morrison?"

I nodded, thinking we all owed the good woman our gratitude, especially when I heard her run on about wedding cakes and flowers and that Murial Cooper had told her the best place to buy bonbons.

When we entered the house, Harriet turned her attention back to me. "And you, my dear, are to do nothing except pick out your wedding gown. A friend of mine owns a little shop, and she's set aside several of her nicest creations for you to choose from. She's ever so clever with a needle and has promised to alter the one you choose in time for the wedding."

She paused at the bottom of the stairs. "With three daughters married, I know all about arranging weddings. The most important thing you must do is enjoy the time before your special day." She nodded for emphasis, her heavy breathing threaded through the nod. "There are plenty of us to see to the arrangements. I want these days to be ones you'll always hold dear."

A lump gathered in my throat when I realized that she and Anne had decided between them to fill the void left by my mother.

While I busied myself with wedding plans, Brock's time was spent helping the police finalize their investigation of Neville Bromfield. Although the task wasn't pleasant, I knew he found satisfaction in bringing out the truth about Neville and my brother.

The next day I selected my wedding gown and patiently stood through the fittings. Rather than one of heavy white satin, I chose a simpler creation of crepe with gauzy lace around the low-cut neckline. The fitted bodice set off my tiny waist, as did the ruffles on the full skirt. Millie thought it was exquisite and declared that she wanted one just like it for her own wedding. No one had to ask who she hoped the groom would be.

When I'd finished with the fitting, Millie preceded Anne and me out of the shop. We hadn't gone many steps when I noticed a man and woman walking toward us. The familiar look of the woman's dress made me take a second look. Recognition came in a burst. "Sarah! Sarah Hewitt."

She and William stopped, "Jessamyne?"

Anne and Millie were forgotten as Sarah and I hugged and tried to speak, our words disjointed and making little sense. Releasing her, I turned and saw William all bronzed and looking well with Jamie and Bethy and Timmy but a few steps behind him. How good it was to see them, the children grown taller and Bethy holding tight to my hand.

Remembering Anne and Millie, I made introductions. "These are my good friends the Hewitts. Remember the family who was so good to me on the ship?"

"Aye," Anne acknowledged. "Jessamyne had naught but praise for ye and yer kindness to her."

"This is Anne McKade and her daughter Millie. Like you, they've been very good to me. In fact, I'm soon to become part of their family." Seeing Sarah's brows raise, I hurried to explain about my impending marriage to Brock. "He's a wonderful man—one I'd love for you to meet. Would it be possible for you to attend the wedding? I know you live some miles from Melbourne, but—"

"Not so far as to prevent us from comin'," Sarah insisted. Taking my hand, she leaned close. "Did I not tell ye the Lord has good things in store for ye? I have much I'd like to share with ye . . . that is if ye'd like to listen. Not now, of course, but later."

I nodded. "I'd love to."

After exchanging addresses, Anne gave William directions to Harriet's church.

"We'll see you on Friday, then."

Love washed over me as I waved to the family who'd befriended me on the long voyage from England. There was no one else I'd sooner have at my wedding.

"What delightful people," Anne murmured. "At Tanybrae when ye told me they belonged to a strange religion, I thought that they might be a wee odd, but they're—"

"Delightful," I finished for her.

"I wonder what she wants to tell you?" Millie put in.

"And if their strange religion might have answers to our questions," Anne added.

I shook my head. "That I don't know. But coming from Sarah, I'm sure it will be good. I've met few women with more faith."

* * *

The day of my wedding dawned bright and fair. As they'd done on the night of the New Year's Ball, Anne and Millie helped me into my white gown and adjusted the veil caught with a cluster of silk orange blossoms on my hair.

When they'd finished, Anne put a hand into her pocket, her eyes on mine rather than the dress, their gray depth filled with love. "What little I had of my mother's, I already gave to Millicent. But I wanted to give ye a wee somethin' to let ye know of my love and to welcome ye into the family."

With this she drew a strand of shimmering pearls out of her pocket. "They come from Angus as well, for 'twas him that bought and gave them to me more'n ten years ago."

I stared at her, too overcome to speak. "I can't take them," I finally got out. "Not your gift from Angus."

"And now a gift to ye . . . a token of his love to both of us. If my husband could be here today, I ken he'd be as pleased as I am to welcome ye into the McKade family this way."

I pulled Anne close, felt the dampness of her tears mingle with mine, this sweet, practical woman who'd soon be my mother. "Thank you," I finally managed to say. "I'll always hold them dear."

Fingering the pearls, I looked at myself in the mirror. I felt happiness and satisfaction in the vibrant young woman who gazed back at me from the glass, her blue eyes and black curls setting off the filmy whiteness of her veil.

Millie leaned her head close. "I hope I'll look as lovely as you do on my wedding day." Turning to her mother, she asked, "Do you think Chris will propose to me before the year's out?"

Anne laughed. "Judgin' by the way he was moonin' over ye yesterday, I think there's every chance ye'll get yer wish." Glancing at me, Anne asked if I were ready.

"All except for the Bible." I opened a drawer and took out Mother's Bible with her name inside the leather cover and the blue ribbon still marking the page. Covering the book with a white handkerchief that also bore her initials, I left the room.

Making my way downstairs, I hoped Brock would be waiting at the bottom, his eyes filled with warmth and admiration. But Harriet had shoed him away, declaring that it brought bad luck if the groom saw his bride in wedding clothes before she came down the aisle.

When we reached the waiting carriage, Henry and Dan were there to help us, both dressed in dark frock coats and tall hats in honor of the occasion. Although Anne and Millie were dressed in the same gowns they'd worn to the New Year's Ball, each had purchased a new hat for the wedding—Millie's a creation of apricot flowers and Anne's a sedate arrangement of filmy gray lace and net.

Sunlight shining on the tall spire of the church caught my attention. We were almost there. A smile touched my lips and stayed there as Henry helped me out of the carriage, his puckish face nodding as if it were all his doing that the wonderful day had finally arrived.

I remember little of what happened next, only a mingling of nervousness and anticipation as the chords of the organ swelled and I walked down the aisle to Brock, who stood tall and handsome beside the minister. My eyes rested fleetingly on the Hewitts, who watched from a pew, faces smiling.

I wouldn't let myself think of Robert. I turned my thoughts instead to Anne and Millie, who were my family now—Millie with Chris beside her, smiling as radiantly as if she were the bride, and Anne with her face showing softness and love.

My fingers tightened on Mother's Bible and handkerchief to pull the memory of her around me. Father too—each one a vital part of the woman whose eyes sought the face of the man she loved.

My reply to the minister's words was soft, Brock's resonant, his hand steady as he slid a circlet of gold onto my finger. I lifted my face and felt the softness of his lips on mine—my joy complete as I became his wife.

* * *

Two days later, Brock and I looked out from a low bluff onto the broad expanse of Port Phillip Bay. The air was balmy, and a slight wind lifted the water in deep blue ripples. In just six short months my life had turned full circle. The waves that had flung me angrily onto Australia's rocky shore now combed with white breakers on the shimmering water.

"Happy?" Brock asked.

I nodded from the back of the mare on which I sat, the smile I gave him an extension of the deep joy and contentment that had been mine these last two days. The Grand Hotel had provided the nest where I became one with Brock, the warmth of lying in his arms and waking up next to him a bliss I'd never experienced before.

This morning we'd left Melbourne, Brock on Night Flyer and me on Adam's chestnut mare, my dream of riding at Brock's side finally a reality. My hands were encased in the kid gloves he'd given me, and I held the carved handle of the riding crop.

With a click of his tongue, Brock started Night Flyer down the embankment. I followed on the mare, knowing I would gladly follow and be with him for the rest of my life.

When he reached the beach, Brock urged the stallion into a canter, its long legs stretching effortlessly as they galloped across the damp sand. I rode at a more leisurely pace, content to savor the fact that I was at last in a saddle, my hand confidently holding the reins.

Seeming to dislike our separation, Brock reined in the stallion where the sand met the waves and set the animal on a course back to me. My eyes took in the outline of his dark jacket and hat along with the assurance with which he rode the stallion.

The memory of the dream I'd had on the boat flooded my mind along with expectancy and wonder. He'd come at last, the man I loved. Excitement pulsed along my spine, and I felt an answering quiver run along the back of the mare. I patted her neck to quiet her while my eyes remained on Brock and Night Flyer as they left the foaming breakers and came across the sand. Reaching me, he reined in the horse, his eyes holding mine in a gaze as intimate as an embrace. When he reached to brush a tendril of black hair away from my face, I didn't move or breathe.

The world seemed to stop for a heartbeat; even the restless waves lapping at our horses' hooves stilled. I leaned toward him and he to me, and when our lips met, the knowledge that Brock McKade was mine and I his became the fulfillment of all my dreams.

AUTHOR NOTES

The Melbourne Cup has been Australia's premier horse race since the mid 1800s. Like our Kentucky Derby and the Ascot races in England, it is a national event. The Melbourne Cup as portrayed in this novel is purely a work of fiction.

For those wishing to learn more about Australia in the 1800s, the following books are excellent sources:

1. *Catherine: The Diary of Catherine Currie 1873–1908 in Victoria and Gippsland*

2. *The Golden Age: History of Victoria Colony 1851–1865,* by Geoffrey Melbourne Serle

3. *Melbourne: The Biography of a City,* by W. H. Newnham

4. *Victoria's Heritage,* by Alan George Shaw

5. *Pioneer Women, Pioneer Land,* by Susanna DeVries-Evans

6. *The Aboriginals,* by R.M. Gibbs

7. *Notes on Gippsland History,* by George Cox

About the Author

Books have always been an important part of Carol Warburton's life. In addition to writing several books, she worked thirteen years for the Salt Lake County Library. Her novels have been set in the United States, Mexico, and Australia, and she is presently writing one set in Ireland. She and her husband Roy live in West Jordan, Utah.